THE COFFEE BUG

Hunter Silvastorm

To order additional copies of this book, contact:
Xlibris Corporation
1-888-795-4274
www.Xlibris.com
Orders@Xlibris.com
39013

Reviews

"The relentless march of the story's gripping suspense begins to build from the first page. This book is guaranteed to have you sitting on the edge of your seat!"
Emily Wexler, Book Reviews, Barwick Journal

"This may be a novel, but we had better pay attention to what Hunter Silvastorm is telling us."
Cynthia Magnus, Librarian, Mayfield Library

"I've recommended this book to everyone I know. It's an amazing page-turner."
Rob Delaney, Dept. of Biological Sciences, Pritchard College

"Hunter Silvastorm has discovered the formula for writing the perfect suspense / thriller. I'm already looking forward to his next one."
John Bessel

"Hunter Silvastorm is, unquestionably, an incredible author. However, he should also receive kudos for his amazing ability as a psychologist. His character development and, especially their interaction to one another, is the best that I have ever read."
Trace Steuben, Reviews—Literary Journal

"The level of suspense that permeates this story is phenomenal. It's probably the most exciting book that I've ever read."
Lee Bradenton

"The Coffee Bug" is more than just a good book. Mr. Silvastorm has created characters that are so real, I fully expect to meet them at the supermarket. Even though the plot revolves around a very serious issue, Hunter Silvastorm has not forgotten that humor is a natural part of life."
Joseph Paglia, Smithsonian

"The Coffee Bug" is absolutely the best suspense thriller since "Jurassic Park."
Harmon Williamson

"Hunter Silvastorm shines a bright light on the controversy surrounding genetic engineering and cloning. His book is so well written, that we can't stop talking about it."

Fred and Anita Szabo

"I predict that The Coffee Bug will be a blockbuster on the Big Screen within one year."

Eleanor McDougal

"My advice to all those who are about to read "The Coffee Bug," is not to read the epilogue before you finish reading the book."

Erica Parmenter

"You may have strong opinions about the new science of biotechnology, but Hunter Silvastorm's novel, The Coffee Bug, will make your jaw drop and open your eyes to both sides of the argument."

Damien Furst, Ventura Ledger

" . . . even though it was late at night, I found myself boo-ing the villains and cheering the hero and heroine! Now, that's the mark of a great book. Three cheers for Hunter Silvastorm and The Coffee Bug!"

Lia Mazzotti, American Consulate—Rome, Italy

"Every one of Hunter's characters were so real that they managed to step out of this novel and come alive."

Jenna Hirsch

Dedication:

For Mom and Dad

A wise man once said, "If I had a choice, I would choose luck over brains every time." Luckily for me, I was the product of two people who each possessed a most perfect gene-pool.

Hunter Silvastorm

"The most exciting phrase to hear in science, the one that heralds new discoveries, is not 'Eureka,' (I found it) but 'That's funny.'"
Isaac Asimov (1920-1992)

"Adapt or perish, now as ever, is Nature's inexorable imperative."
H.G. Wells (1866-1946)

"Something in the insect seems to be alien to the habits, morals, and psychology of this world. It's as if it had come from some other planet, more monstrous, more energetic, more insensate, more atrocious, more infernal than our own."
Maurice Maeterlinck, Nobel Laureate, 18621949

PROLOGUE

The Baby Boomers talk about the 1950's as a time of laughter, frivolity and Rock and Roll. The description is almost dead-on. The American family wandered around in a dream-like state punctuated only with the exciting, but fleeting moments of "I Love Lucy," Elvis Presley, and the "Pillow Talk" movies starring Rock Hudson and Doris Day. The New York Yankees, along with their big guns, Joe DiMaggio and Mickey Mantle, added an extra facet to the lustrous gemstone that was "The Fifties."

People had, for the most part, idealized their lives. They drove to work in their post-war Chevy Bel Airs, or Ford Fairlanes and came home to their cozy, one-bathroom homes. The conversations that took place around the dining room table were shallow, mundane chats that ricocheted off the bumpers of an uncomplicated life known as The Past and The Present. The mind-set of the 50's was not conducive to a vision of the future. During that time in our history, people had to work hard at bringing solemnity into their lives. There was a war going on in Korea, but television had not yet learned how to bring it into American living rooms as it did, years later, during the Vietnam experience. Besides, the Korean War had been happening on the other side of the world and too far away to be a serious contender for introspection. No one was even sure how to pronounce cities such as Seoul or Pyongyang. If a resident of The Fifties wanted profound and somber moments, it was much easier to turn to Hollywood. Productions such as "From Here to Eternity" and "On the Waterfront" offered plenty of sober moments, and presented an opportunity to have five minutes of adult dialogue. It was the effort of actors, writers, producers, and directors that provided the drama necessary to round out everybody's life.

Little did they know that the future was about to enter like a steamroller.

In the midst of that modern Age of Innocence, there was an unfolding event; an extraordinary, albeit obscure, event. It was Professors James Dewey Watson and Francis Crick's discovery of the structure of DNA, the famous "Double-Helix," or microscopic building blocks of life.

The scientific breakthrough was a momentous occasion but, strangely enough, almost nobody was paying attention. Until that point in time, scientists theorized that all living things were made up of genes. And genes were, after all, the one thing that transmitted the characteristics of living organisms from one generation to the next. Yet, it wasn't until Doctors Watson and Crick created an actual model of the DNA that life began to change.

The last four words bear repeating: "Life began to change." Figuratively and literally. Think about it. Jet aircraft have changed the speed at which we live our lives. Telecommunications have changed the way we conduct our lives. Computers have changed our style of life, but biotechnology, specifically gene-splicing, has changed the very fabric of life itself.

And therein lies the dilemma. What happens when scientists alter life in a fashion that nature had not intended? What are the ramifications? Thanks to Watson and Crick, we know for certain that a single strand of DNA is composed of billions of parts and that its complexity is most uncommon and unrivaled. With that multifarious puzzle bubbling just beneath the surface, consider the following event that occurred in our recent history.

In the third week of May 1979, a geneticist named Darrell Botsworth was working in his laboratory located sixteen miles south of the Tombigbee River that runs through downtown Mobile, Alabama. He was conducting experiments that involved the splicing of certain genes from one species of frog to another.

Something went wrong. Terribly wrong.

His assistant, a young woman, Jeanne Price, who was a Doctoral candidate in molecular biology at nearby Tulane University, was found dead at the edge of a marsh. In later interviews with the noted microbiologist, Dr. Norman Friedman, Miss Price was referred to as " . . . a brilliant theoretician who had been promised a position with Schering-Plough Pharmaceuticals upon her graduation."

The coroner for Pritchard County, Alabama, Dr. John Mastebeau, stated that Miss Price's death was due to drowning. When the authorities went to question Professor Botsworth, they found him dead as well. He was lying on the floor in his laboratory, located some six miles from where Miss Price's body had been found. Botsworth's death was deemed to have been from a heart attack. It should be noted that the young man was fit and trim and, six weeks prior, had celebrated his thirty-sixth birthday.

An autopsy was performed on Jeanne Price. The results were freakish. More than three dozen tiny frogs were found lodged throughout her windpipe, esophagus, stomach, bowels, and lower intestines. A rather large egg sac was discovered in her vaginal area. The medical examiner's report described the odd find as, " . . . *a gelatinous material, approximately 12 centimeters in diameter, that looks strikingly like an amphibian egg-sac about to hatch.*" Darrell Botsworth was buried without the benefit of an immediate autopsy.

Then, in the spring of 1980, another strange thing happened in the vicinity surrounding Professor Botsworth's laboratory. A real estate broker, Chris Whitcomb, was showing the abandoned property to prospective clients. As they approached the isolated building, they were amazed to see it surrounded by tens of thousands of frogs. They tried to walk to the entrance of the building, but the frogs had literally made a carpet of themselves. It became impossible to proceed without stepping on vast numbers of the creatures.

Even though Whitcomb called the local health department, the wheels of bureaucracy turn slowly, and several months slipped by before suspicions grew. There was a growing awareness that the mystery of the congregating frogs was related to the genetic experiments of Professor Darrell Botsworth.

By September 1980, there were numerous reports, from various parts of the Southern United States that frogs were dying by the millions. Newspaper articles were cropping up all over detailing the unexplained phenomenon. The geographical epicenter of this oddity seemed to be the marshy area where the dead body of Jeanne Price had been found.

Interviews with scholars and scientists, police and bureaucrats could not determine the reason for the unprecedented deaths of the frogs. The Centers for Disease Control, the C.D.C., was called in to investigate. There were reports that the organization was able to backtrack the event and zero in on Professor Botsworth's laboratory. The Atlanta-based C.D.C. brought in some scientists familiar with biotechnology and, together, they poured over the remnants of Botsworth's titillating notes.

A feature article appeared in the October 22nd issue of the *Pritchard County Tribune* stating that during an interview with Dr. Thomas Cardoza of the C.D.C., he, (Cardoza) admitted to being aware of a gene-splicing experiment that had gone wrong. The article, written by the newspaper editor, Matthew Delahanty, stated:

> . . . *Dr. Cardoza went on to say, 'From what we can gather, Professor Botsworth was attempting to manipulate the genetic makeup of the frogs. However, there weren't enough of his notes to determine what, exactly, he was trying to accomplish.'*
>
> When Dr. Cardoza was questioned as to what he and the C.D.C. felt went wrong, he answered, *'It seems rather clear to us that Professor Botsworth did not anticipate the simple fact that natural mutations occur when species reproduce in the wild.'*
>
> Asked to elaborate, Dr. Cardoza gave the following explanation: *'When frogs mate with each other, we know what we're going to get. When spiders mate, we also know what to expect. But, if you engineer a new life-form by combining the DNA of a frog and a spider, what will happen when the offspring escapes out of the laboratory? What manner of mutation will you get when this new species finds a way to reproduce?'*

CHAPTER ONE

FLORIDA

February

"It is the ultimate act of sin!" He hissed the words through his teeth, while his lips curled in a sneer. If it weren't for the small microphone that sat high on the lapel of his sharkskin suit, the audience would have been unable to hear that last sentence.

He paused to assess the reaction of the crowd. Many were vigorously nodding their heads in approval.

"How dare these people," he called out. "How dare they think that they can put their mortal hands into the Lord's mixing bowls of creation? Where do these sinners get their audacity?"

A lone voice rose from the audience. "Tell us, Brother!" cried a man caught up in the fervor of the sermon.

The preacher shot him a glance, held it for a second and swept his eyes over the rest of the crowd. For a February night in Florida, it was unusually humid. Sweat glistened on the faces of the men and women seated under the tent.

Softly, the preacher asked, "Where do these transgressors get such ideas?" Then, he raised his voice incrementally, as he asked the next two questions. "What makes these offenders of our faith think that they have the *right* to create life-forms in the laboratory? Don't they realize that they are destroying our world?"

Murmurs were building throughout the sea of faces.

"Killing our children?" he boomed.

A man in the front row cried out in desperation. "Oh, Lord!"

"Not the children!" pleaded a young mother sitting on the edge of her metal folding chair, rocking a wide-eyed child.

The preacher began to feel the room responding. His fiery rhetoric was skipping across the audience like electrical charges. The steaminess of the night coupled with the energy of his sermon was starting to take noticeable effect.

While some of the women had their hands clasped in prayer, a few of the men were pumping their fists.

The Preacher, Brother Timothy, raised his decibel level even higher as he shouted, "These people are adulterers! The worst kind of vermin! They rape the Lord's own offspring in the name of science! Their warped ideas crawled out of a black pit, and they have the nerve to call it genetic engineering! It should be called . . . . vulgar blasphemy!"

Chants of "Yea" and "Oh Lord," were coming from various congregants in the crowd. Several people were pleading, "Save us, Brother Timothy!" and "Show us the way!"

Brother Timothy Goodman sensed that he was close. He almost had the audience under his complete control.

Urging his flock to the edge of passion, he raised his arms in the air and asked, "What evil-doer has conjured up these horrendous lies?"

Several rows back, a cluster of believers stood and pleaded for Brother Timothy to give them the answer and save their souls. Other parishioners rose to their feet.

Brother Timothy rasped, "Who is guiding the hand of these rapists, as they turn the Lord's bounty into monsters?"

A few people began crying in fearful anticipation of the answer. Everybody was afraid of the future depicted by the preacher's sermon.

Brother Timothy seethed his final two questions. "Who is it that walks our Earth and takes pleasure by inflicting pain and suffering? Who is it that grins at the sight of mutated children?"

The reaction of the audience was growing in intensity.

The house lights dimmed, and a lone spotlight illuminated Brother Timothy. It had the effect of a lightning bolt, and the crowd fell silent.

Standing on center stage, Brother Timothy stood perfectly still. Only his eyes moved, as he scanned the faces of the men and women who were holding their collective breath.

Suddenly, he spat the answer, "Satan, himself!"

The reaction was immediate and spontaneous. The entire audience, consisting of about two hundred souls, began a yearning cry for salvation. Two people, overcome with their epiphany, fell to the floor. One young man lay in the center aisle, while his body jerked spastically as if in the throes of an epileptic seizure.

Ignoring the chants, the pleas, and the wild gyrations, Brother Timothy continued. He pontificated about the Devil coming to Earth in strange forms. He told his parishioners that the scientists were the manifestation of the Devil, and that they were doing Satan's own work. Brother Timothy convinced his followers that their responsibility was to help prevent this kind of blasphemy.

"It must come to an end!" demanded the preacher. "It must be removed like a cancer! The Lord never intended for us to create new life in a glass test tube. The Lord moves in mysterious ways, and we need to love and cherish the Lord!"

A small chorus of four women broke into the first strains of "Hallelujah," as the music of an off-stage organ burst through a pair of big speakers. Each time Brother Timothy invoked the name of the Lord, the organ sprang to life for a single sustained note, and the chorus chanted "Hallelujah."

Between measures of the music, Brother Timothy told his worshippers that money was needed to fight the Devil. He urged them to reach deeply into their pockets and draw out "Gold for God's work."

Hannah Carpenter sat in the last row, next to the center aisle. A micro-cassette recorder, partially camouflaged by some tissues, was in her hand. She had driven four hours from West Palm Beach to attend the Pentecostal meeting and to hear Brother Timothy cast his spell. In spite of being impressed with the preacher's presentation, Hannah discovered that she was not prepared for the audience's reaction. Although she knew that tent revivals tended to be raucous affairs filled with zealots crying out for salvation, the fervor of the crowd went beyond her expectations. Being surrounded by the action added to her shock. It was one thing to watch some file footage of this sort of phenomenon, but quite another to be in the middle of all the electrifying passion. Brother Timothy's growing reputation for bringing audiences to a fever pitch had been verified.

As a seasoned reporter working for one of Florida's major newspapers, Hannah Carpenter had fought for this assignment. The resurgence of Tent Revivals, with their controversial overtones and undertones, were becoming a hot topic. Additionally, Hannah was going to get the golden opportunity to interview Brother Timothy Goodman.

Driving back to the hotel, Hannah hit the play button and listened as the micro-cassette replayed a portion of the sermon. It took a while before she realized that there was something about the preacher's presentation that was bothersome. However, pinpointing it was like trying to discern a single instrument in a vast symphony orchestra. It could have been Brother Timothy's style, or mannerisms that were teasing her sensibilities. Perhaps, it was simply his attitude. Whatever it was, she couldn't put her finger on it.

Hannah's interview with Brother Timothy was set for noon the next day. She had many questions and was already mentally staging the meeting, sequencing her subjects in order to draw him out. She didn't want to conduct this session and come away thinking that she had missed something important.

CHAPTER TWO

CALIFORNIA

Most of the long stainless steel tables in the lab were literally covered with scientific equipment. Rick Ballinger sat at his "desk," which was actually a table with an acrylic countertop known as Corian. Strewn with several piles of paper and a couple of scientific manuals, the desk also held a thick textbook titled *Molecular Biology* that doubled as a paperweight. To feel more at home, Rick had finagled his boss, Dr. Douglas Matsushita, into allowing the installation of a desk phone, rather than the standard wall-mounted model.

Nursing a cup of cold coffee, Rick read over a handful of faxes that had come in during the night. He had recently celebrated his thirtieth birthday and two of the transmissions were belated good wishes from colleagues. Rick looked a lot younger than his age. He was only five foot six and barely needed to shave daily. When he did take razor in hand, it was only to crop off the meager stubble around his chin. Known as "Rick" to most of his friends and acquaintances, he only used his given name, Richard, during more formal introductions. The only exception was his mother who loathed nicknames and always referred to him as Richard.

Rick's angular face was handsome, boasting a wide mouth and two dimples that had matured just enough to cause women to take a second glance. An unruly cowlick in the front of his hair added to his boyish charm. He was slim and fit and tried to stay in shape by jogging. Despite good intentions, his work at the lab took precedence and, more often than not, he postponed his daily run with the hope of starting fresh the next day.

The second hand on the big faced clock was just sweeping past seven forty-five a.m. when Ashley Eberhardt came through the door. "Y'know, Rick," she said, "it doesn't seem to make a difference what time I get here. You're always here before me. Do you sleep here or something?"

Rick looked up from his reading and took a sip of his coffee. "Good morning to you, too," he said.

Putting her purse away, Ashley said, "Miguel is going to be late this morning. He was supposed to pick me up, but he called real early to tell me his car is on the verge of losing its entrails. He said he'd try to be here by noon."

"I must have had a premonition," replied Rick. "I checked his workstation this morning, and he didn't prepare either of the G-L samples like you asked him."

Ashley was in the middle of donning her white lab coat and stopped to give a grunt of exasperation. "He is such a shit! I asked him specifically to prepare those samples. He *knew* that we were going to do the overlay today and run the CO_2 test again. So, now what are we supposed to do?"

"We'll be okay," replied Rick casually. "I got here early enough to get both of them set up. It'll take a couple of hours to cook, but we'll be able to jump on them by noontime. One o'clock, the latest."

Ashley glanced up at the wall clock and tried to do a quick calculation of Rick's arrival time. "Say! Just how early did you get here?"

Rick smiled, but ignored Ashley's question. "When Miguel does get here," he said, "I want him to get started in a different direction. We're going to tackle the Palestine Project again."

"Crap!" said Ashley. "I was hoping that would just go away."

"No such luck," he said. "It's like a mosquito in your room at night. Just annoying enough to keep you from falling asleep."

"Yeah. You're right," she said. "But, you ought to consider what we're going to do with Miguel. He's missing a lot of work, and when he is here, he spends his time drinking coffee and making personal calls, for Christ's sake."

"Well," said Rick with a little smile, "you're the First Assistant. That's your job."

"Yeah, right," said Ashley, buttoning her lab coat. "You know what my solution would be?"

Rick chuckled, "Uh huh. You would beat him into oatmeal-mush with a two-by-four.

Ashley nodded and smiled approvingly at the suggestion.

"Too heavy-handed," said Rick. "Besides, we don't want to fire him. He adds a certain vitality to the place. I mean, after all, we do a lot of serious stuff around here, and I look forward to his blue collar sense of humor."

Ashley grunted. "His blue collar sense of humor, as you call it, is nothing more than a series of raunchy porn jokes about two midget prostitutes and a Texan with a cattle prod."

Rick smiled.

Ashley continued. "Truth is that you probably don't want to end up being the only guy amongst all us women."

The laboratory, for which the pair was responsible, presently employed six people, with Rick and Miguel being the only men. "I don't know about that," said Rick. "Some men would pray for the chance to be the only man among all you beautiful women."

"Careful, now," stated Ashley. "If you start drooling, Sarah is going to come in here and kick your ass!"

Rick chuckled and nodded.

Pasadena, California was home to a sizeable number of businesses that dealt with the cutting edge of technology. In this quasi-scientific Mecca, corporations structured around engineering, the environment and aerospace abounded.

Having spread its original borders, Pasadena was now considered a suburb of Los Angeles. It had many claims to fame, including the New Year's Day Rose Parade and Rose Bowl football game. The city was also known for the Pasadena Playhouse as well as the famous Civic Auditorium, a cavernous theatre whose patrons witnessed the annual presentations of the prestigious Emmy Awards.

However, it was the ongoing technological advances billowing out of Pasadena that took center stage on a more regular basis. The L.A. suburb also housed Cal-Tech and its affiliate, the Jet Propulsion Laboratory. Since NASA was one of the main sponsors of the J.P.L., all the national networks kept a presence in Pasadena.

The majority of the city's corporations had strong public relations departments, all vying for the attention of the ever-present cadre of reporters. In turn, the media responded by keeping them in the limelight. News stories came and went, but good reporters were always alert to controversial trends. The latest storm was in the field of biotechnology. Within that scientific community, there seemed to be a growing polarization between people who differed on the pros and cons of GE, or genetic engineering.

Rick was an employee of Envirogen, one of the growing list of biotech companies. Although it was located in the foothills of the Sierra Madres, the San Gabriel Mountains were visible against the eastern horizon. Some of the newer businesses had gathered into industrial parks with buildings high enough to peek over the tops of the trees. They included aerospace corporations such as J.P.L., dot-coms such as Earthlink, and biotechs such as Envirogen.

Over the last four years, Envirogen had grown at an astonishing rate. With more than three hundred employees housed inside their three-story building, the company's officers and investors were very pleased. Envirogen had a strong foothold in its niche market. The colorful corporate brochures boasted about a management team of highly degreed and published individuals. For their work with genetically engineered organisms, their names were recognized in cities such as Washington, D.C. and Stockholm, Sweden.

Rick Ballinger's title was Laboratory Supervisor. He, along with his first assistant, supervised a staff of four to six technicians,

Rick and Ashley went about their morning chores. A few minutes after eight, three techs, Nancy, Darlene and Lynn, arrived and exchanged pleasantries before tackling their assignments.

It was just after ten a.m. and Ashley was in the middle of telling Rick about her sister. "I mean, I love her and all that, but she doesn't talk about anything else. Her divorce has been totally devastating."

"Try distracting her," offered Rick. "After all, there are tons of things to do right here in Pasadena, let alone L.A."

"I have been," lamented Ashley. "I've tried everything. I'm at the end of my rope. Last night we went to eat at *Bistro 45*, you know, the one out on South Mentor. Anyway, she spots some guy who reminds her of her ex-husband and she starts to cry."

"I thought you told me she got divorced quite awhile ago," said Rick, trying to clarify the timeline.

"It's been ten months!" exclaimed Ashley with an exasperated gesture. "So anyway, listen to this. She starts to cry. Kind of quiet at first, but then, she begins to sob. Next thing you know, she's wailing like a banshee in labor, and everyone is looking at us. I'm trying to calm her down, but she's inconsolable. I didn't know where to hide. Can you believe it? It's been almost a year since he walked out. It should be enough already, don't you think?"

Rick asked, "So, how much longer will she be staying with you?"

"I don't know," replied Ashley with obvious frustration. "She was supposed to be with me for two weeks, but now it's been almost a month. I mean, don't get me wrong, my brother-in-law was no prize. To tell you the truth, he was a class-A prick. What guy brings his young slutty girlfriend home with him just to tell his wife he's leaving? Don't you think that kind of sucks?"

Rick chose not to answer.

"He destroyed her!" said Ashley, her voice rising once again. "I mean, he took away every ounce of self-esteem my sister had! I would have shot him! I would have blown a big hole in his god-damned chest. But my sister didn't have the strength!"

"And besides," said Rick with a disarming grin, "she's not mean and vicious like you are, you little spitfire!"

Ashley looked at Rick and realized immediately that she had been standing on the proverbial soapbox, spouting venom. She glanced over at Lynn, Nancy, and Darlene who were holding in their laughter. As Ashley began to chuckle, it released a flood of giggles from everyone. Turning to face Rick, she asked, "You really think I'm a spitfire?"

Rick said, "I would hate to be the guy who was married to your sister. Sooner or later you would find a way to castrate him."

"Castrate him? Say, there's an idea that has . . ."

The phone rang. Rick was still smiling as he picked it up and said, "Forum Lab, Rick Ballinger."

In order to avoid an impersonal work environment, each of the corporation's thirty labs had been given a name, rather than a numeric designation. Most of the names had ancient Greek or Roman derivations. While others claimed names such as Marathon, Augustus, Centurion and Trojan, Rick's lab was known as Forum.

"Rick, it's Doug," said the voice on the other end of the line. The caller was Rick's boss, Douglas Matsushita, who was one of genetic engineering's original *wunderkinds*. He had received his Doctorate at the University of California, Berkeley and remained there as a member of a scientific research group that was the progenitor of Envirogen.

"Morning, Doug," Rick began. "The answer to the question you missed yesterday was 'Sir Alec Guinness.' I thought you were a big *Star Wars* fan. What happened?"

"You guys deliberately asked me that question when you knew I would be distracted by the girl in the thong. But that's not why I called."

"What's up?" asked Rick.

"Our two-o'clock," stated Matsushita, referring to the most current of Envirogen's many meetings, "has been moved up to eleven-thirty."

"Eleven-thirty?" questioned Rick. "There goes my lunch date."

"Don't worry," consoled Matsushita. "We're having lunch brought in. Pizza, I think."

Rick was accustomed to the schedule of multiple meetings. The field of biotechnology was relatively young, and because of things such as new discoveries, recent innovations, and bureaucratic regulations, memos and meetings became an integral part of the daily regimen.

"It's not the food I'm worried about," said Rick. "It's Sarah's reaction."

"Well," stated Matsushita, "it's not like she's an outsider. She'll understand."

"Any change in the subject matter?" asked Rick.

"No," replied Matsushita. "The time was changed just to accommodate a scheduling glitch. Bring along your latest results from the Foxboro Project."

"All right," acknowledged Rick, glancing up at the wall clock. "See you in about an hour."

Walking over to Darlene's workstation, Rick took a moment to check her progress on a particular task. He was in the middle of adjusting the rotation speed of the separator when the phone rang again.

Ashley picked up the call and announced her greeting.

"Hi Ashley. It's Sarah. Is Rick available?"

"Sure Sarah. Hold on a sec." Ashley called to Rick, letting him know who was on the line.

"Tell her to hold on for half a minute," said Rick.

Doctor Sarah Levine was Rick's girlfriend. She worked on the third floor of the Envirogen building in the Department of Life Sciences. Recently, Sarah had returned from a symposium in New York where she had given a series of lectures that revolved around her research. The subject of her published paper was the migration of the *Solenopsis invicta* commonly known as the fire ant.

"Sarah? You still there?" asked Rick into the receiver.

"Don't you know you're not supposed to keep a lady waiting?" said Sarah, pretending to be insulted. "Especially a lady who treats you as well as I do."

"Sorry sweetheart," said Rick, "but when I heard it was you, I got so excited that I began to hyper ventilate and had to be revived."

Sarah Levine had a big smile on her face. She was hopelessly in love with Rick whose boyish charm never ceased to please her. "What time are you coming to get me?" she asked.

"Bad news," said Rick. "Lunch is officially cancelled. I've got a meeting to attend."

"I thought your meeting wasn't until two o'clock."

"Doug just called," explained Rick. "The meeting has been moved up to eleven-thirty."

Sarah mimicked a sinister voice as she said, "The evil Dr. Matsushita's goal in life is to keep us apart." Pleadingly, she asked, "Any chance we can have lunch afterwards?"

"No," Rick lamented. "They're bringing in pizza or something. It sounds like it's going to be a marathon session."

"Damn," exclaimed Sarah. "I wanted to discuss the upcoming Passover Holiday."

"How about if we talk about it over dinner tonight?"

"I can't," replied Sarah. "We're getting a shipment of critters sometime after seven and I'll have to be here until at least nine."

"Well, what's the big deal?" asked Rick. "We'll just plan on doing Passover with your parents."

Rick and Sarah had been living together for the past seven months. Very much in love, they seemed to make a perfect couple. The subject of marriage had been a recurring theme in many of their recent conversations. However, since neither Rick nor Sarah had met the other's parents, the two of them decided that the upcoming holidays would be the best time.

Rick's mother, Stephanie Ballinger, had always celebrated Easter with Rick, her only child. On the other side, Sarah's parents were Marvin and Esther Levine of Los Angeles by way of the Bronx, New York. Having traditionally celebrated Passover with the family, they fully expected Sarah to attend.

"The problem," reminded Sarah, "is that Passover and Easter both fall on the same weekend."

Rick simply said, "Oh."

"I know it's only the beginning of February, and we still have two months to work this out but . . ."

Rick finished her thought. "But you would rather put out the flame of a little matchstick now than a raging forest fire later."

"Very well put, lover," said Sarah.

CHAPTER THREE

FLORIDA

Freshly shucked oysters are not for everyone. It takes time to develop a taste for such a delicacy. Sometimes it takes years. It is sad to think that there are still some poor, unfortunate people who never get to experience the delight of rolling a raw oyster around the inside of their mouths.

"Good God, Brad! How can you eat that shit?"

Brad Bishop, who was holding a small, three-tined fork laden with a plump, ice-cold oyster, just stared at the man who had spoken those words.

Brad's lunch guest, Harry Goodenow, still had his face scrunched up as he continued, "Don't you realize that it looks like a pulverized piece of . . ."

Brad interrupted by holding up his free hand. "Harry, if you try to ruin my lunch, I'm going to beat you silly. When I get through with you, you'll look like this oyster!"

Harry chuckled.

Brad popped the tidbit into his mouth and closed his eyes, savoring the delicate flavor. He was having lunch at one of his favorite haunts, a small restaurant on the north end of Palm Beach. *Paul's Dockside* was a cozy place open daily for lunch and dinner.

"Do you want to get in a couple of sets of tennis after lunch?" asked Harry, stirring his iced tea.

"Tennis?" said Brad incredulously.

"Sure," answered Harry. "We could be over at my place in ten minutes and I could watch you have a heart attack trying to run down my drop-shots."

"Harry," admonished Brad, "this is Tuesday. I've got to work. You know, earn a living? Some of us less fortunate souls don't have your bank account. Or your bank for that matter."

"Oh, come now," chided Harry. "I happen to know that you have a considerable little nest egg."

"My nest egg, as you call it," said Brad, "is the kind that needs constant refueling."

27

"Don't forget," said Harry, ignoring Brad's last remark, "that I happen to be privy to how much money you invested in Tarwell Networks when it was selling for fourteen dollars. If I recall correctly, you sold it all just before it hit two hundred bucks a share."

Brad tried to interject, but his mouthful of oyster prevented it.

"Not to mention that other stock I put you in," said Harry. "Ellington Technologies. Remember?"

Harry knew the stock market well enough to regularly choose winners. Thus, with his trading account at Harry's bank, Brad was very appreciative of his friend's talent and counsel.

"You made a bundle buying it at sixty cents and selling out at seven dollars a share, didn't you?"

"Harry," said Brad, trying his best to sound annoyed, but fighting an encroaching smile, "Your expertise in picking winners doesn't give you the right to stick your nose into my wallet. That being said, I still can't spend the afternoon playing tennis."

"Why not? I know you can afford it."

Brad said, "It's called a responsible work ethic. Something that is woefully missing from your character."

"That may be so, my dear Bradstone, but I have tons of charm and loads of money to take their place."

Brad smiled. Harry had a dry wit that fit well with Brad's sense of humor. Besides, the taste of oysters at this time of year was perfect, and sharing good food with good friends was one of life's pleasures.

Brad was an insurance investigator who contracted his services out to several major companies. Although he examined theft, fire, and accident for a variety of customers, a sizeable number of his claimants resided in posh Palm Beach. Because of the value of their losses, they tended to be somewhat demanding, and it often created a stressful workday. As a result, Brad looked forward to sharing an occasional repast with his friend Harry.

The lunchtime crowd was beginning to thin. The restaurant had its own set of docks that allowed the mooring of up to eight boats simultaneously. At this time of year, with the population swollen by the "snowbirds," the availability of tables and boat slips was generally scarce.

Snowbirds was the endearing term that Floridians applied to the wintertime transients who flocked to the area. They began to arrive in a trickle after Labor Day. As soon as the Thanksgiving weekend ended, the number of snowbirds emigrating from colder climates ballooned. Then came the Christmas-New Years onslaught, when the floodgates opened and Floridians braced themselves for the hordes of new residents.

Sheryl came over to the table. "Well. Look at you two," she said good-naturedly. "It's like the Bishop-Goodenow Show."

Harry looked up, a dour expression on his face. "You make us sound like a vaudeville team, Sheryl. And the truth is, neither one of us poor souls can sing a lick."

"Speak for yourself, Harry," said Sheryl. "I've heard Brad do a very passable rendition of "Wasting Away in Margaritaville.'"

Harry pointed at Brad as he said, "Sheryl, are you talking about this Brad Bishop?"

"The very same," replied Sheryl. "If I'm not mistaken, Brad, I recall you having consumed a number of my 'Tequila Squealers' just before you broke into song."

A smile enveloped Brad's face as he said, "Now Sheryl, you promised me that incident would remain our secret."

Brad was a handsome man in his mid thirties. His longish crop of light brown hair tended to streak blond from the Florida sun. Notably charming, he was quick to smile and to put people around him at ease. He kept himself in good physical condition by working out regularly. Although Brad liked the competitiveness of sports, he rarely had time to play. Still, he took pride in whatever athletic ability he had.

Changing the subject, Sheryl asked if the service and food were satisfactory. After paying the woman a compliment, Brad said, "I think it's your turn to buy lunch, Harry."

"Didn't I buy last time?"

"No, Harry," reminded Brad. "If you recall, I was here with Maxine hoping to have a quiet, romantic hour with her when you barged in and sat down. Uninvited, I might add."

"Oh yeah," said Harry, a lecherous look brightening his face. "Right. She was wearing that . . . blouse that was tied into a knot just below those beautiful, round, firm . . ."

Sheryl cut off Harry's words by placing her hand over his mouth. "Uh . . . hold it Harry. I just want to know whose tab to put this on."

Brad laughed. "Pay for lunch, Harry and get your own girl."

Harry Goodenow had a round face that sat under a balding pate. The man's best feature were his eyes, which were bright blue and sparkled with expression. "Hmmph," he muttered.

Sheryl thanked them for coming and walked back to the register to ring up the lunch bill on Harry's tab. As was the custom between the two friends, one paid the bill while the other left the gratuity.

While Brad was counting off the tip, his cell phone vibrated against his waist. He put the money on the table before checking the identity of the caller. The number belonged to Stephanie Carlton-Ballinger, a recurrent client who always seemed to be frustrated about some problem in her life. Brad suddenly realized that at least two months had elapsed since they had last spoken. Even though Stephanie thought the world of him, she could sometimes be a bit overbearing. Brad decided to return her call once he got back to his office.

"Is that another of your exotic lady friends?" asked Harry, moving his eyebrows up and down lasciviously.

Brad re-hooked the cell phone to his belt. "Harry, why do you insist on taking such a salacious interest in my sex life?"

"Because," said Harry, "lately all my girlfriends have been roly-polys with the sex appeal of a dog biscuit. You seem to have cornered the market on 'seductively appetizing,' and I would love to be able to have some of that action."

Brad led the way to the parking lot. "I'm not sure I agree with you," said Brad. "It seems to me that Harriet is a fine-looking woman with a lot going for her."

"Harriet is beginning to bore me," said Harry. "Her days are taken up with shopping or frittering away at the spa, and her evenings are spent at one fund-raiser or another. Besides, our names are too much alike. Harry and Harriet. Sounds like a joke."

Harry's new Mercedes Benz sedan was parked next to Brad's black Lincoln S.U.V. The contrast in their choice of vehicles reflected the difference in their individual styles. "Well, so much for your days and evenings," said Brad, unlocking the door with his remote sensor. "But, that still leaves you with all those steamy nights."

Harry stopped in his tracks. "Oh puh-leeze!" he remarked. "Harriet is so stiff and cold she insists on wearing chain-mail battle dress to bed. Do you have any idea what hoops I have to jump through just to get her naked?"

Brad was laughing as he started his engine. "Harry, you've already given me more information than I wanted to know." Putting the big vehicle into gear, Brad said, "I'll talk to you later, buddy,"

Pulling into traffic, Brad glanced in his rearview mirror. Harry was still standing alongside his Mercedes, seemingly deep in thought. Brad just shook his head and smiled.

CHAPTER FOUR

CHICAGO

The door slammed shut with the force of a battering ram, making everyone jump as the noise shot through the room. One young man, sipping a glass of ice water, jerked spastically at the sudden sound and spilled a good portion of it down his chin and onto his shirt and tie.

Bruce Kreitzer stood at the head of a big oak conference table. He had been addressing the sixteen men and women who were sitting around its perimeter. Kreitzer was in the middle of reading sales figures when his head snapped up at the sound of the slamming door. His eyes focused on the looming figure of Josef Ubermann who strode to the front of the room. Kreitzer stepped aside and, without exchanging a word, allowed Mr. Ubermann to take the podium.

Ubermann was silent for a very long time as his gaze slowly swept around the table. Most staff members who caught his gaze could not hold it. Reflexively, they shifted in their seat and cast their eyes downward.

The big man's presence always sent a little fright-tremor through Bruce Kreitzer. Ubermann was a big man, tall and broad, with a barrel chest and no waist. He looked older than his years due to premature jowls that sagged on a square face. Kreitzer took a silent step backward when Ubermann began to speak. His voice seemed to be scraping along a washboard in a tunnel. However, his opening sentence was spoken in a surprising whisper. "You all are a piss-poor excuse for a group of professional salesmen." He took another long moment before continuing. "I am well aware," he said, still speaking in a strained but controlled manner, "of the diminishing sales results that all of you have been posting each month."

At that point, Kreitzer noted a distinct change in the man's voice. He could hear the anger rumbling just beneath the surface. "Don't you think for one second," said Ubermann, through clenched teeth, "that I'm not aware of everything that goes on in my firm."

Kreitzer felt a cold wave grip his innards as Ubermann shot him a dagger-like glance. The big man refocused his attention on a young woman sitting near the

31

far end of the conference table. "Miss Markowitz!" he snapped. "Can you hear me?"

Shelley Markowitz looked up. She blanched realizing that, for some unknown reason, he had singled her out. "Yes, Mr. Ubermann," she stammered. "I can hear you."

Ubermann boomed, "Well, it doesn't look as though you're paying any god-damned attention to anything I'm saying!"

Everyone turned to stare at the young woman.

"Well? Are you?" he shouted again, not giving her a chance to respond.

Kreitzer had a momentary rush of compassion. For his part, he noticed from the beginning that the Markowitz girl had really nice breasts which always managed to turn him on. As a result, he found it disheartening to watch her struggle through this verbal abuse. Despite that feeling, Kreitzer had no intention of butting heads with his boss. Instead. He just watched as the woman's cheeks flushed and her eyes filled with tears. For a moment, she lost the ability to think coherently. Josef Ubermann was president of the firm that featured his family name. He had a notorious reputation as a tyrant, impossible to work for and given to fits of rage. Everyone in the company made it a practice to stay out of his way.

The young woman's inability to respond was the catalyst for a real blowup. Ubermann hollered, "This is exactly the kind of bullshit I'm talking about! You people are supposed to be good salesmen! You people are supposed to be professionals! This firm was counting on you to be persuasive, glib, and . . ." He struggled for another adjective. " . . . and articulate, for Christ's sake! But instead," he gestured with his hands to encompass everyone in the room, "look who we have here. People who can't speak. My own sales staff, tongue-tied like god-damn mutes!"

Miss Markowitz had removed her glasses and was dabbing at her eyes with a tissue.

"And, now what!" yelled Ubermann pushing an exasperated palm in her direction. "Now, I've got a freakin' cry-baby on my hands! Does this look like a professional salesman to any of you?"

Ubermann paused for only a second. "Well? Does it?"

He scoured the faces in the room, not really expecting a reply. He looked at Kreitzer who was standing board-stiff along the left wall. "Mr. Kreitzer?" he yelled. "Do they look like a competent group of professionals to you?"

"No sir, Mr. Ubermann," replied Kreitzer in military fashion. "They certainly do not."

"Well you're the one who's responsible for them!" he said, momentarily pointing his finger. He looked back to the seated men and women. "So, now what the hell am I supposed to do? Nurse-maid a bunch of god-damned crybabies?"

Unable to compose herself, Miss Markowitz stood up to leave the meeting.

"Sit down, Miss Markowitz!" ordered Ubermann. "I haven't given you permission to leave yet!"

The young woman tried to object, but her throat felt constricted, and she couldn't get any words out.

"You're still employed here, young lady," he spat, "and you and the rest of your kindergarten class here are going to damn well listen to what I have to say."

Markowitz sat and listened. They all listened, allowing the man's abuse to pelt them like hailstones.

Hell-bent on instilling fear into the hearts and minds of his commodity traders, Ubermann's tirade continued for another forty minutes. What he didn't say was that the solvency of his business depended on their success. He was at his wit's end, and this lengthy harangue was born out of desperation.

He ended the meeting with the stern warning. "Next month's sales figures will determine your future with this firm." He spoke deliberately, making sure that everyone in the room understood the implications of his edict. "If there is no improvement," he paused for effect, "you're gone!"

Only the sound of breathing could be heard.

"Now, get out of here," he said dismissing them from the meeting, "and go do the job you were hired to do."

There was an immediate exodus. Everybody scrambled to put some distance between himself and Josef Ubermann. Bruce Kreitzer was among the crowd moving to exit the room.

"Mr. Kreitzer!" called out Ubermann.

Bruce Kreitzer turned, his face blanching.

"You stay!" ordered Ubermann.

CHAPTER FIVE

CHICAGO

"You're supposed to be the god-damned vice president of this company!" shouted Ubermann. "I was relying on you to make this happen!"

The conference room was empty except for Josef Ubermann and Bruce Kreitzer. Despite the hour-long, bluster-filled lecture he had just bestowed upon his sales staff, Ubermann's clothes looked recently cleaned and pressed. Kreitzer, on the other hand, appeared like someone just emerging from a vibrating sauna.

"But, Uncle Joe," said Kreitzer pleadingly, "you told me I was only going to be in charge of the salespeople. Isn't that what you said?"

"Don't call me Uncle Joe while we're in the office. You call me Mr. Ubermann like everyone else. I've told you that a million times. You can call me Uncle, if and when we're having Thanksgiving dinner with your mother. Otherwise, get off of that 'uncle' bullshit."

"Sorry, Mr. Ubermann," said Kreitzer contritely.

"And, as far as your responsibilities are concerned, I made you vice president of marketing. That means, the whole marketing department, you moron!"

Kreitzer nodded his head. "Marketing," he said as if he understood.

"I pay you two hundred-thousand dollars a year," reminded Ubermann. "For that kind of money, I expect you to take the bull by the horns and do the job you're paid to do. You're in charge of marketing. So, make something happen."

Kreitzer had been Vice President of Josef Ubermann Commodities Trading Group for the past seven months. His salary was one hundred-seventy-thousand dollars, not the two hundred-thousand that Ubermann mentioned. Even though Kreitzer liked the authority and control that came with his new position, he was unsure of his duties. His prior experience had been two-fold. First, he had received his sales training on a used car lot and, eventually, worked his way up to sales manager for *Cal-City Kia,* a dealership whose reputation bordered on piracy. After receiving numerous complaints about his management style, he left the auto industry and took a job as a boiler-room telemarketer for *Goddard and Bench,* a full line brokerage house.

Even before Kreitzer took the job, he was aware that his uncle was expecting a lot. Uncle Joe had continually made mention of the tough methods prevalent in auto sales management, and made it clear that he expected his nephew to use that same demanding style.

However, finding himself way in over his head, Kreitzer turned to the one thing that he knew best, the wielding of power. To Bruce Kreitzer, the title of V.P. signified that he held the crown and scepter and everyone else was there to do his bidding. Anybody who balked at his demands or complained about him personally was fired. Simple as that. Not fully understanding the meaning of "marketing," Kreitzer relied on a hustler's mentality when it came to selling. He was limited by its two rules: close the sale any way you can, and cover your ass later. His efforts to coordinate advertising, sales and training were woefully inadequate. Worse still, his shortcomings added to the company's slide in profitability. Kreitzer found that trading commodities was quite different from trading stocks and bonds and certainly a far cry from selling used cars. Even though the volatility in prices of futures was not as dramatic as those on the New York Stock Exchange or NASDAQ, the risks of investing were a lot higher. With futures, investors could buy on huge margins, up to ninety percent. For only a hundred-thousand dollars, a person could buy a million dollars worth of a single commodity.

Trying to defend his actions, Kreitzer said, "The biggest complaint I get from all the salesmen is that they don't feel like they can rely on our research department."

Ubermann threw his hands up in frustration. "You're not getting this, Brucie-boy!" he said as he stood up and jammed his chair back under the table. "Our problem goes deeper than the candy-assed whimpering of a bunch of incompetent salespeople! Our problem is solvency, god-dammit! Solvency!"

"What do you mean?" asked Kreitzer.

Ubermann leaned forward, coming close to Kreitzer's face. "We're broke, you imbecile. We have no working capital. Now, do you understand? We're almost on the balls of our ass!"

There was a long silence as Ubermann walked to the window and stared out at the skyline of downtown Chicago.

Kreitzer wondered if he should ask how this could have happened, but thought better of it. "What do you want me to do?" he asked instead.

Ubermann turned to face him. "Be aggressive," he said. "Be aggressive with the salespeople. Be aggressive with the research department. We've got to find ourselves a winner."

"How aggressive do you want me to be?" asked Kreitzer.

That was a key question. Aggressiveness in the commodities market took on different faces, often with ominous consequences.

In the seventies, the notorious Hunt brothers from Texas tried to corner the market in silver. As the United States was relaxing price controls in gold and silver, it allowed the wealthy Hunt brothers to profit from the opportunity. If they bought enough silver, they would be able to control the market. Having the ability to dictate prices could empower them to make a billion dollar fortune. However, their timing was bad. The Board of Trade sent out a "margin call" forcing the Hunts into bankruptcy.

In the eighties, another shady individual devised a scheme to make tens of millions of dollars. The character, named Jesse Balaban, was eventually arrested and convicted of injecting some unknown substance into hundreds of hogs. Upon investigation of the crime, it was discovered that, prior to his midnight escapades, Mr. Balaban had made sizeable investments in pork belly futures. He hoped that by killing off a large number of hogs, the forces of supply and demand would drive the pork belly futures sky high, thereby making him a fortune. The industry was peppered with similar stories of unscrupulous investors.

"Do whatever has to be done," growled Ubermann. "I don't give a rat's ass about what you do. Just do it!"

Kreitzer nodded his head.

Ubermann continued. "If you tell me to invest in corn futures, I want to know that you plan on blowing up every god-damn corn silo in America. I really don't care what you do. Believe me, I won't lose a single night's sleep over it. Just as long as you understand, if we don't turn things around in a hurry, we're both in trouble.

CHAPTER SIX

FLORIDA

Hannah Carpenter stepped out of the bathroom. She had one towel wrapped around her body and another trussed turban-like around her head. Droplets of water from her morning shower still dotted her exposed arms and legs. The television was blaring something about the excitement of owning a new Ford pickup truck. The brashness of the commercial motivated Hannah to change the channel to CNN Headline News.

Hannah returned to the bathroom to blow-dry her hair and apply her makeup. With a small hand towel, Hannah wiped the condensation from the mirror and took a moment to study her reflection. At five foot, ten inches in her bare feet, she was a statuesque woman. Her dark auburn hair was medium length and framed a squarish face with high cheekbones and full lips. Although Hannah was not inclined to exercise regularly, her sensible eating habits and energetic lifestyle gave her a lithe figure and shapely legs.

Almost thirty years old, Hannah had become dissatisfied with the speed and track of her career. She had been working for the *Sun Coast Ledger* for just over four years, and had hoped to be a headline reporter by this time. Focus and intensity were two of Hannah's better qualities, but they were also the reasons that her editor, Sidney Aarons, said she was not yet ready for the big-time. Mr. Aarons had indicated, during several of Hannah's reviews, that she tended to become so focused on the pursuit of a single point that she failed to see the entire picture. At first, the comments bruised her ego and she argued bitterly over the "incongruity of those remarks." However, with the passage of time along with her editor-in-chief's continued constructive criticism, Hannah began to reevaluate her shortcomings. A semiannual review was due at the end of the month, and Hannah hoped to convince Sidney that she was ready for the City Desk.

Hannah leaned close to the mirror to catch a glimpse of an errant eyelash. Although the woman was humbled by the compliments of others, she glowed when the flattery referred to her eyes. The deep blue-green of a stormy sea had been inherited from her father. Admiring words never failed to bring a smile of fond remembrance.

Hannah's father, Dennis Carpenter, had achieved a measure of fame in the sixties as a young photographer for *Life Magazine*. He had shot some exquisitely poignant moments during the height of the Civil Rights Movement. After winning a Pulitzer Prize for his achievement, he went on to become a photographer for *National Geographic*. During those early years, Hannah didn't see much of her father due to his extensive travel. There were occasional postcards with exotic postmarks, and short, handwritten notes that she treasured. Even less frequent were his phone calls. Still, she idolized her father without ever really getting to know him.

Tragedy struck while Dennis Carpenter was on assignment shooting photographs of a post-war Afghanistan. A stray bullet from some unknown assailant mortally wounded young Dennis. He died within twenty-four hours. Shock was Hannah's only emotion, and it turned her inward, effectively blocking out the rest of the world. Only ten years old, it took years for meaning to come back into her life. As her confidence and self-esteem re-emerged, so did the compliments.

Hannah's beauty was inevitable. Her father had been a handsome man, very tall with rugged good looks. However, Hannah's classic lines were inherited from her mother. Five years before Hannah was born, her mother, Rebecca Blumenfeld, known by her stage name, Becky Bloom, had been voted Miss Indiana. Ultimately, she became third runner-up in the Miss America Pageant. After her husband's tragic death, Hannah's mother, whom everybody still called Becky, remarried. Hannah was then thirteen years old.

It wasn't until she had gone away to college that Hannah came into her own. She made new friends and immersed herself in the experience of learning. Discovering her creative side, she blossomed while studying literature and journalism. During her final three years of college, Hannah received a steady stream of recognition for her writing skills. By graduation, she had compiled an outstanding résumé, and had no trouble getting a job as a reporter.

Dressing for the day, Hannah thought about the things she had to do, She paused as she recalled the events of the previous evening. Portions of Brother Timothy's sermon had invaded her dreams. Now, even in the light of day, certain phrases continued to strike at her sensibilities, making her wince as though listening to the sound of a cracked bell.

Hannah put on the finishing touches, including small gold floral earrings and a matching necklace that accentuated her navy suit. With Brother Timothy's interview more than three hours away, she ordered room service breakfast and began to listen to the tape recording of last night's sermon.

*   *   *

Brother Timothy was being patient. "These interviews are a good thing, Verne," said the preacher. "The more people who can hear my message, the better off we'll be."

"I dunno," said Verne, speaking slowly in his Carolina drawl, "It's just that these reporter people are so pushy and uppity. I think they try to make us look like fools."

Verne Smenken was a believer. He believed in God, he believed in the power of heaven, and he believed in Brother Timothy. He idolized the man and everything he stood for.

Brother Timothy sipped his coffee. Dabbing at his lips with a white linen napkin, he said, "I know, Verne. I know we have no control over the things that these reporters write in their newspapers and magazines, but we have to remember, our goal is to pass on *His* word."

Verne blinked his eyes when Brother Timothy invoked the Lord's name. At five-foot-seven, Verne was a wiry man with a small face and beady eyes. With eyebrows so light, they seemed almost nonexistent, and cheeks so sallow that they cast dark shadows, the man looked like a member of a chain-gang. Awed with the relationship that Brother Timothy had with God, Smenken felt that the Lord must have had good reason to speak directly to the preacher.

Brother Timothy went on. "You and I know that there is evil in this world. Isn't that right, Verne?"

Verne nodded his head.

"We also know that not everyone can see the evil that lurks around every corner. Isn't that also right, Verne?"

Verne nodded again, this time emitting a soft "uh-huh."

Placing the flat of both hands on the white linen tablecloth, Brother Timothy spoke deliberately. "And now, evil has taken on a new form. This time, evil looks just like a scientist in a white lab coat doing experiments with DNA."

Verne Smenken was becoming more animated as he bobbed his head in affirmation.

"These scientists," stated Brother Timothy, "are messing with God's own formula for life, and it's our responsibility to let everyone know."

Verne spoke. "We have to try and stop them."

Brother Timothy reached for his coffee before settling back into the chair. "That's right, my friend. And one way to do that is to tell as many people as possible about how the world will be destroyed if we allow these scientists to continue."

"Who's this reporter that's coming here today?" asked Verne.

"Her name is Ms. Carpenter. Hannah Carpenter. She's with the *Sun Coast Ledger*, which is a very influential newspaper."

"Can you get her to write the truth?" asked Verne, his accent deepening to match his worry. "Y'know, and not make us look like a bunch of hillbillies?"

Brother Timothy smiled a thin smile. "Well, first of all Verne, I'll stress the importance of the Lord's truth. Your job is to make sure all the recording equipment is working properly. I want to record every word of this upcoming interview. If she should misquote me or try to denigrate us in any way, we can attack her legally for slander."

"Right," said Verne, nodding his head. "Attack her."

CHAPTER SEVEN

FLORIDA

B rad Bishop had a multitude of things to do once he returned to his office. The pile of work involved some two dozen ongoing claims for missing property, including expensive watches from *Rolex*, diamond rings from *Cartier* and jeweled necklaces from *Harry Winston*. Handling investigations into theft or damage to rare musical instruments, antique manuscripts and art masterpieces were also within Brad's domain. He employed a number of people, including one who handled restoration of fine art. Even though Brad's main focus was on the administrative end of the business, he enjoyed maintaining a personal relationship with a few of his customers.

A graduate of FSU in Tallahassee, Florida, Brad had gone on to Georgetown University Law School in Washington, D.C. and passed the bar three years later. Then, he applied to the Federal Bureau of Investigation. A letter of recommendation to the FBI, written by one of Brad's professors, included the passage:

"Mr. Bishop possesses a fine analytical mind that has the capacity to comprehend abstract puzzles and fit the pieces together with ease."

The letter helped Brad land the job with the FBI. After spending three years as a Special Agent, Brad mastered the art and science of undercover investigation. Additionally, his law degree put him in the position of outdistancing his competition.

These days business was good, and Brad had recently moved his offices into larger quarters. From the fortieth floor, the view from Brad's office was breathtaking. It overlooked the Intercoastal Waterway and offered a picture postcard view of the famous Breakers Hotel.

Nestled into a narrow strip of land surrounded by Lake Worth and the Atlantic Ocean, Palm Beach lay on Florida's southeastern coast, about an hour north of Miami. The island boasted wealth to the point of opulence, and exclusivity to the point of restriction. Its residents included names like Kennedy, Rockefeller and Carnegie. Wide-eyed tourists paraded through the affluent shopping area of

Worth Avenue. Sometimes, if the alignment of the stars were just right, one could catch glimpses of kings, queens and Arabian sheiks.

One of Brad's clients had called during his lunch. The woman, Stephanie Carlton-Ballinger, **of Greenwich, Connecticut and Palm Beach, Florida had been widowed for fifteen years. Upon her husband's death, Stephanie inherited a very sizeable estate on Connecticut's south shore, an impressive mansion on the island of Palm Beach, and a financial portfolio that included several hundred million dollars in cash and securities.** Brad and Stephanie had met years before when the young man was first starting his business. Having lost a valuable diamond ring, she had put in a claim with her insurance company, and Brad had come to investigate. While doing background checks on Stephanie's domestic staff, Brad had discovered that one of the newly hired maids had a criminal record. A search of the woman's quarters uncovered the errant diamond along with four other pieces of Stephanie's jewelry that she didn't even know were missing. Instantly, Stephanie became Brad's best advocate. It wasn't long before Brad's business enjoyed a substantial and sustained growth.

In addition, once Stephanie found out that Brad was also a lawyer, she became a regular source of business. Her life seemed to be a series of crises. Each time a pesky dilemma reared its head, Stephanie called Brad. Most of the jobs that he did for her were trivial such as a fender-bender on one of her luxury cars or a background-check on a prospective employee. Even so, whenever he completed a job, his number-one fan always showered him with compliments.

Brad had become aware that Stephanie had developed a dependency on him. Since he also knew that Stephanie could be very demanding of his time, Brad charged her accordingly. She never questioned his fee or expenses. For that, he was very grateful.

Walking into his office, Brad was greeted with, "This is the way you run a business?" The woman offering the caustic salutation was Rose Goldberg, Brad's executive secretary, office manager and right-hand for the past six years.

"Hi Rose," said Brad nonchalantly. "Any calls?"

Rose ignored his question. "Do you realize that you've spent two whole hours with that no-goodnik banker, Harry Goodenow? How do you expect to get ahead in this world?"

Brad plopped one corner of his butt onto her desk and smiled brightly. "Hi Rose," he repeated. "Any calls?"

About two decades older than Brad, Rose Goldberg was the stereo-typical Jewish mother, always stressing important values to her children. Sometimes, she treated Brad as though he were one of her own. There were occasions when she went too far, and Brad had to reel her in. However, having Rose in a position of power had very distinct advantages. She could run interference better than a pro football halfback. Since she protected Brad at all costs and was so efficient at her job, Brad often wondered what he would do without her.

"I assume," said Rose, lifting her nose in the air and uttering her question with dripping sarcasm, "you have already heard from Ms. Stephanie Carlton-Ballinger?"

"Yup," replied Brad. "She left a message on my cell phone."

"Only one message?" asked Rose while she gathered a stack of pink message slips. "That woman has called here eight times since you've been gone. Eight times! And the last five of those times, she accused me of not giving you the messages!"

"Aw, c'mon," said Brad with a devilish grin. "You must be exaggerating." Brad knew full well that Rose was not exaggerating in the least, but he was goading her into a mild tirade. "That woman is as sweet as sugar."

Rose wasn't in the mood. It was obvious that Brad was twisting her tail and she wanted no part of it. She stared at Brad for a moment before saying, "I hate that woman."

There had been a personality clash from the very beginning. Generally even-tempered, Rose could get along with almost anyone. However, the first face-to-face meeting of Rose and Stephanie produced a shower of hot sparks. Each woman came away with a powerful dislike of the other. Over the years, the rift widened, and Brad found himself smack in the middle of it. He balanced the clash by adhering to two rules. First, he made certain never to agree with either one of them when told how rotten the other one was. Secondly, he tried to arrange appointments with Stephanie so that there would be the least possible interaction between the two women. For that reason, Brad had decided to give his cell phone number directly to Stephanie.

"Well," said Brad, "she obviously has a burr under her saddle. She'll be my first call.

Brad's inner office was a spacious affair. In addition to the panorama visible from the two big picture windows, the room featured a magnificent desk made of burled walnut. This piece of furniture held an incongruous item; a blue Nerf-ball in a little glass well. The knick-knack was a gift from his friend, Harry, and came with a card stating, "To help alleviate the stress." In the other half of the office, there was a conversation pit consisting of a love seat, three chairs and a coffee table. Brad sat behind his desk and dialed Stephanie's number.

"Good afternoon," said a man with a clipped British accent. "Carlton-Ballinger residence."

Brad did not recognize the man's voice. Knowing Stephanie as he did, Brad understood why she could not keep her help for any length of time. "Hello," answered Brad. "This is Brad Bishop returning Ms. Ballinger's call."

"Oh, yes sir," said the Brit. "Ms. Ballin . . . uh, Ms. Carlton-Ballinger has been expecting your call. One moment, please."

Brad heard an electronic click followed by music meant to entertain the waiting caller. Out of habit, he picked up the Nerf-ball and began squeezing it.

Neil Diamond was halfway through singing "September Morn" when Stephanie came on the line. "You haven't been trying to avoid me now, have you Brad?"

"Avoid you?" asked Brad. "Are you kidding? Stephanie, you're like great cheesecake at the end of a meal, and I never avoid dessert."

"I prefer to think of myself as the appetizer," retorted Stephanie.

"Yeah, well, okay," conceded Brad. "But you sure look a lot better than escargot."

Stephanie giggled. A fifty-two-year-old widow, she considered herself one of the "beautiful people." The woman spent a lot of time, energy and money keeping herself in starlet mode. Hair salons, body waxing and personal trainers took up a good portion of her life. She had also become close friends with the doctors who performed cosmetic surgery on her face, thighs, hips, breasts and tummy.

"Brad, dear," said Stephanie, "I left a message for you almost four hours ago. Why did you take so long to get back to me?"

Brad picked up one of the pink message slips and checked the time of Stephanie's first call. Then, he said, "No fair exaggerating, Stephanie. Your first call came in at one-thirty-eight this afternoon. That was less than two hours ago." Brad found it worked wonders if he quickly put a lid on her embellishments. Hesitating a moment, he added a white lie of his own. "Besides, I was in a meeting and got delayed in a little snowbird traffic."

Brad had just touched upon one of Stephanie's pet peeves. "Isn't it awful," she lamented, "when our beautiful Garden of Eden is spoiled every winter by the hordes of New York Jews that come here and infest our island?"

Brad was caught a little off guard. He knew that Stephanie was somewhat intolerant of minorities, but this was a strong comment, even for her. Brad suspected it had something to do with the eight phone conversations between herself and Rose Goldberg. "Now, Stephanie," chided Brad, "we have to be tolerant of our tourists. Jews and Gentiles alike. It isn't nice to refer to them as an infestation."

"Well, some of them are just so . . . . Jewish," added Stephanie.

"Anyway," said Brad, changing the subject, "I got your call. What's going on?"

"A dire emergency has popped up in my life. Quite serious. Quite serious indeed. We'll need to set a time to discuss it."

Brad said, "Give me a hint."

"This isn't something to go into over the phone. We'll need to discuss this in person."

They each took out an appointment book and promptly agreed upon a date and time. Stephanie suggested meeting for lunch at "The Club," which was her reference to Donald Trump's *Mar-a-Lago Club*.

"I understand that Mr. Trump has redesigned the interior," said Brad.

"Whoever did it," gushed Stephanie, "was sheer genius. But there's more, dear boy. The club also has a new chef. Yves Champilione from the famous *Cordon Bleu* cooking school. Just wait until you've tried his bouillabaisse. You'll just die."

CHAPTER EIGHT

CALIFORNIA

The conference room was on the third floor of the Envirogen building. It was large and well appointed and featured an atrium effect with one wall made entirely of glass. The huge windows encompassed two-thirds of the vertical wall before angling up into the ceiling. To prevent a greenhouse effect, air conditioners pumped massive amounts of cool air, which was circulated by oversized ceiling fans. The centerpiece of the room was a polished pecan conference table designed to seat eighteen people with perimeter space for twice that many.

The spectacular view included the stately Angeles National Forest to the north and the peaked San Gabriel Mountains to the east. The result was an open and bright meeting room that set a positive tone for business.

However, this day would see a more intimate setting. Rick Ballinger was one of only five attendees. Dr. Doug Matsushita, who headed up the oversight committee for Rick's research, sat to the right of Herb Knoll. Herb, a no-nonsense guy, was the Director of Accounting for Envirogen and answered directly to the Chief Financial Officer. Mr. Knoll's responsibility was to make sure that the costs of doing business were held in check, he also saw to it that the research results yielded sufficient profits to satisfy his boss, the Board of Directors and the stockholders.

Besides Rick there were two other lab supervisors in the room. Donna Kingston was in charge of the Spartan Lab and Mel Fishman headed a team in Plato's Lab. Rick, along with Donna and Mel, represented the cream of the crop of about thirty supervisors.

The biotech industry, a high-flying sector of the economy, was pocked with companies on the verge of great things. However, many of the corporations seemed to have difficulty turning a profit. This teetering financial status was an ever-present danger. As a result, whenever a group of biotech scientists completed the research *and* generate a finished product that actually got to market, the team was noticed. When the end result produced a healthy financial gain, the scientists were praised, paraded and given very special attention.

Such was the case with Rick, Donna and Mel. They, along with everyone else at Envirogen, knew that they were the best. That being said, an interesting set of circumstances had evolved. An edgy competitiveness had developed among the three supervisors. Although it was highlighted by a sophomoric sense of good-natured kidding, it was, nevertheless, a serious rivalry.

Rick, the last to arrive, pulled out a chair. "Hey," he said to Mel and Donna. "What are you two guys doing here? I thought that the janitorial committee is supposed to meet down in the basement." Rick, satisfied with his punch-line, plopped into his seat.

Donna spoke with great deliberation and concern when she said, "Uh, Rick . . . Mel put super glue on the seat of that chair."

For just a moment, Rick blanched. Mel began to cackle, Donna put her head in her hands, and Doug snickered. Rick knew he'd been had. Only Herb Knoll failed to see the humor.

Doug Matsushita, still grinning, called the meeting to order. "All right. Hold it down people, and let's get started. Herb and I need to get a complete update on a few of your projects. We want to know the status of your primary, secondary and tertiary undertakings."

Mel raised his hand as though he were in grammar school. With mock innocence he said, "Wait a minute, Doug. Are you suggesting we just forget about our quaternary and quintinary projects?"

Herb Knoll had a puzzled look on his face. "I don't think those are real words." Turning to Doug, he asked, "Are those real words?"

The four of them snickered at Herb's lack of humor, and Doug continued. "Okay, okay. We'll keep it simple. We also want you to tell us what you might need in order to wrap those projects up in a timely fashion. If you need any additional equipment, manpower, supplies, etcetera, let us know, now."

Herb half stood up from his seat. Sternly, he said, "Just because you say you might need those things, doesn't mean you'll necessarily get them, you understand. It only means we'll take it under advisement." He sat back down, adding weakly, "Cost control."

"Lighten up Herb," said Doug. "It's just the five of us." Even though Doug Matsushita represented management, he was first and foremost a research scientist. He felt a camaraderie towards Rick and the others. Herb, on the other hand, had no scientific training. His job was seeing to the money end of the business.

Doug continued. "We have a new client about to come on board. It's the State of Georgia."

Rick said, "Let me guess. They'd like us to show them how to grow cotton balls the size of watermelons."

"With no boll weevils," added Donna.

"Or maybe," said Mel gleefully, "they want us to take the engineering students from Georgia Tech and . . ."

Doug interrupted. "Okay! Enough already. It's not cotton balls or boll weevils. It's kudzu."

"What's a kudzu?" asked Mel.

Donna said, "It sounds like an oral hygiene problem."

Rick sat back and said seriously, "It's a vine-like plant. But more than just a clinging type like ivy, this one has a smothering quality to it. Its thick leaves are quite broad and it grows rapidly. So, it quickly kills off the trees that it attacks."

"Hey! No fair!" complained Mel. "Rick had advanced knowledge of this meeting. Donna and I weren't given the opportunity to do our homework on this kudzu stuff."

"No one was given any advance information," said Doug, annoyed at the interruption.

Donna lightly slapped Mel on the back of his head. "You are being such a baby, Mel."

"Yeah, Mel," agreed Rick.

"Then, how did you know about kudzu?" asked Mel. "Huh, Mr. Botanist?"

"I did an ROTC rotation at Fort Benning," answered Rick. The army base is located in Columbus, Georgia. I remember the kudzu problem was rampant all around that area and that was back about ten years ago."

Doug went on. "Right," he said. "Well, kudzu is a serious problem throughout the State of Georgia. Now, it seems to be affecting its agricultural stocks. Specifically, its export markets in peaches and pecans."

Donna said, "So now, Georgia wants us to step in and genetically manufacture a cure."

"Exactly," said Doug. "They're very anxious to make this happen. So anxious in fact, that they're willing to start us off with a fee of about twelve million dollars for research and development."

Herb shuffled some papers. "This is a real plum for Envirogen." He spoke as though he were addressing a group of children on a tour. "The Board will be very pleased to see this little project come to fruition. And, that's just the start, you know. The possibilities for making money are endless."

Doug held up his hand to prevent any snide remarks from the three scientists. "First things first," he said. "Let's get back to basics. I don't want any of you dropping the ball on what you're doing now."

Rick thought about the purpose of the meeting. This procedure was unusual. In the past, Doug had always conducted this sort of thing on a one-on-one basis, never with all the supervisors in the same room trading notes. Rick and Donna exchanged a glance while Mel, sporting a puzzled frown, raised his hand once again.

"What's your question, Mel?" asked Doug.

"What's this meeting all about? Some sort of brainstorming session?"

"Brainstorming?" repeated Doug. "No. I want to see where each of you is with regard to your present projects. I need a calendar; a schedule of when and how the new research will begin."

Rick asked, "What are you saying, Doug?"

"I'm saying that eventually I want the three of you working on this together. Y'know, if two heads are better than one . . ."

Unsmiling, Donna finished the phrase. "Then three heads make a troll."

Doug ignored Donna's remark. "Our marketing division will be closing the deal with the State of Georgia shortly. I was hoping that one of you would be finished with your primary project by that time, and ready to begin this Kudzu Project."

With those words, the lighthearted atmosphere in the conference room took a distinct turn. Rick, along with Mel and Donna, knew instantly that the "Team Leader" position was up for grabs. With each of them having a proven record of success, it wouldn't make any difference to Doug or Herb which of the three would be in charge of the Kudzu Project. Suddenly, it was obvious that the position of project supervisor would fall to whoever was available first.

Rick and Doug had maintained a personal friendship for the last three years. Even though the two had shared a lot of good laughs, Rick realized that his boss was not going to select a team leader based on that. However, Rick was hoping that his close association, along with his ability to produce, might tip the scales in his favor. Rick also knew that whoever claimed the prestigious title of Team Leader could use it to climb Envirogen's career ladder.

Rick opened his briefcase and spread out the data sheets in front of him. There were three projects for which his team was responsible. One was a long-term research undertaking designed to be a "filler." Consequently, his group would get to it, if and when time allowed.

Another of the studies, titled The Palestine Project, involved a series of trial and error experiments. Its focus was a search for an elusive enzyme that might be used in a new family of drugs designed for Cystic Fibrosis. Rick's team was not the only group working on it. A dozen other supervisors were involved in the same project. The problem was the vast number of possible combinations of DNA inter-splicing. A figure that approached the trillions. As such, it was possible that the Palestine Project could go on forever without ever reaching a conclusion. Rick knew it was something else that could be placed on the back burner.

The remaining study, titled the Foxboro Project, was the main focus of the work being done in Forum Lab. It was the one job that had to be completed before Rick could be selected to head the Kudzu Project. "Foxboro" was named for the Foxboro Brewing Company, headquartered in the Massachusetts town of the same name. The company had started as a micro-brewery and within a few short years, its beer had developed a reputation that took it to national distribution. With a line of six different beers, Foxboro Brewing produced about seven hundred million dollars in annual sales. They had contracted with Envirogen to discover a means to enhance the flavors in the hops, thereby adding new groups of beer to their line.

The job had fallen to Rick and his team. After a month or so of going around in circles and doing what every Brewmaster does, Rick decided to look at the problem from a different perspective. He had asked Doug Matsushita to arrange a meeting with the partners of Foxboro Brewing Company. When Rick addressed the group, he said, "Gentlemen, instead of enhancing flavors with the intent of increasing the product mix, let's consider an entirely different approach."

Fascinated with the field of biotechnology, Rick's audience had listened attentively.

"What if there was a way," Rick had said, "to speed up the brewing process? Wouldn't that translate into greater profits? After all, it takes time to brew a good beer. If you could brew the same quality of beer in less time, think about how much more profitable that would be."

It didn't take long for the beer meisters to realize the advantages of manufacturing their product in less time than their competition. The idea became a contract. Foxboro agreed to pay Envirogen a hefty sum of money for the research and development of such a process.

Rick was ecstatic at his success, for he had an ace up his sleeve. His blueprint was to create a new life-form that would speed up the fermentation process. Knowing how he was going to approach the problem and feeling that success was imminent, Rick had put his plan into motion.

Donna had finished giving Doug and Herb an update of her primary and secondary projects. She asked for additional manpower and equipment in order to expedite the completion of her work.

Herb balked at every request. One of his favorite comments was, "You're not generating enough revenue to warrant all those expensive things."

There were times during her presentation that Doug backed Donna's requisitions. On other items, Doug sided with Herb.

All the while, Rick paid very close attention to Donna as she spoke. It was obvious that she was at least a month away from completing her work.

The meeting dragged on. Pizza arrived in time for lunch but, for the most part, sat in the center of the conference table getting cold.

In the middle of Mel's presentation, there was a minor point of contradiction. When Doug questioned it, Mel became defensive, and it quickly boiled over into a loud debate. Mel had been struggling to make a point that, with a little cooperation, he could be done with all his present assignments in two weeks. Doug, on the other hand, knew better. As such, he asked Mel several questions that the supervisor found difficult to answer without painting himself into a corner. Mel's problem was that he was an overachiever. Each of the thirty Envirogen supervisors was responsible for only one primary project. However, Mel, wishing to show that he could handle more than anybody else, had taken on two. Now, whining that he had more work than Rick or Donna, Mel pleaded for Doug to reassign one of his projects. When Doug refused, Mel became upset.

Voices were raised until Herb stepped in and calmed things down by saying, "Look, Mel. We are not going to make a decision today about who takes over the Kudzu Project. Doug and I will assess all your input . . . I'm talking about the input from all three of you, and we'll make our decision sometime down the line." Then, Herb suggested a twenty-minute break while they cleared away the pizza and brewed some fresh coffee.

Finally, around two p.m. it was Rick's turn to offer an update as to his lab's status. He began by dismissing two of the three projects with which his team was involved.

Donna interrupted. "Wait a minute! My team is also working on the Palestine Project. If Rick is allowed to, off-handedly, dismiss the importance of finding a cure for cystic fibrosis, then I should be given the same consideration."

All eyes shifted from Donna to Doug.

Doug simply said, "All right."

Rick continued. "That leaves the Foxboro Project."

"Okay," acknowledged Doug. "How's that one going?"

"We're on the down slope now," answered Rick. "We've got the key to accelerating the fermentation process. I've taken the liberty of calling the new life-form, '*Quadballingermyces*.'" Rick smiled and waited for a response.

Naming a new life-form was akin to earning a gold medal. Since it represented all the effort required to accomplish such a feat, it was a badge that the recipient wore proudly. It also meant that, in a sense, you had a shot at immortality. If the creation or invention proved to be an integral part of something important, and your name was indelibly associated with that discovery, it could become a household word. Examples of such fame included Jonas Salk and his Salk vaccine and Louis Pasteur and his process of pasteurization.

"We'll make sure to get it filed," said Doug. "Go on."

"Well," said Rick, "My team spent a lot of hours researching the basic process, and doing a great job narrowing the field of various fungi that we could use as interjectors." Rick was a good team leader who always gave credit to his group. It was a glaring contrast with Mel Fishman, who always presented his findings as though he were the only one who had done the work.

Rick continued. "So far, we're doing pretty well. The team has been testing the new 'myces,' and have set up about a hundred and fifty control groups."

Herb Knoll cleared his throat. "I don't understand," he said. "What do 'mice' have to do with the fermenting of beer?"

A little chuckling floated around the room caused by Herb's ignorance of basic biology.

"He's referring to yeast," explained Doug.

Rick added, "Specifically, saccharomyces. It's the main ingredient in the fermentation process."

"So, what did you create?" asked Herb wide-eyed.

"A new form of yeast," Rick explained. "You see, the problem, as I saw it, was how long it took for fermentation to occur. I figured that if the fermentation process could be sped up, that would greatly enhance the manufacturing process and allow for the production of a lot more beer. Therefore, it would be more profitable for Foxboro."

Herb asked, "So, how did you do it?"

"I found a fungus that produces considerably more enzymes than the average. As a result, it metabolizes and decomposes very rapidly. We extracted some specific DNA from that fungus and spliced it into the saccharomyces, you know, the regular yeast. In that way, the new yeast became more efficient."

"Tell me how that's done," said Herb.

Rick looked at Doug. "Do we have time to go into this?"

Doug shrugged. "Go ahead, but keep it short."

"Okay," said Rick. "You take the yeast, saccharomyces, and feed it a starch rich diet. In this case, it was shredded potatoes. That causes the haploid cells to become diploid cells. Then, we sit back and wait for mitosis to occur."

"Mitosis?" questioned Herb.

"Cell division," explained Doug. "Don't you remember 'mitosis' from your eighth-grade science classes?"

Herb nodded as though he did remember.

Rick continued. "In the middle of mitosis, the cell temporarily becomes a quadriploid. That's the critical moment. At that exact time, the new cell is captured and a strand of DNA from the fungus is spliced in. The new life-form, which I call *Quadballingermyces*, has four sets of chromosomes rather than the usual two. Now, the fermentation process occurs at almost twice the normal speed."

"Jeez," said Herb, shaking his head in amazement.

Rick moved his focus back to Doug, "Anyway, the DNA splicing portion of the project is complete. Now, all we're doing is testing."

"Excellent," stated Doug. "Then you should be complete in . . . what . . . two weeks or so?"

"Maybe," said Rick hesitantly. "We've run into a minor glitch."

"What is it?" asked Doug.

"When we started the testing on the control group, everything went fine for a while." Rick flipped through some pages in his notes looking for a particular passage. "Here it is," he said. "At G.A.-16, the results showed an elevated level of CO_2."

"What do you call 'an elevated level'?" asked Doug.

Before Rick could answer, Mel jumped into the conversation. "You said your tech found a fungus and you extracted DNA from it. What fungus, exactly?" he asked with a probing tone.

Rick looked at Mel and then back to Doug. With exaggerated patience, Rick answered Mel's question. "Plasmodia."

"Plasmodia?" shouted Mel. He spun in his chair to face Doug. "That's the shit that gives people malaria, Doug! It sounds to me like he's got to go back to the drawing board."

Mel was looking for an opening. Any problem that would cause a delay in Rick's work would give Mel a chance to catch up and pass him. "How could you have used plasmodia, Rick?" asked Mel with an air of incredulity. "Didn't you realize it was deadly?"

With squared shoulders and pulse pounding in his temples, Rick addressed Mel. "You're out of line, Mel. And, you don't know what you're talking about!"

"Doug," pleaded Mel, "believe me when I tell you that plasmodia is dangerous. It's . . ."

Doug held up his hand, cutting off Mel's words. "Relax Mel," he said. "I'll ask the questions." Turning back to Rick, he asked, "What's with the plasmodia?"

"First of all," said Rick, still upset from Mel's inquisition. "I am not using the parasite that infects the anopheles mosquito, which is *Plasmodia falciparum*. On the contrary, I am using a one-celled mold spore with a similar name. It's called simply *Plasmodia unacera*." Rick addressed Mel. "And if you had done your homework, Mel, you wouldn't have had to embarrass yourself by shouting out such nonsense."

Seemingly satisfied, Doug asked his next question. "So what do you think is causing the high levels of CO_2?"

"I'm not sure," replied Rick. "Fact is, the plasmodia I've used has been known to cause some blight in cabbages and similar vegetation. That may be the reason for the elevated levels of the gas. So, it's going to require more testing."

Donna Kington, who had been sitting quietly for some time, now interjected, "Isn't CO_2 a natural by-product of fermentation?"

Rick nodded his head. "Yeah," he said. "It is."

"So what's the big deal?" stated Donna impatiently. "CO_2 is CO_2. Let's get on with the meeting."

"All right," said Doug. "Do your testing. If anything else unusual crops up, let me know."

"Wait a minute!" cried Mel. "Is that the end of it?"

Doug took a deep breath and said, "All right, Mel. State your piece."

"Okay," said Mel as he stood up. "What I'm going to say is important. We're dealing with some pretty serious stuff here. We're creating new life-forms in this building. It's imperative for us to be aware of our responsibility. If we make a mistake . . ." Mel made two fists and pointed both thumbs toward the ground. "That could be the end of it. Our actions could cause a disaster. Just think about *Ceratocystis ulmi*."

"What the devil is that?" asked Herb.

Mel said, "That's the fungus responsible for Dutch Elm disease. It's been wiping out all the elm trees in Europe and in the United States since World War II. And, how about Ergot? I'll bet you haven't considered Ergot, have you?"

Mel's dissertation was rocketing far beyond Herb's comprehension. He spread his hands in a helpless gesture and looked at Doug for an explanation.

Doug explained, "Ergot is the fungus that causes 'ergotism,' also known as 'St. Anthony's Fire.'"

"That's right," said Mel feeling vindicated. "And there's no known cure for that disease. The Ergot fungus contains lysergic acid. That's the main ingredient in LSD."

Doug lost his patience. "Enough, Mel," he said. "You're off on a tangent, and it doesn't have any bearing on the present discussion."

With Doug's chastising words, Mel felt as though he was about to lose momentum. In desperation, he turned to Herb Knoll. "Herb, surely you see the danger in using something that could be deadly?"

Before Herb had a chance to gather his thoughts, Doug responded. "C'mon, Mel. Cut out the dramatics. You know as well as anybody that more than half the drugs on the market have a downside. More than half of them will kill you as quickly as they'll help you, if they're not used properly."

"Yeah," countered Mel, "but take into consideration . . ."

Mel's words were cut off when Doug said, "The Ergot you're referring to . . . the one that causes 'St. Anthony's Fire,' is used every day to help induce labor. It's also prescribed to stop migraine headaches and hemorrhaging. So come down off your soapbox, Mel."

Mel sat down.

Hoping to add the closing comment, Rick said, "Besides, my people are doing all the necessary testing. We've still got a way to go, but we'll get there."

Herb asked, "Will it produce profits?"

"It most certainly will," answered Rick.

Doug concurred. "Big profits."

Herb seemed pleased. "Good," he stated simply.

Rick used the moment to ask for two additional technicians, as well as a new centrifuge, a separator, and a considerable amount of agar, the medium for growing cultures.

Herb stood and looked at his watch. "I think Doug and I have all the information we need in order to go ahead. I want to thank the three of you for keeping us informed. And Rick, it sounds like you're doing a fine job on that . . . beer thing. I've been getting good feedback. Those folks in Foxboro are very excited about the culmination of your project." Herb glanced at Mel before continuing. "And, whenever one of our clients is eager to throw a lot of money at us, we need to accommodate them. So, let's not worry about a little carbon dioxide, especially when it's a natural by-product of making beer in the first place. Besides, cars and trucks spew that stuff into the air all the time. A little more isn't going to hurt the environment." Herb put his notes and papers together and walked out of the room, signaling that the meeting was over.

Donna was the first to speak. "Cars and trucks spewing carbon dioxide?" she asked rhetorically. "He is such a dolt."

Mel removed his glasses and wiped one lens with a tissue. In a gravelly tone filled with frustration, he said, "Once again, dear friends, science takes a backseat to money."

CHAPTER NINE

CALIFORNIA

Mel Fishman gathered his papers and left without ever looking at Rick or Donna. He was smarting from having lost his battle with Doug Matsushita, a hurt made even worse because it happened if front of his peers.

Doug was getting ready to walk out the door as well. "Rick, when you get back to your lab, check your schedule for this coming Thursday and call me. We need to talk about the two new techs you've asked for."

"Sure, Doug. I'll call you later."

The door closed, leaving Rick and Donna alone. Rick said, "Thanks, Donna."

Donna's head snapped up. "For what?"

"For coming to my defense when I was explaining my CO_2 results."

"Listen, Rick," said Donna closing her briefcase, "The more I think about it, the more pissed off I get."

"What are you talking about?" asked Rick.

"I think it's great that they want their three shining stars working on this kudzu thing, but I don't think Doug and Herb have looked at it from all angles."

"What do you mean?" Rick asked sitting back down in his chair.

Donna's anger became evident as she said, "You, me, and Mel, are the best damn supervisors in this joint. Now all of a sudden, two of us are going to become underlings! What kind of bullshit is that? Doug has definitely not thought this through."

"Underlings?" said Rick incredulously. "That's not what he wants, Donna. Doug wants the three of us to work together as equals. Like a triumvirate, of sorts."

Donna said, "Well, the reality of it is that one of us is going to have to be in charge. And that one person is going to be you, by virtue of the fact that your schedule frees you up first. That leaves me and Mel as the underlings. You can sugar-coat it all you want, but the truth is, ultimately, we'll be working for you."

Rick was shaking his head. "Donna. I really do believe he wants us to collaborate on this."

"Oh, Rick," said Donna, like a parent losing patience with a child. "Wake up." Don't you see it?"

Rick just stared blankly.

"Look," she explained. "Don't you sometimes collaborate equally with your first assistant? What's her name? Ashley?"

"Yes. So?"

"When we attend all these back-to-back meetings, do you bring Ashley along? Do I bring my first assistant just because we work together? Of course not. The fact is that the three of us may end up working on this Kudzu Project, but only one of us will be coming to the meetings. It'll just be you, Rick. Just the team leader."

Rick exhaled audibly. "Look, Donna. I'll admit that I hadn't thought of it that way, but I think that Doug and Herb are just looking to get the biggest bang for their buck. I never . . ."

Donna interrupted. "This is nothing against you, Rick, God knows, if I had to work under someone's supervision, I certainly would pick you over that asshole, Fishman. He's such a pompous, smarmy son of a bitch."

Rick just nodded.

Donna continued. "And, that explains why I came to your so-called defense. I can't stand the idea of Mel Fishman being my boss. It's obvious that with my present workload, I'm not going to be selected. So, you're my next choice. It's that simple."

"Well, okay," Rick said. "Thanks anyway."

"And I'll tell you something else," said Donna. "As soon as Mel realizes what's in store for him, he's going to raise a dust cloud, too."

Rick just shook his head. "I'm going to have to think about what you're saying."

Donna stared for a long moment. "You do that, Rick."

They walked out of the conference room together. Donna turned right and headed down the hall towards her lab, while Rick turned left towards the elevator. The door to the stairwell opened and out walked Stan Briscoe, one of the other lab supervisors. As they approached each other Rick noticed a Cheshire cat grin on Stan's face.

"Hey, Rick," called Stan. "Weren't you just in a meeting with Mel Fishman?"

The question was unexpected and made Rick stop in his tracks. "Yeah, I was, Stan. What's up?"

Mel Fishman's popularity was limited to management. Since he had the ability to produce results and profits, he was held in high esteem. On the other hand, Mel's peers had a very different opinion.

"I just saw him in the stairwell," said Stan in between a couple of mean-spirited chuckles, "and he looked like someone dragging his dick through the mud. What the hell happened in there?"

Rick couldn't help but smile. Stan's comment seemed apropos, but Rick thought it might be wiser to keep the information to himself. "Who knows," answered Rick, swallowing the white lie. "He gets pissed at the drop of a hat. Could've been anything that set him off."

"Ain't that the truth," agreed Stan. "The little prick runs hot and cold like a prostitute in an Eskimo village."

Rick's grin widened.

"See you later, buddy," said Stan.

Rick took the stairs down two flights. Coming out through the stairwell door, he thought he heard loud voices. Walking down the hall toward Forum Lab, the sound of a blaring argument was unmistakable. Rick entered his lab and momentarily stood frozen in disbelief. His first assistant, Ashley Eberhardt, was standing nose to nose with Miguel Ortiz, one of Rick's lab techs.

Ashley was screaming at the man. "You are fucking useless, Miguel!" she hollered. "I get more work out of a god-damned cockroach than I get out of you!"

Miguel Ortiz had his arms at his sides, but his hands were balled into fists. Leaning forward, his face was very close to Ashley's. Anger was making his Mexican accent more pronounced. "You must be on the rag or something!" he yelled in return. "Don't talk to me!"

Rick said, "Hey you two!" but they were so deep into their argument that they were oblivious to Rick's presence.

Ashley shouted, "All you do all day is drink coffee and think about your whores! You think with your dick, you ugly shit! And I'm sure it's no bigger than your brain!"

Miguel, nowhere near as glib as Ashley, was doomed to lose this war of words. There was a moment's hesitation before Miguel railed back. "You are one black-hearted bitch! You know that?"

Rick turned to Lynn, Nancy and Darlene who stood helplessly at their workstations. They looked frightened and none seemed willing to offer an explanation.

Turning back to Ashley and Miguel, Rick stepped forward. "Whoa! Whoa!" he shouted. His loud command caught the attention of the two combatants, and both turned to look at him.

"Back off!" commanded Rick. "Back off, the both of you!" he said again as he stepped in between them. "What the hell is going on here?" he demanded.

Miguel took a step back. Ashley was shaking visibly and showing the first signs of crying. "I'm going home, Rick," she said between gulps of air.

"Ashley," Rick said firmly. "Wait a minute, will you?"

"No!" she blurted, as she struggled to remove her lab coat. "I will not wait a minute! I will not wait even one god-damned minute!"

"Ashley," pleaded Rick. "At least give me a clue as to what precipitated this . . . fiasco."

Ashley's wristwatch had somehow become entangled with one sleeve of her lab coat. She was forced to yank at it repeatedly until it finally came loose. In the struggle, the sleeve was turned inside out, creating an even greater frustration for the woman. She stomped to the door and half turned, glaring at Miguel. Then, she looked at Rick and said through clenched teeth, "You figure it out!"

The door slammed behind her.

Rick turned to Miguel. "What the hell was that all about?"

"Aw c'mon, man," moaned Miguel. "What is this? I'm the only one left, so I'm the one gonna get in trouble?"

"Don't give me, 'aw c'mon,'" said Rick sounding very stern. "I want to know what went on here."

"It's that Ashley bitch, man," said Miguel.

"What's that supposed to mean?"

"She been on my case for months, man," said Miguel with his head bowed. "That bitch don't let up for a minute."

Rick was frustrated at not getting a straight answer. He turned to Nancy, Lynn and Darlene and said, "Wouldn't you all like to take a break? Maybe, twenty minutes or so?"

The three women didn't say a word. They grabbed their purses and left hurriedly.

Rick waited until they left before pulling over two wheeled office chairs and offered one to Miguel. They both sat down.

Miguel Ortiz had grown up in the barrios of Southern California. For most of his life, he had known only the Mexican neighborhoods where poverty was prevalent and crime was common. After landing a job with Envirogen's maintenance department, four years earlier, Miguel was quickly promoted. His supervisor recognized that the Mexican had a talent for fixing all sorts of things, including some newly acquired, sophisticated equipment. Soon, he was working in Rick Ballinger's lab. Miguel's job was that of a "gopher," the title given to a worker whose responsibility it was to fetch things for everybody. Even though Rick had promoted Miguel to "technician" status and managed to get him an off-cycle merit raise, he still lived like one of the *Mojados*. Better known as "wetbacks" and delinquents, the *Mojados* resided in the slums and spent their time in the streets.

"Okay Miguel," began Rick. "We're alone, and I'm giving you a chance to tell your side of the story first. Let's hear it."

Miguel started by asking Rick to just forget the incident, saying it didn't mean anything. Rick would have no part of that evasive game and insisted that Miguel reveal the reason for the argument. "Miguel," said Rick, ""if you're not willing to tell me what happened, then I'm going to be forced to believe Ashley's version. And, whatever action I take will be based solely on her explanation. Is that what you want?"

There was a long silence before Miguel spoke. "It's just that she don't ever let go of you. She's like a gutter-whore, y'know? She don't never say, like, thank-you. She don't say shit. She just chews on my ear with her filthy mouth, know what I mean?"

"So, what was the argument about?"

"I must be stupid or somethin'," said Miguel seemingly ignoring Rick's question. "I been drivin' that slut to work every morning, and I ain't never asked for nothin'. I mean nothin'. No gas, no wear and tear . . . nothin'. And today, when I come into work, she jumps all over my ass."

Rick was beginning to show obvious frustration. "You know something, Miguel, you're not telling me anything. You're talking in circles. I'm asking you specifically what triggered that argument, and you're telling me what an awful woman you think she is."

Rick sat forward, hoping that his prodding would motivate Miguel into an explanation. When Miguel did not respond, Rick said, "Okay, Miguel. So here's how it's going to be. You go home. I'll call you to come back to work once I get to the bottom of this. And only if I think you can fit in and do your job."

Miguel looked up, his face turning red with anger. "What the fuck!" he blurted. "Are you firing me? Is that what the hell you're doin'?"

Rick had not seen this side of Miguel and became slightly alarmed at his reaction. "Not yet, Miguel," he said cautiously. "But I won't tolerate this kind of behavior in my lab. I'm going to make a decision . . ."

The telephone interrupted Rick's thoughts. He stopped in mid-sentence and looked at it, contemplating whether to answer it. He looked back at Miguel. "I was saying . . ."

As the phone continued ringing, Miguel stood up quickly. The swift action caused Rick's heart to skip a beat. For a fleeting moment, he envisioned a physical confrontation with Miguel. Alarmed, Rick stood up so abruptly that his wheeled chair skidded backward and slammed into a steel table causing the clang of metal against metal.

"Answer your fuckin' phone, you pussy!" said Miguel. "It's probably that Ashley bitch, gonna cry on you!" Then, he headed for the door.

Rick watched as Miguel walked out of the laboratory. Crossing the room to the ringing telephone, he picked it up.

"Uh . . . Hello?" Rick stammered. "Um . . . Forum Lab," he corrected.

"Rick? Is everything okay?" It was Sarah Levine, Rick's fiancée.

"To be honest with you, Sarah," he said as he sat down and ran a hand through his hair, "I'm not sure."

"Why? What's going on?" asked Sarah, a hint of concern in her voice.

"Oh, not much," he said with veiled sarcasm and a ragged breath. "On the one hand, Doug and Herb may have just handed me an assignment that's going to be the envy of all the other lab supervisors. On the other hand, I'm standing in the middle of my lab, which happens to be totally devoid of any technicians."

"What are you talking about?" asked Sarah. "What happened?"

"Ashley and Miguel just beat each other bloody, and the other three ran out of here fearing for their lives."

CHAPTER TEN

CALIFORNIA

It was a medium-sized white panel truck with Old English style lettering stenciled on the driver's side door. The words read, "Stevenson Associates." The transport service specialized in catering to odd and eclectic shippers who delivered curious and bizarre merchandise to a select group of extraordinary customers. On this night, the customer was Envirogen.

Sarah Levine stood at the loading dock, cradling a clipboard in her left arm. The driver had just taken the last of two small cartons from the van and placed them on a big table in the receiving area. Each box was only about a foot-and-a-half square and covered with brightly colored labels marked "Fragile," "Perishable," and "Live Specimens."

The driver handed Sarah two forms and said, "You gotta sign both of them, babe."

Sarah raised an eyebrow and glanced sideways at the driver. Never having met him before, his casual use of the title, "babe," surprised her. She carefully inspected the cartons, looking for any signs of damage, signaling that the items packed inside might be harmed. Finding no visible imperfections, she checked off the appropriate box on each of the forms and continued to scrutinize the shipment.

"Hey, babe. You gonna take long doin' this?" asked the driver. "It's getting late and I got a bunch more stops to make."

Sarah Levine, who had been born and raised in the Bronx, claimed ownership to a rich New York City accent. Initial impressions were not always favorable when people first listened to her speak. However, Sarah had a few things going for her. She was witty, pretty, and possessed an international reputation as an expert in her field. It had been a long time since anyone had referred to her as babe.

Sarah had received her Master's degree in entomology from Cornell University and her Ph.D. from Princeton. These days, her world was far removed from the Bronx. Brazen taxi drivers and whistling construction workers, who might have called out "Hey baby," had long ago been replaced with serious people and men of letters who attended biological symposiums, and referred to Sarah as "Doctor."

Sarah stared at the driver for a beat or two. "Naa," she answered, choosing to ignore his impertinence. "This won't take long," she said as she cut through the packing tape. "I'm just going to make sure that all the little critters in these boxes are still alive. You know, buzzing and crawling and stuff."

"Buzzing and crawling?" said the driver, his face scrunched up as though he just had eaten something rotten. "What the hell is in there?"

Sarah looked up and couldn't help but smile at the look on the man's face. "Insects," she enunciated with dramatic deliberation. "Hundreds of live insects."

"No shit!" he remarked. "Live insects?"

Both cartons were divided into twelve separate sections. In each compartment there was a vial specifically designed to hold one or more of a particular species of insect. Several of the glass jars were meant for only a single, large insect, such as the common tarantula spider.

"Yup," said Sarah nonchalantly checking each container. "Live insects."

"Shi-it!" said the driver, with a shiver. "You got a creepy job, lady. How the hell do you do it?"

"Mostly, I take drugs," said Sarah straight-faced. Having finished looking at each of the vials, she was satisfied that the mortality rate was low enough to accept the shipment as is.

The driver watched as Sarah replaced the glass jars. "Say," he asked, "do any of those things ever get loose?"

After signing off on both forms, Sarah handed them to the driver. He reached for the documents, but was fixated on the bugs. Sarah watched his expression. Man was still a primitive beast, she thought. Despite eons of trekking through jungles and forests inhabited by countless billions of insects, man still had an intrinsic fear of the little creatures. This delivery driver, who just moments ago boldly referred to her as a "babe," was now ready to run. Picking up the vial that imprisoned the big tarantula, she unscrewed the top. The hairy spider reluctantly lumbered out of his makeshift cage and stopped in the middle of the table.

Sarah looked at the driver for his reaction. He had taken a cautionary step backward and held out one hand as if warding off an evil spirit. "What the hell you doin'?" he asked in a trembling voice.

As Sarah scooped the tarantula back into the safety of its enclosure, she said casually, "There was supposed to be another one of these spiders, but he seems to be missing." She gestured toward the white van. "Probably somewhere in your truck."

The driver's mouth fell open. He stared alternately at Sarah and his van. Finally he said, "You gotta be shittin' me!"

Sarah lifted both cartons and started to walk back to her lab. She called out a warning over her shoulder, while trying to suppress a giggle, "Just be careful. You probably won't find him for a while. He'll hide somewhere, but eventually you'll see him somewhere up front. Tarantula spiders like to ride up front with the drivers." Sarah turned to push the door open with her elbow. "They like the light coming through the windshield."

Reluctant to even take a step towards his van, he called out, "What the hell am I supposed to do?"

"Well, whatever you do, just don't let him get up your pant-leg," advised Sarah as she took a step into the hallway and let the door to the receiving dock close. No longer able to stifle it, she broke into laughter.

Dr. Sarah Levine was the corporate entomologist at Envirogen. In addition to her role as resident bug expert, she ran the Life Sciences Division of the company. Her department was home to a chemist, a zoologist, a botanist and three technicians, all of whom answered to her.

Life Sciences main purpose was to work with all the lab supervisors on their various projects. Sarah's responsibilities were not only that of department supervisor, but also included her own project. It was a task that involved her working with Bennett Pharmaceuticals, a giant drug conglomerate based just north of Los Angeles. The goal was to uncover natural compounds that could aid in cosmetic surgery.

The telephone was ringing as Sarah came through the door of the room known as "The Zoo." Not much bigger than a twelve-by-twelve cubicle, it housed all the live specimens. Although presently residence to only a handful of white mice and an aquarium full of frogs, one side had cages large enough to accommodate dogs and monkeys, while the other side displayed a bank of glass containers, capable of holding an odd and varied collection of insects.

Plopping the cartons unceremoniously onto the counter, Sarah picked up the phone. "And who might you be?" she asked into the receiver. Since it was after hours, there was no need for daytime formality.

"Hi Sarah," said Rick. "I called before and it just rang a long time. Is everything all right?"

"Yeah sweetheart," she replied. "Everything is okay. I was out on the loading dock, checking in a shipment of critters with an impertinent delivery man who kept calling me 'babe.'"

"May I assume that the delivery man is now on the way to his next stop?"

Sarah smiled. "Perhaps," she answered cryptically. "But I wouldn't be surprised if he was still standing out there tomorrow morning."

"Oh, no. What did you do to that poor guy? Staple his feet to the loading dock?"

Sarah giggled. "I was just teaching him a little respect."

Rick tried changing the subject. "Coming home soon?"

"In about an hour," she replied. Then, still enjoying the memory of her practical joke, she laughed and said, "You should have seen the look on the guy's face when I told him there was a tarantula spider loose in his delivery truck."

"You're going straight to hell, Sarah," said Rick with half-hearted conviction. "Someday somebody's going to drop dead of a heart attack right in front of you. You know that?"

Sarah took her turn at switching topics and asked, "Did you eat dinner yet?"

"No," said Rick. "I was hoping, if you weren't going to be too late, we could grab a bite together."

"Good," said Sarah, aware of the many hours since her lunch. "It shouldn't take me too long. I'll try and be home in maybe . . . forty minutes. So, what have you been up to?"

"My mother called," said Rick. "We were on the phone for over an hour."

Waiting to see if Rick would elaborate, Sarah asked, "Did she say anything about Easter?"

"Yup. Sure did."

"And, did you tell her about our plans?"

The relationship between Sarah and Rick was growing stronger every day. Their status as co-workers had led to a friendship which, in turn, led to frequent dating. Several months prior, Rick moved into Sarah's townhouse. They were very much in love. However, knowing that they would one day marry, Sarah made a point of discussing the potential problems they would have to face. The big one was that Sarah Levine was Jewish and Richard Ballinger was not.

"I did," said Rick.

"And . . . ?"

Rick said, "And, as expected, it did not go over very well."

"Then what?" she coaxed. "Did you stick to your guns?"

"Come on, Sarah. Give me some credit!"

"Well, it's just that you've said yourself how demanding and manipulative your mother can be."

"Oh, she tried, Sarah. God knows she tried. She wanted the address of your folk's house in L.A. so that she could arrange a cross-burning on their lawn."

"Be serious," said Sarah, ignoring his dark humor. "What did she say?"

"She got me to agree to come visit her the weekend after Easter."

"The weekend after? Damn!" said Sarah suddenly remembering a scheduling conflict. "I won't be able to make it. I've got to be in Seattle for the conference."

"Not to worry Sarah. She didn't invite you."

*   *   *

Besides casting a melon-colored glow onto the side of Maria's face, the orange script, with its illuminated neon lettering announced that the name of the club was "El Ranchero." Smaller letters, no less glaring, promised "Hot music" and "Cool drinks." Maria was wearing a white tank top that exposed the cinnamon tones of her bare arms and shoulders. It was cut to reveal her midriff from just under her breasts to a point seductively below her navel. A pair of denim shorts, clinging tightly to her hips, had a flowery ruffle sewn on the bottom of each leg. The shorts were cut high in the back, allowing a tempting glimpse of her butt-cheek. The men who frequented "El Ranchero" didn't seem to mind a bit.

Miguel Ortiz noticed the sign's reflection on Maria. Having consumed enough liquor to have a really good buzz, he was fascinated by the color of her skin, which had taken on the shadings of a faded cantaloupe.

He shook his head as if trying to clear his thoughts. "Come walk with me, woman," said Miguel as he stuffed his hands into his pockets. He hunched his shoulders against a momentary shiver that gripped him despite the seventy-degree temperature.

Maria draped her right hand over Miguel's shoulder and fell into step. "You had some bad day today," she said softly. She slipped her free hand inside the open front of his shirt and rubbed his chest. "You deserve better than that, *mi querido*."

Having related the events of the day, Miguel had managed to resurrect his anger over Rick Ballinger for threatening Miguel's job. "So what if I get pissed at that Ashley bitch? That's none of Rick's business! He should have just left it alone! But no. That little prick had to keep on pushing! Just like Ashley! Always pushing me! The two of them never seem to let go!"

"It'll be all right," said Maria, softly.

Miguel ignored her prediction. "Everybody's always pushing me," he stated.

"I know, baby," cooed Maria. "I know."

"I like my job," he continued. "Y'know that? I like my job. I do important work there. A lot of important work."

"I know you do, baby," acknowledged Maria. "I love it when you tell me all about your work. It makes me proud of you."

69

Miguel glanced at Maria and saw the sincerity in her dark eyes. He studied her lips. They were full, inviting and sensuous. Now, slightly parted, her teeth shone white behind the raspberry lipstick. She was gorgeous. Managing a crooked smile, Miguel put his left hand around her waist as they walked.

Despite being Miguel's steady girlfriend, Maria had been working the streets since she was fifteen. Her first seven years as a prostitute were hell, as she struggled with the competition of the other whores. Even though there were pimps who treated her fairly well, she had a couple who turned out to be bad people. They cheated her, beat her, and made her do things that she regretted. Maria had endured more of the same from many of her customers, men who pawed at her like Neanderthals, licking their lips as though she were the drumstick on a long-awaited Thanksgiving turkey. in spite of all that, Maria had qualities that she turned to her advantage. Enticing because of her seemingly childlike innocence, she had the face and figure of a teenager. Notwithstanding, she was street smart. Whenever she had a customer who treated her well and paid without a hassle, she made sure to keep him as a client. Maria felt that Miguel was smart. Too smart to be hanging around with the other Mexicans who were not going anywhere. His enthusiasm for his work excited Maria, and she would ask dozens of questions whenever he talked about a new project taking place in the lab. Never thinking that her questions were stupid, Miguel took the time to explain what Maria didn't understand.

Later that night, they lay naked in each other's arms, breathing regularly now that the throes of passion had subsided. Maria adjusted her pillow to bring her face close to Miguel's. With her fingertips, she gently combed the hair off his forehead and asked, "Baby? You ain't gonna quit your job, are ya?"

In the half light of the room, Miguel continued to stare at the ceiling. "Well, I'll tell you this," he said, "I ain't gonna give that Ashley bitch no more rides to work. That's for sure."

CHAPTER ELEVEN

FLORIDA

Somewhat anxious about her interview, with Brother Timothy Goodman, Hannah Carpenter had arrived at the Marriott Hotel fifteen minutes before her scheduled appointment. Despite having interviewed a number of prominent people who were better known to the public than Brother Timothy, Hannah was intrigued by the man's charisma.

The front desk took Hannah's name and phoned Brother Timothy's suite. Informed that someone would come to escort her upstairs, Hannah made herself comfortable, choosing a seat closest to the elevator. A large painting, reminiscent of one in her stepfather's study, caught her eye. After a moment, Hannah averted her gaze.

Hannah was barely a teenager when her mother remarried. The three of them moved to Palm Beach, Florida where Hannah experienced living in relative comfort. Although it might not have been considered a mansion, it was a very large home complete with a pool, a garden and a full-time maid. Her stepfather seemed to be a fairly generous man, and Hannah didn't want for much. However, despite all the amenities, she never felt totally comfortable or completely safe. Hannah's mother assumed that her daughter's discontent was due to her little girl's unfulfilled love for her real father. The truth, however, was a dark secret that Hannah kept buried for years.

Hannah's stepfather had, on several occasions, attempted to fondle her. Whenever she did something naughty, her stepfather would threaten to relate the incident to her mother. Often near tears, Hannah would plead with her stepfather not to tell of her misbehavior. In turn, he hugged and stroked her until she squirmed away fearful and confused. It took several years of this sexual trauma before her level of caution and wariness became Hannah's protector. She learned how to avoid her stepfather and still maintain a cordial relationship with the man. The last thing she wanted was to hurt her mother, and confessing the sexual abuse would have done just that. It became Hannah's secret.

Hannah looked at her watch. Precisely fifteen minutes had passed when a young dark-haired girl, who proved to be miserly with her words, introduced herself as Leila and escorted Hannah to her audience with Brother Timothy.

"Leila's such a pretty name," said Hannah breaking the silence as they waited for the elevator.

"Thank you," said the young girl, without turning her head in acknowledgment.

Hannah guessed Leila's age to be sixteen or seventeen. The teenager seemed very serious for such a young person. "Are you familiar with Leila Barros?" asked Hannah. "The Olympic volleyball player from Brazil?"

They stepped into the elevator and Leila pushed the button for the sixth floor. Never taking her eyes off the control panel, she shook her head slightly and said, "No."

Hannah tried a different approach. "Are you related to Brother Timothy?" she asked. "His daughter, or something?"

This time, Leila briefly glanced at her questioner, shook her head again, and uttered her single word response, "No."

The remainder of the elevator ride proceeded in silence. After accompanying Hannah into Brother Timothy's two-room suite, Leila walked into the adjoining room and never reappeared.

The living room portion of the suite was typical. On one wall, there was a chair and desk that held a telephone, fax and computer. Dominating the room were a sofa, love seat and two chairs, arranged in a tight conversation pit. In the center of the grouping, sat a beige coffee table with a pot of freshly brewed coffee and china service for two.

As Hannah walked into the room, Brother Timothy Goodman looked up from reading a fax. Extending his hand, he said, "Miss Carpenter. Welcome, and thank you for being so prompt."

Hannah was immediately taken aback by his voice. At this moment, he was the epitome of a soft-spoken, country-bred southern gentleman. Nothing at all like the voice that fired thunderous volleys at the Pentecostal parishioners who were gathered under the tent the previous night.

Hannah quickly composed herself. "Thank you, Reverend. Is it all right if I call you Reverend Goodman?"

Brother Timothy had one of the brightest smiles Hannah had ever seen. She couldn't help but smile in return.

"Please make yourself comfortable, and call me Brother Timothy. My parishioners have given me that name, and I'm quite at ease with it."

They both sat down, Hannah choosing a chair and Brother Timothy sitting on the love seat at the end closest to her. He filled two cups with the aromatic brew and asked about her preference for creamers and sweeteners.

With pleasantries out of the way, Hannah got down to business. She set up her tape recorder, turned it on and placed it on the coffee table. Next, she took out her yellow legal pad with all her notes and began the interview. "My paper is very interested in the resurgence of revival meetings. All through the middle of the nineteen hundreds there were tent revivals in every vacant corn field. But, during the so-called enlightenment of the sixties and seventies, they seemed to die out. Now, here you are, leading the charge back to tent revivals. How do you account for that?"

Brother Timothy continued to stare at Hannah. His eyes roamed over her face, studying the details. Once again, he smiled. It was absolutely effervescent and Hannah smiled back.

"May I call you Hannah?" he asked.

"Oh. Yes, of course," she said, her cheeks beginning to flush.

"You're not at all like other reporters," he said. "I was expecting the usual drivel. You know: where I was born, where I grew up, where I went to school. That sort of thing. But you're obviously an exception. And a beautiful exception at that."

Surprised at the warmth in her face, Hannah felt the need to take a sip of coffee. Brother Timothy was a handsome man. Middle forties and tall, he had a square face with a rugged jaw line. Dark, deep eyes were softened with very long eyelashes. The most striking feature was his hair. Mostly black, it had a contrasting streak of light gray, almost white, that cut through the middle.

"Thank you, Brother Timothy," Hannah said, placing her cup in the saucer. "But you see, I already have your bio, although I do have one or two questions about that. So, I thought you and I could get right to the heart of the matter."

"Well in that case, my dear Hannah," he said, "my purpose is not to resurrect the tent revivals. The meetings I conduct are nothing more than an opportunity to deliver my message."

"But you seem to have sparked a renewed interest in this kind of thing. People are beginning to come out of the woodwork just to hear you. Don't you realize that you're the catalyst in all of this?"

Brother Timothy sat back and crossed his leg. Anticipating a long, detailed answer, Hannah also sat back and crossed her legs. Unfortunately, while doing so, she accidentally kicked the coffee table. The rattling cups and saucers momentarily distracted Brother Timothy from his thoughts. Before he had a chance to begin again, a man emerged from the adjoining room. Silent, he stood staring at the two of them.

Brother Timothy refocused. "Miss Carpenter? I'd like you to meet my assistant, Verne Smenken. Verne has been with me since . . . forever." He turned to Smenken. "Verne? Say hello to Hannah Carpenter from the *Sun Coast Ledger.*"

"How do you do, ma'am," Verne said straight-faced and without inflection.

"What can we do for you, Verne?" asked Brother Timothy.

"I heard the dishes rattling," he said without taking his eyes off Hannah. "I thought you might need me to clean up a bit."

Brother Timothy glanced at the coffee cups. They seemed fine. He looked back at Smenken who was still staring at Hannah. "Yes. Of course," said Brother Timothy as he stood up. "Go ahead and tidy up a bit, Verne. Miss Carpenter and I will continue our discussion over here." Brother Timothy stood and slid a wooden, straight backed chair to the opposite side of the desk. Once she was reseated, Hannah was facing away from Verne Smenken and was unable to see what he was doing.

Brother Timothy said, "Hannah, if you would be so kind as to please repeat your question." The Preacher glanced over Hannah's shoulder at Smenken. The man was on his hands and knees resecuring the hidden microphone that allowed the secret recording of the interview.

Hannah said, "I was saying that revival meetings are becoming all the rage again, and a lot of people are pointing to you as the inspiration. Is this what you were hoping for?"

"To be known as an 'inspiration . . . ' Well, that's something. Wouldn't you say?"

Hannah nodded. "My editor thinks that you could wind up on the cover of *Time Magazine*. That means, at the very least, your popularity is growing. How would you account for that?"

"You've heard my message," said Brother Timothy, more as a statement than a question.

"Yes," replied Hannah. "I was there last night."

Brother Timothy squinted and was silent for several seconds. "Oh, yes," he said nodding his head. "Back row. On the aisle. You were wearing a blue print sundress."

Hannah raised her eyebrows, shocked at his ability to have picked her out. "There must have been a couple hundred people in attendance. How did you . . . ?"

Brother Timothy interrupted. "I try to be aware of everything that goes on around me."

Hannah tried to absorb the significance of his comment.

"Since you were there," he continued, "and heard my message, I'm sure you understand why so many people come and listen. They want to hear the word of the Lord. They want to believe in His word."

"But hasn't that always been the case?" asked Hannah. "Isn't that why people go to church in the first place?"

Brother Timothy looked surprised. "Churches don't offer the truth," he said, addressing her naiveté. "Those robed men who stand at the pulpits of America only speak about what the church wants them to speak about. They merely recite the doctrine of the church. Their Sunday sermons are just empty words. They think they're being politically correct when, fact is, they're afraid to tell the truth."

"And you tell the truth," stated Hannah.

"My truth is God's truth," said Brother Timothy, his voice dropping half an octave. "I'm merely God's messenger. God wants everyone to be aware that there is evil in this world." Brother Timothy took on a more relaxed attitude as he added, "The evil I speak about is the Devil, himself. And the Devil, in this case, has taken on the form of a scientist doing experiments in genetic engineering."

"So, you put the fear of God into those people," said Hannah. "Is that why they come? Do people want to be frightened? Do people come to listen for the same reason they go to see scary movies?"

Brother Timothy stared at Hannah. She was aware that her question bordered on disrespect. She waited.

The voice of Verne Smenken made them both turn their heads. "Y'all can come sit back down here now," he said softly. Smenken had rearranged the coffee table so that Hannah and Brother Timothy would have more leg room. They moved back to their original seats. Hannah expected Smenken to disappear to the adjoining room. Instead, he sat at the desk, claiming Brother Timothy's former chair. She noted that Brother Timothy did not object to Smenken's presence.

"The fear of God," said Brother Timothy quietly. "That's a bad expression. There's never a reason to fear God. There are only reasons to love Him. Now, the Devil, on the other hand . . ." He stopped himself, rethinking how he wanted to proceed. "You want to know why so many people are coming to hear me speak?"

Hannah nodded.

"They come because nobody else is telling them the truth. They come because they can't hear the truth spoken on their television sets, and they can't read the truth in their newspapers. The media only relates what they themselves receive in the form of press releases. But what I do, Hannah Carpenter, is cut through the lies. I cut through the smoke screen of the so-called wonder drugs and the whispered secrets of financial gain, and I tell the truth. God's truth."

"And that is . . . ?"

"That there is an inherent danger in genetic engineering. It must be stopped or it will destroy the world."

"You realize, of course," said Hannah, "that you have a lot of detractors. Some very prominent people are saying that you prey on the uneducated, the country bumpkins of Middle America."

Hannah glanced at Smenken as the man cleared his throat.

She turned back to Brother Timothy. "How do you respond to that?"

"You haven't done your homework, young lady," admonished Brother Timothy. He sat forward and rattled off four names in succession. The first was the Dean of Bell-Norman University. The second was a well known professor of bio-engineering at U.C.L.A. The third was a nationally syndicated talk-show host, and last was United States Congressman, Lee Clark, also an outspoken critic of the new science. "Certainly there are detractors against what I preach. That's because I pose a threat to disrupt their cash flow. But, as you can see, I have my share of supporters."

The interview continued. Throwing her questions like punches, Hannah kept trying to uncover the secret of the man's allure.

Brother Timothy was using this meeting as a means to hammer home his message that the creation of new life-forms must rest solely in the hands of the Lord. Any attempt to alter God's plan would open the doors to Hell and allow the Devil free access to mankind.

Focused solely on the interview, Hannah was unaware that an entire hour had slipped past. Her fascination was more with the man himself than with his message. Smooth and poised, Brother Timothy was making his points with facts, sincerity, and an occasional disarming smile.

"I'm sure you're aware," said Brother Timothy, "that most of the countries in Europe have outlawed the importation of genetically altered foods from the United States."

"Yes, of course," replied Hannah. "But isn't that a kind of mass hysteria? It's like, when there's a drought or a flood; you can make farm folks think that it's their own fault for not believing in God. Aren't you using this new-age genetic engineering thing in the same way the dust-bowl preachers of the thirties used the drought?"

"You're missing the point, Hannah." Brother Timothy leaned forward. "Scientists have known for years that simple things like Tylenol, aspirin and other over-the-counter medicines can do irreparable harm to the body. Read the small print on the drug company's own literature."

"What's your point?" asked Hannah.

"My point is: science has spent the last fifty years trying to find out why some people die when they ingest these everyday medicines. Researchers still have no answers. Do they pull their products off the shelf? No. Do they stop manufacturing these deadly pills? No. What they do, is forge ahead. Create more things that they don't fully understand. Create more things that will kill off humanity. Nobody knows the long-term effects of eating genetically engineered foods. Nobody. But that's not the worst part. The worst part are the GMO's. The genetically manufactured organisms. They're being manufactured and unleashed to our world at an alarming rate. And we are about to pay a terrible price for that. These new organisms will multiply. And, they will multiply into numbers the scientists didn't expect. But then . . ." Brother Timothy held up one finger to accentuate his point. "But then, they will mutate. All species do. And they will mutate in ways that will surprise us. Even shock us. And the scientists will no longer be able to control them. That is when the end will come."

Hannah found herself sitting on the edge of her seat. She took a breath and smiled weakly. "You're good, Brother Timothy," she said nodding her head as her smile broadened. "You managed to give me the shivers. Between last night's sermon and this interview, I can understand why so many people are drawn to you."

Brother Timothy looked at his watch.

Hannah spoke apologetically. "I know we've gone past our allotted time, but there are more questions I'd like to ask you. How about if we meet later? Maybe for dinner?"

"No," came an answer from the corner of the room.

Hannah had forgotten Verne Smenken's presence, and his pronouncement startled her.

The man took a step towards them. "Brother Timothy won't be available for another interview."

Hannah looked at Brother Timothy for confirmation.

He turned to Smenken, held his gaze for a moment and turned back to Hannah. "Verne is right, my dear Hannah. We're going to be leaving this afternoon."

"Well," ventured Hannah, "where's your next stop? Maybe I can meet up with you there."

"Hannah, you've been delightful," said Brother Timothy, reaching across to take her hand. "And I think I would enjoy that. But we're getting ready to leave for California. To be precise, I'll be staying in Los Angeles. I'm scheduled to give a sermon at the Civic Auditorium in Pasadena."

Brother Timothy's hand was warm, and Hannah found his touch to be tender and reassuring.

"Pasadena?" repeated Hannah. "Isn't that the unofficial Mecca for genetic engineering?"

"That's correct," answered Brother Timothy. "What better place to deliver my message."

"Hmm," she mused as she looked into his eyes. "Like Daniel walking into the lion's den."

CHAPTER TWELVE

CALIFORNIA

The name of the restaurant was *Belinda's Garden.* Bright and cheerful, it reflected the management's aim to get its entire dining room staff to do a passable impersonation of "Rebecca of Sunnybrook Farm." Each waitress wore a ruffled skirt and frilly white blouse partially covered by an apron bursting with an explosion of colorful flowers. Rick and Sarah's server had blonde hair done up in a matching pair of ribboned pigtails.

After serving the main courses, the waitress asked if Rick or Sarah needed anything else. Because the menu was strictly vegetarian and well-suited to Rick's taste, the restaurant was one of Rick's favorites. Sarah, on the other hand, would have preferred something more substantial than sprouts, cucumbers and radicchio. She looked up from her dinner plate and pleadingly asked, "Any chance of getting a side order of hot pastrami on rye?"

The waitress giggled and left.

Rick had finished giving Sarah an overview on the dreadful fight that had occurred earlier between Miguel Ortiz and Ashley Eberhardt. He summed it up by saying, "I'm really out of my league on this one. I'm a scientist, for God's sake, not a referee."

"You're also a supervisor," said Sarah. "You're supposed to be able to manage your people."

"I'm supposed to supervise their work," said Rick defensively. "Not their battles. I create their work, organize it, and hand it out as assignments. I didn't anticipate that I'd have to be breaking up school yard fights."

"So, what *did* happen? What precipitated it?"

Rick said, "I don't know. Ashley refused to tell me what happened and left in a huff. That's when I think I screwed up."

"Screwed up? How?"

Rick related the events in detail. He told her how he got into Miguel's face and demanded to know what happened. "Just like Ashley, Miguel didn't want to talk about it either. But, did I leave it alone? Nooo." Rick stretched out the one word answer like a refrain from a song. "I kept hammering away at him, flexing my management muscles, and all that time, I was painting him into a corner."

"No wonder he got pissed at you," said Sarah. "You're lucky he didn't haul off and cold-cock you."

Rick nodded. "At one point, I actually thought he was going to do just that. I threatened to fire him and things got a little dicey. We were standing nose to nose and I was sure he was going to pummel me into the basement."

"Then what happened?"

Rick took a deep breath and sadly shook his head. "He was speaking Spanish but, just before he left, I think he made some kind of reference to my mother and a goat."

Sarah giggled. She loved this man with his off-beat sense of humor and was always thankful that they had found each other. "Now, what are you going to do?" asked Sarah.

"I think I've made an executive decision," he replied.

"And that is . . . ?"

"Ask you what you think I should do."

Sarah thought for only a moment before saying, "Talk to Ashley in the morning. If she still wants to leave it alone, well then, leave it alone. All I would do is call both of them into your office and tell them that you've decided not to pursue the issue. Explain that you hope they will have a cordial working relationship. You might add that you won't tolerate any more disruptions in your lab."

"You see!" said Rick, jubilantly. "That's why I need you! You're brilliant! How about we record what you just said and I can sit them both in a room and merely play the tape. I wouldn't even have to be there."

They both laughed.

Rick took a sip of his raspberry iced tea and asked, "How are things going in your part of the building?"

"Quite good," answered Sarah, nodding briskly. Her expression changed slightly as she added, "Well, except for the Bennett Pharmaceutical Project."

Rick glanced up from a poised forkful of greens. "Why? What's happening?"

"What isn't happening would be a better question."

Envirogen's contract with Bennett Pharmaceuticals involved a search for a new compound. The giant company, a leader in the field of medications relating to cosmetic surgery, had pioneered the use of bufotoxins.

"All right," agreed Rick. "What isn't happening?"

"Well, I told you about our search for a substitute for bufotoxin, right?"

"Right. Bufotoxin. The poison extracted from frogs."

"Not frogs," corrected Sarah. "Toads. Specifically, a species known as *Bufo marinus,* or more commonly, the Cane Toad. The little devils have these pockets called parotoid and dorsal glands just behind their eyes and along the bumps on their backs. Those are the things that are filled with the poison."

Rick swallowed a mouthful and said, "I recall seeing a couple of those babies the last time I visited your Zoo. I also remember you telling me that the poison is used when people treat themselves to a face-lift."

"Correct," agreed Sarah. "The toxin has a sclerotic effect. It sort of expands the vessels under the skin. Seems to work pretty well in taking out wrinkles."

"Sounds like something worth its weight in gold," replied Rick.

Sarah nodded in agreement. "It is. However, the problem is its toxicity. It's so highly poisonous that manufacturers and surgeons are afraid of it. That's why they have us looking for a substitute."

"And so far, you're not having any luck," stated Rick.

"Not yet. I've got both Kelly and Kim working on the project," said Sarah, referring to the biologist and chemist who were part of her staff. "I probably have them spending too much time on it, but the damn thing has now become a quest."

"You'll find the solution, Sarah. You always do."

Sarah changed the subject. "How was your meeting with Doug?"

"Extremely positive," said Rick. "Well, except for Mel Fishman and his seventh-grade competitiveness."

"What do you mean?"

Rick pointed out how unusual it was for Doug Matsushita to hand out a new assignment the way he did. "He always meets with a supervisor one-on-one, checks out their progress, and decides whether or not to give the guy additional work. But, calling me in, along with Mel and Donna, definitely caused some waves."

Sarah raised her eyebrows and waited.

Rick told her how Fishman had tried to convince Doug and Herb that the Foxboro Project was dangerous.

"Dangerous, huh?" she repeated. "What was he basing his assumptions on?"

"Well, I mentioned that there was an unexplained increase in CO_2 production, and he took that fact and ran with it. He got way off base, spouting stuff about St. Anthony's Fire, Dutch Elm disease, and LSD. Doug finally had to shut him up."

"So, what did Doug say about the carbon dioxide? Did he recommend anything radical?"

"No. On the contrary, Herb Knoll asked if the Foxboro project was going to generate profits. When I said, 'yes,' Doug jumped in and added the phrase, 'very profitable.' After that, Herb gave me his blessing by saying something like, 'Damn the carbon dioxide and full speed ahead!'"

Sarah stopped eating, and sat up straight. As an employee of the same corporation, Sarah was quite familiar with the notorious Mr. Knoll and his reputation for cost cutting. "Herb Knoll," she mused softly. "Mister Bottom Line. To him, science is nothing more than an expanding balance sheet. Someday, the Board of Directors will realize that the scientists at Envirogen are serious people. And, that we're doing things that could alter the world we live in. Maybe then, the Board will pay more attention to the effects of our scientific experiments rather than the effect of our stock price on the NASDAQ."

Rick nodded as he added a fine dusting of fresh ground peppercorns to his salad. "You are so right,"

Sarah asked, "What's the new project that's being handed out?"

"It's being labeled the Kudzu Project. The State of Georgia wants us to develop a way to eradicate the kudzu vine, which is growing out of control and killing their peach and pecan exports. The project looks as though it's shaping up to become a major coup because of the amount of money that's involved. Not only up-front money, but Herb said it'll generate hundreds of millions of dollars because we'll be able to modify the GMO's and sell them elsewhere."

"GMO's?" Sarah asked with concern. G.M.O. were the initials standing for Genetically Manufactured Organism, a life-form created in a laboratory. "What kind of GMO's?"

"Bugs," stated Rick. "The plan is to engineer some kind of new bug to take care of the problem." Rick added, "That means you and I will be working together again."

As Envirogen's resident entomologist, Sarah Levine was always notified when research projects required the use of insects. Sarah would work closely with the project supervisors, offering final approval for the choices of insects to be used. "Nobody has said anything to me yet," she pointed out.

"It's all too premature," said Rick with a wave of his hand. Doug said they won't even be signing the contracts for another week or so."

While Rick busied himself eating the cucumbers from around the edge of his plate, Sarah lay deep in thought. "Sometimes I wonder," she began slowly, "just how far we're going to take this thing."

"What are you talking about?" asked Rick with a mouthful of greens.

"I'm talking about the GMO's," Sarah answered, her eyes narrowing. "I mean, everyday, one of you guys take a perfectly good insect and change it into a new species. But to what end?"

Rick looked at her blankly.

Sarah held up her hand, warding off any counter-argument. "Don't get me wrong. I realize that a contract with the State of Georgia could make millions for Envirogen and, in the process, pump up our stock price. But, I'm guessing that eventually there's going to be a price to pay for all of this."

"You're talking about mutations, aren't you?"

Sarah nodded her head. "It's something we should consider," she said. "Maybe nothing will happen for five years, or five hundred years, but eventually it'll blow up in our faces."

"Hey. You're supposed to be a world-renowned entomologist. You can't go around sounding like you're part of the fringe group."

"I know, I know," she said, frustrated with her own train of thought. "But listen to me for just a sec. When the internal combustion engine was invented, nobody worried about the exhaust created as a by-product. After all, the amount was insignificant. Such a teeny, tiny bit of noxious fumes being puffed out into our atmosphere. What possible harm could there have been in that, right?"

"I see where you're going," said Rick.

"Exactly," said Sarah, warming up to her impromptu theory. "Our atmosphere is trillions, no make that quadrillions of cubic yards in size. There was almost an infinite amount of clean, fresh air. So of course, nobody was worried about a little bit of car exhaust polluting it. But now, just a hundred years later, people are beginning to panic. Some scientists are saying it's already too late to reverse the trend and, as a result of that kind of pollution, the greenhouse effect may end up destroying our beautiful planet."

"So, what are you saying? If I solve the kudzu problem for the State of Georgia, the Earth goes up in a ball of flames?"

"I'm saying that if we continue to create life-forms that normally don't exist in nature, sooner or later one of them will mutate into something that might do irreparable harm."

Rick gave a crooked little smile. "Aren't you taking this a little too far, Sarah?"

"Um . . . maybe," she said. Then added, "Probably."

"Whew," said Rick, feigning mopping his brow. "For a second, I thought you had been listening to Mel Fishman's doomsday scenarios."

Sarah said, "Okay, okay. I'll be good. She took a bite of her salad before asking, "Now, does this mean that you're going to head the project?"

"Looks like. Donna is bogged down with a stickler, and Mel, in his desire to prove to everyone that he is really 'Superman,' has taken on too many projects. Now, he can't possibly be ready to take on another. I think I'm going to win this one by default."

Sarah smiled warmly. "Don't sell yourself short, my cuteness. You've got more talent than you give yourself credit for." Her smile broadened and she added, "A lot more."

Rick looked at her. She had a round face that he found adorable and full lips that he found inviting. Her hazel eyes sparkled with the delight of a little girl at the circus. Sarah's cheeks, which always seemed to have a rosy glow, added to her picture of youthful innocence. Despite the look of an ingénue, Sarah was a consummate lover. Full bodied and voluptuous, she gave herself completely to Rick and tried her best to keep him happy and satisfied.

"A lot more talent, huh?" repeated Rick lasciviously. "Want to go home and let me show you just how good I really am?"

"Speaking of your talent, Rick Ballinger, we need to determine how successful you've been in discussing our plans with your mother."

Rick exhaled loudly. "You sure know how to kill a moment, Sarah."

'I'm being serious, Rick. Easter and Passover are less than two months away, and if you and I are going to have a life together, we need to discuss how we can incorporate our parents into it. Now, please tell me the details of the conversation with your mother."

Pushing his dinner plate away, Rick rolled his eyes. "Like I told you earlier, it didn't go well. When I told her we were going to be in L.A. with your folks for Passover, she flipped. She kept saying, 'What do you mean?' and reminded me that spending Easter together had become *our* tradition."

"By 'our tradition' she was referring to the Christian tradition, right?"

"Yes," said Rick nodding sadly. "I think she's convinced that you're personally responsible for crucifying Christ."

Sarah leaned forward. "Did you explain the seriousness of our relationship? That you plan on making me her daughter-in-law?"

Rick raised his eyebrows. Sarah never ceased to amaze him. She had a way with words that always seemed to make a distinct point. He wished he had thought of that exact phrase when he spoke to his mother. "I didn't exactly put it that way. But, I did tell her that you and I were living together and that I'm in love with you."

"And her response was . . . ?"

Rick rubbed his face with both hands before responding. "She said, and I quote, 'But didn't you say she was a Jew?'"

Sarah put her elbow on the table and rested her chin in her hand. "Oh, Rick," she lamented. "How are we ever going to break down that barrier?"

"By your coming with me the weekend after we visit your folks. Once she meets you, she'll fall in love with you just like I did."

"Thank you, lover," she said. "But there are two problems. "In the first place, you said your mother didn't invite me, and secondly, I have to be in Seattle that weekend for the conference."

"Look, Sarah, we're just going to have to bust the door down on this one. I mean, just show up in her living room. If we wait for a formal invitation, it might never come. So, cancel your trip to Seattle and come with me to Palm Beach."

"I can't do it that weekend," she said pleadingly. "It's the International Entomological Meeting, and I'm slated to be one of the two keynote speakers. And besides that, I've waited a year and a half to meet Dr. Kaminski, and he's agreed to fly to Seattle for the express purpose of meeting with me."

"Ah, yes," Rick pontificated. "Dr. Jacobus Kaminski, the infamous bug hunter, who searches tirelessly for strange insects in remote jungles of the world. Just exactly what is his area of expertise?"

"He bills himself as a 'Chemical Prospector.' He looks for bugs that have a natural chemical defense mechanism. Some estimates say there's over a million species out there that have that ability. Anyway, the big chemical companies pay him a lot of money to do what he does."

"You mean that he catches bugs that have their own insect repellent, huh?"

Sarah nodded her head. "Exactly. But not only repelling other insects. Some insects have chemical defenses that are so potent they can chase away birds, snakes and small rodents.

Rick suddenly squinted his eyes. "Say . . . are you two having an affair?"

"Oh sure," said Sarah with a sneer. "He's fifty years old, shaggy, unkempt beard, and he probably smells like the back end of a dung beetle. Yes sir. Sounds like my kind of man."

They both chuckled.

When the laughter subsided, Sarah said, "Why don't you call your mother back and reschedule the trip for a time convenient for all three of us?"

Rick took a deep breath. "I love my mother dearly," he stated, "but she's such a hardnose. I'm not sure it'll make a difference."

"Well then, what do you suggest?"

"I'm afraid the only thing that'll make a difference is if I come home with a Gentile girl. How do you say that in Yiddish?"

A wry expression filled Sarah's face. "A *shiksa*," she replied.

CHAPTER THIRTEEN

FLORIDA

J ust prior to the turn of the Century, the billionaire, Donald Trump, had purchased the extraordinary mansion known as *Mar-a-Lago*, and turned it into an exclusively private club for the jet-setters of Palm Beach. Originally, it had been the home of Marjorie Merriwether Post, the heiress to the Post Cereal fortune, and her second husband, a very wealthy man in his own right, Mr. E.F. Hutton. The Spanish style castle sprawls from Lake Worth on the west, to the Atlantic Ocean on the east. It includes one hundred and eighteen rooms and a seventy-five foot tower that would have been perfect for Rapunzel's long tresses. For an annual membership that hovers precariously close to six-figures, one is granted the right to hobnob, golf or dine among the rich, the famous, and the powerful. The mansion features silks and tapestries from around the world, frescoes and sculptures created by the masters, and botanical gardens filled with flowers that are a treat to one's senses. A world-renowned chef supervises the kitchen. Among his world-class gastronomic creations is a recipe for bouillabaisse that has won many gold medals during international competitions. Stephanie Carlton-Ballinger loved that bouillabaisse.

Stephanie's luncheon guest, Brad Bishop, stood second in a short line waiting his turn to announce himself. A matronly woman was pleading with the maitre'd for a table next to the one where Jay Leno was seated.

"I assure you, madam," said the tuxedoed host, "that is not Jay Leno. Allow me to seat you at a table overlooking the gardens."

"Are you sure that's not Jay Leno?" asked the woman, peering over the top of her glasses.

The maitre'd grabbed a menu and tried to coax the woman to follow him to the table he had selected. "Jay Leno is a white haired gentleman who must be close to sixty by now," he said. Lowering his voice, the host added, "The gentleman you're referring to can't be more than thirty-five years old."

The woman persisted. "He sure looks like the guy from "The Tonight Show." Turning to Brad, she pointed and asked, "Does that guy look like Jay Leno to you?"

Brad glanced at the exasperated maitre'd who was rolling his eyes. Then, Brad followed the woman's outstretched finger to the diner in question and said reassuringly, "Absolutely not Ma'am. Definitely not Jay Leno."

Satisfied, the woman allowed herself to be led away to her table.

She hadn't gone any more than ten steps when Brad called out, "I think it's Tom Cruise."

In an attempt to confirm what Brad had said, the poor woman struggled to stop and turn. However, the maitre'd had a good grip on her arm and was able to pull her along to the other side of the dining room.

Returning to find Brad waiting with a cocky smile, the annoyed maitre'd said, "I suppose you thought that was funny."

Brad shrugged, "Just trying to make her day more interesting." Brad gave his name to the man and asked if Ms. Carlton-Ballinger had arrived. In response, the maitre'd escorted Brad to a semiprivate area of the dining room that was nestled into a quiet corner. Surrounding it was a magnificent wall mural depicting a European village scene replete with quaint shoppes, laughing children, and an outdoor café.

Already seated, Stephanie was sipping a glass of Riesling. Her sleeveless dress was patterned with diffused clouds of soft pastels, while a wide sash of blue silk wrapped her waist. Hanging on the back of her chair was a broad brimmed straw hat that sported a matching blue silk band, which covered a portion of the crown and flowed off to one side.

"Stephanie," remarked Brad, "you should be modeling for *Vogue* in that outfit."

"You always say the right thing, my dear Brad."

Sitting down, Brad said, "It's been months, Stephanie. What have you been up to?"

"Oh, the usual. Here and there. Three weeks ago I flew to Milan to shop for shoes. I swear, only the Italians understand how to make great shoes."

Brad smiled. Stephanie was deliberately casual about her extravagances, and he always felt somewhat entertained when the woman detailed her lavish lifestyle. "Now that your closets are restocked, what's been keeping you busy?"

Stephanie said, "My friends have been arriving in droves, and I've just been flitting from one afternoon tea to another." She leaned toward Brad and lowered her voice to a whisper. "Look over there," she motioned with her head. "Do you see that woman with the green sweater and short skirt?"

Brad knew that Stephanie thrived on gossip. From her conspiratorial tone, it was obvious that she was about to indulge him again. He looked toward the indicated direction and spotted the woman to whom Stephanie was referring. The stunning hard bodied blonde appeared to be in her late twenties and close to six-feet tall. Not taking his eyes off the beautiful creature, Brad said, "Yeah. I see her. What's her story?"

"You remember Jeremy Grainger, don't you?"

Brad furrowed his brow, trying to recall the name. "Isn't he the old guy in the catalog business?"

"Yes," she whispered like a schoolgirl.

"So, what's the connection?"

"That's his mistress," she declared.

Brad sat upright. "What? Are you sure?"

Stephanie nodded her head excitedly.

"Oh, good Lord!" remarked Brad. "Old man Grainger must be pushing eighty. If he truly manages to get that woman into his bed, he'll be dead of a heart attack before they even finish their foreplay!"

Stephanie was giggling as she replied, "All my friends are saying the same thing. Effie said that when they make love, he must be wired to a defibrillator! Isn't that clever?"

A waiter came to take their drink order. Both requested iced tea, with Stephanie specifying jasmine.

Unfolding his napkin, Brad asked, "And how is your social life? Any new suitors this season?"

Stephanie smiled smugly. "Just before Christmas, I went down to my condo in San Juan and met a man in the Caribe Hilton casino. His name is Raphael Boñez, and he's a Bolivian industrialist. Very debonair, and very romantic. We've seen each other several times since then."

"Do you want me to run a check on him?" offered Brad.

"Oh, that won't be necessary," said Stephanie. "The man is so honest, so sincere. His poor wife died during childbirth twenty-five years ago. It was very sad to hear him tell the story."

"What kind of an industrialist is he?"

"He has a big manufacturing plant in southern Puerto Rico that builds shopping carts. He sells them to supermarkets all over the world; Publix, Albertson's, Kroger's, everywhere. He's very successful."

"I'm glad to hear that," said Brad, "but you've had me check out every man you've dated for the last six years. Why the hesitation with this guy?"

"I don't know," said Stephanie, searching for a rational answer. "It's just that . . ."

"It's just, what?" coaxed Brad.

"It's just that he makes me feel . . . different. That's all."

Brad smiled at the faraway look in her eyes. "Listen Stephanie. I represent the practical side of your life. Those junior high school butterflies that you're feeling shouldn't have anything to do with my running a check on the man."

"Oh, I suppose it's all right."

"Okay," said Brad reinforcing her decision. "If he's that public of a figure, it'll be a no-brainer to look him up. I won't even charge you for the service."

"All right. Go ahead."

Brad took out a small note pad and jotted down the man's name and telephone number. Stephanie didn't remember the name of his manufacturing company. As Brad finished writing, the waiter arrived with the iced teas, and asked to take their lunch orders.

Stephanie said, "You must try the bouillabaisse, darling. It is simply not to be believed."

Brad continued to study the menu. "I love seafood, but that's going to be a little too garlicky for my taste today."

"But, there's only a hint of garlic," assured Stephanie.

Brad smiled. "I think I'll stick with something lighter such as . . ." Turning to the waiter, Brad asked, "Any complaints about the quiche with the Portobello mushrooms and Colby cheese?"

"Complaints?" questioned the waiter dryly. "We never get complaints."

"Okay," nodded Brad. "If you say so. I'll have the quiche and a small tossed salad with peppercorn dressing on the side."

As the waiter left to enter their orders, Stephanie said, "No garlic, eh? Do you plan on cavorting with some new young chippie this afternoon, or are you still dating that voluptuous Maxine?"

Over the past few years, Brad had acquired what he deemed to be an ill-deserved reputation for being a lady's man. Even though there had only been a limited number of women in his life, a pattern had emerged. Brad would date one woman for several months before he began to feel the pressure of commitment. The problem was threefold. First, after seeing a woman exclusively for a period of time, Brad would become disillusioned with her emerging personality and would give up on the idea of anything long-term. Consequently, people whom he had not seen in a while would suddenly be aware of another new female hanging on to Brad's arm. The second thing that added to his title as a bon vivant was that each of these women was spectacularly beautiful. The third problem had to do

THE COFFEE BUG

with Brad's perception of an ideal relationship. Some time ago, life had thrown him a bad curve, and it had taken many years of painful guilt and many nights of bad dreams to overcome the tragedy.

"Maxine and I have moved away from anything serious," said Brad, studying the ice cubes in his glass. "It just wasn't meant to be."

"Knowing you as I do, dear boy, I'm sure it won't take you long to discover your next conquest."

Brad ignored Stephanie's comment and asked curiously, "This Bolivian industrialist of yours . . . is he the reason you wanted to see me?"

"No."

"You mentioned a 'dire emergency.' Now would be as good a time as any to tell me what it is."

"It's Richard."

"Richard? Your son? I thought you told me he's living in California."

"Yes," confirmed Stephanie. "Just outside of L.A. Pasadena to be exact."

"What's the emergency?" asked Brad. "Is he all right?"

"I'm not really sure," answered Stephanie, frowning. "I don't know where his head is these days."

Brad sensed her concern. He leaned forward and said, "Suppose you just tell me what's going on. Take your time."

Stephanie began, "He's managed to get himself involved with this woman. Her name is Sarah. Sarah . . . *Levine*."

The emphatic enunciation of the woman's last name spoke volumes about Stephanie's non-acceptance of minorities. Nonetheless, for the moment, Brad decided to listen patiently.

"He called and told me he wants to bring her to Florida to introduce us." There was a note of desperation creeping into Stephanie's voice. "I just don't know what to do."

A long moment of silence ensued as Brad put together the ramifications of what Stephanie was saying. "Am I right in assuming that this will be the first time Richard will be bringing someone home to meet momma?"

Stephanie just nodded.

"And you're not ready for it," he stated.

"I don't think *he's* ready for it," corrected Stephanie. "My sweet Richard is just a child. Did you know that he actually encourages others to call him 'Rick?'" He's simply not . . ."

Brad interrupted. "What do you mean 'just a child?' He's almost as old as I am."

"He's more like a schoolboy," lamented Stephanie. "His whole life has been devoted to learning. Do you know he has separate master's degrees in biology,

91

genetics and bioengineering? And, he's presently working on his doctorate. When it comes to life, he's like a baby. He's not ready for this."

Brad shook his head. "I think you're the one who's not ready for this."

"Well, I'm not," she said emphatically.

"All right," said Brad, putting both elbows on the table and leaning close. "Let's have a serious discussion here. If this woman's name weren't 'Levine,' would you be more amenable to the idea?"

"Of course, I would," said Stephanie. "You know how these Jews are. They're just so opportunistic. Always looking for a crack to crawl through. They want to be a part of a society that they don't belong to. First, they slipped into Palm Beach in the middle of the night and muscled their way into my country club. Now, one of them has her hooks into my son. I cannot condone that."

Brad knew better than to try and break down Stephanie's long standing intolerance of Jewish people. Despite being an unreasonable prejudice, it had been ingrained in her from some distant past and seemed to stiffen with time. Over the years, Brad chose to ignore her anti-Semitism unless he became directly affected.

He shook his head in disbelief. "Tell me, Stephanie, what exactly are you hoping that I can do for you?"

Stephanie's eyes hardened. "I want you to investigate this woman. Investigate the hell out of her. Check out her background, look into her finances, see if she's lied about her education, and dig up any skeletons in her closet. Find out anything that will expose her for what she really is."

Brad leaned back, mulling over Stephanie's request. The waiter arrived with their lunch plates and set them down with a flourish before departing.

Brad sat forward and said, "As far as Richard's girlfriend is concerned, do you have any reason to suspect that she's not who she claims to be?"

"Jews always exaggerate. They shave points off their golf handicap, they brag only about their winnings in the stock market, and everything they buy is always wholesale. They're all the same."

"You're not being nice, Stephanie," admonished Brad, wagging his finger. "If you keep this up, you'll turn into a bitter old lady with lines in your face."

"Oh please, Brad. You've got to help me. He's my only child, for God's sake."

Brad took a bite of his lunch but didn't seem as hungry as he had been a few minutes earlier. As an insurance investigator, Brad had access to information that allowed him to uncover details about anyone. Having spent three years as a special agent for the FBI, he had acquired the contacts and the skills needed to dig as deeply as necessary.

"And what if I don't find anything?" asked Brad. "What if this Sarah Levine woman turns out to be everything that Richard said she is? Then what?"

"Well . . . good for her."

"No. I mean, what if it turns out that she's perfect, and that Richard has actually found the woman of his dreams? What are you going to do then?"

Stephanie hesitated a long moment, as she mulled over that possibility. Perplexed, she moved her hand to her lips. "I don't know," she said, welling up emotionally at the prospect.

"If you don't climb down off this anti-Semitic high horse you're on, you'll be running the very real risk of losing your son."

Stephanie took a corner of her napkin and touched it lightly just under her lashes. "What am I supposed to do? Help me, Brad." She sniffled and dabbed at her eye once more before looking at her napkin, which revealed a minuscule smudge of eyeliner.

"I'll run a check on her. But, if I don't turn up anything, it's up to you to take the next step."

"Which is . . . ?"

"Accept her into your home."

Stephanie pursed her lips. "I'll try," she said, nodding.

"Accept her into your home and let your son know that you're happy for him."

"I can try and do that."

"And embrace this woman."

"Embrace her?"

"Yeah! Give her a big hug and kiss and welcome her into the family."

Stephanie slowly contorted her face into a suspicious squint. "Now you're really pushing it, Buster."

CHAPTER FOURTEEN

FLORIDA

A stenciled sign on the glass door announced, "Sidney Aarons, Editor in Chief." In the South Florida newspaper market, the *Sun Coast Ledger* was second only to the *Miami Herald*. Sidney's office was typical of any big city newspaper editor. With its glass partitions on two sides, he had an unobstructed view of the daily goings-on. The beehive of activity included a myriad of reporters, editors, copywriters, all scurrying purposefully in a flourishing publishing environment.

Hannah Carpenter sat in one of the half-dozen chairs spread about Sidney Aaron's office, waiting patiently, while the editor barked orders into the telephone. Square face and jutting jaw, Aarons came across as a powerful man. The sleeves of his white shirt were rolled halfway up his forearms, revealing a thick mat of dark hair that added to his rugged masculinity. His forceful presence had a second dimension. He loomed over his world, taking an active role in every aspect of his newspaper business.

Completing his phone call, Aarons redirected his attention to Hannah. "As I was saying," he said, taking a sip from his monogrammed coffee mug, "your piece is okay. Not great, but okay. I had Donnie do a little red pencil editing. So, go over it and make the changes. I'll run it this Sunday."

"You don't like it." Hannah stated with a hint of disappointment and a pinch of defiance.

Aarons said, "It's not a question of my not liking it. I said it was okay. It's just that I know you're capable of so much more."

"I covered all the bases, Sidney," said Hannah defensively. "Don't you think my article will give our readers a better understanding of the 'Brother Timothy' phenomenon?"

"Not the point," he said, dismissing her comment with a wave of his hand. "You did an adequate job of explaining what's going on in the tent revivals. Your description of the hootin' and hollerin' wasn't too bad. And you managed to paint a fairly decent portrait of Brother Timothy spitting lightning bolts every time he opened his mouth. All of that was . . . okay. But, like so many times before, Hannah, you're not opening your eyes. You're not taking in the rest of the picture."

Hannah threw her hands up in frustration. "What do you want from me, Sidney? You give me an assignment, you spell out what it is you're looking for, and I do it. You just never seem to be satisfied with anything I do. What more do you . . ."

Hannah's words were cut off by the ringing of the phone on his desk. He picked it up and snapped, "What?"

Although the phone call was only a brief interruption, it gave Hannah time to stew over being admonished. She felt like a stepchild who could never quite measure up. She had heard him grant an occasional "well-done" to some of the other reporters, but she never seemed to be the recipient of such praise.

Again, Sidney hung up the phone and picked up the conversation as though there hadn't been any interruption. "What do I want from you? I'll tell you what I want from you. I want you to open your eyes when you're working. I want you to open your ears when you're conducting an interview. I want you to be aware of the big picture, the things that aren't so obvious. Understand?"

"I understand that you weren't clear in your instructions when you gave me this assignment."

"Hannah," pleaded Aarons, leaning back in his chair and spreading his arms. "You're a big girl now. College is over. Here you are playing in the big leagues with the big boys, and you're still talking about life in Journalism 101."

"Okay," she said, sitting forward in her seat. "Explain that to me."

"Listen. When I give you an assignment, it's just an idea, a notion, barely an outline. You're the reporter. You're supposed to do the research and then write the article. You're the one who should be filling in the blanks. Now, here's the problem: You're too focused on your task. So much so that you're not paying any attention to what's going on around you."

Aarons paused, but Hannah didn't give any indication that she was understanding his meaning.

"Now, follow me, Hannah. This Brother Timothy is a real Elmer Gantry guy, isn't he?"

"Elmer Gantry?"

Aarons immediately realized he had used the wrong analogy. Since there was a thirty-year age difference between himself and Hannah, she was too young to be familiar with the notorious depression era preacher. "Elmer Gantry was a character who was portrayed in the movies by Burt Lancaster. He was just like Brother Timothy, a firebrand, a Holy Roller who was capable of stirring up an audience to a fever pitch."

"Oh," Hannah said, nodding.

"Anyway, your piece was about the man's ability to cast a spell over his audience. You wrote about their reaction to his style, his command of the moment, didn't you?"

Hannah sighed. "Isn't that what you asked for?"

"Yes. I did, but . . ."

The glass door to the office opened, and a middle-aged woman poked her head in and said, "Just reminding you, Sidney. You've got to be downtown at two-thirty."

"All right, Nina," acknowledged Aarons. "I'm getting ready to leave."

"The Honorable Mayor really gets pissed when you're late," said Nina, as she closed the door behind her.

"So, let me ask you a question," said Aarons, redirecting his attention to Hannah. "Do you think those people who were sitting under Brother Timothy's tent were all mesmerized by his commanding style, or do you think maybe, just maybe, the Preacher had a legitimate message?"

"Are you suggesting that his talking with God is for real?"

Sidney tapped his desk impatiently. "His other message, Hannah. The subject of his sermon."

Hannah's face wrinkled into disbelief. "Are you serious? Are you saying that Brother Timothy's shtick about the 'Devil's-gonna-get-you' is legitimate? Just because some scientist is doing genetic research?"

Preparing to put on his suit jacket, Sidney stood and began rolling down his sleeves. He looked at her squarely and answered, "Yes. I do."

Hannah was irritated by this new twist in instructions. "That's what my story should have been about?" she asked incredulously.

"What I'm saying, Hannah, is that you should be the kind of reporter who has the ability to tune in to that. Don't be so focused. Loosen up. You have to learn to become a better listener. That way, if another story comes popping out of the original story, you're ready to pounce on it."

Hannah knew she only had a few moments to clear this up. "So now what? What do you want me to do with my story?"

"Nothing. After I run it, I want you to do a follow-up." Aarons put on his jacket and headed for the door.

"A follow-up on Brother Timothy's message?"

With Hannah on his heels, Aarons began walking briskly through the newsroom. "Exactly," he said.

At the elevator, Aarons pushed the down button.

"Well, I don't think there's a story there," she said.

The doors opened and they both entered. "Fine," said Aarons with a slight note of exasperation. "You said that Brother Timothy is on his way to Los Angeles?"

"Yes. Pasadena, actually."

The elevator opened into the building's spacious lobby. Aarons said, "Since you don't think there's a story there, I'm going to send Henry Drummond to do it. He'll find a story."

Hannah's mouth fell open at the mention of Drummond's name. "Henry Drummond?" she protested. "Why are you doing this to me? You don't even like him!"

Stopping at the information desk, Aarons plopped his briefcase onto a waist-high shelf. As he unlatched and opened the attaché to retrieve something, he said, "Frankly, I hate the sonofabitch, but he's a damn good reporter. He can find a story under any rock. And that's what I'm looking for here."

The reality of this situation was barreling toward her like a runaway freight train, and Hannah was becoming concerned. Suddenly realizing that Sidney might be thinking her incapable of handling the assignment, she hastily backtracked. "Okay Sidney," she said, holding both hands in front of her in a gesture of surrender, "I'll go out to Pasadena and do the follow-up on Brother Timothy."

"Too late, Hannah," snapped Aarons decisively. "You had your chance."

Hannah was speechless.

Snapping his briefcase shut, Aarons said, "But, I'll tell you what I want you to do. Drummond is going to need some advance research. So, I want you to look up a particular website. It's called 'The Mean Gene.'" Aarons began walking away. He called over his shoulder, "Make sure Drummond gets everything he needs for the story."

Hannah stood dumbfounded as she watched Sidney march to the exit. He was twenty feet away when she called out, "What the hell just happened? Did you just demote me to Drummond's research assistant?"

Without turning around or breaking stride, Aarons waved a goodbye. Then, he disappeared out the main entrance and into the limousine that awaited him.

Hannah was stunned. Aarons' decision to send Henry Drummond to do the follow-up story was disastrous. It was disastrous to her ego and certainly to her career. Despite being an excellent reporter, Drummond had the reputation of doing things unethically. The personality clash between Aarons and Drummond had lasted for at least as long as Hannah had been employed. She was shocked at Aarons' choice of Drummond, especially in light of how Sidney felt about the man.

The elevator ride upstairs did nothing to alleviate Hannah's confusion and frustration. With her nose feeling blocked, she knew that she was on the verge of tears. Hannah made her way directly into the ladies' room, where she sat on a bench in front of the mirror while she rummaged through her pockets for a tissue. Finding none, she went to grab a paper towel, when the door opened and Ann Silkwood entered. "Silky," as she was known, worked in the payroll department. Since one of her duties involved the twice monthly handing out of employee paychecks, everyone recognized her. Hannah and Silky had always had a friendly relationship. Although they had discussed getting together, they had never socialized outside of work.

"Hey baby," said Silky, concerned at seeing the distress on Hannah's face. "What the hell happened? Are you all right?"

Hannah plopped back down on the bench and the tears began flowing in earnest. "No. I'm not all right," she cried. "I just lost my job."

"Oh shit!" said Silky helplessly. "You got fired?"

"No. I didn't get fired," corrected Hannah, wiping her nose. "Sidney demoted me to research assistant."

Silky sat down next to Hannah and gently rubbed her neck and shoulders. "What happened, baby? Tell me."

Stopping occasionally to blow her nose, Hannah tearfully told her story. After talking for the better part of fifteen minutes, Hannah was calmer.

Silky stood and stared down at Hannah. "Can we talk?" she asked rhetorically. "Man to man?"

Hannah managed a weak smile as she said, "I don't think either of us could pass the physical, but sure, go ahead."

Silky ignored Hannah's attempt at humor. "Y'know I think the world of you Hannah, but I gotta tell you. You are your own worst enemy, girl. All these problems you're talking about . . . ? This mess you're in right now . . . ? It's your own doing."

"What are you saying?"

"You're sitting in a pile of shit right now, wondering why you smell so bad. And the truth is, you were the one who created the pile of shit."

Hannah stared blankly.

Silky continued. "This may be a big newspaper, but working here is like working in a small town. Everybody knows your business. And, since everyone knows how talented you are, we're all wondering why you're not listening to Sidney whenever he takes the time to teach you something. Some of the gossips around the office think it's because you hate men. And some of them think it's because you think you're too good for everybody. There's even a story going around that you had an affair with Sidney, and now you're pissed at him because he wouldn't leave his wife."

Hannah managed a faint smile. She swallowed and said, "What do you think, Silky?"

"I think you're talented enough to win a god-damned Pulitzer. That's what I think. But before that can happen, you've got to get both feet planted firmly on the ground and start being a *mensch.*"

"A *mensch?*" repeated Hannah, surprised at Silky's choice of metaphors.

"Look, baby. Sidney is a great teacher, and the advice he's giving you, he doesn't give to just anybody. Listen to him."

Hannah blew her nose.

Silky continued. "Remember what it was like to be a journalism student?"

Hannah nodded.

"Well, you've got to get back to that and put yourself into receptive-mode. Pay attention to the things that Sidney tells you. Believe me when I tell you this, Hannah. For whatever reason, he has your best interests at heart."

*　　*　　*

Brad Bishop was sitting at his desk when his secretary, Rose Goldberg, returned from lunch.

"How was lunch?" he asked.

"My lunch? Huh!" she grunted sarcastically. "All my meals are a waste of time. You spend money for a doctor and all he tells you is that your cholesterol is too high. Don't eat eggs, don't eat chopped liver, and stay away from the skin on a chicken. Then, he shakes his finger and tells me to be careful because my triglycerides are off the scale. So now, I'm not allowed any butter, no mayonnaise, no nothing! Not even a salted cashew nut! Don't ask me how my lunch was." She put one hand on her hip and switched subjects. "Better you should tell me what happened with your fancy-shmancy lunch at *Mar-a-Lago* with Queen Stephanie."

"She sends her love."

"Yeah. Right," replied Rose, her face screwed up in disbelief. "And the Pope wants me to conduct mass at the Vatican."

Brad smiled. "There are two new people," he said, "who have popped into her life. She's requesting background checks on each of them. Standard stuff, mostly, but I want you to include an FBI file on both of them."

"What happened? Did she fire all her domestics? Does she suspect that a distant relative might be a rabbi?"

Brad put down the pamphlet he was reading and said, "C'mon now, Rose. It's bad enough listening to Stephanie pick on you without listening to you pick on her."

"All right. All right," said Rose, looking skyward. "God forgive me. I'll try to behave. So, who are these people we're checking out?"

Brad relayed the details of the lunchtime meeting with Stephanie Ballinger. When it came to business, he kept no secrets from Rose. He told Rose about Stephanie's concern over her son's new girlfriend, Sarah, and Stephanie's new boyfriend, Raphael.

"Well, I can understand this Raphael character," said Rose. "He's just one more name in a long list of suitors, but what's with her son's girlfriend? Stephanie's never had us do a background check on any of *his* girlfriends. What's up with that?"

Brad thought for a moment before answering. "Promise not to give me any grief?" he asked.

"What? You're asking me to make you some kind of promise even before you answer my question?" Rose pulled a chair close to Brad's desk and sat down saying, "Oh boy. This is going to be good."

"Remember," reminded Brad, "no grief."

"All right, already," agreed Rose. "No grief. Now, what's up with her son's girlfriend?"

"She's Jewish."

"Bitch!" shrieked Rose.

Brad wagged his finger at her and said, "You promised . . ."

"That woman is impossible. She should have been a Gestapo Agent!"

"Well," said Brad, "the good news is that I managed to calm her down a bit. I actually got her to promise me that if we didn't turn up anything unethical or criminal, she would accept this Sarah Levine as a daughter-in-law."

"Whoop-dee-doo, Brad. Does that really seem like a big deal to you?"

"Hey. It's something," he said with mock pride. "Who knows? Next time, I may actually get her to convert to Judaism."

"Right," said Rose sarcastically. "She'll be third in line behind Louis Farrakhan and Osama bin Laden!"

CHAPTER FIFTEEN

CHICAGO

Bruce Kreitzer hung up the phone, swiveled his chair to face the window, and stared blankly at the Chicago skyline. The lanky six-footer had a triangular face, which ended rather sharply at his chin. His gene pool had given him skinny fingers, long legs, and big feet. His oversized shoes would often induce a rash of tittering whenever he strode past the secretarial pool.

Walking out his office door, Kreitzer paused at his secretary's desk. Abby looked up. "Can I get you something, Mr. Kreitzer?"

Glancing across the hallway, he scanned the cubicles which housed the sales department. "Nope. Just checking to see who's here," he answered absently. Without looking at Abby, he said, "Tell Shelley Markowitz I want to see her." Then, spinning on his heel, Kreitzer went back into his office.

Making her way over to the trader's cubicle, Abby waited for Shelley to get off the phone before telling her of Kreitzer's request.

"What now?" asked Shelley, worry lines creeping across her forehead.

"He didn't say," said Abby. "Just asked me to send you in."

Shelley grabbed the three files on her desk. Each had the name of a customer with whom she had recently spoken. The folders contained documentation of sizeable buy orders, one for soybean futures and one each for corn and oil futures. She didn't want to miss the opportunity to let Kreitzer know about her recent successes. With Abby in tow, Shelley took a deep breath, approached Kreitzer's door, knocked and waited.

Abby said, "Go right in, Shelley. He's expecting you."

Opening the door, Shelley stepped into Kreitzer's office and stood just inside the doorway. Although he was sitting at his desk and on the phone, his chair was swiveled so that his back was turned. At the sound of the opening door, Kreitzer spun in his chair and said into the receiver, "Hold on a sec, will ya?" Then, to Shelley, he said, "Come in. Come in. Close the door and sit down. Be with you in a minute." Just as quickly, he turned back around and continued his phone conversation.

Doing as she was told, Shelley moved to one of the two chairs in front of Kreitzer's desk. She sat down, crossed her legs and adjusted her skirt. Abruptly, she became acutely aware of the brevity of her hemline.

Finishing his conversation, Kreitzer hung up the phone. Oddly, he just stared at Shelley as though his mind were locked onto some enigmatic puzzle.

Shelley remained silent until she felt uncomfortable. "You asked to see me, Mr. Kreitzer?"

"Yeah. Right," said Kreitzer. "Shelley Markowitz," he said, refocusing on the moment.

"Yes, Mr. Kreitzer?"

"You've been having a kind of a rough time of it here, haven't you?"

"I'm . . . uh . . . it's been okay," she said hesitantly.

"I mean with overall slumping sales and you not making your quota for the past . . ."

Shelley interrupted. "Things are definitely improving, Mr. Kreitzer." Taking the customer files from her lap, she stood and extended them. "I just closed three nice orders. A really big one for soybeans and a couple others for corn and oil futures. Over a hundred thirty thousand dollars in all. So, things are starting to turn around. I'm feeling pretty good about it."

Kreitzer took the offered files and dropped them, unopened, on his desk. "Good. I'm glad to hear it, but, y'know, a couple of sales don't pay the rent. I'm talking about the big picture, Shelley. I'm talking about your future with the firm."

Shelley just stared, trying to comprehend his words. Feeling a slight spasm in the pit of her stomach, she said, "Am I being fired, Mr. Kreitzer?"

A strange smile spread across Kreitzer's face. "Fired? Hell no. You're not being fired."

Shelley took a halting breath but wasn't able to release her tension.

Kreitzer said, "I just don't think the sales department is for you."

"You don't?"

"Let's face it, Shelley. There's a lot of pressure that comes with that job. And, when quotas aren't met, you're in for a rash of shit, and you don't handle that too well, do you?"

Shelley sat there uncommitted.

"And last week's sales meeting with Mr. Ubermann? He rode you pretty hard. Let's face it, you're not cut out for that kind of abuse."

"What are you suggesting?" she asked.

Kreitzer stood and walked around to the front of his desk. Plopping one cheek of his skinny rump onto the edge, he let his foot dangle. "I'm gonna get you involved in some other stuff. You and I are going to be doing a lot of one-on-one."

Shelley felt uneasy as she asked, "Such as?"

Kreitzer bounced up off the desk and grabbed the arm of the chair next to Shelley. Sliding it close to the young woman, he sat down. "All right. Let me give you an idea of what's involved." Kreitzer spelled out her first assignment. There was an upcoming meeting in Pasadena, California. It was a symposium conducted by the Securities and Exchange Commission regarding the ethics of trading in commodities. At least one representative from each licensed brokerage house had to attend, and Bruce Kreitzer had selected himself to represent Ubermann Commodities Trading Group. "I want you to make all the arrangements; hotel, airlines, car rental, restaurant reservations, all that stuff."

"No disrespect, Mr. Kreitzer, but I'm working on commissions. If I take a lot of time to do all those things, I won't have enough time to devote to sales."

"Hey!" exclaimed Kreitzer, with a quick non-descript gesture of his hand. "You ain't listening. Forget sales. You ain't gonna be in the sales department any more."

"But what about Abby? Isn't it her job to make all your reservations?"

Kreitzer's eyes narrowed, wondering why Shelley wasn't understanding. "I don't want you to be my secretary, for Christ's sake. I'm making you my assistant. Giving you a raise and everything."

"Really?"

"Yeah. Really." Kreitzer changed gears. "What did you make last year?" he asked rhetorically, before answering his own question. "I looked it up. Just under forty-two thousand, right? Well, your new title is gonna be Assistant Marketing Manager, and your salary is going to be a straight fifty G's. No more commissions."

Shelley hesitated. The job description didn't fit the offered salary. "Fifty thousand a year," she repeated, "and you want me to make airline and hotel reservations. What about Abby?"

"Nope. You don't understand. I'm just having you do that as a way of getting your feet wet. Abby will still be responsible for doing all that reservations stuff. Your job will be to set up the meetings and attend them with me. Like, you'll be coming with me to the SEC meeting in Pasadena. That kind of thing."

"Travel together? With you?"

Kreitzer reached over and took Shelley's hand. "Yeah, Shelley. It'll be fun."

Shelley tried to ease her hand away, but Kreitzer had interlaced his fingers with hers. "Uh . . . what kind of arrangements did you have in mind?" she asked nervously.

A lascivious smile slowly spread across Kreitzer's face. "King-size bed, mirrored ceilings, maybe the honeymoon suite . . ."

Shelley's shocked look gave Kreitzer a laugh. Backing off from his semi-serious teasing, he added, "Stop worrying, baby. Make the reservations for two adjoining rooms." He let go of her hand, patted her thigh and stood to grab a brochure. Handing it to her, he said, "This is the information on the SEC meeting. It's at the Hilton Conference Center in downtown Pasadena. Get us out there the day before and, like I said, book two adjoining rooms. After that's done, get back with me and I'll give you a list of people I want to meet with while we're out there."

While studying the brochure, Shelley was startled when Kreitzer put his hand under her chin and lifted it. Their eyes met.

Softly, he said, "This is a brand new opportunity for you, Shelley. I've had my eye on you. You're smart and you're beautiful. This is your chance to be somebody, play with the big boys. Be cooperative, and you could really go places. Know what I mean?"

Shelley attempted to stand, but Kreitzer's nearness made it awkward. As he reached out to help her to her feet, Shelley felt the back of his hand brush across her breast. Kreitzer was standing so close, she could feel his breath on her face. "Mr. Kreitzer," she said as she maneuvered herself away from him and the chair, "your proposal came at me rather unexpectedly. I'm going to need a little time to think about it."

Kreitzer put a long arm around her shoulder, draping his hand just inches from her breast. "No problem, baby," he said as he walked her to the door. "But don't take too long. I've got to fill the position, and you're my first choice. So, let me know tomorrow."

"Okay. I'll do that."

Kreitzer gave her shoulder a squeeze before running his hand down her back and ending with a playful slap on her butt.

Shelley opened the door and left.

Pleased with himself, Kreitzer walked back to his desk, confident that Shelley would take the promotion. He chuckled as he envisioned himself and Shelley playing a couple of rounds of Slap-the-Frog.

Kreitzer punched the button on his speaker phone, bringing the dial tone to an audible pitch. Someone picked up after two rings.

"Yeah?" the voice said gruffly.

"This is Kreitzer. Let me speak to Mr. Pignatano."

"Who are you?" the speaker demanded, not having paid attention to Kreitzer's introduction.

"Kreitzer," he repeated. "Bruce Kreitzer."

"Hold on," said the man, grudgingly.

Mr. Pignatano was none other than Paulie "Porky" Pignatano, a powerful, well known Mafia underboss. The focus of his organization which was limited to the Chicago area, included bookmaking, extortion, and drugs.

When it came to his world, Porky Pignatano was a traditionalist. He demanded obedience from his people. Fortunately, his staff included throwbacks to a time of the absolute rule of the "Don," Godfathers who held the seat of power and were surrounded by respect and devotion.

A voice, heavy with a Chicago accent, blared out of the speaker phone. "You got my money?"

Startled, Kreitzer sat upright, shifting his mind into gear. "Hey, how you doing, Mr. Pignatano?" he asked, sidestepping the man's question.

"You got my money, Kreitzer?" he repeated, ignoring Kreitzer's salutations.

"Yeah, I got your money, Mr. Pignatano," acknowledged Kreitzer. "But, I'm calling you about more important matters. I've got a big deal going. Really big, and I need to talk to you about it."

When he spoke again, Pignatano raised his voice. "Listen, you skinny little weasel! All I want to know is, do you have my money?"

Kreitzer lurched forward, reaching for the button on the phone that would take Pignatano off the speaker. The last thing Kreitzer wanted was for Abby, or anybody in the outer office, to hear the disrespect that was just thrown at him. Kreitzer picked up the hand set and answered. "Hey, Porky. Take it easy, will ya? I said, I had your money and . . ."

Pignatano interrupted. "Don't you call me Porky, you little shit! You ain't earned the right! Understand? Now, do you have my god-damn money? All of it? All forty-three thousand two hundred?"

There was a momentary silence as Kreitzer did some quick mental calculations. "Listen, Mr. Pignatano. I've got twenty-five . . . uh, make that twenty-six grand I can give you, day after tomorrow. Give me a break, would ya?"

Pignatano took on a softer tone. "Brucie, Brucie, Brucie," he said patronizingly. "You know the rules, and I've already made an exception for you. I can't make no more exceptions. If you ain't got all my money, don't worry about it. Just pay me the vig, and were okay for another week."

The "vig" that Pignatano referred to is an insidious catch-22 system that the Mafia has used for many years. Nicknamed for vigorish, or the interest rate that a person owes on a loan, the vig works like this: A man borrows a hundred dollars from a Mafia loan-shark and promises to pay it back in one week. The interest, or "vig," is twenty-five percent per week which means that, come Friday, the borrower has to pay back one hundred twenty-five dollars. It's a simple arrangement except for one catch. If the borrower doesn't have the entire sum by Friday, the loan shark says, "No problem. Just pay me this week's vig of twenty-five dollars. Then, next Friday, when you pay back the loan, you'll pay me the one hundred dollars, plus the next week's vig of an additional twenty-five dollars." In this manner, if the borrower doesn't have the entire amount, he is forced into a never-ending cycle of debt.

The problem was Kreitzer's need to bet on sporting events, mostly professional football, basketball and baseball. Over time, he had won quite a bit of money but, as luck would have it, he had lost much more. His gambling debt had continued to rise until, a month and a half prior, it reached a staggering thirty thousand dollars. Consequently, his vig had grown proportionately, and he now had one week to pay back the thirty thousand plus interest. For over six weeks, poor Kreitzer had been unable to come up with the entire thirty-seven thousand five hundred. Now, he had no choice. He had pleaded his case to Pignatano who had taken a measure of pity and reduced the interest rate, or vig to twenty percent. Even with the five percent decrease, Kreitzer had to cough up six thousand dollars weekly just to pay the interest. To make matters worse, he had missed another payment.

Kreitzer felt as though he were being buried alive. Desperation had brought him to this point. Josef Ubermann had commanded him to take some sort of action that would assure the financial future of the firm. Undoubtedly, it would involve dealings on the wrong side of the law but something that would turn a very healthy profit. In order to dig his way out from under the punishing weight of a new seven thousand dollar weekly vig, Kreitzer was willing to make Pignatano a part of the scheme.

Kreitzer pleaded, "Mr. Pignatano. You know what I do for a living, right? You know that I'm vice president of a firm that trades commodities. Right?"

"What are you telling me? You want to make me a partner?"

There was a long silence before Kreitzer said, "In a manner of speaking, yes."

"Okay. Keep talking. But, this better be good."

Kreitzer went on to explain that, as the vice president, he was the man in charge, the one person who could make things happen. He was working on a special project that was going to bring in a lot of money. "I mean, a whole lot of money," he emphasized.

"What do you call a whole lot of money?" asked Pignatano, his curiosity piqued.

"Your share alone would be more than five million dollars."

"Kreitzer, you little prick. You're blowing smoke up my ass. You ain't got no . . ."

Kreitzer interrupted. "No, no, no, Mr. Pignatano. It's legit. I swear. My boss, Josef Ubermann, the Chairman of the Board, for Christ's sake, told me to get this done. This deal is definitely going to happen. Definitely. And I'm giving you a chance to be a part of it."

Pignatano mulled it over silently before saying, "You talking five million or more, eh? Okay. So, what's the deal?"

Kreitzer outlined the scheme, briefing Pignatano on the workings of the commodities business and how small changes in prices could yield huge profits. Using an example, Kreitzer explained how a well planned fire in a couple of strategic warehouses could devastate the reserves of a commodity such as lumber, thereby driving the price sky high. Pignatano had questions and that made Kreitzer feel as though he were making some headway.

Pignatano wanted to know why everybody didn't do it. Kreitzer replied that, besides being illegal, it was unethical and dangerous. "If you're caught, you lose your license to trade and you could go to jail."

"And what happens to the money you made from burning down the lumber warehouses?" asked Pignatano.

"That's the really good part," chuckled Kreitzer. "You get to keep the money. If you're caught and the government prosecutes you, they always slap your hand and make you pay a small fine. But for some reason, they never take away your money. Your profits are always credited to your account. Pretty neat, huh?"

"You've done this before?" asked Pignatano.

"No," answered Kreitzer indignantly. "We haven't done this before."

"Why not?"

"We're a legitimate firm," explained Kreitzer. "We do business on the up and up."

"So, if you guys are such big mucky-mucks doing business on the up and up, why would you want to set fire to somebody's warehouse?"

Kreitzer lowered his voice to a conspiratorial level. "Because the firm is in financial trouble. We're in deep shit, Mr. Pignatano."

The Mafia Boss hesitated before saying, "So, if you guys haven't done something like that, who has? Anybody been getting away with it?"

"I'll give you a good example," said Kreitzer. "The Gulf War. You remember the Gulf War back in 1990?"

"What about it?"

"We went after Saddam Hussein because he set fire to the Kuwaiti oil fields, remember? Well, did you ever wonder why the hell he would do a thing like that? What did he hope to gain by blowing up all the refineries and destroying so much of the world's oil production?"

Pignatano didn't get to kingpin status because he was stupid. On the contrary, Paulie Pignatano was the kind of man who could recognize an opportunity when he saw one. "You're telling me, Sadaam Hussein first bought up oil futures and then set fire to the oil fields?"

"Exactly," said Kreitzer excitedly. "The price of oil went up immediately. Even while our planes were still in the air, Hussein made billions! Tens of billions of dollars."

"And you're telling me that the sonofabitch got to keep it?" asked Pignatano, starting to get caught up in the scheme.

"You bet he did," stated Kreitzer emphatically. "Until we hung the prick, he was one of the wealthiest sonsabitches on the planet. It was a brilliant move. What Hussein did was pure genius."

"Okay, Kreitzer," said Pignatano hesitatingly, "what's your plan? What kind of fire are you going to set?"

"I'm working on it," he said. "But, I need your help. I'm going out of town next week but, when I get back, I want to sit down with you and go over the details of the plan."

"Sure. Okay, but in the meantime, you still owe me over forty thousand dollars."

"What I'm asking, Mr. Pignatano," ventured Kreitzer, "is that you put the money I owe you on hold. Bringing you in on a deal like this is way bigger than the forty g's I owe you. Right?"

"Look at it from my point of view," said Pignatano. "You owe me a lot of money. Now, you're asking me to walk away from a vig of better than seven grand a week. And for what? Some bullshit you've just given me over the telephone? C'mon. You've got to do better than that. But I'll tell you what. Meet with me face to face. Show me something that'll convince me to let you off the hook. If you do that, I'll think about it."

The conversation ended with the two men agreeing to meet for lunch in two days.

Hanging up, Kreitzer took a folded piece of paper out of his wallet. He smoothed out the creases before looking at his watch. It was ten-thirty a.m. in Chicago, which would make it eight-thirty a.m. in Pasadena, California. An acceptable time to call. Dialing the number on the little piece of paper, he listened as an answering machine clicked on, and a sultry voice said, "This is Maria. I've been waiting for your call. Just leave me your name and number and allow me to whisk you away."

Kreitzer spoke to the machine. "Hey baby. This is Bruce Kreitzer. Y'know, Big Bad Bruce. I'm gonna be in Pasadena on the sixth. I'll be staying at the Hilton on Los Robles for about four or five days. Give me a call at the office, baby, and let's plan on you and me getting together . . . know what I mean?"

After hanging up, Kreitzer rubbed his hands together. He felt good. He had managed to buy a little time from the loan sharks. Soon, he would be in sunny California and, before he could finish splashing on his aftershave, pretty little Maria would be in his bed. Smiling and nodding, he decided to treat himself to a shopping trip for one of those big silver belt buckles he loved so much.

CHAPTER SIXTEEN

CALIFORNIA

Maria felt the bed being jostled when Miguel Ortiz got up. It was a little before seven in the morning, and Maria kept drifting in and out of her pre-dawn slumber. She caught the occasional sounds of Miguel's routine as he prepared to go to work. Managing to fall back to sleep during Miguel's shower, Maria was abruptly reawakened when he plopped down on one corner of the bed and put on his socks and shoes.

It had been sometime after midnight when Maria had come home and found Miguel already asleep. Her previous evening had been occupied with an out of town customer. The client, who had taken Maria to a nightclub, decided to cut out early in favor of bringing her back to his hotel room. Because the man was paunchy and sedentary and probably limited his exercise to answering a telephone, their sexual escapades lasted only twenty minutes from start to finish. After collecting her fee, she left. Everyone was happy. Her client was happy to have had a young, beautiful woman hanging on his arm and happier still to have had the pleasure of her supple body in his bed. Maria was also happy to have made some easy money from a customer who treated her gently and with respect.

The morning flooded back into Maria's consciousness as she felt the bed jostle again when Miguel, shoes laced, bounced up off the mattress. She listened as he walked to the kitchen and popped the top of a Coke can.

Shortly, Miguel returned to the bedroom and stood in the doorway. Assuming that she wasn't asleep, he said, "I'm going to work now. I'll see you later."

Eyes closed, Maria grunted her acknowledgment. She could hear his fading footsteps clip-clopping down the single flight of stairs that led to the street. Pulling the covers up under her chin, she promptly fell back to sleep.

Miguel was tolerant of the fact that his girlfriend, Maria, was a prostitute and, by unspoken agreement, he never said a word about her lifestyle. These days he had other things on his mind. His job at Envirogen had always been a source of pride, something more that just a job. Miguel had been promoted, and that, in itself, was a unique accomplishment. The friends and neighbors he had grown up with always seemed stuck in dead-end jobs that yielded nothing more than a meager paycheck. However, Miguel's elevated status brought a new outlook to the work he did for a living. Suddenly, he became aware of the satisfaction that comes with a job well done.

All that being said, there was a bump in the road by the name of Ashley Eberhardt, Miguel's supervisor. Their personalities clashed like fire and water. Even though he occasionally went out of his way to give her a lift to work, she was totally unappreciative. When his daily tasks involved working alone, things were better. However, if he was given a job that put them in close proximity, the air was filled with backbiting and disparaging remarks. Consequently, those workdays became long and tiring.

The worst of Miguel's episodes occurred when, one week prior, he had his blowup with Ashley. Unable to take it anymore, he lost his temper, and recalled having to control an urge to slap her across the mouth. Although Ashley didn't realize it, she was saved by the sudden appearance of Rick Ballinger, the lab supervisor. Rick's interference made the situation go from bad to worse. In mere minutes, Miguel was locked in the new struggle of trying desperately to defend his actions. Before Miguel knew what was happening, he found himself in jeopardy of being fired.

Now, in addition to hating Ashley for making his life miserable, he hated Rick Ballinger for being such an asshole. For Miguel, all that was left was an irrelevant job and a burning desire to strike back.

Around ten a.m., Maria finally rolled out of bed. She made her way to the bathroom before going to the kitchen to brew a half pot of coffee. Still rubbing the sleep from her eyes, she went into the second bedroom and saw the red light blinking on the answering machine. Turning up the volume and punching the play button, she listened.

'Hey baby,' it blared. 'This is Bruce Kreitzer. Y'know, Big Bad Bruce. I'm going to be in Pasadena on the sixth of next month.'

The message continued with Kreitzer spelling out the length of his visit and the name of the hotel at which he planned to stay. Maria closed her eyes and pictured the skinny, angular Bruce Kreitzer. She had been his escort on two occasions over the past year and a half and vividly recalled the odd smell his body emitted when he perspired during sex.

The answering machine played the last of his message: ' . . . let's plan on you and me getting together, know what I mean?'

*   *   *

"Forum Lab," said Rick Ballinger into the telephone.

"Glad I caught you before you left for your meeting," said Sarah Levine. "I've got some preliminary information for you on the kudzu plant. It's good stuff, Rick. Real good stuff. They'll be impressed, and it'll make you sound like the genius you are."

Rick's meeting with Doug Matsushita, and Herb Knoll had been arranged for the purpose of finalizing the takeover of the new Kudzu Project.

"Okay. Whachya got?" asked Rick.

Sarah recited a laundry list of facts about the kudzu plant, including its scientific classification, general composition and history. "It turns out," she concluded, "that kudzu is not native to the United States. It was originally brought into this country in the late eighteen hundreds from Asia. Some say China and others say Japan, but definitely Asian. So, my guess is that over in the Orient, where kudzu has to tolerate native predators, such as Oriental bugs that feast on its roots and leaves and bark, the plant stayed in check. But, here in this country, no such controls exist. As a result, kudzu has been spreading unchecked for over a hundred years."

Rick had been taking notes as Sarah spoke. "Good information, Sarah. Anything else?"

"I've learned that the root system of the plant is very high in carbohydrates. You should look into the possibility of introducing some kind of mold that will thrive on the roots. In the meantime, I'll check into which species of Asian insects thrive on eating kudzu. I'll keep you posted."

While Rick and Sarah talked, the rest of Forum Lab's team showed up to start their day. With only occasional chatter, they concentrated on their tasks. Ever since the blowup between Ashley and Miguel, an unspoken tension lingered in the air.

Rick hung up and called out "good-morning" to his staff. Pleasant salutations were offered in return. The notable exception came from Miguel who only grumbled his greeting. Rick decided to chalk up Miguel's grunts to the man not being a morning person. It usually took Miguel a couple of hours and a pot-and-a-half of coffee before he became fully conversational.

A newly hired technician, named Britney, was working alongside Darlene and Nancy. Although Britney lacked the experience of the others, Forum Lab needed another body to help wrap up the existing projects. Human Resources had hired Britney while Rick had been in San Diego for a two day seminar. The responsibility for interviewing her had fallen to Ashley.

Shutting his briefcase, Rick called out to everybody, "Off to another meeting. See you all in about two hours." Then, to Ashley he said, "I'm running a little late. Come walk with me to the elevator."

Ashley closed the door behind them and walked down the hall with Rick. "What's up?" she asked.

"When I got in this morning," he began, "I checked the workstations. I noticed that Britney has been filling out the Frequency Distribution Tables incorrectly. It looks like she's entering median values instead of the standard deviation values. It's really going to screw things up when we get to the time-lapse sequencing. Would you please work with her on that?"

A disgusted look came across Ashley's face.

"What's wrong?" asked Rick.

"I screwed up," said Ashley, shaking her head. "I should have spotted it when I interviewed her. The girl is such a blonde. She can't walk and chew gum at the same time. I can't even allow her to take ten-minute coffee breaks anymore."

"Why not?" asked Rick.

"It takes too much time to retrain her," answered Ashley with a deadpan.

Rick smiled at her dark humor. "That bad, eh?"

"I went over the stat tables with her on Monday. Even though the concept took a while to sink in, it looked like she finally got it." Ashley paused. "At least I thought so. Guess not."

"Is she going to make it, or are we going to have to replace her?"

"I'm not sure yet," sighed Ashley. "But the odds are stacking up against her. She's like a teeny-bopper, snapping her gum and bouncing around to some music that only she can hear."

Rick raised his eyebrows.

Ashley concluded with, "I'll try again to get her to focus on what she's supposed to be doing."

Rick preferred walking up the two flights to Doug's office, rather than riding the elevator. They paused at the stairwell entrance. "Okay," he said, changing subjects. "What's happening with you and Miguel? Have you two managed to bury the hatchet?"

"Well, we haven't been firing shots at each other, if that's what you mean."

"Frankly," said Rick, "I'm concerned about his attitude. I'm on my way to a meeting with Doug and Herb. They're about to hand me an assignment that could prove to be the company's biggest payday. If we do a good job, it'll put our team head and shoulders above everybody else. I just want to make sure that it's smooth sailing between you and Miguel."

"I've got a news flash for you, Rick. The problem ain't so much between me and Miguel. The problem is between you and Miguel."

"Me and Miguel?" asked Rick, shocked at the implication.

"Yeah," she confirmed. "Miguel and I have swept most of our problems under the rug. But, he's really pissed at you."

Rick's mouth fell open.

Ashley continued. "Nancy told me that Miguel thinks you've got no backbone. Says, he's still ticked off because you threatened to fire him. Is that true?"

Rick tried to smooth down his unruly cowlick. "Right after you stormed out of the lab," recalled Rick. "I tried to get Miguel to tell me what happened, but he refused. That irked me. I may have said something about ' . . . rethinking his position.' I don't really remember."

"Well, to Miguel, that meant you were about to fire him."

"Yeah," said Rick, trying to recall the details. "He really got upset. To be honest, I thought he was going to take a swing at me."

Maybe you should talk to him," suggested Ashley. "Y'know, clear the air."

"Yeah," said Rick. "That's probably a good idea. But, right now, I've got to go. I'll see you later."

Ashley watched as Rick took the stairs two at a time.

Rick's meeting went well, despite he and Doug spending most of it listening to Herb discuss the contracts that had recently been signed with the State of Georgia. Herb's excitement was visible as he explained that the Georgia legislature had already allocated a lot of money for this project. If Envirogen were able to produce successive results, the multi-million dollar deal would lead to millions more.

"Right now," said Herb, "it looks like the Department of Agriculture is holding all the cards. And the politicians are running scared."

"That's kind of unusual, isn't it?" asked Rick. "Usually, it's the other way around."

Doug Matsushita interjected. "Well, it seems that the farmers are worried about their export crops. There's a huge lobby in the state capital from the pecan and peach industries, and the growers have been putting the pressure on the politicians to do something about the kudzu problem. If nothing is done, the kudzu will wipe out half of the state's exports. That, in turn, will erode the state's tax base. So, the politicians realize that their jobs are on the line."

"Hence," stated Rick, "open access to the state's coffers."

"Right," agreed Herb. "And this is just the beginning. There must be other kinds of pest plants out there. I don't know . . . maybe poison ivy or ragweed or something that's messing up somebody else's export crop. What do you think?"

"I've got some good news for you Herb," said Rick, recalling the conversation he had with Sarah. "Georgia isn't the only state with the kudzu problem. Turns out that kudzu is running rampant all through the Southeast. Alabama, Florida, the Carolinas . . ."

Herb interrupted. "You see Doug? This is the kind of research that we need. Not just test tubes and beakers, but meat and potato stuff like what Rick just said. That's the kind of information that could make us millions. Hell, billions!"

Rick smiled, as Herb took the ball and ran with it.

Herb continued. "I mean, we waited for the State of Georgia to come to us with this problem. But, what's wrong with our own marketing people going to the other Southeastern states and making the proposition to them?" Not giving either man a chance to respond, Herb answered, "Nothing! Our people need to become more aggressive, more proactive. There's a tremendous amount of money to be had out there. We've got to go out there and get it."

"Sounds right, Herb," offered Doug. "And you're the guy who can make it happen."

Herb nodded his head vigorously. "Damn right. There's no reason why we can't have the same kind of deal with each of those states."

The idea was beginning to take shape. Expanding on it, Herb turned to Rick and said, "I want you to meet with Ray Travers. He's the vice president of the marketing department."

"I know," said Rick.

Herb continued. "I want you to tell him what you just told me. Then, we'll be able to go after . . ."

"Hold on," said Doug, holding up a hand and curbing Herb's enthusiasm. "One step at a time."

"What are you talking about?"

Doug explained. "Let's get the Kudzu Project going first. Once a solution is found, then, you'll have a product that can be sold to other state governments. If you go right now to the State of Alabama, for instance, all you're offering is a hope and a prayer. But, if you wait until we have an actual organism that can eradicate the kudzu, you'll have a bargaining chip that could double or triple our profits. Make sense?"

Herb's eyes went wide at the mention of doubling or tripling the company's profits. "Right," he said. "Good point. What we need to do is forge ahead. Full steam."

Herb sat up and faced Rick. "How do you plan on doing this?"

"I've been doing some preliminary research on *Pueraria lobata*," said Rick . . ."

"What?" asked Herb quizzically.

"*Pueraria lobata*," repeated Rick. "It's the Latin classification for kudzu."
Herb nodded, seeming to comprehend.

"Anyway, I've come up with some interesting data. First of all, the root system is very high in carbohydrates. So, I'm going to have my team do a printout on various molds that thrive most efficiently on starch. Also, since the plant only grows in warmer climates, I'm going to consider various fungi that might do well on the leaves or vines. Lastly, it turns out that kudzu isn't native to our country. It was imported from Asia in the late eighteen hundreds. So, I'm having Sarah Levine, the entomologist, check into whatever Oriental insects might be keeping the plants under control."

"Excellent, Rick," said Herb as though the project was already complete. To Doug, he said, "We've obviously got the right man on the job. Good work." Turning back to Rick, Herb said, "You need to get to work, young man. Go create your thing, your mold, your fungus, your bugs, whatever. I'll see to it that you have whatever you need."

With Herb in such a generous mood, Rick would have loved to conclude the meeting. However, there was another subject to be discussed. "Look," he said, "I'm almost ready to take on the Kudzu Project, but we're having some difficulty wrapping up the Foxboro Beer job."

"What's the problem?" asked Doug.

"It's the CO_2 levels. They're still too high."

Leaning back in his chair, Doug contemplated the dilemma. "Have you tried an oxygen inhibitor?" he asked.

Before Rick could respond, Herb interrupted. "Hey. Haven't we discussed this already?"

"We have," said Rick. "When we were . . ."

Herb spoke over top of Rick's sentence. "So, what's the big deal?" he said impatiently. "A little carbon monoxide? C'mon. Let's get the Foxboro Beer project off the table. Let's just give it to them and don't worry so much about a little air pollution. Fact is, they'll be happy as a pig in shit because we were able to increase their beer production. Doug, you need to see that Rick gets a clean slate to work from. When we're talking about millions of dollars, none of us should be worried about a little CO_2."

Rick glanced at Doug who shrugged his shoulders in resignation. Herb Knoll was a man who spent all of his time working to improve Envirogen's bottom line. His knowledge of basic science seemed nonexistent as shown by his repeated reference to CO_2 as carbon monoxide. He didn't seem to grasp the significance of the potential problem. Or perhaps, he chose to ignore the carbon dioxide issue in favor of profits. Perhaps, Mel Fishman was right when he said that science always takes a backseat to money.

CHAPTER SEVENTEEN

FLORIDA

S outheast Florida in the winter months was weather perfect. Daytime temperatures hovered in the shirtsleeve range, while the humidity, which would become oppressive in midsummer, now felt quite comfortable. The sky, dotted with billowing puffs of cotton, was always a deep tropical blue. It was paradise.

Rather than taking the tunnel from the covered parking lot to the offices of the *Sun Coast Ledger*, Hannah Carpenter walked along the palm-lined sidewalk. Before going to work, she wanted to take a moment to enjoy the warm sunshine and balmy breezes. Pausing at the big glass entry doors, she gathered in the view of the Intercoastal waterway that separated her from Palm Beach and the Atlantic Ocean. Hannah breathed deeply, trying to capture a hint of the briny aroma that sometimes hung in the air. Satisfied, she entered the building.

Crossing the spacious lobby, Hannah scanned the wall of clocks, each showing the correct time in one of fifteen different cities around the globe. Yesterday, she had received a note from her Editor-in-Chief, Sidney Aarons, stating that he wanted to have a meeting with her this morning at eight-thirty. Hurrying to her desk to start her day, Hannah clicked on her e-mail before checking to see if there were any new faxes or telephone messages. Although she busied herself with routine tasks, Hannah was preoccupied with the upcoming meeting. Ever since their last go-around when Sidney had intimated that she was about to be demoted, feelings of stress and self-recrimination had become an integral part of her life. The thought of having to do the bidding of such a weasely asshole as Henry Drummond left her completely cold. Hannah had decided that, if Sidney insisted on her becoming Drummond's assistant, she would quit.

Eight-thirty came quickly, and Hannah, feeling anxious, hurried to her meeting. Through the big glass walls of his office, she could see Sidney, shirtsleeves rolled up and tie hanging loose under an unbuttoned collar. As usual, his hands were occupied, a telephone in one and a coffee cup in the other.

Aarons saw her approaching and nodded his head, signaling permission for her to enter. Hannah's first surprise was that she and Aarons were alone in this meeting. No sign of Henry Drummond. There had been a nagging worry that the agenda for this meeting was going to be a collaborative effort between Aarons and Drummond to lay down the ground rules for Hannah's new responsibilities. Now, knowing that there were only the two of them, Hannah was more inclined, even anxious, to speak her mind. She waited for Aarons to get off the telephone.

"This phone hasn't stopped since seven o'clock this morning," said Aarons replacing the receiver into its cradle. "Let's make this quick before it rings again."

The Editor-in-Chief's secretary would never "hold all calls," unless Sidney deemed the meeting to be of great urgency. Otherwise, employees, Hannah included, had to be prepared for the constant jangling of the telephone.

"All right Sidney," began Hannah. "About Henry Drummond . . ."

Aarons jumped in, speaking overtop of Hannah. "Right. Henry Drummond," he said with a sudden new direction of thought. "I've got him working on the Home Depot warehouse fires. Looks like arson."

Hannah ignored the news of Drummond's assignment and sat forward in her seat. "I don't think you were very fair when you said that you wanted me to . . ."

Aarons was already shaking his head. "I didn't call you in here to discuss fair or not fair. We all have a job to do and we need to get it done. That includes you."

Hannah felt as though she had been punched in the stomach. Knowing that Aarons had already made up his mind about her demotion, Hannah felt queasy. Although she tried to come to grips with this ego-buster, the thought of being demoted got her hackles up. "I didn't join this newspaper just to do Drummond's scut work, Sidney. I expected to be the kind of reporter . . ."

Aarons felt a flash of anger. With his free hand, he slapped the desktop. With his other, he plopped down his coffee cup so forcefully that some of the contents spilled onto a stack of newspapers. "Why the hell are you always fighting me?" he asked, his voice raised in frustration. "I'm your boss, damn it!" Momentarily, he turned his attention to the puddle of coffee that was quickly being absorbed by other scattered documents surrounding the wet newspaper. "Shit," he muttered. "Will you look at this."

Hannah stood up. "Well, if you're going to make me work for Drummond, then I quit!" she stated emphatically.

Aarons also stood up. "You are one pain in the ass! You know that? One colossal pain in the ass! I ought to let you quit. I ought to let you walk out that door, but y'know what?"

"What?" Hannah seethed angrily.

"I want you to sit down and shut up for one minute," he said, pointing his finger at her face. "Just shut up, and try not to make a damned fool of yourself. Got it?"

Sitting down again, Hannah folded her arms across her chest.

Aarons stepped from behind his desk and strode to the window. Pausing to calm himself, he gazed out at the Atlantic seascape.

Hannah could see him take a deep breath.

Aarons turned to her and said, "I spend more time with you than with any other reporter on my staff. You know that? Tell me, Miss Carpenter, why do you think that is?"

Hannah started to answer, but Aarons held up a hand, denying her an opportunity to reply.

"I told you not to speak for one minute," he reminded her. "My question was rhetorical. So, just be quiet and listen. I spend more time with you because I believed you were worth it. I thought you might have the raw talent to be an exceptional reporter. I thought that maybe . . ."

The ringing of the phone cut Aarons off in mid sentence. Picking it up, he carried on a conversation that didn't last anymore than twenty seconds. Hanging up, he punched an intercom button and waited.

"Yes, Sidney?" asked his secretary, Nina.

"Hold all my calls," he ordered.

Hannah was astounded. Sidney Aarons had bestowed an honor by "holding all calls" for the remainder of their meeting. It was an extraordinary moment. His action prompted her to sit upright and to pay very close attention to whatever else he had to say.

Organizing his thoughts, Aarons stared at her for a moment. "I think you have talent. As a matter of fact, I believe you're capable enough to be this newspaper's next Pulitzer. But in order for that to happen, you've got to start paying attention. Writing is one thing. There's no question that you've got what it takes. But, listening is another, and that's your weakness. You don't listen to me, you don't listen to Donnie and it's becoming painfully obvious that you don't listen to the people you're interviewing. Broaden your mind and open your ears, Hannah. Remember, the news business, by its very nature, is fluid. It changes day to day. Hour by hour. Minute by minute for God's sake! A good reporter goes out on assignment and brings back a story. But, a great reporter goes out there, listens carefully to what's being said, and comes back with a blockbuster."

Aarons paused for effect. Satisfied that he had Hannah's attention, he continued. "And that's what I'm trying to teach you. That's why I spend all this time with you."

He walked back around and sat at his desk. "Any questions?"

"Henry Drummond?" asked Hannah timidly.

"Forget Drummond," said Aarons with a wave of his hand. "You're not working with Drummond. I want you to continue on the Brother Timothy story. There's a lot more to it, and I want you to go out there and find it. Understand?"

Knowing that her career was suddenly back on track, Hannah experienced a wave of relief. There would be no demotion and, more importantly, no Henry Drummond. Nodding her head, she tried to hold back tears of elation. "Okay Sidney," she sniffled, as a smile worked its way to the corners of her mouth.

Aarons watched two big alligator tears travel part way down Hannah's cheeks before she dabbed at them with a tissue. Without commenting on her rush of emotions, Aarons continued. "Brother Timothy is becoming news. "He may be spouting his fear-mongering bullshit about genetic engineering, but people are starting to listen. The man has an army of zealots out there who believe every single word that comes out of his mouth. And all this while, Hannah, you're the one with the inside track. He knows you and, hopefully, you've managed to build some kind of rapport."

"Yes," agreed Hannah. "We hit it off quite well. I think he was kind of taken with me, if you know what I mean." Hannah changed the subject. "For the moment, he's in Los Angeles. He plans on splitting his time between L.A. and Pasadena, because, as far as the Devil and genetic engineering are concerned, that's where the action is."

"Okay," said Aarons. "Fly out there and spend a couple of days with him; a week if you have to." Leaning forward for emphasis, he added, "But, listen carefully to what the man is saying, Hannah. There's a real story out there. I have no doubt that you can write it. I just want to feel the same confidence in your ability to uncover it."

Assuming the meeting was over, Hannah stood. "All right, Sidney. I'll go make my reservations."

"Wait. Not so fast."

Hannah sat back down.

"Before you take off, there's someone I want you to interview. Her name is Dr. Indira Jawara. She's a geneticist. Although she's originally from Calcutta, she's the Department Head of Biological Sciences at F.A.U." Aarons was referring to Florida Atlantic University, a sprawling campus located in the heart of Boca Raton, Florida. "She'll give you an insight into the world of gene-splicing that you won't get anywhere else. Indira's one of the few scientists out there who isn't afraid to talk about the negative side of DNA manipulation."

Handing Hannah a sheet of paper containing Dr. Jawara's personal data, Sidney said, "I've known Indira for a number of years. She's made a name for herself because regulatory committees are always calling her in to testify. If you watch C-Span with any regularity, you'll see her. Now go," said Aarons, waving his hand in dismissal. "I've already told Professor Jawara that you'd be calling."

Hannah stood, walked around the desk, and kissed the man on the forehead. "Thank you, Sidney."

"Don't you dare try sucking up to me," he said, leaning away. "I'm still pissed at you. You made me spill my coffee."

CHAPTER EIGHTEEN

FLORIDA

It wasn't until late morning that Brad Bishop had an opportunity to speak with his office manager. Since one of Brad's investigators was out on maternity leave and another was down with the flu, the work had been overwhelming.

Rose Goldberg said, "I've called Office Temps. They're sending us a file clerk. If she's not an idiot or a klutz, we have half a chance. At least, it'll be a warm body."

Ignoring her caustic humor, Brad said, "My main worry is the Motorola case. We still have more than two hundred of their people to interview, and it has to be done by the middle of next week."

Pondering the problem, Rose tapped the side of her pen against her cheek. She brightened and said, "How about Jimmy Toomey? He might be willing to help us out. Especially if I entice him with some donuts."

"Toomey? You think so?"

"Last I heard," said Rose, "he turned sixty-two and retired from the Sheriff's Department. Maybe he'd be willing to work for us part-time like he used to. I can call and ask."

"Sure," agreed Brad, making a note of the decision. "Why not? We need all the help we can get." Brad picked up another sheet of paper and asked, "Also, what's happening with the investigation about the collapsed scaffolding on Clematis Street?"

Rose continued to fill Brad in on the progress of the various active cases. Her efficiency and memory never ceased to amaze him. Over the years, Brad had come to realize that he could ask Rose any question about any case, past or current, and the woman would know the answer.

They were in the middle of their meeting when Sophie, Rose's assistant, poked her head in and announced, "Brad? Mr. Goodenow is on line one. Claims it's urgent."

Sophie, a recent college graduate, had been working for Brad's agency a mere six months. Fair haired and blue eyed, with a stunning figure and dazzling smile, her skills belied the stereotypical dumb blonde.

Rose said, "The only thing urgent with Harry Goodenow is his afternoon martini."

Sophie added, "And his desire to get into my pants."

Brad smiled. "Tell him I'll call him back."

"I tried that," said Sophie. "He insists on talking to you."

Sighing, Brad punched the button activating the speaker phone. "What's up, Harry?" asked Brad, reaching for his Nerf-ball.

Harry's voice filled the office. "Noontime is approaching, dear Bradstone," he said dramatically. "There are rituals to maintain, and I have the munchies."

Brad stopped squeezing his blue Nerf-ball. "That's your big emergency? That's the reason you insisted on interrupting my meeting?"

"I'm hungry, Brad," whined Harry, "and you and I haven't had lunch in over a week. Besides, it's 'season' and *Paul's Dockside* is featuring fresh stone crabs."

It was that time of year. The Dockside Restaurant, like other fine food establishments, brought in succulent stone crabs for aficionados to enjoy. Since the restaurant always did such a fine job preparing the little morsels, wintertime patrons lined up ceremoniously, waiting for their chance to crack the claws and savor the delicacy.

"I'm sorry, Harry," lamented Brad, replacing the blue ball into its well. "I'm short of help and I'm up to my ears in work. We're going to have to do it another time."

Rose interjected. "I have a better idea. Go to lunch with Harry. Nothing's going to fall apart if you go to lunch for an hour."

Harry's voice came through the speaker. "Is that you, Rose?"

"Yes Harry. It's me."

"Rose, Rose. You're an angel of mercy," emoted Harry. "Not only do you possess a sultry beauty, but you are wise beyond your years. Listen to her, Brad. This is a woman who deserves our love and admiration."

"Love and admiration?" repeated Rose. "What are you saying Harry? Are you finally going to ask me out on a date?"

"Oh, sweet Rose," said Harry sadly. "If only I could . . . But, my heart has been promised to Angelina Jolie, and she would kick my *derrière* if she knew you and I were an item."

Brad said, "All right, Harry. Whose turn is it to pay?"

Harry's snicker was laced with evil. "Heh, heh, heh," he cackled. "Your turn. And I intend to eat buckets of those stone crabs. You'll have to take out a second mortgage just to pay for my indulgence."

"In that case, forget it. I definitely can't make it for lunch."

"Hey!" said Harry indignantly. "No weaseling out of it. You know our rules."

Rose spoke into the phone. "Harry, he'll meet you there in a half hour. Now, say 'goodbye' so we can finish our meeting."

"Goodbye, sweet Rose," said Harry. Then, to Brad, "See you at the 'Dockside' in half an hour."

Brad hung up and said, "You sure you don't mind?"

Rose smiled. "Being that I'm Jewish, I'm struggling not to say anything that'll make you feel guilty."

Brad laughed. "Okay. What else do we have to cover before we wrap this up?"

"That's pretty much it," she said, standing. "Oh, there is one more thing."

"What?"

"Your dear friend, Stephanie, the Nazi . . ."

Brad's face took on a dour expression. "What now?"

"You asked for background reports on a couple of people that she's associated with."

"Right," Brad concurred. "Find anything interesting?"

"As a matter of fact, I did. That woman in California, Sarah Levine? She's got a Ph.D. in entomology. Very high up in the world of bugs. From what I could gather, she's very well respected in her field. Stephanie should feel lucky that her son has taken up with that kind of woman. And luckier still that Sarah Levine has agreed to date a boy who's the spawn of Adolph Eichmann."

"Okay. I'll tell her."

"But now, for the interesting news."

Brad sat back. "What?"

"Stephanie's boyfriend? *Señor* Raphael Boñez?"

"Go on," coaxed Brad.

"Initial reports are not promising. A man by that same name has been arrested several times for stealing shopping carts."

"You're kidding."

"Well," hedged Rose, "keep in mind, that's just preliminary information. The Raphael Boñez in my report is not a Bolivian industrialist. On the contrary, he's a Latin hustler living in San Juan, and I'm not positive that he's the same man."

"Oh, yeah? Then, how come I'm starting to sweat?"

Rose shrugged. "There's always the chance that there are two people with the name Raphael Boñez, although that shopping cart connection may be a little too coincidental."

"Please keep checking. I'd like to be absolutely sure before I talk to Stephanie."

Rose started to walk out of Brad's office. "I'll let you know as soon as I can confirm it. But, it sure would give me a warm feeling if I knew for a fact that Queen Stephanie was getting humped by a Puerto Rican con man."

*   *   *

After dialing the Florida Atlantic University campus and punching in the extension to the Department of Biological Sciences, Hannah Carpenter quickly connected with Professor Indira Jawara. Following a pleasant greeting, the Professor not only agreed to the interview, but made a suggestion. "I'll be in your neck of the woods within the hour," said Dr. Jawara. "Since I'll be staying with friends in Palm Beach, how would it be if we did the interview this morning?"

Sometimes, the scheduling of interviews took days of phone calls, compromises, and calendar manipulations. Consequently, Hannah, elated over her good fortune, quickly agreed to the Professor's suggestion.

Dr. Jawara said that she was staying at the home of Countess Erika Unstedt on Palm Beach, and gave the address to Hannah. The Countess was an active member of the Palm Beach social scene. As such, she was a well-known personality whose name and photo had appeared many time in Hannah's newspaper. The sprawling estate was located in the middle of "mansion row" on South Ocean Boulevard. Hannah arrived shortly before ten o'clock. She was greeted by one of the staff who escorted her through the home's interior. The mansion was breathtaking. The foyer, almost overwhelming in its size, featured a thirty-foot ceiling that encased a gigantic skylight. After walking through the impressive structure, Hannah was led to a bank of sliding glass doors that opened onto a spacious patio, which surrounded an Olympic size pool.

Dr. Indira Jawara rose from her chair to greet Hannah. "Good morning Miss Carpenter," she said, extending her hand. "It's nice to meet you. Sidney told me all about you, but he neglected to tell me how beautiful you were."

Hannah thanked Professor Jawara for the compliment and asked how long she had known Sidney Aarons.

"Sidney and I go way back," said Indira with a growing smirk. "All the way back to when he was a slave trader for the Egyptian Pharaohs."

Hannah nodded. "Right. A slave master with a big heart."

Seating themselves under the shade of a broad leafed schiflera tree, the two women chatted amiably about a number of subjects, including Sidney Aarons, and the terrible traffic along Interstate 95. They also agreed to dispense with formalities and call each other by their first names.

Referring to the owner, Hannah said, "I hope this interview won't be an imposition to Countess Erika."

Indira shook her head. "Not at all. I've known Countess Erika for over twenty years. "We were dorm-mates during our undergraduate years at Vassar College, and have been very close friends ever since. I spend a lot of time here, and she insist that I treat this place like my own. So, doing this interview is no problem at all."

Hannah studied Indira Jawara's face as she spoke. Her skin, like finely brushed, light brown suede, looked soft and warm. Dark, deep set eyes seemed to reflect intelligence and anticipation. Except for a few strands of gray that fell across her forehead, the woman's hair was jet black. It was pulled back into a tight sweep and held together with a silk hibiscus flower.

"Sidney said you were from Calcutta," commented Hannah, "but I don't detect any accent."

Indira smiled. "My parents and I came to live here when I was just an infant. My father was an ophthalmologist with a practice in New York City, and my mother was a botanist working for the United Nations. So, growing up in this country and having two parents who spoke English quite well, made it impossible to guess that I was born in India." An impish look crossed Indira's face as she said, "Especially, since I got rid of that red dot on my forehead."

Double-checking Indira's brow, Hannah saw that no sign of the mystical dot remained. Although she had a latent curiosity about its origin and purpose, she decided to save those questions for another time. Instead, she said, "When I called you for this interview, I thought I had the wrong person. You sounded more like a genuine New Yorker than . . ."

Indira's hearty laugh drowned out the rest of the sentence. "That's me," she said. "New York, New York. Subway trains, Nathan's franks, Central Park and the New York Yankees!"

Hannah giggled at the infectiousness of Jawara's laugh. "I think this interview is going to be fun."

"Me too," agreed Professor Jawara. "Where would you like to begin?"

Hannah mentioned the piece she had written about Brother Timothy Goodman.

"I'm familiar with your article," said Indira. "When Sidney called and said that you'd be requesting an interview, he faxed me a copy."

Hannah couldn't help asking, "What did you think of it?"

"It was very well written," said Jawara, carefully choosing her words, "but to be honest, you seemed to be focused more on the tent revival movement than on the message that the Preacher was trying to spread."

"You've heard of Brother Timothy?"

"Are you kidding?" asked Indira, raising her eyebrows. "That's like asking me if I ever heard of Reverend Jerry Fallwell or better yet, Attila the Hun. Brother Timothy is the fire-breathing dragon leading the charge against the dreaded Tiamat."

"Uh . . . I'm not familiar with the dreaded Tiamat."

Professor Jawara smiled. "Most people aren't as honest as you, Hannah. They would just go along, pretending they knew what I was talking about, regardless of the obscurity of my reference."

Jawara paused, thinking that Hannah was about to respond. Instead, Hannah just smiled.

"The story of Tiamat," explained the Professor, "contains the earliest reference to dragons in literature. Tiamat was a character in a Mesopotamian folk tale, written over two thousand years ago. She lived in the netherworld and represented chaos and evil. Eventually, she was slain by a dragon, allowing order to return to the Earth."

"Wow!" said Hannah, impressed with the ancient tidbit of knowledge. "I get the feeling you're just chock full of stuff like that. So, you think Brother Timothy is our modern day dragon slayer?"

"Perhaps David and Goliath would have been a better analogy."

"Which of those is Brother Timothy supposed to be?"

"David, of course," said Jawara, a look of seriousness coming over her. "Goliath, in this case, would be represented by the giant corporations of the world, the industrial mega-plexes that he's battling."

"You think he has a point, don't you?" said Hannah. "Are biotech companies making a mistake by going forward with genetic engineering? Can it really lead to extinction? The end of the Earth?"

Professor Jawara started to speak but, momentarily, held herself in check. "Hannah," she said slowly, "There's a good story here. A story with three sides. There are the Brother Timothys of this world attempting to frighten the masses into awareness, the Fortune 500 companies attempting to make a profit, and the truth. Try not to be the reporter whose only goal is to write sensational headlines."

Hannah stared at Dr. Indira Jawara, a world renowned geneticist with a reputation for poking holes in dogma. She was the sought after Professor who was invited to testify on Capitol Hill about the new wave of biotechnology and its effect on society. Knowing that people flocked to this woman for answers, Hannah suddenly felt as though she had been admonished for asking a dumb question. "I . . . I didn't mean to imply . . ."

Indira interrupted. "The world of genetic engineering isn't black and white, Hannah. There is a myriad of gray that complicates the issues. All I'm saying is,

I'll be happy to give you this interview, but I'm hoping you'll write a balanced piece, not one with an alarming headline saying, 'Professor Jawara says that mankind is doomed!'"

"Agreed," said Hannah with a nod of her head. "Let me rephrase my question. Even though Brother Timothy always speaks to a packed house, and people are glued to his every word, how much of his rhetoric is truth, and how much of it is designed to suck money out of his parishioners?"

"The problem with most of the 'Chicken-Little' crowd is their lack of scientific training. They run around yelling, 'The sky is falling! The sky is falling!' Brother Timothy is one of those. He may be a motivational speaker and have the ability to get people to listen, but he's certainly not a scientist."

"So, you think his message is all smoke and mirrors?"

Jawara sat up straight. "Not *all* smoke and mirrors," she said. "He does present a couple of valid points."

"Okay," said Hannah, warming to the interview, "Tell me some things you agree with and what you think is hokey."

Jawara said, "In every age of our history, there have been those who have tried their level best to stop progress. Go back to the time when folks thought the Earth was flat. Even the great Egyptian mathematician, Ptolemy, advanced the Flat Earth idea. So, when sailors finally set off to explore what was beyond the horizon, there were plenty of people who sat on the shore saying, 'You shouldn't do that. You don't know what dangers are out there. And, because of your reckless behavior, no one knows what disasters will befall the rest of us!' Today, people with the same mind-set scream at the idea of space travel, exploring the oceans, organ replacement surgery, stem-cell research, cloning, the list is endless. Brother Timothy is saying that science should stop this experimentation of gene-splicing because not knowing the outcome frightens him. And, in turn, he frightens others."

"All right," acknowledged Hannah, "that's all well and good, but what about the validity of his rhetoric? Is he saying anything that makes sense?"

The interview was interrupted by a member of the household staff who approached them and asked if either would like some refreshments. He made a couple of suggestions, including juices, soft drinks and iced tea.

"Yes, Nelson," answered Indira. "I'll have some raspberry iced tea."

Nelson turned to Hannah. "And you, Miss Carpenter?" he asked formally.

"Some orange juice, if that'll be all right," she said.

Nelson left to prepare the drinks.

Indira Jawara continued without missing a beat. "Poor Brother Timothy," she said shaking her head. "There are a number of things he says that actually make sense, but he says them for all the wrong reasons. Let me give you a 'for instance.' He says we should stop engineering food crops such as corn and soybeans, because we're sticking our nose into God's business. He claims we should stop creating new life-forms because . . ." Jawara lowered her voice in an attempt to imitate Brother Timothy. " . . . that's the work of the Devil."

Hannah chuckled. "You do that very well," she said.

"Thank you," said Indira, nodding her head in acknowledgement. "I've been practicing." After brushing back a lock of hair, Indira continued. "Now maybe, just maybe, we should consider a slowdown or perhaps even a moratorium. However, that decision should be based on the industry's willingness to take another look at what it's doing. Not because God or the Devil said so."

Hannah stopped scribbling a note. "Do you think the biotech industry would have such a willingness?"

"Let's face it, Hannah. The biggest motivator for scientific research is money. Regardless of what you hear, they no longer do things for the good of society. Corporations aren't interested in helping the poor disadvantaged people of the Third World. Their interests lie in how much money can be generated from a particular project."

"Isn't that kind of cynical?"

"No. Not at all," replied Jawara. "That's the reality of the situation. Do you have any idea how much money is funneled into cancer research? Or the search for finding a cure for diabetes or Alzheimer's? Hundreds and hundreds of millions of dollars. Y'know why?" Without waiting for an answer, Jawara continued. "Because if the scientists are successful, even partially successful, the return on that investment will be in the billions of dollars. Not one or two billion, but rather scores of billions."

Hannah was about to comment, but the Professor cut her off. "On the other hand," continued Indira, "how much money is being spent to find the cure for Crudtzfelt-Jacob disease?"

Wondering if the Professor was pulling her leg, Hannah smiled uneasily. "Come again?" she asked.

"Crudtzfelt-Jacob disease. You probably know it better by its more common name, Mad Cow disease. Anyway, the answer is, practically nothing. Maybe ten bucks. A lot has been written about the malady, but the fact is not enough people are burdened with the curse of the mad cow to warrant the research for a cure."

"Is that why there's so much going on in the rest of the field of biotechnology?"

"Precisely," affirmed the Professor. Then, she asked, "Have you ever heard of Bt corn?"

Hannah's response was interrupted by the reappearance of Nelson, who carried a tray of refreshments. Taking a moment to lay down a tablecloth, he followed it by setting out small dishes and napkins. Before departing, he centered a plate of cookies which included the chocolate chip and oatmeal variety.

"Ooo," cooed Hannah, eyeing the sweets. "They look good."

"A lot more appetizing than Bt corn."

"Absolutely," replied Hannah, remembering Jawara's question. "Isn't Bt corn the kind that's been engineered to . . . to resist . . . um . . . blight and stuff like that?"

"Pretty good, Hannah. Actually, it's been engineered to resist insects. Well, here's the dark side of that story. The corporations that have developed Bt corn have taken it a step further. They were afraid that the farmers would harvest their own seeds from the Bt crop in order to plant next year's crop. That way, the farmers could avoid buying the seeds from the suppliers. So, the big, bad biotech corporations reengineered the corn to produce 'terminator seeds,' or seeds that do not have the ability to produce baby corn."

Indira spread her hands in a gesture of the farmer's futility before continuing. "No new crops from harvested corn. In that way, they force the farmer into purchasing new seeds every year. I realize that a packet of corn seeds doesn't cost an arm and a leg but, on a global scale, it amounts to billions of dollars."

Hannah was surprised by the amount of money to which Jawara alluded. "Billions of dollars in corn seeds?" she questioned.

"Multiple billions," corrected Jawara. "The corn industry is enormous. Remember, it's not just seeds or corn on the cob. Think about Taco Bell, Taco Cabana and all the other tortillas and tacos in the world. Consider the enormous quantity of popcorn that's consumed in movie theaters. Or, how about corn syrup, corn soup and all the frozen TV dinners that have corn as part of the meal?"

Hannah nodded as the light of understanding grew brighter.

"Wait. There's more. The biggest buyers of corn products in the world are *McDonalds, Burger King* and *Kentucky Fried Chicken*. They use corn oil by the ton every single day!"

"I never thought about it like that," said Hannah, awed by the immensity of the subject. "I can see where money is the motivation, but what's wrong with engineering a better corn? Sure, the corporations make more money, but so what? Nobody gets sick or anything, do they?"

With barely a whisper, Indira repeated, "Nobody gets sick." Aloud, she said, "That question is still out on the floor for debate. But here's another important question. Does the environment get sick? Does our fragile eco-system suffer when we produce massive quantities of an unnatural food source?"

"And what's the answer to that riddle, Professor?"

"The honest to goodness answer is, nobody knows. Nothing bad has actually happened that allows us to point and say, 'see, I told you so.' Even though Brother Timothy and his band of zany zealots have been promising doom and gloom, so far . . ." Jawara shrugged submissively. " . . . it's been okay."

Squinting skeptically, Hannah said, "This isn't what I expected from you, Indira. You're supposed to be the one scientist that the corporate moguls hate. Instead, you sound as though you're defending their actions. What's going on?"

Indira smiled helplessly. "The fact is, up to this point, the process of engineering, growing, and harvesting modified crops has been quite successful; a model of what bioengineering can do. I mean, the crops taste just as good, but they have all kinds of added benefits. No need for nasty pesticides. No more ravaging insects. More productive farm land, and more money for the farmers." Jawara paused to take a sip of her iced tea.

"But . . . ?" prompted Hannah.

Jawara continued. "But, there's a growing body of evidence suggesting that bad things are about to happen. Scary things, and the biotech corporations are choosing to ignore them. I'm not saying they should stop what they're doing. It's just that they should be prepared to be held accountable. The biotech giants need to consider putting some long-range thinkers on their payroll. People who can take a hard look into the future and predict the problems that might end up destroying our planet."

"Destroy our planet?" asked Hannah. "What kind of evidence are you talking about?"

"The evidence I'm referring to is frightening stuff, Hannah. It conjures up fears of biblical proportions, such as boils and leprosy. Let me explain. During the process of gene-splicing, there are certain substances used as catalysts for the process. You see, nature has a way of protecting its own. Consequently, there are natural barriers that exist in every living thing. It's those barriers that fight against wrongful reproduction. It's the kind of thing that prevents any offspring from being created by the union of, let's say, a chicken and a giraffe, or an eagle and a frog. So, to circumvent the barrier, the clever and slick geneticist uses a substance that will break down that barrier. One catalyst that's widely used to modify the DNA of a plant comes from a plasmid known as *Agrobacterium tumefaciens*."

"Whoa," declared Hannah. "That's a galaxian word. I don't use words like that when I write my articles."

Jawara, deep into her explanation, barely smiled. "Anyway," continued Jawara, "the point is that this substance produces tumors."

Hannah's eyes went wide. "Tumors? Like lumps in your breast?"

"Exactly. Now, when it comes to engineering various species in the animal kingdom, the problem is magnified. In those cases, the substances used are made from retroviruses that cause cancer and a whole host of other plagues. Are you seeing how the problem is blossoming?"

"Are you telling me that all this stuff is going to cause worldwide epidemics of cancer and the plague?"

"No, Hannah," Jawara said, shaking her head. "Don't misunderstand me. What I'm saying is that the biotech boys have found a way to create new life-forms that do not have that natural barrier. That might make it possible for the new species to pass on its own warped DNA. I'm talking about the DNA that includes a cancer causing gene."

"It sounds positively dangerous," stated Hannah. "Aren't there any government agencies that are aware of this?"

"Not only are they aware, but certain agencies take an active role in encouraging the process. There's a lot of genetic engineering going on with fish. The Departments of the Interior, along with Wildlife Management are promoting this kind of thing. Their motive is that they would rather feed the population with fish from fish farms than from rivers and streams. So, they actually help to fund the process. Now, listen to this. When it comes to engineering fish, the barrier-breakdown substance that has been developed comes from a virus known as Moloney murine leukemic virus. This is the same little bugger that causes leukemia in mice. But keep in mind, there's nothing stopping the virus from doing the same to anyone who ingests the modified fish. To make matters worse, they sometimes add ingredients such as the vesicular stomatitus virus which causes festering lesions in the mouths of cattle, pigs, and human beings. I could keep on going, but I'm sure you can see how this is snowballing into a dangerous situation."

"Oh, my God," remarked Hannah. "I don't understand how all of this genetic engineering can continue." She paused to think of a question. "Why does it continue?"

Jawara leaned back. "Good question. Not only are the corporate decision makers continuing with their handiwork, but the whole field is also expanding. To answer your question, genetic engineering is still barreling along like a runaway roller coaster because everything I just told you is theoretical."

Hannah interrupted. "Theoretical? You mean you're not sure if they're using cancer causing agents?"

Indira emitted a sardonic chuckle. "Oh, there's no question about that part. They're definitely using all that garbage I just mentioned. When I say theoretical, I mean there is no proof that eating the corn will cause cancer or eating the fish will cause leukemia. That's the part that's theoretical. The biotech corporations tell the media that their detractors are just scaring the public. Then, the biotechs tell the government that they have unlocked the secrets of the cornucopia and will be able to feed the poor, starving children of the world. Lastly, they tell their stockholders that they're going to be wealthier than King Midas. Once you manage to get that group to give you an enthusiastic thumbs-up, you're all set."

"I'm overwhelmed," admitted Hannah, shaking her head. "I'm finding it all so fascinating."

"Yes," agreed Indira. "It is both fascinating and overwhelming."

Hannah narrowed her gaze. "Are you predicting worldwide epidemics of cancer and leukemia?"

Indira smiled patiently. "That's the kind of question that comes from a reporter looking to write a sensational headline."

Sheepishly, Hannah replied, "Well, after what you just told me, I think the question is legitimate."

Indira barely nodded before replying, "The answer is, no. I'm not predicting epidemics. I am, however, pointing out that increases in the incidents of cancer and leukemia are merely one possibility. But, keep this in mind, Hannah; the science of genetic engineering is, by its very nature, unpredictable. There are too many variables to contend with. Not enough government controls. No industry-wide regulations. Pressure from investors, cross-pollination, crossbreeding, mutations . . ." Indira hesitated before continuing. "The only thing I'm willing to predict is trouble. You could bet money on it."

Seeing the Professor look at her watch, Hannah said, "I wish we could have more time."

"I know," agreed Jawara. "It's a subject I'm extremely passionate about. But unfortunately, I have an appointment later this afternoon."

"Well, how about we do lunch, and then I'll let you go?"

Checking her watch again, Indira said, "All right. What did you have in mind?"

"I don't care," answered Hannah. "Any place will be fine."

Jawara brightened. "I know a great seafood place on the Intercoastal called Paul's Dockside. Want to give it a try?"

A look of mock horror appeared on Hannah's face. "You'd eat seafood after what you've just told me about fish?"

"When it comes to stone crabs," admitted Jawara, "there's no stopping me. And, they're in season right now."

"I love stone crabs," said Hannah, emphatically. "I could eat them with a steam shovel."

CHAPTER NINETEEN

FLORIDA

P *aul's Dockside* restaurant had an inordinately long line of lunch guests. Paul's girlfriend Sheryl, who, on this day, wore the hat of the hostess, smiled graciously and wrote down each of their names on the 'waiting-to-be-seated' list. She followed that by saying, "It shouldn't be more than twenty to thirty minutes."

Awaiting an available table, Brad Bishop and Harry Goodenow sat at the bar, a mere ten feet from Sheryl's hostess stand. As faithful, year-round customers, the two men received preferential treatment over the snowbirds who only frequented the eatery in the winter months.

The wait gave Harry an opportunity to order a Bloody Mary from the newly hired barmaid, Andrea Pepper. Six-feet tall in sneakers, her long ponytail protruded from under an orange baseball cap with a *Home Depot* logo. Her cropped tee shirt revealed a smooth olive-complexioned midriff and an occasional glimpse of a bellybutton ring. Not more than ten minutes had passed when Sheryl caught Brad's eye, and held up two fingers. It was a signal that a table would soon be ready.

Turning to Harry to pass on the update, Brad hesitated when he saw his friend immersed in a slick pitch. Harry was trying hard to impress the young barmaid with descriptions of his home, his automobiles and his bank account. Like a high school boy asking a girl to the prom, Harry was trying to get Andrea to say, "yes." By the look on her face, his efforts were falling way short of the mark.

Something caught Brad's eye and he turned his attention back to Sheryl's hostess stand. Two women were about to add their names to the list. Brad studied the pair. One was dark skinned and seemed to have the features of a woman born in India or Pakistan. It was hard to guess her age, but Brad estimated it to be in the early forties. In contrast, her companion was in her late twenties or early thirties and strikingly gorgeous. Her auburn hair, full lips, and lithe and graceful figure kept Brad's eyes riveted. He couldn't help but notice how tall she was and glanced down at her shoes to ascertain what part they might be playing. Noting that they were only two-inch heels, Brad calculated her height to be five-foot-ten. He watched and listened as Sheryl told the two women that they would be seated in about a half-hour.

"A half-hour, you say?" asked the dark skinned woman.

"Maybe a little less," answered Sheryl. "I think it's moving quickly."

The woman turned to her tall companion. "Half an hour, Hannah," she said. "I think that might be cutting it a little close. I'd rather not rush through lunch, and I don't want to be late for my afternoon appointment."

Her name was Hannah, mused Brad. Soft sounding and traditional, it was a perfect name for her.

Hannah shrugged. "Whatever you say, Indira. You're the one with the tight schedule."

Upon hearing the unusual name, Harry Goodenow abandoned his fruitless pitch for the attentions of the barmaid and leaned over to see which one of the waiting customers laid claim to the name, "Indira."

Turning to Sheryl, Indira said, "Okay. Put us on the list, but please do whatever you can to get us seated quickly."

"I'll definitely do what I can," said Sheryl, as she picked up her pen. "What's you name?"

"Dr. Jawara."

"How do you spell that?"

Harry interrupted the conversation. "Indira Jawara," he called, stepping forward and extending his hand.

Indira turned at the sound of her name. "Harry, you old curmudgeon," she acknowledged. "What are you doing here?"

Harry shook both her hands warmly. "I would ask you the same thing, Professor, but I suspect that the answer would be identical for both of us. Stone crabs!"

Jawara smiled. "My mouth is watering already, Harry. However, we're being forced to wait a half-hour."

"Allow me to introduce my intrepid companion and stalwart friend, Bradstone Bishop."

Brad stood and walked towards them.

"Brad," said Harry, "this is the world famous Dr. Indira Jawara; scientist, geneticist, author, and scourge of the Fortune 500."

Dr. Jawara shook hands with Brad. "Not all of the Fortune 500 hates me," corrected Jawara. "Only the biotechs."

"I've seen you on television," said Brad. "MSNBC. Tough crowd but, as I recall, you managed to hold your own."

It was Jawara's turn to make introductions. "Brad, Harry, this is Hannah Carpenter. She's a top-notch reporter with the *Sun Coast Ledger*."

Harry maneuvered himself to stand directly in front of Hannah. "An absolute pleasure to meet you, my dear," he said gallantly. "Your beauty is sparkling. You look like starlight in the daytime."

Hannah glanced at Jawara and Brad before breaking into a broad smile. "Thank you, Harry," she said shaking his hand. "I don't think anyone has ever said that to me before."

Sheryl interrupted. "I hate to break this up, boys, but your table is ready. I've got a good one for you. Right on the water."

Brad made a suggestion. "Harry and I would love it if both of you would join us for lunch."

Hannah and Indira looked at each other.

"Please," coaxed Brad. "I'm betting it'll be lively conversation, and this way, you won't have to wait an extra half-hour to enjoy lunch. Besides," he said to Jawara, "it'll give you and Harry a chance to catch up."

"Are you sure you don't mind?" asked Hannah.

Harry surprised Hannah by looping her arm into his and saying, "Sheryl, better make that a table for four."

Following Sheryl to the patio, Harry and Hannah walked arm in arm. They made an odd pair. Although Hannah was considerably taller than Harry, the real contrast was her willowy gracefulness next to his round waddle. For Brad, the visual effect was amusing. Hannah slid into the booth, and Harry shuffled in next to her. Brad and Jawara sat opposite them.

The drinks were ordered and served. While everyone else opted for iced tea, Harry indulged in a martini. The lunch order was a simple affair. Each one ordered a portion of cold stone crabs and extra napkins. The atmosphere encouraged a good-natured camaraderie, as they laughed, talked about seafood, and reviewed area restaurants. They finally agreed that one well-known eatery was terribly overrated and would better serve the public if it were turned into an adult bookstore.

While Brad tried to steer the conversation by asking how Harry and Indira knew each other, Harry's focus was on Hannah. Seemingly enchanted, Harry spent his time repeating the boasts he had used on the barmaid. As for Hannah, she remained very polite and tried not to ignore the other table guests.

Indira Jawara explained that she met Harry when his bank was recommended to her as a place for good mortgage rates and great investment strategies. Harry had offered to personally advise her regarding any "hot" stocks.

Brad asked, "Did he make you any money, or were you forced to go to a soup kitchen for sustenance?"

"Our timing was good," laughed Indira. "I came to Harry right after the bottom fell out of the market. He did manage to pick a couple of winners for me." Raising her glass of iced tea, Indira toasted, "Thank you, Harry."

Changing the subject, Brad said, "You're still involved in biotechnology, aren't you?"

"Oh, you bet," she answered, breaking off a portion of an ice cold claw. "I was in Washington two weeks ago testifying on Capitol Hill and this morning, Hannah was interviewing me on just that subject."

Hannah wiped her hands with a couple of paper napkins. "You've been a perfect interview, Indira. Friendly, informative and fun."

Putting a dollop of cocktail sauce on his plate, Brad said, "It didn't look as though you were having any fun when Chris Matthews was pelting you with questions."

"Showboating S.O.B.," grumbled Jawara. "That was no fun at all. Chris Matthews' interviewing style is like a Gatling gun. He fires his second volley long before you're finished loading your first round."

Brad said, "I remember some other panelists bashing you for saying something like genetic engineering will cause the end of the world. Do you really think that's the case?"

The Professor glanced sideways at Brad as she swallowed a tender morsel. "Nope," she stated. "Not at all. I'm definitely not part of the fringe group. The big biotech companies would love to lump me into that particular category, but I have a different agenda."

"What's that?" asked Brad.

Indira took a sip of iced tea before answering. "I'm just trying to tell it like it is. Regardless of the number of detractors yelling 'halt,' the corporations are going to forge ahead with genetic engineering. My focus is to make them aware of the pitfalls and, hopefully, to point them in a direction that will lead to responsible experimentation."

Hannah added. "I've had the dubious pleasure of talking with some of those so-called 'detractors' who populate the fringe. And I must tell you, Indira is like the lone voice of reason. She even goes so far as to defend the corporate giants on many issues."

"Defend them?" asked Brad, surprised at Hannah's choice of words. "Then, why do they denounce you so vehemently if you're trying to defend them?"

"First of all," answered Jawara, "I only defend that which is defensible. If, on the other hand, they're doing something stupid, I'm the first to let them know.

All that being said, the real reason they come after me is because I'm threatening their wallets, their bottom line."

"Which reminds me," said Harry, pointing his finger in the air for emphasis, "Would you please try to keep me informed if you intend to say something disparaging about a particular corporation? At least, give me some time to sell off my stock."

The other three laughed at Harry's request. Although the banter remained lighthearted for the remaining minutes of the meal, Indira broke the mood when she said she had to leave.

"I'd better be going, too," said Hannah. "My boss doesn't tolerate anything longer than one-hour lunches. He only agreed to take off my leg irons because the rash was becoming unsightly."

"Is your boss Sidney Aarons?" asked Brad.

"Yes. Do you know him?"

Brad smiled coyly. "I'll tell you what, Hannah. If you and I ever do this lunch thing again, I'll put a word in for you. I should be able to get him to agree to an extra five minutes. And, perhaps some ointment for the rash."

"Do you really know him?" she asked again.

Brad nodded. "Yes. Sidney and I have worked together in the past. He's a good guy, but I don't think I would ever want him for my boss."

Hannah smiled warmly at Brad. "I'll keep that information between us. It was very nice meeting you." Turning to Harry, she added, "Nice meeting you, too."

Standing to allow Hannah to slide from the booth, Harry became visibly animated. "Wait," he said. "I would love to have your home phone number, Hannah. You know, get a chance to show you the highlights and magnificence of where I live; this paradise we call Palm Beach."

Graciously, Hannah said, "Thank you, Harry, but my schedule is just horrendous. I never know when I'll be in town or off to the jungles of the Amazon. Why don't you give me yours, and that way, I'll be able to get in touch with you."

After the last of the goodbye's were said, Brad and Harry sat back down to discuss the lunchtime encounter.

"I think she likes me," said Harry.

"I think she was just being polite," corrected Brad. "You might have had a better chance with that young woman if you weren't drooling all over yourself every time you looked at her."

"But she's dazzling, Brad. She's like a finely sculpted piece of art. A Picasso. A Renoir. Did you watch her walk away? I don't think she was wearing any panties, for God's sake!"

Brad laughed. "I can't believe you mentioned Picasso, Renoir, and Hannah's panties in the same breath."

A smug look came to Harry's face. "You're just jealous because I made the move first. I'm the one who's out front this time, and you're just walking in my dust."

"Honestly Harry, I think you'd have better luck if you made a move on Professor Jawara."

"Indira?" exclaimed Harry incredulously. "Have you lost your mind? She's gay!"

Brad's eyes widened. "Indira? A lesbian?"

"Indeed!" stated Harry succinctly. "Hard-as-nails, finger-in-the-dike lesbian. Brilliant woman. Can't take that away from her, but she definitely rides a horse of a different color."

"And where did you come up with that tidbit?"

"Common knowledge, Bradstone, my boy. Common knowledge. She's had a long-term affair with The Countess Erika. Supposedly, it's been going on since they were roomies at Vassar."

Brad narrowed his gaze. "I thought The Countess Erika and her boyfriend were a happy couple."

"You've almost got it right, Brad. You only have to add one adjective: happy *bisexual* couple. That's the perfect description."

"Oh boy," said Brad, shaking his head. "This is much more information than I really wanted to know."

"Sorry to have disillusioned you."

"The disillusionment may be yours," said Brad, as he signed the lunch tab.

"What do you mean?"

"Well," said Brad, preparing to leave, "that means there's a distinct possibility that Hannah and Indira are romantically involved with one another."

There was a long pause as Harry's mouth fell open. "Oh my God!" he whispered, hoarsely. His face scrunched into a wrinkled ball of disbelief before slowly morphing into one of salacious curiosity. "Y'think?" he asked with an edge of hopefulness.

CHAPTER TWENTY

CALIFORNIA

L istening to the caller's instructions, Sarah Levine scribbled her notes swiftly, almost illegibly. "So you think that's what will put us on the right track?" she asked.

"One-hundred percent," stated the voice on the other end of the telephone. "When you determine a way to extract those qualities from the DNA of each species I've mentioned, you'll have your answer to the kudzu problem."

Sarah was elated. "I had a feeling you were going to be helpful, Dr. Kaminski," she said, "but I just didn't realize how knowledgeable you would be on an obscure plant like the kudzu."

"Fortunately," said Kaminski, "I spent three years in China cataloguing insects. Tens of thousands of insects. A person never knows when somebody will come knocking on his brain and ask for something insignificant that's stored inside."

Sarah laughed. Dr. Jacobus Kaminski, a world-class entomologist, had written several texts that were considered benchmarks by other experts in the field. Although his research had been varied, Kaminski's notoriety was as a "chemical prospector." He worked under a highly funded grant from one of the giant chemical corporations that manufactured pesticides. His work involved finding insects with a natural chemical defense mechanism. The idea was to extract and analyze those chemicals and hopefully use them to develop new pesticides.

Sarah was aware that Professor Kaminski was being more than cordial. Because of the fast developing professional rapport, Sarah decided to push her luck. "Perhaps," she began tentatively, "you would allow me to tweak your encyclopedic brain once more."

"You have another question?" he asked.

"I've been given a project," explained Sarah, "that seems to have me stumped. I was hoping that you could suggest or even introduce me to someone with expertise in that field."

"What's the project, Sarah? What are you working on?"

Sarah explained her assignment for Bennett Pharmaceuticals. Rattling off a laundry list of various species of snakes, toads and lizards, Sarah detailed her attempts to find a substitute for bufotoxin. "I have a chemist, a biologist and a botanist at my disposal, and although we've come up with a lot of ideas, we still haven't found a substance to create a sclerotic effect on human skin as efficiently as bufotoxin. Any suggestions?"

"Ah yes," said Kaminski knowingly. "The dreaded cane toad with its lumps and bumps full of poison."

"You're familiar with that particular species?"

"Certainly," answered Kaminski. "Did you know that the cane toad is indigenous to Central America? And that it was brought into Australia for the purpose of controlling the Gobrano beetle?"

Sarah shook her head at the man's endless stream of facts. "No. I didn't know that."

Kaminski went on. "Once that little bulging-eyed amphibian arrived Down Under, it quickly established itself in the environment and became an even bigger pest. Now, because of the popularity of cosmetic surgery, there's this sudden need to harvest its bufotoxin."

"So I've learned," said Sarah.

"Don't you find it amazing that human vanity has reached the point that people will allow a deadly poison to be injected into their face?"

Sarah chuckled. "I hadn't thought of it in quite those terms."

"Well," said Kaminski, switching gears, "we will consider discussing that topic when we meet. For now, let's get back to the problem at hand."

"All right," agreed Sarah.

"The problem, as I see it, is the type of poison exuded by the cane toad."

"What do you mean?"

Kaminski cleared his throat. "The cane toad secretes a vesicular toxin, a very specialized poison. I think you're searching in the wrong direction."

"How so?"

"The snakes and toads and lizards you mentioned all have different poisons. Some have neurotoxins, some have vascular toxins, and others have hemorrhagic toxins. Each is very potent, to be sure, but none is vesicular in nature. Do you know what you need to do, Sarah?"

"Tell me, Professor."

"Look in your own backyard."

There was a palpable pause as Sarah tried to digest his mysterious proposal.

Without waiting for Sarah's reply, Kaminski continued. "Look at insects!" he blurted. "You'll find that kind of poison is commonplace with certain insects."

Sarah was getting excited. "Really? Give me a hint, Professor."

"*Lepidoptera limacodidae acharia*," pontificated Kaminski.

Sarah recognized the Latin classification. "The Saddleback Caterpillar?" she questioned incredulously.

"The one and only."

"I knew the saddleback was poisonous, but I never . . ."

Kaminski interrupted. "That caterpillar has long spines growing on its tail section and each and every one is filled with poison. Not just any poison, mind you, but the specific one you're looking for. Vesicular poison."

Sarah's excitement bubbled over into the remainder of their conversation. She said, "I'm not sure how to thank you for all the information you've given me. But, one thing is certain; I'm looking forward to meeting you at the Seattle symposium."

"Absolutely," said Kaminski. "And since we are going to be friends, let us cease formalities and begin by having you call me 'Jake.'"

In addition to newspapers and magazines lauding his scientific accomplishments, Jacobus Kaminski often appeared on television as the proverbial "expert." Star-struck by his celebrity, Sarah found it difficult to utter her next sentence. "Oh. All right, um . . . . Jake," she stammered. "I suppose you'd better call me Sarah."

"Then, 'Sarah' it shall be," boomed Kaminski.

Sarah replaced the phone into its cradle and leaned back in her chair. Coming back to the moment, she looked at her notes. Pleased as she was with the conversation that had just ended, she was even more excited about passing on the information to her fiancé. Rick had already started his search for the best methods of controlling the wild kudzu vines of Georgia. As Sarah retyped her notes, she smiled thinking about how overjoyed Rick would be that Professor Kaminski knew so much about the kudzu plant.

Waiting for the printer to chug out two copies of her notes, Sarah dialed the extension to Rick's lab. The line was busy. So, like a little schoolgirl with a good report card, Sarah hurried off to show Rick her results.

*   *   *

Rick concentrated on the controls of the sturdy little microwave oven. He was in the middle of showing Darlene how to adjust the controls. He pointed and said, "See here? If you can manage to maintain forty-six Celsius and between eighteen and twenty-two percent humidity, we'll get a nice clean flow."

Nodding her appreciation, Darlene said, "Thank you, Rick,"

Turning to Ashley, Rick said, "I'm starving. I'm going to run upstairs to the cafeteria and grab a sandwich or something. Be back in about a half hour." Just before exiting the lab, the door opened and in walked Sarah. "Perfect timing," said Rick. "I'm on my way to get a bite to eat. Come on. Join me."

Sarah looked at her watch. "Good idea," she said with a broadening smile. "We can talk over lunch."

Normally, Rick preferred taking the stairs up two flights to the cafeteria. However, in the past, when Sarah had tried to accompany him, she found the effort exhausting. Her idea of exercise was to stay home and ride her stationary bicycle only until the pizza and canoli were delivered.

Taking the elevator, Rick said, "You know, Sarah, I planned on whisking you away to Paris for a romantic holiday, but you'll never be able to handle the stairs in the Eiffel Tower!"

Sarah chuckled. "A beach in Tahiti will substitute just fine, Rick. That way, my only exertion will be lifting some exotic tropical concoction with a little umbrella in it."

The doors opened onto the third floor. Standing in front of them was Mel Fishman. Before Rick or Sarah could offer any greeting, Mel pointed a finger at Rick and blurted out, "I was just coming to see you, asshole!"

Rick was taken aback. Despite the competitiveness between them, nothing prepared Rick for Mel's outburst. "What is your problem, Mel?"

"You know damn well what my problem is! That whole thing was a setup, Ballinger, and you know it!"

The elevator door started to close, threatening to leave Fishman standing on the third floor by himself. Making a quick decision, he stepped inside the car and allowed the doors to close behind him. The elevator remained motionless with the three of them inside.

"Mel," pleaded Rick, "for the love of God, I have no idea what you're talking about."

Holding his briefcase in his left hand, Mel used his right to point accusingly. "Kudzu, god-dammit! Kudzu!"

Sarah attempted to mediate the tense situation. "Mel, Mel," she said soothingly. "Take it easy. Nothing is worth a stroke or a heart attack. Let's talk about it rationally."

Fishman's face was beet red and the veins in his neck were protruding. "You stay out of this, Doctor Levine. This is between pretty-boy and me." Turning his attention back to Rick, Mel said, "That was a shit thing you did, Ballinger! You stepped on my neck just to get the Kudzu Project! I ought to kick your ass!"

Bullying was totally out of character for Mel Fishman. He had always given the impression of being a bookish nerd and certainly a pacifist. Although the man was considerably taller than Rick, it was doubtful if Mel could ever claim victory in a fair fight, or even engage in one.

Rick took a step forward. "Mel!" he said sternly. "You're out of line! I had no control over that decision. None at all."

The stationary elevator, reacting to some would-be rider pushing the "call" button, suddenly lurched into motion and began its descent. "Don't give me that horseshit!" said Mel. "You and Doug cooked the whole thing up! All that god-damned showboating in the conference room, and I fell for it!"

Helplessly, Rick glanced at Sarah before turning back to his accuser. "What the hell are you talking about?"

Mel continued. "This decision was made long before we ever went into that meeting. You were briefed on kudzu. You were briefed on everything, weren't you?"

Rick tried again. "For Pete's sake, Mel. Calm down. You're talking foolishness."

"Don't tell me to calm down!" shouted Mel. "I'm not about to let my whole career go down the toilet just because you want me to be one of your flunkies! Bullshit! I mean to tell you . . ."

The elevator came to a stop. The sound of the doors sliding open interrupted Mel's tirade. He looked over his shoulder to see Stanley Briscoe, another of the lab supervisors, standing there with his mouth open. With mushrooming anger, Mel looked back at Rick and shouted his final warning, "If you ruin my career, I'll fucking kill you!" Spinning on his heel, Mel stormed out of the elevator and down the hall.

After watching Mel stride away, Briscoe stepped inside the lift. The elevator car was bathed in silence, as the door closed the three of them inside. Finally, Briscoe nodded his head somberly and said, "God loves him."

Glancing at each other, Rick and Sarah wondered what prompted such a remark.

Briscoe continued. "Of course, everybody else thinks he's a blooming asshole."

CHAPTER TWENTY-ONE

CALIFORNIA

The first fifteen minutes of their lunch hour was spent discussing the Mel Fishman incident. Even though Rick said that he had lost his appetite, Sarah insisted he eat something to prevent lightheadedness. "You're going to be in meetings all afternoon," Sarah reminded him, "and you might not get another chance to have any nourishment."

Reluctantly, Rick nodded his head.

"Get the soup and some crackers," insisted Sarah. "It'll help tide you over."

Standing in the cafeteria line, Rick confessed that he never thought that Mel's frustration would have reached such a fever pitch.

"You know what your problem is?" asked Sarah. Not waiting for Rick's reply, she answered. "You're just too nice a guy. You've never experienced having anyone hate you."

Rick nodded. "Yeah," he said forlornly. "Now it seems like everybody hates me."

"Who's 'everybody?'"

Rick explained. "Miguel Ortiz has been sulking around the lab like a whipped puppy. I was sure that he was still upset with Ashley for the tongue-lashing she gave him. Come to find out, I'm the one he's angry with. I feel like the whole world is beginning to gang up on me."

With their lunch plates in hand, Sarah led the way to a table by the window. "Are you going to mention the Mel Fishman incident to Doug?"

Rick put down his soup spoon. "I suppose I should."

"When do you plan on telling him?"

Rick looked at his watch. "In about an hour. We're supposed to discuss the start up of the Kudzu Project, but this thing with Mel will have to take priority."

Sarah blinked. Rick's mention of the Kudzu Project reminded her of what she wanted to tell him.

Sliding the plate with her half-eaten sandwich to the other side of the table, Sarah arranged her notes in front of her. "Okay," she said, taking a deep breath.

"Talking about Mel Fishman will be the first part of your meeting with Doug. The second half will be the Kudzu Project. Are you ready to talk about that?"

"I sure am," said Rick. "I desperately need the diversion."

Eager to pass on her newly acquired knowledge, Sarah said, "Guess who I spoke to this morning?"

Rick could see the impishness in Sarah's eyes and smiled as he said, "I give up. Who?"

"Professor Jacobus Kaminski."

Rick raised his eyebrows. "Jacobus Kaminski? The Holy Grail?"

"Yes. And guess what he told me?"

Rick squinted as he replied, "That he never graduated high school and that his life as a celebrity is really just a sham."

"No, silly," Sarah giggled. "Since we developed such a nice rapport during our conversation, he told me to call him 'Jake.' Can you imagine? Jake. Isn't that cool?"

"Jake?" asked Rick, feigning jealousy. "What ever happened to respect? Like maybe calling him, Doctor Kaminski? Or perhaps even, Your Eminence? But you're telling me he cut through all the protocol and went straight to 'Jake?' Jeez, Sarah, what does he call you? 'Honey-bunch?'"

Failing to suppress a giggle, Sarah recouped and mentioned Kaminski's suggestion to use the saddleback caterpillar as the source for a new toxin in her Bennett Pharmaceutical project. "The man is amazing," crowed Sarah. "Not only did he suggest the saddleback, but he also explained why the track I was on was doomed to fail."

Rick smiled warmly. "Who are you kidding, Sarah? You could never fail at anything."

Smiling appreciatively, Sarah nevertheless changed subjects and began discussing the Kudzu Project. She informed Rick that Kaminski had spent several years in China working with entomologists from that part of the world. "This man is a gold mine," said Sarah. "He's familiar with tens of thousands of species native to the Orient. But, more importantly, he's a veritable expert on the Chinese kudzu."

"So, I suppose that he had some suggestions for me, too," said Rick. "What were they?"

Although Sarah referred to her notes, she relayed Kaminski's conversation almost verbatim. The Professor's list had included several species that thrive on the Chinese kudzu and ultimately keep the plant under control. "Kaminski told me that he's seen the devastation from kudzu in Georgia and Alabama and that if it weren't for the *Khapra dermestids*, all of China would be knee deep in kudzu vines."

"*Khapra dermestids?*" questioned Rick, squinty-eyed. "Come on, Sarah. Give me a break. I barely remember that spiders are referred to as arachnids. Try it again in plain English."

"Beetles," she simplified with a shrug. "Beetles such as June bugs or Japanese beetles."

"Is that what he suggested? June bugs and Japanese beetles?"

"No. That's just the family and genus. Insects like the Japanese beetle would be too indiscriminate. They'd happily eat your kudzu, but then, after two belches and a half-glass of Chardonnay, they would devour everything else in sight."

"Did he name anything specific that might do the trick?"

"Yes," said Sarah. "He suggested that you start with a little critter called *Lepidoptera paravulgarus descenderae*. It seems to have all the qualities you're looking for."

"There you go again with those ten-dollar words. What's the common name for that bug?"

Slowly, Sarah took on a blank look. "I don't know," she said. "Since it's only native to China, I imagine the locals have a common name for it, but I have no idea what it might be."

"So, how do you pronounce it again?"

Sarah repeated the name. "It's Latin," she said. "It translates into 'Very Ugly Descendent.'"

Rick reached for his pen. "I should probably write that down. I'll need it when I go into my meeting."

Handing Rick a sheet of paper, Sarah declared, "Already done, Rick. This spells out all the preliminary data in sequential order."

Rick perused the information. Then, looking at her with a boyish grin, he said, "You're an angel. Beautiful *and* smart."

With a glow in her cheeks, Sarah continued. "Kaminski said that one of the things that make the paravulgarus an excellent candidate, is that the little devil loves carbohydrates, and the kudzu's root system, similar to potatoes, is loaded with it."

Rick smiled. "So, since the paravulgarus loves potato chips and French fries, we just make sure it doesn't run loose in *McDonalds*."

"Cute, but not to worry," corrected Sarah. "It prefers the carbohydrates of the kudzu root rather than the French fries at Mickey D's."

"Is that the only insect that's keeping the kudzu in check?"

"It's one of them," replied Sarah. "There's also a couple of species of beetle that enjoy eating other parts of the plant. One gets under the outer husk and eats the pulp. Another is a winged variety, similar to a ladybug that makes a meal of the leaves. But the paravulgarus is different. In its larval stage, it burrows underground like a grub and eats the roots."

"And when it's all finished being a grub," asked Rick, raising his eyebrows, "what does it grow up to be?"

"As it matures, it first turns into a caterpillar. An ugly thing with fleshy, swollen lumps along its body and a odd coloration."

"Odd coloration?" repeated Rick.

"Mmmm yes," said Sarah thoughtfully. "Although the creature's entire body is a dull, battleship gray, it has a bright red dot on top of its head."

Narrowing his gaze, Rick asked, "Once that little bugger gets out, what other kind of damage can it do?"

The question immediately took Sarah's mind off the insect's markings. She clearly understood the underlying significance of what he was asking. In the past, it had proven dangerous to introduce new species of insects into a part of the world where they had never existed. Numerous cases exemplified the problem. *Solenopsis invicta*, the ubiquitous and menacing fire ant imported from South America, had spread its insidious colonies to the entire southern half of the United States. Another example of good intentions gone bad occurred in 1922. In an attempt to initiate silk fabric manufacturing in America, a group of industrialists decided to import the silkworm from the Orient. By summer of that year, a quarter-million silkworm caterpillar were being warehoused in Boston. During a violent storm, their cages broke open and the bugs escaped. It wasn't long before the silkworm caterpillars found a way to interbreed with domestic caterpillars. The result has been that, ever since that incident, the Northeastern Region of the United States has been fighting the devastating effect caused by the gypsy moth.

"Good question," she said, leaning forward in her chair. "In the larval stage, the paravulgarus only survives on the kudzu root. Take away that particular food source and the little grubs die. However, once they mature into caterpillars, that becomes another story. So, here's where you come in. You take the paravulgarus and . . ."

Rick finished her thought. "And I add the DNA of some other insect, thereby creating a brand new life-form that, hopefully, won't devour the entire State of Georgia."

"You are just too smart," said Sarah with a grin.

"Okay," said Rick, nodding his head approvingly. "So, whose DNA do we splice into this paravulgarus?"

"Kaminski's suggested that you use the *Elaphidiine taxa*. You'll see that name about two-thirds of the way down that data sheet."

Rick glanced at the information in front of him.

"Note the spelling," said Sarah. "There really are three 'I's' in Elaphidiine."

Rick looked at his watch. "I have a bunch of questions, Sarah, and not much time before my meeting starts. So, just give me the highlights."

Sarah briefed Rick on the group of horned beetles commonly referred to as "wood-borers." Concluding, Sarah said, "Despite the existence of more than six-hundred sub species in that family, Kaminski managed to zero in on one called *Elaphidion skiles*."

"You know Sarah," said Rick dolefully, "if it weren't for these forty-syllable words you keep throwing at me, this project would be a snap."

Realizing that time was at a premium, Sarah smiled briefly and spoke quickly. "Let me tell you why those two insects are good choices for a recombinant DNA procedure. The paravulgarus thrives on kudzu root. Only kudzu root. On the other hand, the Skiles beetle lives its entire life in the larval stage." Sarah paused for emphasis. "Now get this," she said. "After two years as a grub, the Skiles larva emerges as an adult beetle, but it doesn't eat anything. All it does is mate, drop its eggs and die."

Rick grinned. "I guess wild, uninhibited sex can exhaust any species."

"Be serious for a moment," said Sarah. "You don't have much time to learn all this. I feel very strongly that the newly created organism would successfully kill off the kudzu plant without damaging the surrounding ecosystem."

Rick nodded his head. Sarah had just stated one of the primary doctrines of genetic engineering. Responsibility to the safety of the environment. Putting that aside for the moment, Rick worried about the complexity of the procedure that would have to be undertaken. "Has anybody mapped out the genome of either of these bugs?"

"Not the paravulgarus," answered Sarah. "But the Skiles beetle has been completely mapped for quite some time."

"Good," said Rick. "That'll make things easier. I'll only have to figure out which nucleotide to extract from the Skiles beetle. As for the paravulgarus, since I'll only be inserting a nucleotide, all I need to do is locate a reasonable spot along the double helix."

Sarah beamed. "You make it sound so simple, Rick. I'm very proud of you."

Smiling with a shy glow, Rick asked, "Will it be a problem importing either one of those bugs?"

"No. Not at all. The Skiles is native to North America, so that won't pose any sort of problem. And, as for the paravulgarus, I'm permitted to bring in a number of the little critters under code seventy-seven of the government's I.G.S. That's the Importation Guidelines Schedule. As long as my work is for experimentation and study, they give me permission to import them. I'm just not allowed to breed them or sell them."

"This is great, Sarah," he said, putting the unfolded sheet of paper into his briefcase. "It's clear and concise. I think they'll be impressed."

"Go get 'em, Tiger," urged Sarah.

Rick stood to leave. "Y'know, Sarah," he said reflectively "if what we're doing results in producing a new life-form, you and I will get to name it."

The idea had never occurred to Sarah. Suddenly, the prospect of acclaim fascinated her. "Really?" she asked.

Rick nodded. "Yes. I'm serious."

Sarah thought of the work Rick had been doing for the Foxboro Beer Company, and his successful creation of the new fermentation myces. "Like your *Quadballingermyces*?

"Exactly," he said. "Only this time, the christening of the new GMO will reflect both of our names."

"Any suggestions?" she asked, trying to curb a silly grin.

"How about . . ." Rick paused, looking skyward for inspiration. "How about *Ballingeria rex*, slash, *Sarah optera vulgarus*?"

Sarah balled up her paper napkin and threw it at Rick.

CHAPTER TWENTY-TWO

FLORIDA

It had been several days since Hannah had conducted her interview with Dr. Indira Jawara. The professor had opened Hannah's eyes to a world she had not fully understood. A world sharply divided between the pundits who welcomed the benefits of gene-splicing, and the zealots who predicted the end of mankind.

Hannah's continuing research had taken her into the glass and steel edifices of the corporate giants. Having spoken with the public relations officers of companies such as *Cellgene* and *Genentech,* she came away wide-eyed and impressed with all the noble and worthy things these organizations could do. She had gone to the pharmaceuticals, megaliths such as *Merck*, *Eli-Lily* and *Millennium*. There, she was showered with streams of data that proved the benefits of new drugs born in the bioengineering laboratories. After being inundated with such an avalanche of altruism, Hannah, had a clear vision of a future bereft of hunger, pain, and suffering.

It wasn't until quiet moments of reflection that Hannah was able to recall the sobering words of Indira Jawara and the fiery rhetoric of Brother Timothy Goodman who shouted dire prophecies from the other side of the coin. The contrast between the corporate position and the ideology of the naysayers struck Hannah like a lightning bolt.

"You look a whole lot better than you did last week when I met you in the ladies room."

Hannah looked up from her computer screen. The voice belonged to Ann "Silky" Silkwood. "Thank you, Silky," replied Hannah. "I'm feeling a whole lot better, too."

"I've been watching you," said Silky. "You've been putting in a bunch of hours. You don't look like someone who just got demoted."

Hannah smiled broadly. "You were right," she said. "Sidney did have my best interests at heart, after all. Even on the day he threatened to demote me, it was just a scare tactic to get me thinking in the right direction."

"See? What did I tell you? He's more like your father than your boss."

Hannah nodded enthusiastically. "And he's given me a great assignment with lots of research and interviews. I'm eating it up."

"Yeah, but now you don't have any time for a social life."

"Well," said Hannah, responding to the new thought, "you may be right, but this project won't last forever. Besides, I occasionally, get to meet men outside of this office. I'm keeping my options open."

"Oh, yeah?" questioned Silky. "Anybody special?"

"Um . . . too soon to tell," said Hannah with a shy smile.

Silky raised her eyebrows. "Look at you," she said as she studied Hannah's face. "You look like a kid that's about to be asked to her first dance. Give me a hint, would you?"

"Really, Silky. It's way too soon. I mean, he's good looking and seems very nice, but I don't even know if he's available."

"Oh, shit!" said Silky, rolling her eyes in disgust. "Whatever you do, don't get yourself caught in a triangle. I once fell for one of those 'unavailables' and it cost me plenty. Buckets of tears and most of my principles, but mainly my self-esteem."

"You don't have to worry, Silky. I'd never allow myself to get into a situation like that. Nothing good ever comes of it."

Silky looked both ways before leaning forward and whispering, "I don't know about that. When the sex is great, you suddenly forget all the rules set down by Sister Mary Elizabeth and the rest of the Nuns."

Hannah's giggle was interrupted by Donnie, the Feature Editor who called out, "C'mon, Hannah. Sidney's ready for us."

Gathering her notes, Hannah followed Donnie into Sidney's office. Two other reporters were already there.

Sidney Aarons wasted no time getting the meeting started. "This has got to be quick," he stated. "I only have forty minutes. My four o'clock meeting in Fort Lauderdale has suddenly become a two o'clock. So, I can't spend as much time with you people as I had planned. Let's just go over the highlights of what you're doing and see where you are."

With that, each of the reporters presented a synopsis of his feature article. The meeting was going quickly and smoothly with rapid-fire dialogue and furious note-taking.

Suddenly, it was Hannah's turn to make her presentation.

"What have you got, Hannah?" asked Sidney, looking at his watch.

Barely referring to her notes, Hannah gave a rundown of the interviews she had conducted over the past week. She concluded by making a bold suggestion.

"This is turning out to be big, Sidney. Much bigger than I had anticipated. The story cannot be done in a single Sunday supplement. At the very least, it'll have to be a three-parter."

Staring in silence, Sidney pondered what it would mean to run the story for three consecutive Sundays. Finally, he asked, "You actually think that this story might be bigger than just Brother Timothy and his tent revivals?"

His question was a direct reference to Hannah's stubbornness and tunnel vision with the original assignment. Hannah smiled sheepishly. "I'll admit it took a lecture from you to make me look at it again, but it was Dr. Indira Jawara who really opened my eyes."

Donnie interjected. "Jawara? Isn't she the pit bull who's always snapping at the heels of the biotech companies?"

One of the reporters said, "She was on Fox News last week and made mincemeat out of the CEO of *Brandstadt Pharmaceuticals*."

Hannah continued. "There are just too many facets to this story, Sidney. The public needs to be made aware of all sides of this issue."

"How long do you think it's going to take you?"

Hannah said, "I'm leaving for L.A. tomorrow. That'll be the last leg of the interview campaign. I'll be meeting with the former head of *Celera Genomics* and the executive vice president of *Cambridge Antibody Technology*. I'm also firming up my second appointment with Brother Timothy."

Sidney took a gulp of his cold coffee before clarifying his question. "What I meant was how long before your articles are ready for publication?"

"Oh," said Hannah, shuffling through the pile of notes in front of her, "I already have the first draft." She drew out a small sheaf that had been paper-clipped together and handed it to Donnie. "It's the overview of the science," explained Hannah. "I've written it so as to whet the appetite of the readers."

Directing his next question to the feature editor, Sidney asked, "What do you think, Donnie? Is she making any sense?"

Donnie folded his arms across his chest before saying, "Any subject can be pared down to three-thousand words. What makes you think that you'll be able to hold the reader's interest for three weeks?"

"Are you kidding?" exclaimed Hannah. "This stuff is dynamite! First of all, it's all over the news. You can't tune into any channel without hearing something about gene-splicing, cloning or stem-cell research. The public can't get enough of it. But, the real reason for doing a three-parter is that there's way too much information to do in a single piece. It seems as though everybody has something to say on the subject. The interesting thing is, as contradictory as their views may be, they all have valid points. The biotechs talk about doing away with world hunger. The pharmaceuticals want to demonstrate how they can cure diseases. The politicians are out to prove that they know how to save the masses from self-destruction. And Brother Timothy . . . ." Hannah paused before saying, "Well, Brother Timothy just wants to be the one to drive a stake through the heart of the Devil."

Hannah had been directing her comments to Sidney. Now, as she watched him, Sidney turned to Donnie and nodded once.

Donnie stood. "Come children," he said to the three reporters. "We're all done here." Then, gesturing to the spacious newsroom on the other side of the glass partition, Donnie added, "It's time for us to go play in the big sandbox out there."

Still seated, Hannah asked, "Sidney, may I have a word with you in private?"

Sidney relegated some last minute instructions to Donnie before the feature editor left and closed the door. Sidney looked at his watch and said, "I have an appointment, Hannah, and I need to be out of here in less than five minutes."

"I'll make it quick," she agreed. "I just wanted to thank you for . . . um, for . . ."

"What?" asked Sidney impatiently. "Yelling at you? Threatening to demote you?"

Hannah smiled. "Yes," she concurred. "I wanted to thank you for taking the time to help me see my faults. These past several days have been a revelation."

"How so?"

"Well, the subject matter of this assignment has been absolutely fascinating. But the real epiphany came when I asked myself why I hadn't seen this before."

"Good," stated Sidney. "That's the answer I wanted to hear. But remember, Hannah, there has to be an epilogue to this epiphany of yours."

"What do you mean?"

"I can't continually take the time to bitch-slap you whenever you get stubborn or stupid. Now that you see the light and understand how to recognize the big picture, I expect you to continue on this yellow brick road. You following me?"

Hannah nodded. "Now, I want to change the subject and ask you a question."

Pointing to his watch, Sidney said, "Tick-tock, tick-tock."

Hannah sat forward. "On the day when Indira Jawara and I went to lunch, she introduced me to a couple of gentlemen. One was named Harry Goodenow. The other man was Brad Bishop. We all ended up having lunch together."

Sidney interrupted before Hannah could ask her question. "Harry Goodenow, huh? What a piece of work! Did he try to sweet-talk you out of your pantyhose?"

Hannah giggled. "It certainly seemed that way," she acknowledged. "He practically fawned all over me."

"Goodenow's got a roving eye. If there's a pretty girl within a mile, he turns into a bloodhound. As it happens, he owns a very well established and profitable bank. So, on rare occasion, he ends up with some retired model hanging on to his arm. You thinking about dating the man?"

"Good heavens, no," stated Hannah. "But the other fellow, Brad Bishop, seemed quite interesting. He said he knows you."

Sidney nodded. "Right. Bishop. He's a good guy. Brad and I have known each other for a number of years."

"How long has he been married?" asked Hannah.

Sidney's face contorted into pure sarcasm as he repeated Hannah's question in a high-pitched impersonation. "How long has he been married, Sidney?"

Hannah blushed at her obviousness. "Okay. Is he single? Divorced? . . . what?"

Sidney leaned back and momentarily stared at the young woman in front of him. "You may be looking to pick an apple from a tree with no fruit."

Hannah squinted. "What's that supposed to mean?"

"Listen," replied Sidney. "Bishop's a good guy. Hardworking. Smart. He owns an agency that specializes in investigating insurance claims. I think he's pretty successful. And yes, he's single. Never been married."

Hannah seemed to brighten. "Oh?" she mused. "Well, that sounds promising."

Checking his watch once again, Sidney decided he had a few minutes to spare. "Better listen to the rest of the story," he said with an audible sigh.

Hannah clasped her hands.

"Bishop did his postgraduate work at Georgetown University. After getting a Master's Degree in criminal justice, he joined the FBI and spent about three years working as a field agent in the D.C. area. He was very good at it. While he was there, he met a young lady by the name of . . . ." Sidney paused and thought better about revealing more than he had to. "What's the difference," he said with a wave of his hand. "He met a young lady, fell in love, and they got engaged. She was also an agent for the FBI." Once again, Sidney hesitated, wondering if he should be telling this story at all. In a moment, he continued. "Early one morning, both Brad and his fiancée were part of a massive drug raid, a combined effort with the boys from the Drug Enforcement Agency. Things went from bad to worse. Bishop told me that when the firefight broke out, more than a hundred shots were fired. Our side lost four people. Two D.E.A. agents and two from the FBI."

Hannah whispered, "I'm not going to like the ending of this story, am I?"

Sidney shook his head. "No," he agreed. "One of the agents was his fiancée."

Hannah squeezed her hands together until her knuckles were white.

Sidney went on. "The worst part for Brad was that, for the longest time, he thought that it might have been a bullet from his own gun that actually killed her."

Hannah put a hand to her mouth to prevent a sorrowful sound from escaping.

"Who knows whether or not that was the case," said Sidney, "but for a couple of years afterwards, Bishop tended to blame himself for her death."

Hannah was speechless.

Preparing to put on his suit jacket, Sidney stood and rolled down his shirtsleeves. "You thinking of pursuing him?" he asked.

Hannah stood and took a deep breath. Wistfully she said, "I was thinking of getting him to pursue me."

*   *   *

Clutching a yellow legal pad, Rose walked into Brad's office. Unceremoniously, she plopped herself into one of the chairs in front of his desk. "I've got some good news," she said, "and I've got some bad news. Which do you want to hear first?"

Brad put down his pen and sat back. "Okay," he said. "I'll bite. Give me the bad news first."

"The bad news is, yesterday, I went to the Sawgrass Outlet Mall to buy an outfit for Seymour's party, and I came away empty-handed."

Brad just stared at Rose.

Then, indicating an afterthought, Rose raised her hand and said. "Oh yeah, and today, I'm bushed and my feet hurt."

"I can hardly wait for the good news," said Brad.

Eagerly, Rose said, "There are actually two pieces of good news. First, that young woman in California, Sarah Levine, checks out."

"She really is an entomologist?" asked Brad.

"Not 'just' an entomologist," said Rose, referring to her legal pad, "but a big-shot entomologist. She got a Bachelor of Science from Cornell University, a Master of Science from Columbia University and a Doctorate in entomology from the Weitzman Institute in Israel."

"Pretty impressive," said Brad.

"Wait. That's not all. Ms. Levine has been attending the University of Southern California and has completed another doctoral thesis in something called 'Extinction of Species.' In May, she'll be receiving a second PhD, this one in biology. So, how do you like those apples?"

Brad shook his head. "Poor Stephanie has spent a lifetime stunting her own personal growth by being so intolerant of Jews. Maybe something like this will help her grow up."

"Grow up?" exclaimed Rose. "*Zee zol vahxen vee a tzibelah mit eer kohp in drerd.*"

"I give up," said Brad. "What does that mean?

"It's Yiddish. It means, 'May she grow like an onion with her head in the ground.' That's the only kind of growing she should do."

Brad sighed. "Anything else on the Levine woman?"

"You bet," said Rose gleefully. "She's the supervisor of the Department of Life Sciences at a place called Envirogen. That's also where Stephanie's son works,. Anyway, the girl has written two books and will be the keynote speaker at the International Symposium on Entomology in Seattle, Washington next month." Rose put down her legal pad and asked, "How do you like that?"

Brad smiled. "I like that," he said. "It's going to be very interesting when I present that information to Stephanie. I hope she finds it in her heart to be accepting."

Rose started to say something, but quickly changed her mind. Instead, she asked, "Are you ready for part two of my good news?"

"Sure. Go ahead."

"I think Stephanie is getting shtooped by a genuine Puerto Rican no-goodnik!"

Brad sat back and rubbed his eyes. Then, peeking through his fingers, he said, "I guess you're telling me that her boyfriend really isn't a well-mannered Bolivian industrialist."

"I don't think so," said Rose in a lilting sing-song.

Brad reached for his Nerf-ball. "So, exactly how bad of a 'no-goodnik' is he?"

"Big time," said Rose, relishing the moment. "If I've got the right man, Señor Raphael Boñez has been convicted of embezzlement, blackmail, grand-theft-auto and mail fraud. At present, he's under indictment for racketeering and tax evasion." A huge smile spread across Rose's face as she said, "Isn't that funny?"

Brad shot her a dubious look. "I'm afraid I don't share your enthusiasm, Rose."

"Oy, Brad, Brad, Brad, Brad, Brad," said Rose, shaking her head. "Can't you appreciate what's happening here? When somebody long ago first used the phrase, 'poetic justice,' *this* is what he was talking about."

"You may be right, Rose, but my concern is that, no matter what, I end up being the messenger. How in God's name am I going to tell her?"

Reverting to her sing-song, Rose said, "If you want, I'll gladly volunteer."

Brad sat silent for a long moment. Finally, he asked, "Y'know what I need?"

"A glass of schnapps and a steam bath," suggested Rose.

"Not bad," agreed Brad. "But, I was thinking of a serious diversion. I'm ready for another lunch with Harry."

"Harry Goodenow? What's so special about that?"

"The last time Harry and I had lunch, I met a very interesting woman. She's a reporter working for Sidney Aarons. Quite beautiful."

"Who's beautiful? Sidney Aarons?"

Brad gave Rose a wry look. "I'm serious. The woman I met was poised, conversational and very charming."

"What about the girl you're presently dating? Uh . . . Maxine?"

Dismissing the question with a wave of his hand, Brad said, "That's been over for a month. Maxine is moving to New York this weekend. She got a job with a big ad agency."

"So, now it's a reporter working for Sidney Aarons. Okay. What's her name and where have you taken her?"

Brad paused. "Her name is Hannah, and I haven't taken her anywhere yet. We only met for the first time when Harry and I were last having lunch."

Rose scrunched up her face. "What are you telling me? You don't even know if she's married or anything?"

"I don't think she's married," said Brad. "She didn't come across like a married woman."

"So, call her and ask her," suggested Rose.

"Uh . . . . I didn't get her number."

"Call your friend, Sidney. He'll tell you."

Brad brightened. "That's a very good idea, Rose."

CHAPTER TWENTY-THREE

CALIFORNIA

Although it wasn't yet ten p.m., Hannah Carpenter was having difficulty keeping her eyes open and stifling a yawn. Her dinner guest was speaking in a monotone that could have hypnotized the entire West Point Glee Club.

"Now you see, in addition, there's a whole family of medications known as 'beta-blockers.' You can recognize them because they usually end in the letters, 'L-O-L.' Examples of these types include timolol, atenolol, citeralol, propranolol . . ."

"Excuse me, Dr. Lynch," interrupted Hannah. "I hate to do this to you, but I'm going to have to cut this evening short."

"Is everything all right, my dear?" asked her companion.

Hannah nodded as she said, "I'll be fine. It's just that the combination of the day's events have put me off my pace. With my flight from Florida this morning, the delay in Dallas, and the three-hour time change . . . Well, they've all ganged up on me and given me a splitting headache."

"Oh, you poor dear," said Professor Lynch, reaching across the dinner table and taking her hand in his. "Is there anything I can do for you? Massage some part of your body, perhaps?"

"Really, Doctor. I'll be fine." Hannah gently pulled her hand free and added, "A full night's sleep and I'll be good as new."

Cocking his head to one side, Lynch pretended to scold her as he said, "There you go again, Hannah. Always being so formal. Doctor Lynch. Professor Lynch. Now, you know I've asked you to call me, Thurman. After all, I've been calling you, Hannah. So, you're just going to have to reciprocate and refer to me by my first name."

Thurman Lynch, a chemist who had worked for one of the large drug manufacturers, had recently turned sixty-five and was now retired. He was a paunchy man with gray hair and well formed jowls. His sad eyes were topped by brows that continually bounced up and down. Lynch had made a point of mentioning, on at least three occasions, that he was divorced and living the life of a *bon vivant*. That being said, his conversation was limited to two things: Talking about his work and making an unabashed play for Hannah.

"All right, Thurman," obliged Hannah. "I'll try and remember. But for this evening, you'll just have to forgive me."

Reaching once again for her hand, Lynch said, "I could spend a lifetime forgiving you, my dear Hannah."

Without seeming overly repulsed, Hannah demurely slid her hands off the table and onto her lap. "Thank you, Thurman," she said politely. "That was very sweet."

Anxious to end this tiresome exchange and return to the tranquility of her hotel room, Hannah clicked off the micro cassette that had been recording their conversation for the past two and a half hours. She was thankful that they were sitting in the restaurant of the hotel in which she was staying, for it meant that she could be in her room in just a matter of minutes.

Lynch watched as Hannah put the recorder back into her pocketbook. His eyebrows began an animated dance as he asked, "Does this mean we can now discuss a romantic interlude without the fear of it ending up in print?"

Shaking her head at Lynch's persistence, Hannah hoped her exasperated look would send the clear signal that she was not interested in pursuing that subject. Without answering his question, Hannah stood as she said, "Now, if you'll excuse me, Thurman, I'm going to head upstairs."

Lynch stood at the same time. "Allow me to accompany you to your door," he said gallantly.

"Please don't bother, Thurman. I'll be fine."

Professor Lynch capitulated. "I understand," he said. "It's been a hectic day for you. But tomorrow is another day. I can call you in the morning, and we can make plans to do this again."

The man didn't seem to realize that his advances were unwelcome. "Thurman," she said more firmly, "I'm only going to be in town for a few days, and my calendar is full. I have meetings scheduled for every meal of the day." Hannah held out her hand and added, "So, once again, let me thank you for your time. Good night, Thurman."

Thurman Lynch took her hand and, with a flourish, kissed it. "In the words of George Bernard Shaw," he said dreamily, 'parting is such sweet sorrow.'"

Turning to make her way to the elevators at the opposite end of the lobby, Hannah rolled her eyes at his incorrect reference. 'So what if he doesn't know Shakespeare,' she mused to herself.

It had been Sidney Aarons who had arranged Hannah's meeting with Lynch, and Aarons had predicted that Lynch would be " . . . a tough interview." Sure enough, each time Hannah managed to squeeze in a question, Thurman Lynch would either rattle off an encyclopedic array of gobbledygook that had little to do with her original query, or he would use the opportunity to attempt sweeping Hannah off her feet. During a dissertation on yellow jaundice, the Professor used the moment to tell Hannah, " . . . the color of your velvety skin, my dear, is the perfect blend of cinnamon and vanilla." The words of adoration, although somewhat flowery, might have been appreciated except for the lecherous pump handle action of his eyebrows as he added, " . . . and I'll wager it tastes just as good." The interview had seemed interminable.

Back in her room, Hannah slipped into her nightgown and sat at the desk. With her laptop open, she was ready to transcribe her notes. Hannah turned on the cassette recorder and searched for the one section of the interview which she had found intriguing.

Hannah started and stopped the tape several times before finding the part of the conversation that she wanted to hear again. As the recorder replayed their voices, Hannah listened to herself say, "That sounds as though it would be a terrible idea."

Lynch's response came through the machine, saying, "Allow me to describe the absolute worst example of greed. It started when a colleague told me that his laboratory had developed a cure for diabetes."

"A cure for diabetes?" repeated an astonished Hannah.

"Do you understand the nature of diabetes?"

"Yes, I think so," ventured Hannah. "It occurs when a person has lost the ability to produce insulin. Right?"

Lynch shrugged. "A little over-simplified, but it'll do. Anyway, my colleague . . ."

"What's your colleague's name?" asked Hannah.

"I'm afraid I can't reveal that information to you at this time."

"When will you be able to tell me?" asked Hannah.

"Once you and I become intimate," cooed Lynch, "I'll gladly reveal everything."

There was another long pause on the recorder, followed by Hannah saying, "Go on with your story, Doctor. The one about your colleague."

"Very well," agreed Lynch, reluctantly. "My colleague had been directing a group of bioengineers and together, they managed to regrow beta islet cells. Their research had progressed to the point of conducting experiments on mice. With great success, I might add."

"Define 'great success.'"

"Injections of the DNA promoted the regrowth of new beta islet cells that were actually capable of producing their own insulin."

"What are you saying?" asked Hannah.

"I'm saying that he found a cure for diabetes. He bypassed the treatment of the symptoms and went straight to the cure."

"A cure for diabetes?" said Hannah cynically. Wouldn't that be . . . . monumental?"

"Of course it was monumental! Diabetes has been a scourge on mankind for thousands of years."

"So, how come I never heard of this cure?"

Lynch cleared his throat. "About two weeks after he told me, he vanished."

"Vanished," repeated Hannah.

"Yes," said Lynch. "Disappeared. And his papers disappeared along with him. As a matter of fact, all his research papers vanished. Nothing remained. Not in his office. Not in his home. Not anywhere."

"Is there any way that I can corroborate this story?"

"Only by the fact of his disappearance, dear Hannah. There is no remaining proof of what I've just told you."

"Do you think it was foul play?"

"Unquestionably."

"And the motive for getting rid of him . . . ?"

Lynch replied, "Once again, it was that ugly emblem of capitalism: Profits."

"Are you kidding?" asked Hannah incredulously. "They could have sold that cure to every single person who has diabetes. They could have sold millions of them, worldwide. Wouldn't that have generated profits?"

"Unfortunately, nowhere near what they're presently making on the sale of insulin related products."

"Really?"

"Oh yes, my sweet innocent Hannah. Think about this. There are more than twenty million diabetics just in the United States. Some estimates of the world's diabetic population are upwards of two-hundred million. Now, take the average cost to the diabetic of five dollars per day. That's based on all the diabetes-related paraphernalia used by those poor souls. I'm talking about the insulin, the pills, needles, alcohol swipes, blood monitors, test strips . . ."

Remembering Lynch's unending laundry list, Hannah fast forwarded through the tape. When she hit the "play" button, it restarted with Lynch saying, " . . . costs that are considerably higher. However, for simplicity's sake, I'm using an average of five dollars a day per person. Now, if you take that five dollars and multiply it by two hundred million diabetics, you get an astounding dollar value that exceeds a billion dollars a day."

A pause ensued before Hannah heard herself say, "Oh, my."

Lynch's voice dropped half an octave. "Now, my dear, sweet Hannah, I'd like to change the subject and talk about us. I was hoping that perhaps you and I might indulge . . ."

Hannah clicked off the recorder. She recalled that this was the part of the interview at which he offered to teach her an exotically sensual game he called "Fly-in-the-Buttermilk."

Despite his licentious behavior, the chemist presented a side of genetic engineering that she had not previously considered. The concept of a dark side of corporate profiteering had struck a chord. From the many interviews that Hannah had conducted over the past ten days, she noted an emerging pattern. It seemed that the bulk of the information that she was collecting was negative. Stories about cloning predicted its disastrous effect on our society. Points of view regarding designer babies foretold of its ruinous consequences on families. Indira Jawara warned of the dangers in creating GMO's. And now, Thurman Lynch admonished pharmaceuticals for their unrestrained greed. When it came to the subject of genetic engineering, Hannah realized how easy it was to find the critics. As a reporter, Hannah was one of the best. Although some accused her of sensationalism, she had an aptitude for keeping the readers glued to each of her paragraphs. The three-part article would enable her to delve into the dark side of the issue and spice up the story with predictions of legal wrangling, moral dilemmas, and ghastly genetic mutations. It was just the sort of thing that would sell newspapers and bring attention to her talents.

Of the remaining three interviews that Hannah had scheduled, two were with high ranking executives in the biotech industry. The third, and the one she eagerly anticipated, was with Brother Timothy Goodman. Hannah smiled at the recollection of her previous interview with Brother Timothy. She had mistakenly held fast to a single-minded focus on the Preacher's role as the leader of the tent-revival movement. Her two most vivid memories of that meeting were the incredibly charismatic presence of Brother Timothy and, by contrast, her sense of foreboding when she met the Preacher's aide, Verne Smenken. Eager as she was to reinterview Brother Timothy, Hannah hoped that Verne Smenken would not be there.

*   *   *

"I must be on the verge of dying," complained Winston Sattherwaite, with a flourish of both hands. "My back hurts, I have a headache, and I think I'm going blind. I've got to get out of here before I crumble into sawdust."

"Good idea," agreed Sarah Levine. "As soon as I finish this last page, I'm going home, too."

"Well," said Winston, "if you promise, promise, promise that it's only going to be the one page, I'll wait for you."

Winston Sattherwaite was the resident botanist who worked in Sarah's Life Sciences Department. Because of his prematurely graying hair, the man gave off an initial impression of being much older than his forty years. However, Winston's unlined face and youthful gait were enough to dispel the picture of a silver-haired senior. Looks aside, Winston was a complainer. He constantly whined about the ever-mounting workload, the unappreciative attitude of Envirogen's management, and the myriad of aches and pains that seemed to come and go elusively. Despite being a negative hypochondriac, he was a professional scientist and an accomplished botanist.

Winston Sattherwaite was gay. It was not a subject he discussed openly, preferring to keep his personal life to himself. However, as human nature sometimes dictates, others did the talking instead. With his hips and thighs oversized to the point of being disproportionate to the rest of his body, Sattherwaite presented an odd physique. He tended to display a wide range of feminine characteristics, including a frenetic, lilting quality to his voice and a pronounced swinging of his buttocks as he walked. In addition, early on during his two-year tenure with Envirogen, the man had been spotted in a gay bar. The combination of all those things made him a focal point of office chatter.

Sarah thought his dry sense of humor was endearing. "You don't have to do that," she replied. "I'll be all right."

It was approaching eight p.m. and the two scientists had been at their posts for almost twelve hours. "Oh, please!" exclaimed Winston. "Don't you put up such a brave front with me. You know there's been a rash of vandalism in the area. I'll wait for you to finish."

"That's very kind of you, Winston, but what do you plan on doing if we're approached by a band of vandals?"

Winston's eyes went wide. Obviously, he hadn't really thought of that possibility. "Oh, my goodness! I . . . I don't know. I suppose I'll just have to frighten them away."

"Frighten them away?" asked Sarah. "With what?"

"Just look at me, Sarah. I'm hideous! I could frighten anybody!"

Sarah laughed. "You're not hideous, Winston. But not to worry. Arm in arm, we'll venture out into the parking lot and kick some ass if we have to."

Winston beamed. "You are such a stalwart," he said with pride. "I simply love it."

In less than five minutes, Sarah had finished typing the last of her notes. She clicked the "save" icon before copying the information onto a disc. Shutting down her computer, Sarah remembered that she had wanted to check on the insects that were received the previous evening. "Before we go," she called to Winston, "I just want to take a peek in the Zoo."

Winston sighed audibly. "You are such a mother hen but, all right, let's go."

"You don't have to come with me. I'll just be a minute."

"If I sit here any longer," moaned Winston, "I'll get pins and needles in my tush, and my joints will stiffen up. It'll be better if I come with you."

They walked down a short hallway which ended at three doors. The two on the left were restrooms, each appropriately labeled in Spanish, *"Caballeros"* and *"Damas."* The door on the right had a different designation. A framed sign, prominently displayed in its center, read, "The Zoo." Serving as not much more than a holding area, the Zoo was temporary home to the live specimens requested by Envirogen's laboratories.

With Winston following closely behind, Sarah entered the room. A quick, practiced glance told her that everything seemed to be in order. A rhesus monkey grabbed onto the bars of its cage and emitted a low, mournful sound. Its cry conjured a vision of an animal that seemed to know its days were numbered. The monkey's desperate wail set off a cacophony of squeals from a dozen white mice caged nearby. Sarah turned her attention to the newest arrivals at the Zoo, a trio of insects that she had recently ordered for herself and Rick.

"I hate coming in here," said Winston. "All those creepy-crawlies give me the shivers, and it always smells like the underside of a dirty litter box."

Sarah was immersed in her own thoughts. She walked toward the far wall where the insects were housed. "That's the monkey's fault," said Sarah, distractedly. "The monkey doesn't know it yet, but it's off to Stanley Briscoe's lab first thing in the morning."

"Thank God," said Winston with exaggerated relief. "Filthy beast."

The three different groups of insects were the direct result of the telephone conversation between Sarah and Jacobus Kaminski. The man had suggested the saddleback caterpillar for use in Sarah's project with Bennett Pharmaceuticals, while the two remaining species were recommended for the purpose of creating a new GMO that would solve the kudzu problem.

After approaching the glass enclosure that held the saddlebacks, Sarah peered in at its occupants. Winston, standing safely behind the woman, peeked over her shoulder. "Eeeww . . . !" he uttered in a frightful whisper. "What are those things?"

"Caterpillars," answered Sarah. "Poisonous caterpillars."

A uniform coloring made the caterpillars look almost identical. Over an inch in length, the front and rear of each insect was brown, while a more dramatic set of colors highlighted its midsection. A deep purple spot sat in the middle of a bright green swatch, creating the illusion of a caterpillar wearing a saddle. Despite two horns protruding from its head, viewers were more horrified by the sight of several needle-like spikes that rose menacingly from its tail.

"Poisonous?" repeated Winston, an edge of terror in his voice. "Oh, my God!"

Sarah felt his hands on her back as he squared himself directly behind her for protection. "It's all right, Winston. The caterpillars are confined to this . . . ." Sarah paused. She had been counting the number of caterpillars housed in the glass pen. The previous day on the loading dock, she had counted and confirmed receiving one dozen of the multi-legged creatures. Now, however, a quick tally revealed only eleven. "Mmmm," she muttered.

"What's wrong, Sarah?" asked Winston, furtively. "What's happening?"

Sarah straightened up. "One of them seems to be missing."

Alarmed, Winston cried, "Missing?" Panic engulfed him, and he began dancing in a tight circle, desperately searching for the errant bug. In a voice tight with fear, he chanted "Oh my God! Oh my God!"

Ignoring Winston's wild gyrations, Sarah was intent on finding the wayward saddleback. Concentrating on the series of glass containers, she, nevertheless, inspected the floor and the underside of the counter as she inched forward.

Winston suddenly squealed. "Sarah, Sarah! I think it's on me! Oh, my God, I think it's on me!"

Sarah spun to look. "Where?" she demanded. "Where is it?"

"On my back! On my neck! In my hair! Oh, my God! They're all over me!"

Winston was still high on his toes, doing an odd hop and spin. His twirling motion gave Sarah a chance to view his body without her having to walk around him.

Seeing no sign of even a single caterpillar, Sarah lost her patience. "Winston!" she called sternly. "Stop it! There's nothing on you! Nothing!"

"Are you certain? Please, please tell me you're certain."

"Why don't you go and wait for me outside? And stop being such a baby."

Winston shook his head. "Uh-uh. No way. I am not going out there alone."

"Then, stop carrying on," ordered Sarah, "and help me look for this thing."

Turning her attention back to the table, Sarah, once again, felt Winston's hands on her back.

"What's that over there?" whispered Winston, pointing.

Following the direction of his finger, Sarah saw that he was pointing to the container that held the paravulgarus. Her view was partially blocked by a metal strip on the corner of the glass enclosure. Moving slightly to her right, Sarah was startled to see the saddleback caterpillar inside the wrong container. Moreover, it was milling around and stepping over the overtly squirming grubs!

"Is that it?" hissed Winston. "Is that the poisonous caterpillar?"

Sarah nodded her confirmation. "It sure is," she said. Stepping toward the displaced saddleback, she mumbled, "Now, how did you get way over here?"

Winston's voice was a rasping whisper laced with tremors. "He's eating the other bugs, isn't he? He's injecting them with his poison and eating them. Right?"

"Take a deep breath and settle down," coaxed Sarah. "The saddleback may be poisonous, but it's strictly a vegetarian. I don't think it's interested in eating the paravulgarus." After picking up a small pair of forceps, Sarah locked on to the roving saddleback. Gingerly, she marched it back to its own cage.

"Now, can we please get out of here?" pleaded Winston.

"Yes. In a minute," answered Sarah. "I just want to make sure the saddlebacks stay put." The glass container that held the spiny tailed caterpillars had tall steep sides. It seemed almost impossible that one of them could have escaped by climbing up and over the edge. Playing it safe, Sarah put a heavy lid on the saddleback's container. Turning to check on the paravulgarus, Sarah said, "I really can't afford to lose any of these. The distributor in China shipped far fewer than I ordered."

Sarah was troubled. With only eight viable specimens of the kudzu-eating insects, she worried about any harm that might have been caused by the lone, intrusive saddleback. The tiny paravulgarus were like hatchlings, defenseless and totally at risk. Emitting a sigh of hope over their health and longevity, she proceeded to examine each one of them for movement. Moments later, Sarah exhaled a note of relief and said, "Looks okay. It doesn't appear as though any damage was done."

"Now, can we get out of here?" repeated Winston, seemingly near tears.

With Winston leading the way, Sarah turned off the light and closed the door before making her way back to the office to collect her purse.

Winston was quickly recovering from his traumatic encounter. "So," he said with a ragged breath, "if the saddleback wasn't eating the little bug, what was it doing?"

"I don't know," admitted Sarah. "It just seemed to be laying on top of it."

They were walking toward the exit when Winston stopped in his tracks. "Oh, my God!" he said with a flash of insightfulness. "They were shamelessly fornicating, weren't they?"

Sarah chuckled. She looped her arm through his and pulled him along. "Come on, big guy. Do your job and protect us as we venture out into the night."

CHAPTER TWENTY-FOUR

CHICAGO

Bruce Kreitzer sat at his desk studying a list of college basketball games that were scheduled to be played over the following week. Alongside of each of the participating schools was something called a point-spread. Somewhere in the smoke-shrouded gambling Mecca, sat the supreme beings, known as the odds makers. These were the gurus who measured the skills of the individual players and analyzed the nuances of the competition. Then, they drew their pentagrams, recited their incantations, and ultimately predetermined the probable winner of each game. These masterminds of sports had the ability to predict how many points would separate the winner from the loser. That difference in score was known throughout the world of gambling as the point-spread.

Kreitzer loved to bet on almost anything, but especially on college sports. Although he had his share of good days when he picked a series of winners, lately, the bad days far outnumbered the good ones and his gambling debts had become an oppressive burden. Kreitzer was skirting the edge of a fifty thousand dollar liability. The enormity of the situation would, at times, cause a shortness of breath along with a feeling of welling panic.

The intercom on Kreitzer's desk came to life when his secretary, Abby, announced, "Mr. Kreitzer? You have a call on line two."

So as not to lose his place on the odds list, Kreitzer put his finger on the spot. "Who is it?" he asked gruffly.

"It's Mr. Pignatano," announced Abby. "I told him you were busy, but he . . ." Abby decided not to finish her sentence. "He's on line two, Mr. Kreitzer."

Bruce Kreitzer closed his eyes and took a deep breath. He knew the reason for Porky Pignatano's call and had been dreading it. Despite hating the idea of being yelled at and humiliated, Kreitzer answered the phone with a cheery, "Good morning, Mr. Pignatano."

"You missed your payment, Brucie-boy," said Porky Pignatano with an air of finality.

"Yeah, I know," replied Kreitzer. "But it's just for a few days. I get paid this Friday. I'll be stopping over and . . ."

Pignatano cut him off. "Don't give me any of your happy horseshit," he said impatiently. "You know the rules. If you can't pay the debt, just pay the vig."

"Okay, Mr. Pignatano. No problem. I'll be over. Uh . . . how much is it right now?"

Kreitzer could hear Porky Pignatano say something to somebody nearby, but could not decipher the words. Suddenly, he heard the Mafia boss bark, "Not that piece of paper, you idiot! The other one." Kreitzer closed his eyes and waited.

"Okay, Brucie-boy," said Pignatano. "Here it is. You're up to fifty-one-thousand, eight-hundred."

Instantly, Kreitzer felt a clamminess come over him. The debt seemed overwhelming. His temples began to throb and Pignatano's voice began to fade as though someone had turned down the volume.

Kreitzer struggled to catch his breath. Slowly, he again became aware of Pignatano speaking. The loan shark's words began to register as Kreitzer heard him say, " . . . digging deep, you slime ball. You following me?"

"Yes," said Kreitzer swallowing hard.

Pignatano continued. "So, twenty percent comes to ten-thousand, three-hundred and sixty bucks. I'll expect to see you over here no later than four o'clock." Pignatano raised his voice for his final command. "Cash in hand!"

The dollar amount hit Kreitzer like a punch in the stomach. He knew he owed a lot in principal, but the interest that was due was staggering. Ten-thousand dollars was interest for just one week. Feeling the stirrings of panic, he muttered, "Oh shit." Then, aloud, "Are you sure?"

"Am *I* sure?" asked Pignatano incredulously. He raised his voice while repeating the question. "Am I sure? Who the fuck do you think you're talking to?"

Kreitzer backtracked immediately. "No, no, Mr. Pignatano. I'm sorry. I didn't mean it that way. It's just that I didn't realize . . ."

Paulie Pignatano interrupted again. "Ten-thousand, three-hundred and sixty bucks. Four o'clock this afternoon."

"Please, Mr. Pignatano. I'm not going to have the full ten grand by this afternoon. Please. I get paid this Friday. I'll have the money this Friday. I'll pay you the full ten-grand on Friday."

Paulie Pignatano hesitated.

Kreitzer continued. "And remember the deal we talked about? Remember? I said I would make you a part of it, remember? We're talking five-million bucks. Your end of it. Five-million bucks!"

"Y'know what, Brucie-boy? I'm getting sick and tired of your bullshit. You got more stories than my grandmother. You got five-million bucks? Bring it over here with you on Friday, you skinny shit. Otherwise, just shut up. And y'know what else? Fifty grand, hard cash in my pocket is a whole lot better than a five-million dollar promise from a miserable lying fuck like you!"

"Mr. Pignatano . . . please . . ."

"I don't want to hear it, Brucie-boy. You got 'til Friday. That's it. After that, you deal with Bruno." Without saying anything more, Paulie Pignatano cut the connection.

Kreitzer put both elbows on his desk and rested his throbbing head in his hands. Pignatano's reference to "Bruno" was ominous. Bruno Mordello, a.k.a. "The Enforcer," was on Pignatano's payroll for the express purpose of collecting the "uncollectables." In the past, Kreitzer had gone to Porky's headquarters, a remodeled restaurant that had been renamed the Neapolitan South Side Social Club. Even though the well stocked bar always seemed to have a half-dozen, unsmiling, cruel-looking people milling around, one stood out from the others. He was a massive, round-shouldered man known as Bruno Mordello.

Just three inches away from a height of seven feet, Bruno could make your blood clot just by looking at you. When he stood straight, he looked like Goliath with hands big enough to palm a watermelon. Having the features of a Cyclops on thorazine, Bruno always made Kreitzer nervous by coldly staring out from under a Neanderthal brow. His reputation was unquestioned.

Kreitzer stood and began to pace. He was in trouble. He couldn't see any way of putting together ten-thousand dollars by Friday. His mind ran the gamut from begging, to borrowing, to stealing, but kept on coming up blank. Staring out the window at a cloud-covered Chicago skyline, Kreitzer's thoughts were interrupted by his intercom.

Once again, it was Abby. "Mr. Kreitzer?" she asked tentatively.

Kreitzer's nose was beginning to run. "What now?" he asked as he wiped it with his fingers.

"If you have a moment, Shelley Markowitz wants to talk to you."

Kreitzer took a deep breath. He was more than ready for a visit from a pretty girl like Shelley. Since he had offered her a promotion and the opportunity to accompany him to Los Angeles, he was looking forward to her appreciative acceptance.

After giving permission for Shelley to enter, Kreitzer used both hands to brush his hair off his sweaty forehead. As the young woman stepped in, Kreitzer said, "Close the door, Shelley, and come on in and sit down."

Shelley said, "I'm only going to be a minute. I'm just . . . ." She stopped in mid-sentence and stared at Kreitzer. "Are you all right, Mr. Kreitzer?"

"Yeah. Sure, I'm fine," he retorted quickly. "Why? What's the matter?"

"You look like you just ran a race, or something."

Moments before, Kreitzer had fought desperately to stifle a panic attack. Having broken out in a cold sweat, his face was now red and big circles of perspiration appeared under each arm. "Ahh, it's nothing," he lied. "I was just doing some push-ups. Got to stay in shape, y'know. Anyway, did you come to tell me you're taking me up on my offer?"

In an attempt to overcome the intimidation she always felt in the presence of Bruce Kreitzer, Shelley had rehearsed her reply. "Actually no, Mr. Kreitzer," she said with a gulp that she hoped he wouldn't notice.

"What are you talking about? What do you mean, 'no?'"

"I've decided to leave the firm," she said with a little more assertiveness. "Sears has agreed to rehire me. I just wanted you to know."

Kreitzer stood up and started to walk out from around his desk. "Let's talk about this, Shelley. I figured you were going to jump at this opportunity."

Shelley had hoped to keep the conversation short and to the point. She dreaded the thought of being in close proximity to the man and having to endure his lewd groping. "Mr. Kreitzer," she said, holding up her hand and taking a step backward. Her gestures stopped him in his tracks. "Please," she continued. "You can't talk me out of this. I've already made up my mind."

Kreitzer was upset. Still reeling from his conversation with Porky Pignatano, Kreitzer was in no mood for additional negatives. "God dammit, Shelley! What the hell are you doing?" Raising his voice, Kreitzer continued. "You're throwing away a golden opportunity, for Christ's sake! I mean, what is it? The money? Is that it? You want more money?"

The shrillness of Kreitzer's voice cracked Shelley's fragile veneer. Tears welled up in her eyes as she began to step backwards toward the door. "I've got to go, Mr. Kreitzer. Thank you for the opportunity, but I've got to go." Shelley turned and walked quickly across the expanse of carpet.

"Wait!" shouted Kreitzer as Shelley crossed the threshold. "Would you just hold your horses?"

Shelley kept going.

Kreitzer took several long loping strides and yelled, "Will you just listen for one god-damned minute?" He stood flatfooted and watched Shelley half-run down the hall. "Shit!" he spat in frustration. "Shit!" he repeated. Kreitzer glanced at Abby who had witnessed the young woman's escape. Abby had an odd expression on her face. "What?" barked Kreitzer.

"Mr. Ubermann wants to see you in his office right away."

Kreitzer felt as though his world was being bombarded. Uncontrolled forces were detonating one explosion after another, and it was beginning to take its toll. Kreitzer tried to take a deep breath, but it did nothing to assuage his sense of impending doom. "He wants to see me? Are you sure?"

"Yes sir," acknowledged Abby. "As soon as you're free."

Kreitzer went back into his office to retrieve his suit jacket. As beads of sweat reappeared on his brow, he felt a weakness come to his knees. Holding his jacket in his hand, Kreitzer took a moment to sit and compose himself before facing his uncle.

Despite having trouble thinking clearly, Kreitzer formulated a solution to his problem, albeit one that he dreaded implementing. To get the loan sharks off his back, Kreitzer would have to ask his uncle for an advance on his salary.

Josef Ubermann had just hung up the phone. With a grim look etched on his face, he stood and walked to the east window. The CEO gazed out at the panorama of the Chicago skyline. On most days, this particular view was inspirational, but for this moment, he just stared, unseeing.

Ubermann was seething over the telephone conversation that had just taken place. The bank that held the paper on Ubermann's firm had called and made it clear that it was no longer interested in hearing excuses about missed payments. After listening to the bank president firmly lay down the guidelines for the future, Ubermann tried to negotiate. Instead of considering any of his compromises, the bank presented an ultimatum. Ubermann Commodity Trading Group had ninety days to bring its account up to date, or the bank would institute its own controls. Any resulting actions would be bad, but the worst case scenario was that Ubermann might end up being forced out entirely. It was a desperate time.

Kreitzer knocked lightly and entered. "You wanted to see me, Mr. Ubermann?"

Ubermann turned away from the window and stared at Bruce Kreitzer. The CEO disliked his nephew. Always had. If it weren't for Ubermann's sister badgering him into hiring her only son, Kreitzer would still be selling used cars. "I want to know what kind of progress you've made," asked Ubermann sternly.

Kreitzer's head was still reeling from his crumbling state of affairs. "Progress?" he asked. "You mean in the research department?"

Ubermann was exasperated. "No. I don't mean the research department. Close the god-damned door! Then, we'll talk."

Doing as directed, Kreitzer shuffled to a chair in front of the massive desk. Sitting down, he asked, "Progress on what?"

Ubermann made a wild gesture with one hand. "You are becoming more useless as each day goes by," he said shaking his head. He sat behind his desk before continuing. "Last week, I told you we were in financial trouble. Do you remember that?"

Kreitzer nodded quickly. "Yes. I remember."

"And, do you recall me telling you that we needed to take some steps to assure a profitable future?"

Kreitzer just nodded his consensus.

"We need to move on that," stated Ubermann. "So, I want to know what you've done so far."

Because Kreitzer had been so wrapped up in his personal problems, his uncle's mandate to "take the bull by the horns" had vaporized. Now suddenly, Kreitzer needed to come up with an idea. Any idea.

"Uh . . . I got a couple of things in the hopper," lied Kreitzer. "I just need some time to work out the details."

Seemingly overtaken with exhaustion, Ubermann slumped back in his chair. "We don't have any time," he said quietly. There was a long, uncomfortable silence. Suddenly, the commodities mogul sat up again and spoke severely. "I don't care if it's just an idea. Tell me what you've got planned. I want to know."

Kreitzer's mind was racing. He had no plan. His morning had started terribly, and now it was getting worse. "Uncle Joe," said Kreitzer soothingly. "You don't want to know what the plan is. Believe me, the less you know, the better off you'll be."

Ubermann looked at his nephew incredulously. "It's just the two of us in here," he said. "And besides, my office isn't bugged. So, what are you talking about?"

"All I'm saying, Uncle Joe, is that you don't need to know about anything illegal. If what I'm doing ever gets traced back to the firm, you don't know anything. You're not involved."

"Traced back to the firm?" questioned Ubermann with a narrowing gaze. A long, uncomfortable interval passed before he spoke again. "Are you wired?" he asked venomously.

"Huh?"

"Are you recording this conversation, you little weasel?"

Not expecting that reaction, Kreitzer, looking dumfounded, spread his hands in a helpless gesture.

Ubermann stood, pointed and demanded, "Stand up! Get up and take off your shirt! I want to see if you're wired!"

"Wired? Jesus Christ, Uncle Joe! I would never . . ."

Ubermann cut him off. "Don't give me any of that 'Uncle Joe' bullshit, you little prick. Just do as I tell you. Stand up and take off your shirt!"

Having trouble comprehending the moment, Kreitzer sat stock still and glassy-eyed. Slowly, he became aware of taking short, shallow breaths. His headache returned with such a vengeance, he was sure that he would begin bleeding from his eyeballs.

Ubermann broke the spell by shouting, "Do it! Now!"

Kreitzer stood and removed his shirt. In one horrendous morning he had been insulted, threatened and rejected. Now, on top of everything else, he was half naked and humiliated. It seemed like an eternity before Kreitzer heard his uncle order him to get dressed.

Reseating himself, Ubermann again demanded the details of Kreitzer's plan to force a rise in the price of some commodity.

The strip search episode had given Kreitzer a little time to think of a story that would appease his Uncle. "I've been talking to Porky Pignatano," he said. "The man's got pretty good connections with some people who can help make this happen."

Everybody who followed the news knew of the Mafia Underboss. Additionally, Ubermann was aware that his nephew was a gambler and had occasional dealings with the crime lord. "Okay. So, you've been talking to Pignatano. Has he said anything useful?"

Kreitzer offered the germ of an idea. "Porky thinks that we can do something with lumber futures."

Ubermann relaxed the squint in his eyes and said, "Go on."

Seeing a spark of interest on Ubermann's face, Kreitzer sensed he was on the right track. He knew that his uncle would have scoffed at the idea if he thought it had come from his nephew. However, saying that disrupting the lumber industry was Porky Pignatano's brainstorm, gave the scheme some credibility. "Yeah," embellished Kreitzer. "Porky said he happens to know the main warehouses for *Georgia Pacific* and *Weyerhauser*. He thinks that a couple of well-placed matches could light up the country's biggest bonfire."

Ubermann sat quietly for a long time. finally, he asked, "You think you can get it done?"

"We're still working on it, Uncle Joe. We're supposed to be getting together in the next couple of days. I'll be able to tell you more after that."

Leaning forward, Ubermann lowered his voice. "If you can make this happen, I've got to start buying lumber futures while the price is still low."

Kreitzer was back in control. Greed had gripped his uncle and Kreitzer knew it. The plan was simple. Buy lumber futures at the present price. Next, set fire to a good portion of the nation's lumber supply. That action would cause the price to rise sharply. Then, sell off your holdings at an enormous profit. Seeing Ubermann's wheels turning, Kreitzer said, "Hold off a while longer. Give us a chance to see if it really can work."

"What are you telling me?" asked Ubermann. "It might not work?"

"No. All I'm saying is that this is just one idea. Porky's got a couple of others. They're all sounding pretty good. Let me have my meeting with him and then I'll let you know."

"All right," agreed Ubermann.

Kreitzer breathed a sigh of relief. For the moment, he was off the hook.

Ubermann went on. "In the meantime, I just got the new sales figures this morning. Ever since that meeting where I beat the shit out of everybody on our sales staff, I've been anxious to see who might have taken me seriously."

"Anybody standing out from the crowd?" asked Kreitzer.

"Yes. That little Jewish girl, Shelley Markowitz. She's really turned things around."

Kreitzer blanched. He suddenly became fearful of having to tell Ubermann that Shelley had just quit. Ubermann would be furious and demand to know why. Kreitzer couldn't possibly tell him the truth. "No kidding," stated Kreitzer weakly.

"When are you having your next sales meeting?"

"Uh . . . when I get back from the conference in Pasadena."

"Let me know," ordered Ubermann. "I want to be in on that meeting. Maybe I'll give her some kind of award. 'Most Improved' or something. Show her off to the others as an example of what diligence and hard work can do."

Not knowing how to maneuver himself out of this dilemma, Kreitzer stammered, "Okay. No problem."

"All right," stated Ubermann with an air of finality. "One more thing."

"What's that?" asked Kreitzer, still on edge.

"I'm cutting your salary."

Kreitzer just blinked.

"Until we get this company back on sound financial footing, I'm cutting your salary in half."

"Wait a minute, Uncle Joe," pleaded Kreitzer. "Half my salary? Oh, my God! I won't be able to make it."

Ubermann became disgusted. "Stop your god-damned bellyaching, Bruce. Just tighten your belt, for Christ's sake. Stop eating out every night at *Morton's Steak House* and cut back on your gambling. You'll be fine."

"No, no," whined Kreitzer. "You don't understand. I have some . . . . some obligations. Obligations I've got to meet. I was going to ask you for an advance on my salary."

"Advance? What are you? An imbecile? Didn't you hear what I was just telling you? We're in financial trouble, for Christ's sake."

"But . . . but if my income is cut in half, I can't . . ."

"Jee-zus!" complained Ubermann with a look of abhorrence. "Stop with that adolescent sniveling, would you? Try to be a man, for God's sake. Suck it up!"

Kreitzer was devastated. Desperately, he tried to plead his case, but Ubermann was adamant. The only reprieve his uncle gave was to say that the salary cut would be temporary. "As soon as you and Pignatano make it happen, and we get healthy again, your salary will go back up."

Kreitzer was numb.

"And, if you do a really good job, there'll be a bonus in it for you. A substantial bonus."

With the meeting over, Kreitzer found himself sitting back at his desk, feeling overwhelmed. Since the start of the morning, trouble had come in wave after wave and now, he understood the fearful suffering of a drowning victim. His ears seemed to be blocked, muffling all sounds. Even his vision was out of focus, making it difficult to concentrate on any one thing.

Abby had watched her boss walk zombie-like past her and into his office. She had never seen Mr. Kreitzer look quite so haggard. Even though she didn't care much for the man, she was basically a compassionate woman and felt a need to see if he were all right. Abby walked the few steps to his office door and knocked. There was no answer. Knocking again and then opening the door, Abby entered uninvited.

Kreitzer was at his desk, seemingly unaware of her presence.

"Are you all right, Mr. Kreitzer," asked Abby. "Can I do anything? Get you something?"

Kreitzer tried hard to fight through his fog. He looked at Abby and slowly focused on what she was asking. "What?" he asked.

"I wanted to know if I could get you anything."

"Yes," said Kreitzer after a long pause. "Get me on the first flight to L.A. tomorrow morning."

"The conference doesn't start until Monday morning," reminded Abby. "I already have you booked on a flight this Sunday."

"Change it. Get me out of Chicago as soon as you can."

CHAPTER TWENTY-FIVE

CALIFORNIA

R ick Ballinger had a look of revulsion on his face. "Those are some disgusting-looking little bug!"

Agreeing, Sarah smiled and nodded.

Rick continued. "I've seen some of the insects that you deal with and, I must say, a few of them have some fascinating qualities. The praying mantis, for instance, or those colorful scarab beetles, all have a kind of nobility. But those slimy slugs . . ." Rick struggled to think of a perfect description. "Those obnoxious little puppies look like body waste."

Sarah's smile broadened. "Would you say that they were aptly named?"

"Aptly named?" repeated Rick.

"Yes. *Paravulgarus descenderae*," quoted Sarah.

"Right. I remember," said Rick. "But what did you say it translated to?"

"Descended from the very vulgar," stated Sarah dramatically. "Or something close to that."

Rick nodded vigorously. "Right. Vulgar. At least, that portion of its name is right on. If we weren't about to eat dinner, I would tell you exactly what I think it looks . . . ."

Sarah reached out and tried to put her hand over his mouth. "Don't you dare, Rick Ballinger! I don't want to hear any more of your nauseating little descriptions when I'm about to eat."

"In that case," said Rick, feigning insult, "I have nothing further to say."

Rick and Sarah, sitting at a window seat in *Belinda's Garden,* had just ordered their dinners. The evening's specialty was "Cornucopia Croquettes." It was concocted from a variety of six exotic beans that were chopped, minced and sautéed with a conglomeration of spices, designed to mimic the taste of salmon. Rick loved it.

To Sarah's palate, the imitation failed miserably. Despite a preference for Chinese or Italian cuisine, Sarah recognized the long hours that Rick had been putting in, and felt that he deserved, at least for this one evening, to choose the restaurant.

For the past four days, Rick had been diligently slaving away on the Kudzu Project. His work began in earnest when Sarah had presented him with the two species of insect necessary to do the recombinant DNA procedure. Although she had ordered thirty-six of the paravulgarus, only eleven of the gray larvae were received. Furthermore, three were dead on arrival, leaving only eight viable specimens. Sarah had better luck with the other half of Rick's requirement, the little wood borer that she referred to as the Skiles beetle.

Since the process of splicing the DNA of two divergent species required such a concentrated effort, Rick had been working twelve-hour days. It was only now, almost a week later, that Rick was first beginning to feel relaxed.

"Tell me how everything went," urged Sarah. "You've been so secretive the past several days, and I'm anxious to hear what you have to say. I felt badly that I was only able to give you eight of the paravulgarus. How did you make out?"

Before Rick could answer, their regular waitress, a bubbly, pigtailed beauty, skipped her way to the table and served their dinners. Rick began eating immediately, while Sarah took a moment to study her plate of romaine lettuce, tomato chunks, broccoli florettes, and julienne carrots. Around the perimeter of those vegetables were mounds of bamboo shoots, cucumbers, hearts of palm, and guacamole. Looking at her salad, she dreamed of a spicy Szechuan tureen full of General Tso's Chicken. Listlessly, she picked at the tomatoes in front of her.

After a half-dozen forkfuls, Rick was ready to answer her query. "No question that I could have used more than eight of the little buggers but, as it's turning out, it looks as though eight is going to be enough."

"Did all eight survive the procedure?"

"Lost two," said Rick with a mouthful of mock salmon. "But the remaining six are all doing well."

"You know, you almost didn't have any," stated Sarah.

"Really? How come?"

"It was strange," she began. "The day before I gave you the bugs I went into the Zoo to check on all the critters. I found that one of the saddleback caterpillars had somehow made its way into your container of grubs."

"No kidding. What was it doing there?"

"I don't know," answered Sarah. "It was funny when I thought about it afterward. Winston was with me. When I said that one of the poisonous caterpillars was missing, he carried on like a frightened little girl!"

"That must have been a sight to see," said Rick.

"And then," continued Sarah, "when Winston saw the saddleback mounted on top of the paravulgarus . . ." Sarah began to laugh.

"What?" asked Rick, starting to snicker as a result of Sarah's infectious laughter. "What happened?"

"He was shocked," giggled Sarah. "He pointed and gasped that the two bugs were shamelessly fornicating!" Sarah continued to chuckle at the memory. "He can be so comical without even realizing it."

They chatted briefly about Winston Sattherwaite's eccentricities before Sarah brought the conversation back to the Kudzu Project. With the edge taken off his hunger, Rick delved into the details of his attempt to create a transgenic organism, a life-form born out of the combining of separate DNA's.

"My initial problem," explained Rick, "was finding the proper vector."

Vectors, another name for a carrying agent, were instrumental in the process of splicing DNA. The procedure required taking the DNA from a donor and mixing it with a suitable carrying agent before inserting it into a host. In most cases, vectors were chosen from specific viruses that had the necessary properties to carry DNA to its destination.

"With the two bugs being different species," said Sarah, "I wondered if that might have posed a problem. What vector did you end up using?"

Outlining the steps of his search, Rick explained how he had earmarked and then discarded several different viruses before hitting upon the answer. "My biggest worry was that I had only eight chances to find the key. If I killed off all eight of the little snots, I'd be back at square one."

"So . . . ?"

"So, I remembered a research paper written by Professor Judith Rappaport. Her subject dealt with a problem that was similar to mine. I looked it up and discovered that she had some luck using the influenza virus."

"Influenza?" questioned Sarah, a smile spreading across her face. "No kidding. Did all the little larvae begin sneezing?"

Using his best Rocky Balboa imitation, Rick put down his fork and said, "Hey! I'm talkin' some serious stuff here."

They both began laughing.

A few moments later, Rick resumed his explanation. "Anyway, the influenza virus seemed to have a debilitating effect on the nucleotides of the donor bug." Rick hesitated, thinking about how to best continue the tale. "Not a terrible effect," he clarified, "but just enough to tell me two things." Rick paused to take a sip of his orange-cranberry iced tea.

"And, what two things were those?"

"That, although the influenza virus wasn't my answer, I was on the right track. I did some more research and found something else. Professor Rappaport had uncovered a derivative of the *streptococcus*, a shy, quiet little guy called *calageria*."

"*Calageria?*" asked Sarah. "I've never heard of it."

"It's a retrovirus that hasn't made any headlines because it doesn't seem to do any harm. Even though it's associated with the notorious one that causes strep throat, by itself, the *calageria* is dormant. So, I tried it."

"And . . . ?" coaxed Sarah.

Rick shrugged. "So far, so good. Like I said, all the little transgenic organisms are alive and wriggling. I've started the cloning process, and now it's just a waiting game."

Sarah took a breath. "When will you know if you've been successful?"

"A wise man once said, 'Success is the progressive realization of a worthy ideal.' So, under that definition, I'm experiencing success every day. A lot of the credit goes to you."

"Thank you," said Sarah. "But if you don't mind, I'll stand in the background. This is your turn in the spotlight."

"Maybe so," replied Rick. "But we do work well together. You chose insects with the necessary qualities, and I discovered a viral vector that seems to be working. Even after the trauma of receiving an injection of the DNA, the new organisms are still alive. Not only that, but they're eating."

Sarah asked, "What did you give them to munch on?"

"I have them feasting on a diet of kudzu root and sugar-water that Ashley whipped up in a blender."

"It all sounds wonderful, Rick. But, what about the field trials? Will you have to go to Georgia to do that?"

"Yes. I'll definitely have to go to Georgia. I want to oversee this project firsthand. But, when that'll take place, is up to the new life-forms.

"What do you mean?"

Rick said, "It really depends on how fast the cloning process can increase their numbers. I'd like to start with a trial run of about a thousand. That'll give me a good statistical base for my study. It'll also allow me to see just how hungry these little suckers are for the kudzu root."

"Just make sure you cover that sweet, pinchable ass of yours," cautioned Sarah.

"Cover my ass? Why? Do you know something I don't?"

"No," replied Sarah. "It's just that things can go wrong, and you need to protect yourself. That's all I'm saying."

Rick smiled condescendingly. "You're turning into a worrywart, Sarah. It's going to be fine. Think about it; you specifically selected bugs that wouldn't harm the environment. The new organism will only eat kudzu, and the adult dies as soon as it has sex. How much more can we ask?"

Sarah leaned forward. "The problem in this discussion is that I'm an entomologist and you're a geneticist. You live for the day that you can create a GMO. Regardless of the cost of that birth, most geneticists forge ahead, blindly mind you, in their quest to grow new and exotic life-forms."

Rick's inevitable protest was cut off by Sarah holding up her hand. "Wait," she said. "Let me finish."

Rick sat back and listened.

Sarah continued. "As an entomologist, I work with the widest variety of animal life on the planet, namely insects. And unlike any other animal, insects evolve with greater rapidity. They adapt to all kinds of variables. Weather, pesticides, radiation . . . . nothing stops them. They adapt, they change, they even mutate, for God's sake! And, it's all so unpredictable."

It was Rick's turn to lean forward. He lowered his voice and said, "You know, Sarah, if this works, and I think it will, it could make me famous. Famous!" he re-emphasized. "The thing I did for Foxboro Beer, my '*Quadballingermyces*' creation, will pale by comparison. The only people who might get to know my process of beer fermentation will be the brewmasters who use it. That's it. Nobody else will be interested. But this . . ." Rick paused, searching for his next words. "This could be big. Very big. My method for controlling pest plants could land me interviews on the *Today Show* or *Good Morning America*. Just think about all the problem plants that people fight to get rid of. Kudzu, maleleuca, leafy spurge, miconia, crabgrass, dandelions, I mean the list is endless. I could become known worldwide!"

Sarah gave a wry smile. "Are we going to have to clear a space on the mantle for your Oscar, your Emmy, and your Nobel Prize?"

Rick blinked, abruptly becoming aware that he may have expressed his aspirations a little too fervently. Still in all, he was disconcerted that his girlfriend could burst his bubble so cynically. "You know what your problem is?" he asked.

Sarah placed both her elbows on the table and rested her chin in her hands. "What do you think my problem is, lover?"

"You hate this restaurant and you won't be happy until I get you a piece of chocolate layer cake for dessert!"

*   *   *

Closing the cover of her laptop, Hannah yawned softly and stretched luxuriously until a slight twinge in her shoulder blade stifled the action. It had been more than twenty-one hours since she had last slept. Having put up with the tumult of last-minute packing and the stress of inevitable flight delays, Hannah was beat. On top of all that, her interview with the monotonous and lecherous Thurman Lynch had left her exhausted.

The Marriott Hotel had provided a comfortable and well appointed room. Removing the bedspread and turning down the blanket, Hannah caressed the crisp white sheets and realized that she was more than ready for bed. Hoping to hear the final news of the day, she clicked on the TV. Hannah removed her jewelry while a deep, masculine voice, emanating from the television, confidently told the viewers why they should purchase a Chevy truck. Removing her makeup in the bathroom, Hannah could hear bits and pieces of the next commercial, a public service announcement that had something to do with protecting California's children.

While Hannah was brushing her teeth, she heard a woman's voice say, "Welcome back to 'L.A. Newsmakers.' I'm Amanda Dale."

Unable to get her desired one-minute synopsis of the headlines, Hannah decided to shut off the television. Coming out of the bathroom, she heard the moderator say, " . . . and for those of you just joining us, my guests include Brother Timothy Goodman, a highly respected and vocal critic of genetic engineering, Harvey Teitlebaum, an attorney for a Beverly Hills based organization known as Citizens for Responsible Cloning, and Doctor Morris Culpepper, a Professor of genetics at UCLA and author of . . ."

Suddenly, fully alert, Hannah plopped down on the corner of the bed. As Amanda Dale presented the agenda of the late night panel discussion, Hannah realized how right Sidney Aarons had been when he predicted that Brother Timothy was going to get a lot of press and " . . . just might end up on the cover of *Time Magazine.*" Hannah made a mental note to bring up the Preacher's television appearance the following day during their scheduled interview.

The studio set consisted of a "V-shaped" table in front of a mural depicting an unrecognizable skyline. Amanda Dale was seated at the point of the inverted "V" with the show's guests on both sides of the host. Brother Timothy and the attorney named Teitlebaum were seated side by side on her left, while Professor Culpepper occupied the lone chair on her right.

Teitlebaum was agitated as he said, "If you would just stop and think about it for a moment, you'd realize that the Citizens for Responsible Cloning is the vehicle that can push modern medicine light-years into the future."

Brother Timothy was shaking his head. "You are rushing headlong into Dante's Inferno. Our first step should be to stop and think about what we have accomplished so far. If we take the time to understand the ramifications of what we're doing today, it will become safer for us to step into tomorrow."

"The problem with all you fundamentalists," said Teitlebaum, waving his finger, "is that you want to turn the clock back to the last century. We're living in a time of rockets and cell phones and computers. You can't control the lives of Americans with a horse and buggy . . ."

Brother Timothy's commanding voice silenced the attorney's statement. "Have you forgotten that God is in control? It is He who ultimately lays down the rules. It's God who controls our lives. Not cell phones."

Hannah could sense the tension on the set and wondered what had transpired between the panelists before the commercial break.

Amanda Dale intervened by turning to her right and asking, "Professor Culpepper, what's your opinion of the Citizens for Responsible Cloning?"

Culpepper was deliberate. He paused two full seconds before answering. In a television panel discussion format, those two seconds were an eternity. It broke the momentum of the dialogue and caused the excitement of the dispute to flounder. "I think Mr. Teitlebaum's organization is quite harmless."

Amanda looked into the camera and blinked. She wasn't sure whether to pursue Culpepper's strange answer or to go back to the other side of the table where she knew the attorney and the Preacher would continue to bicker. Venturing a follow-up question for the Professor, she asked, "Harmless? Why do you classify the C.R.C. as harmless? Are you saying that there is no downside to cloning?"

Again, the hesitation. "All I'm saying," clarified Culpepper, "is what the C.R.C. is proposing is pure science fiction. I've read their press releases, and what those people are talking about, can't be done. The organization resembles a group of children planning a trip to the great galaxy Andromeda. There is no science, presently or on the drawing board, that can accomplish their goals."

Frustrated, Teitlebaum half stood and pointed a stabbing finger at Culpepper. "You obviously don't know anything about our organization. Where did you read those so-called press releases? Tabloid Confidential? If you really want to learn about what we do, I'll make personal arrangements to . . ."

Brother Timothy turned and spoke to Amanda. "Professor Culpepper is right. The C.R.C. is nothing more than irresponsible daydreamers giving false hope to people with serious medical problems."

The next instant changed the tempo of the show. With no one supporting his side of the argument, Teitlebaum had been fighting an uphill battle. Furthermore, the moderator, Amanda Dale, was posing her questions so as to make it sound as though the C.R.C. was a group of irrational eggheads. On top of all that were Brother Timothy's constant interruptions. Revealing an obvious loss of temper, Teitlebaum spun to face the Preacher. Unfortunately, the attorney's extended hand inadvertently clipped the side of Brother Timothy's face. Simultaneously, Teitlebaum barked, "I'm not finished talking!"

"How dare you slap me!" bellowed Brother Timothy. "I was directing my comments to Miss Dale until your idiotic ramblings told everyone . . ."

Teitlebaum stood fully erect. "Who are you calling an idiot?"

Brother Timothy jumped to his feet, and now, the two men were standing nose to nose. Not wanting to miss anything, Hannah came off the bed and knelt in front of the TV screen.

"You've been making an ass of yourself all evening!" shouted Brother Timothy.

Amanda Dale was standing. "Gentlemen, please."

The voices of the two men became more strident.

Amanda tried again. "Gentlemen," she begged. "Please sit down."

Oblivious to her pleas, Teitlebaum reacted only to the insult of being called an ass. Red-faced, he screamed back at Brother Timothy, "And you're a god-damned, two-bit Holy Roller with nothing . . ."

Teitlebaum's invectives were drowned out by a cacophony of voices from the show's participants as well as from off-camera stagehands. In the middle of the shouting match, Hannah's eyes went to the right side of the screen where three newcomers suddenly appeared within camera range. To Hannah, it appeared as though Brother Timothy and Harvey Teitlebaum were about to be physically separated by the trio. However, before they had a chance to intervene, Teitlebaum completely lost his self-control and pushed Brother Timothy squarely in the chest. The action caused the Preacher to rock backwards and to become entangled with his chair. Hannah gasped as Brother Timothy tumbled over and fell onto the floor. For a split second, it looked as though Teitlebaum was preparing to leap onto the Preacher when, unexpectedly, there was a flash of a metal folding chair coming down, hard and fast towards the attorney. With the impact of a piledriver, the blow caught Teitlebaum on the back of his head and shoulders and instantly crumpled the man to his knees. Jumping onto Teitlebaum's back, the unidentified assailant, fists flailing like a windmill gone mad, began pummeling the attorney's head.

Hannah was experiencing total disbelief. Holding her face and uttering "Oh my God," she shuffled nervously in front of the TV and watched the dramatic action unfold. The camera kept rolling as more people came into view. Then, pandemonium exploded when a blonde, teenage girl, wielding what looked like a broomstick, came barreling onto center stage. Hannah couldn't be certain whether the girl was going after the man with the battering fists or after the attorney who was pinned underneath him. The set was suddenly swarming with about a dozen new people, all rushing to put an end to the melee. One man subdued the blonde who was about to uncork her makeshift bat, while two other bystanders grabbed the once chair-wielding pugilist who was now using Teitlebaum's head as a punching bag. As they pulled the two-fisted firebrand upright, Hannah let out a short, uncontrollable cry. Struggling against his captors, the combatant kicked viciously at Teitlebaum's leg, catching him in the thigh. Hannah watched the aggressor writhe and snarl like a cornered animal. Still, there was no mistaking the face of Brother Timothy's right-hand man. It was the creep who had been introduced to Hannah as Verne Smenken.

CHAPTER TWENTY-SIX

FLORIDA

"*Nu?*" asked Rose Goldberg, pulling over a chair. "What happened?"

Brad looked up, a blank expression on his face. "What do you mean, 'what happened'? What are you asking me?"

"I'm talking about Miss Stephanie 'Prima Donna' Ballinger," reminded Rose. "What did she say about her future daughter-in-law being a Jew?"

Brad put down his appointment calendar and sat back with a sigh of exasperation. He took a moment to rub his face before answering. "You just can't wait for this to happen, can you?"

"Are you kidding?" asked Rose with wicked delight. "I'm living just for that moment. I'd give up a year's salary for a videotape of you telling her the news."

Brad shook his head. "Vengeful woman," he uttered.

"*Oy* Brad," lamented Rose, "you don't know the half of it. I'd be willing to give up chocolate, for God's sake, if I could just be there when you tell her she's been getting shtooped by a Puerto Rican no-goodnik with a rap-sheet that . . ."

Holding up his hand, Brad cut her off. "I get the picture. But, you'll be sad to learn that I have some bad news for you."

"Wha-at?" whined Rose.

"This thing is becoming an obsession with you," chided Brad. "And I have no intention of playing into your wickedness. It's bad enough that I have to listen to the anti-Semitic comments of a client without having you spouting your vindictiveness into my other ear."

Disappointed, Rose slumped in her chair.

"Furthermore," continued Brad, "I have no intention of telling you any of the details of our meeting. You'll just have to use your imagination."

Rose stood up. "Fine," she said feigning insult. "Be a spoilsport. See if I care." She walked out the door and disappeared around the corner. As Brad reopened his appointment book, Rose popped her head back into the door and said, "By the way, Harry Goodenow called and said he'll meet you at Paul's Dockside at exactly twelve-thirty."

Glancing at his watch, Brad said, "Thank you," as Rose vanished again.

Within seconds, Rose's head reappeared in the doorway.

"What now?" asked Brad.

"If Stephanie is pregnant with a Puerto Rican love child, you'd at least tell me that much, wouldn't you?"

Brad picked up the Nerf-ball and threw it in the direction of the door. Rose disappeared, as the ball bounced off the wall and fell harmlessly to the floor.

*　　*　　*

Paul's Dockside was crowded but, as usual, Sheryl had taken special care of her good customers. After only a ten minute wait, she seated Brad and Harry at a waterside table. The drinks were served before Harry began lamenting his current relationship and listing the reasons he needed to end his affair with Harriet.

"Harry," retorted Brad, "those are some of the lamest excuses I've ever heard. If you want to break up with the woman, just end it. Be a man and end it."

"Easier said than done," replied Harry, stirring his martini with an olive-laden toothpick. "I've tried doing this before, but she's determined to hang on and make my life miserable."

"You've got to be strong, Harry. Just tell her it's over. She'll understand that."

"It's not that simple," whined Harry. "I tried that about a week ago, and all I got in return was a tongue-lashing."

Brad tried to control an encroaching smile. "May I assume that 'tongue-lashing' in this instance doesn't refer to anything sexual?"

Harry looked up at his friend. "From your mouth to God's ear," he replied wistfully.

Brad became serious. "We've been friends for a long time, Harry. At the risk of hurting your feelings, I'd like to make an observation."

"Are you going to take Harriet's side in this?"

"All I want to say," began Brad, "is that you have two very distinct personalities. When it comes to business, you're commanding. You're well reasoned and forceful."

"So far you're not hurting my feelings."

Brad continued. "But when it comes to your personal life, especially relationships with the fair sex, you become mush. You let women walk all over you."

Harry sadly nodded his agreement. "I know. As a matter of fact, a couple of days ago Harriet accused me of not having any backbone. What am I going to do, Brad? Help me."

"Things are that bad, huh?"

"Terrible," stressed Harry.

"Must be," concurred Brad. "I've never known you to drop a woman unless you have someone else waiting in the wings. You must want to get rid of her very badly."

Harry didn't reply.

Brad waited for Harry to say something. Anything. When he didn't, Brad cocked his head and narrowed his gaze. "You haven't told me everything, have you?"

Harry looked up from his drink. He had the look of a little boy caught in a lie. "It's just that there's someone else I'd rather be with," he confessed.

"I knew it!" stated Brad slapping the table. "Who is she?"

"Andrea."

"Who?" questioned Brad.

"Andrea Pepper. The barmaid in this place."

"Andrea?" asked Brad incredulously. "Six-foot-tall Andrea?"

Harry nodded enthusiastically.

"Harry! What are you doing? She's just a kid!"

"She's old enough to be a barmaid, and she's hotter than a jalapeño pepper!"

Brad was dumbstruck. A long moment of silence was finally broken by the waitress who came to take their orders. Harry requested another martini along with a dish of crab stuffed Mahi-Mahi, while Brad chose the luncheon special of broiled shrimp and scallops. Waiting until the waitress was out of earshot, Brad looked at Harry and said, "The last time we were in here, I saw you make a play for Andrea. However, I distinctly recall her rebuffing your advances. It sure looked to me as though you didn't have a chance in hell with that girl. What happened since then?"

"Persistence, my dear friend," said Harry smugly. "Persistence and a promise to take her to a . . ." Harry closed his eyes and said, "God forgive me, a rock concert next week."

Brad spoke with disbelief. "Incredible," he groaned. "Harry Goodenow at a rock concert! You're a purist, Harry. An aficionado of the classics. If you take Andrea to a place full of screaming teenagers, you'll never forgive yourself."

"Oh yes, I will! I'll feel forgiveness as soon as I get her back to my place and into my bed."

"Ahh," said Brad with renewed understanding. "That's the reason you want Harriet to be gone, isn't it?"

Harry shifted gears. "You know what your trouble is?"

"I'm sure you're going to tell me."

"You're jaded."

"Jaded?" questioned Brad.

"Right. Jaded. All your girlfriends are gorgeous. One more beautiful than the next. You've never had to put up with the likes of a Harriet or a Cecilia. Remember Cecilia?"

Brad acknowledged his recollection of the fortyish frump.

"My lot in life," continued Harry, "has been a collection of pudgy women with drooping boobs and too much perfume. Your companions, on the other hand, have been an endless stream of centerfolds. You've never longed for a woman with the body of an Andrea Pepper. You open your eyes in the middle of the night and there they are, lying right there beside you. You wake up and go to the bathroom in the morning and they're right there, stepping out of your shower with droplets of water beading up all over their naked bodies." Harry nodded affirmatively at his own commentary. "That's what I mean when I say you're jaded."

Brad took a deep breath and resigned himself to the fact that Harry was committed to two goals. First, to get Harriet, the shrew, packed and out of his house. And second, to get Andrea, the barmaid, unpacked and settled into his bedroom. The two men continued to speak about the subject until their lunches were served. With each man concentrating on taking the edge off his hunger, eating took precedence for the next few minutes.

Harry was first to speak. "What do you know about trading in futures?"

Brad was thankful that Harry had moved off the topics of love, sex, and rock concerts. "Not too much. Why do you ask?"

"I have some new depositors at my bank. One in particular is privy to a wealth of information regarding commodities in the futures market. I think this man is going to be invaluable for making some successful trades in that area. I'd like you to get involved."

"I have no problem with that," said Brad. "Just tell me what issues to invest in, and I'll do the rest."

"That's all well and good," replied Harry, "but there's a seminar on the in's and out's of the commodities market that I'd like you to attend."

"When is it?"

"This afternoon, from three to five. You'll learn how to . . ."

Brad interrupted. "No can do, Harry. I've got a conflicting appointment this afternoon and I cannot get out of it. What other day are they going to give it?"

Harry was clearly disappointed. "Unfortunately, this is the last in the series. I don't know when they'll do it again. Are you certain you can't cancel your appointment?"

Brad considered the prospect of having to inform Stephanie Ballinger about her son's girlfriend. Worse yet, the thought of telling Stephanie that her lover was a con man made Brad cringe. "Truth is, Harry, given a choice, I'd gladly take the seminar over what I have to do, but there's just no way I can get out of it."

"That means, if a situation comes along that looks as though it will reap rewards, you might be investing blindly."

Brad smiled. "Thank you for your concern, old friend, but I've been investing blindly for years. As my adviser, you've been my eyes and ears. If you say it looks like a good investment, that's good enough for me."

"I appreciate your vote of confidence. I shall continue to keep you informed of potential winners. In the meantime, be prepared to invest in one or two commodity futures."

*　　*　　*

Brad arrived at Stephanie's home with a feeling of trepidation. The woman's guarded attitude and unwavering gaze confirmed the difficulty of his job. Suspecting that the news he was about to convey might illicit anger, or at least a few colorful metaphors, Brad had insisted that they talk in the privacy of her den.

Watching Brad close the double doors to the room, Stephanie knew that bad news was imminent. "Am I going to need a drink?" she asked.

Brad handed her a photograph. "Perhaps," he said. "But first, tell me if you recognize this man."

Stephanie barely glanced at the photo before acknowledging that it was her Latin suitor, Raphael Boñez.

"In that case," Brad stated, "a drink might be a good idea." Crossing the room to the wet bar, Brad poured two glasses of 18-year old Macallan over ice. He had put a lot of thought into the order in which he would convey the two items of bad news. Hoping to end the meeting on a high note, Brad decided to first broach the subject of Stephanie's newest lover.

Without ever taking a sip of her Scotch, Stephanie listened intently as Brad spoke about the so-called Bolivian industrialist who had stolen her heart. Midway through Raphael's rap sheet, Stephanie stood and began pacing the floor. When Brad revealed that *Señor* Boñez was not from Bolivia, but rather a resident of the slums of San Juan, she stood and hollered in frustration. "God dammit!"

Brad let her vent off steam. He understood that, although her immediate fury would die down, the flames of her hostility would burn hot for a long time.

After expressing her desire to surgically remove the con-man's testicles with a pair of dull pinking shears, Stephanie broke into tears. Heaving sobs racked her body as big, wet tears rolled down her cheeks.

Taking Stephanie in his arms, Brad held her and said softly, "I'm sorry it didn't work out."

Stephanie cried for the next several minutes. When she finally pulled away from Brad's arms, a combination of eye makeup and salty tears had left a spotted reminder of her grief on the front of Brad's shirt. "Do you know why I'm taking this so hard?" she asked, as she sat on the edge of the love seat.

"Because you were in love," offered Brad.

"Hell no! Maybe that would have happened in time, but I hadn't fallen in love yet. No." Stephanie sniffled and grabbed a fresh tissue. "The thing that's really killing me is my shame. I'm embarrassed as all hell." Choking up, Stephanie added, "I feel like I can never show my face . . ." Then, she began crying anew.

Brad sat next to her. "Listen, Stephanie. Nobody has to know. This can remain between the two of us and that tissue you're holding. Nobody around here knows anything about this Raphael Boñez character. So, you don't have to lock yourself in a closet and hide. Keep it simple. Just tell your friends that he misrepresented himself. No one will be the wiser."

Stephanie blew her nose into the tissue. "You think it might be that simple?"

"Absolutely. And, I'll tell you what else. I have a contact in San Juan who used to be the Deputy Chief of Police. You give me the vitals on this slug, Boñez. His current telephone number, names of any relatives, or where he hangs out. I'll pass that on to my buddy, and within the week, they'll have his ass in jail. Guaranteed."

Stephanie liked the idea. It gave her solace at a time she desperately needed it. More importantly, Brad's suggestion gave her a way to strike back.

Seeing her take a big swallow of the Scotch, Brad asked, "Do you want me to refresh your drink?"

"Why?" asked Stephanie. "Is there more bad news?"

"On the contrary," said Brad in a lilting tone. "I've got some good news about Richard's girlfriend."

"Is she dead?"

Brad wagged his finger. "Be nice, Stephanie. I realize that you're still smarting over the news I just gave you, but try not to let it overshadow the positives about your son."

Stephanie took a shaky breath and another swallow of her drink. "You're right," she said nodding. "I'm sorry."

Brad went on to tell Stephanie about Sarah Levine. Speaking glowingly about her credentials, he concluded, " . . . and, she'll be the keynote speaker at a very prestigious international symposium in Seattle. There'll be hundreds of prominent scientists from around the world." Brad paused a moment before saying, "The woman sounds pretty good, doesn't she?"

Stephanie shrugged.

"C'mon Stephanie," urged Brad. "Let's try and be a little more enthusiastic. After all, this Sarah Levine may become your daughter-in-law."

Stephanie stared at Brad. Matrimony was a thought that she was trying hard not to consider. "I don't see how that could happen. She's Jewish. There isn't a Catholic Priest in all of Palm Beach who would marry them."

Deciding to hit her with a shot of reality, Brad said, "Oh, yeah? What if they decide to get married by a Rabbi? In a synagogue?"

Stephanie's eyes narrowed into slits. "What the hell are you talking about? They can't do that."

"It won't be up to you, Stephanie. It's a decision that Richard and Sarah will have to make."

Stephanie stood and began pacing. Marching between the wet-bar and the love seat, she fought with this unwelcome possibility. After the third round-trip, she turned to face Brad. Placing her hands defiantly on her hips, she stated, "Well, you're not going to catch me wearing any stupid-looking skullcap."

Undeterred by her intractability, Brad smiled and said, "Hey, Stephanie . . . if it's good enough for the Pope, it should be good enough for you."

CHAPTER TWENTY-SEVEN

CALIFORNIA

Hannah's last interview with Brother Timothy had been at the *Marriott Hotel* in Orlando. In just a few short weeks, life had changed for the Preacher. Even before his appearance on *L.A. Newsmakers, with Amanda Dale*, articles had been written about him, photographs of him had appeared in national magazines, and his sermons were so well attended that city fire marshals needed to be present. There was no question that the twinkling phenomenon known as fame had lit up the life of Brother Timothy Goodman. As often happens with fame, fortune was following closely behind.

Brother Timothy was presently quartered at the exclusive *Peninsula Beverly Hills*. The spaciousness and opulence of the hotel's lobby were breathtaking. Even the drive over had been spectacular. Once she got off the 405 Freeway and exited onto Santa Monica Boulevard, she noticed the change in scenery. As breathtaking as that looked, it wasn't until she turned east on Wilshire Boulevard that wealth revealed itself unabashedly. Beverly Hills was truly the Shangri-La of the modern age.

Trying not to look as though she were an out-of-town tourist, Hannah approached the front desk and stole a glance at the enormous array of crystal chandeliers that adorned the ceiling. The place reeked of money.

Hannah was third on line to give her name to the receptionist. After that, she would wait in the lobby to be escorted to Brother Timothy's suite. She casually looked to her left and caught her breath. The movie actor, George Clooney, was just entering a doorway, not more than twenty feet away. Star struck, she watched the door, hoping that the Hollywood idol would reemerge. Hannah slowly became aware of a woman's voice reiterating, "May I help the next person in line?"

Turning forward, Hannah realized that she was the object of the repeated question. "Yes," she said, stepping up with a blush on her cheeks. "I'm Hannah Carpenter. I have an appointment with Brother Timothy Goodman."

Hannah did not have long to wait before a familiar face soon stepped out of the elevator. She was the same teenager whom Hannah had seen the previous night on

L.A. Newsmakers. She was the blonde who had run out on stage swinging a metal broomstick. Hannah remembered someone having grabbed the girl, preventing her from pummeling the combatants during the scuffle.

"Hi," greeted the blonde. "Are you Miss Carpenter?"

"Yes," answered Hannah with a broadening grin. "I am."

"I'm Melanie."

Hannah stood up and nodded. "I remember you from last night," she said. "That was quite a raging battle, and you looked like someone who was ready to jump into the middle of it."

"Oops," replied the teenager, a little embarrassed at having been recognized. "It wasn't something I was hoping to be remembered for. It's just that when I saw Brother Timothy go down . . . . well . . . . y'know."

"Well, it's nice to meet you, Melanie," said Hannah extending her hand. "Did anybody get hurt?"

"Bumps and bruises," retorted Melanie. "That's about it."

"What about Brother Timothy? Is he okay?"

Melanie hesitated. "Um . . . Brother Timothy told me not to talk with you. He said I should just come down here and bring you upstairs."

"Really? How come?"

"He just likes it when . . ." Melanie stopped in mid-sentence to think of a reply. Then, she looked at Hannah and said, "If you have everything, I'll take you upstairs."

They made their way to the elevator and rode up in silence. Hannah thought back to her original interview with Brother Timothy in Orlando. There, she was greeted by a different young girl, a dark-haired teenager named Leila. Hannah had asked Leila if she were related to Brother Timothy and recalled getting a strange look from the young lady. It was as though the relationship that existed between her and the Preacher was common knowledge to everyone except Hannah. Hannah thought it curious that Brother Timothy needed to surround himself with pretty, female adolescents. They got off the elevator on the fifth floor and began the long walk to the suite. Attempting to revive the conversation, Hannah asked, "How do you like California? What do you think of Beverly Hills?"

Melanie glanced back at Hannah. "Oh, I used to live around here. I've already seen all the tourist sights."

It was a lot more conversation than Hannah had managed to elicit from Leila, her Orlando escort. Trying to expand on their little chat, Hannah asked, "Tell me Melanie, how long have you known Brother Timothy?"

"Oh, wow," replied the teenager, chuckling at the memory. "Me and Brother Timothy go way back. We were once on a . . ." Once again, Melanie bit off her words. Her smile faded as she thought better about telling the tale. The two women continued down the hallway in silence. "It's just around the corner," said Melanie. "Brother Timothy's waiting."

As Melanie opened the door, Brother Timothy stood to greet them. "How very nice to see you again, Hannah," said Brother Timothy, extending his hand. "You look even lovelier than I remember."

Letting go of any pretentiousness, Hannah broke into a broad grin. The Preacher's charm and infectious smile made her glad that she, once again, had an opportunity to interview him.

As Melanie disappeared into the adjoining room, Hannah took Brother Timothy's hand and said, "Thank you Brother Timothy. All compliments gratefully accepted."

Brother Timothy poured coffee while they made themselves comfortable. "I want to thank you," he said, sliding over her cup and saucer.

"For what?" asked Hannah.

"After interviewing me for the first time, many reporters tend to portray me as some sort of kook. You, on the other hand, wrote a very good piece about the work I'm trying to accomplish, and I wanted to thank you for it. That being said, I must apologize for this interview."

"Oh? Why is that?"

"I realize that I told you we'd have an hour together. Unfortunately, I neglected to take into consideration that, in about thirty minutes, I must leave for a photo session. I'm sorry."

Hannah was disappointed. Secretly, she had hoped to extend the interview beyond the allotted hour. "Did Melanie forget to remind you of that appointment?"

Brother Timothy's eyebrows went up. "Melanie?" he asked as if he weren't sure he had heard the right name. "No, no. Melanie has other duties. I rely on Verne to keep my calendar straight. You remember Verne, don't you?"

Hannah did indeed remember Verne Smenken. She recalled him from the first interview when he seemed to slither in, ostensibly to clean up the coffee table, and remained for the duration of the interview. Hannah had not forgotten the uncomfortable feeling that ran through her when she realized that the sinister-looking man wasn't taking his eyes off her. Most recently was the previous night's television show where Verne Smenken suddenly appeared from stage left and came to Brother Timothy's defense by viciously attacking one of the other panelists. "I was watching television last night," said Hannah softly. "I saw what happened. Are you all right? Was anyone seriously hurt?"

Brother Timothy shook his head sadly. "An unfortunate incident," he said. "But, I'm fine. I just got a little tangled up with my chair."

"Your friend, Verne Smenken, put on quite a show. Is he all right?"

Brother Timothy sipped his coffee and thought about his answer. "Verne is a passionate young man. And, he's also very loyal. It was that combination of qualities that led him to rush to my defense so . . . exuberantly."

"Exuberantly?" said Hannah with a smirk. "I don't mean to be disrespectful, Brother Timothy, but his actions seemed a tad more violent than exuberant. What happened to that Teitlebaum guy? He looked to be in pretty bad shape."

Brother Timothy nodded. "Yes. Harvey Teitlebaum. He's in the hospital. He needed a couple of stitches in the back of his head, and now he's undergoing some tests to rule out any neck injuries. It's some nasty business, and the attorneys on both sides are already hard at work."

"And Verne . . . ?"

Brother Timothy leaned forward and touched his bottom lip. "Tell me, Hannah. Is this what you came to talk to me about? Is this the new purpose of your interview?"

Hannah should not have been surprised by the question, but she was. Although she had hoped that a rapport had been established between the Preacher and herself, not enough time had passed for a meaningful friendship to have developed. Still, Hannah was taken aback by the Preacher's cynicism. "No. Not at all," she said with a twinge of disappointment. "The purpose of this interview today is to get to the heart of your message. I'm only asking questions about last night's fiasco because I happened to see it. As far as that incident is concerned, I have no intention of writing anything except the facts."

Brother Timothy sat back. "I see. I want you to understand that part of my guarded stance is due to the flood of phone calls I've received. There seems to be ten reporters calling from every tabloid just because they smell blood. I suppose I shouldn't be putting you in the same category as the rest of the wolf pack."

Hannah said, "Apology accepted," but her mind was racing with memories of a time past. It was Brother Timothy's attitude that she found so disturbing. Something in his manner brought back the turbulent emotions of her adolescence. The subtle reprimands of her stepfather before he took young Hannah in his arms and . . .

Hannah shook away the cobwebs. "So, is Verne all right?" she asked.

Brother Timothy took a deep breath. "Presently, Verne is in jail. The initial charge of attempted murder has already been reduced to assault and battery. I have our lawyers down at the courthouse arranging bail. He'll be released to my custody which is just fine. In time, the dust will settle and he'll be all right."

"And you'll be able to refocus on your work."

"Exactly, "agreed Brother Timothy. "My message is still paramount."

"Right," said Hannah, adjusting her position and sitting upright. "That leads to some questions I'd like to ask you."

"Ask away," he said, taking another sip of his coffee.

Hannah began. "Your message has been very consistent. You've been hammering away at the biotech moguls and the genetic engineers. You've been shouting from the mountaintop that everything they do is really the work of the Devil."

Brother Timothy nodded his head.

"When you mention the 'Devil,' are you using that word as a substitute for 'harm,' or 'dread,' or 'evil?' Or are you being more literal and referring to the Devil as the actual manifestation of the deity in charge of hell?"

Brother Timothy sat pensively and stared at his questioner. Over the years, he had heard his share of disdain from the Doubting Thomases of the world, people who didn't share his belief in the existence of Hell or the Devil. Sitting forward, the Preacher said, "First of all, one must never refer to the Devil as a deity. The word grants an elevated position with far too much reverence, and the Devil is not deserving. As for mentioning his name, I use it to exemplify all levels of evil. War, pestilence, the seven deadly sins, Armageddon . . . . anything that can cause grief for mankind. But, I also refer to the Devil as an entity. He's a powerful force, one that can come to us in many disguises. We must always remain vigilant, or he'll find a way into our midst."

"You haven't actually seen the Devil, have you?"

Brother Timothy suddenly broke into a wide smile. "Do you know the difference between a sleazy tabloid reporter and you?"

Momentarily taken aback, Hannah was surprised at the comparison. However, the Preacher's smile was disarming and Hannah found herself smiling along with him. "Are you about to say something that's going to make me feel bad?"

"No, no. Not at all," said Brother Timothy. "I was going to compliment you on how you worded your question. A tabloid reporter would have asked, when was the last time you actually spoke with Satan?' At least you, my dear Hannah, gave me the benefit of the doubt."

"So, what you're saying is that we should all look for signs of the Devil, right?"

"That is definitely part of it," agreed Brother Timothy. "The Devil leaves a blood-trail in his wake."

"But how do we know which disaster is the work of the Devil? I mean, if I happen to trip and fall down a flight of stairs, does that mean Satan actually pushed me, or was it just bad luck? Surely, not every bad thing is the fault of the Devil."

Brother Timothy said, "In the case of genetic experimentation, there is no question that the mark of the Devil is on it."

Hannah started to say something, but hesitated a moment before asking, "May I ask you a favor?"

Brother Timothy narrowed his gaze. "Certainly," he said. "What can I do for you?"

"The next time the Devil causes trouble, would you point it out to me?"

Brother Timothy studied her face, looking for any sign of mockery. "You're serious, aren't you?"

"Yes, I'm serious. But don't misunderstand. You haven't made me a believer. I just want you to point out the Devil so that you and I can move to the next level of our dialogue."

There was a pause as he mulled over her words. "Yes, Hannah," he said with a smile. "I'll do that for you." Brother Timothy sat back and crossed his legs. "Do you realize," he said, "if any other reporter were asking that favor, I would have him escorted out for being disrespectful?"

"Are you being bombarded by the press?"

"Oh," sighed the Preacher, "you don't know the half of it."

"I think I understand," said Hannah. "After all, I'm a reporter, and you, sir, are big news. How do you like your fifteen minutes of fame?"

Brother Timothy chuckled. "The truth is that I find myself on the edge of losing fame and gaining notoriety. I wasn't really looking for either."

"Maybe not, but it sure beats talking to a tent full of people in the middle of a cow pasture, doesn't it?"

A grin came to the corners of the Preacher's lips but quickly disappeared. "Relaying the Lord's message to fellow believers still gives me great satisfaction. However, the biggest difference in the past couple of weeks has been the media. I'm talking about responsible people like you, Hannah, and others from the nation's major publications. By putting me on the front page, so to speak, you have become my reluctant disciples. You've made things much easier for me."

"So, where do you go from here?" asked Hannah.

"Brother Timothy paused. "I've been giving that a great deal of thought," he said. "Although a lot more people are beginning to hear what I have to say, I realize that until now, it hasn't changed the status quo. I've been praying for guidance. I'm hoping that the Lord will shed some light and show me the way to reach a bigger forum." Brother Timothy sat forward. "Since you're a reporter, Hannah, let me ask you a question. If you needed to get a message across to . . ."

The Preacher's sentence was interrupted by the appearance of Melanie who emerged from the adjoining room. "Excuse me, Brother Timothy," she said softly. "You have a phone call."

"Who is it, Melanie?"

"It's a Mr. Michael Meltzer. He says he's a producer of a television show on MSNBC."

"Oh? Did he mention the name of the show?"

"Yes," she replied. "It's called *Hardball with Chris Matthews.*"

"Tell him I'll be right with him."

Brother Timothy turned to his interviewer. Before the Preacher could beg her pardon, Hannah said, "Sounds as though your prayers may have been answered."

*   *   *

Rick Ballinger took the stance of a ringmaster at a circus. "Ladies and Gentleman," he announced grandly. "Allow me to formally introduce the newest member of transgenic larvae, the one and only *Paravulgarus eliphidion skiles.*"

The entire staff of Forum Lab was gathered around the stainless steel table, gawking at the three Petri dishes that contained the tiny, grayish grubs.

Ashley Eberhardt was first to comment. "Damn big name for a bunch of little nothings."

Rick had worked long and hard to get to this point. After genetically engineering the new species, his role became that of a nursemaid. Having started with only eight original specimens, Rick knew that there wasn't any room for error or bad luck. Consequently, he spent his time fostering to the six "newborns." Working at a pace of more than eighteen hours a day, he constantly checked things such as the fermentation of the food source, the ambient temperature and humidity of the air, and the pH value of the culture medium. Additionally, he watched the larvae for signs of reassuring movement. Now, late this Friday afternoon, Rick felt confident enough about the organisms' survival to assemble his staff and to showcase his accomplishment.

"Well," explained Rick, "the name is only temporary. Since it's a GMO, we'll be filing for a patent under a new name. Something shorter, but yet, catchy."

Miguel offered an absurd suggestion. "How about 'Pedro?'" he said, eliciting a smattering of giggles.

Darlene made a face. "I think they look like maggots."

Miguel sipped the coffee from his Styrofoam cup and added, "There's a guy in my neighborhood that everybody calls 'Maggot.' He kind of looks like one of those bugs."

Ignoring Miguel's comment, Rick answered Darlene's observation. "They are maggots," he said with a smile. "But, hopefully, they won't remain maggots for very long."

Lynn asked, "Really? What's going to happen?"

"In a couple of weeks," replied Rick, "they'll start a process of molting."

Darlene still had a nauseated twist to her face. "Molting? Oh, Jeez."

Ashley piped up. "Molting their skins? You mean, like a snake?"

Nancy, Britney, and Juanita all began squealing in horror. Lynn took a half-step backward and asked, "Are these things going to grow up to be snakes?"

"Oh, yeah!" said Miguel, jumping at the opportunity to tease the women. "Slippery, slimy snakes with poison. You girls are going to have to really check your lockers in the morning. You never know."

Rick offered a short laugh. "No. Not snakes. Caterpillars. Miguel is just trying to frighten you. They'll shed their skins several times and grow into little caterpillars."

Chuckling over the women's reaction to his comment, Miguel gingerly balanced his coffee cup as the hot liquid sloshed close to the rim.

Ashley said, "If each of those . . . . things shed their skin several times, there'll be a lot of loose skins lying around. What do you do with them?"

Rick shrugged. "I'm not sure. There's a distinct possibility that the little critters will eat them. But if not, then one of us will have to clean out the cages, so to speak."

Darlene shook her head. "Uh-uh."

Juanita added, "Not me, brother."

Miguel spoke with mock wickedness. "Don't worry, Juanita. I'll do it. I'll take out the dead skins and put them in your potato salad. You won't even know they're there until you bite into something crunchy."

Contorting her face, Juanita slapped Miguel's shoulder as she said, "Miguel! You pig!"

Juanita's slap coupled with Miguel's quick motion to twist out of the way, caused the coffee cup to slip out of his hand. It hit the edge of the metal table and, like a fountain spraying its flume, splashed its dark brown liquid over the three Petri dishes that held the newly created organisms. The little gathering of technicians held their collective breath, as the cup crashed to the floor and spilled the balance of its contents.

All eyes darted between Rick and Miguel. "Hey man," said Miguel, "I'm sorry. I didn't mean . . . . it just slipped . . ."

Rick froze for just a moment. Without looking up, he called, "Ashley. Get me some paper towels. Quick!"

Miguel turned his attention to Juanita. "What are you? Stupid or something?" he scolded. "What the hell did you make me spill my coffee for?"

Juanita looked helplessly at Rick. "Oh, my God. I didn't mean to . . ."

Ashley came rushing over with a handful of paper towels. Handing the bulk of them to Rick, she first removed several sheets for herself and began wiping the area around the specimen containers.

Rick tore off a small corner from a single sheet and rolled it into a cigarette shape. He took a moment to study the coffee droplets before saying, "Don't worry about it, Juanita. It isn't your fault." Glancing directly at Miguel, he added, "It isn't anybody's fault." Then, Rick took the pencil-shaped piece of absorbent towel and dabbed it into the little puddles of coffee scattered among the fragile larval specimens.

Seeing the success of Rick's contraption, Ashley began rolling her own similar shapes. Stealing a sideways glance at Miguel, she muttered, "Stupid."

"Hey, Ashley," said Miguel, annoyed at her name-calling. "It was an accident. Okay? Why you picking on me?"

Friction had been rebuilding between them for some time. "Because," said Ashley, "what you did was stupid. You shouldn't have been drinking coffee around this table."

Miguel raised his voice defensively. "Hey! I'm drinking coffee all the time. You didn't never tell me not to . . ."

Rick interrupted. "Both of you, cut it out. It'll be all right." Refocusing, he continued to blot at the areas surrounding the grubs. Glancing up and seeing concern on all the faces, he said reassuringly, "Don't worry, guys. Go on back to your workstations. Ashley and I will finish up here. Everything will be all right." Silently, Rick added, 'I hope.'

The assembled staff dispersed and shuffled back to their respective corner of the lab. Ashley watched as Rick dabbed delicately at a droplet of coffee that had landed on top of one of the maggots. Whispering, she asked, "Will they really be okay?"

"I don't know."

Ashley was sympathetic. "Is there anything we can do to counteract this?"

Rick sighed and stood up straight. "The real problem is that all of this is brand new. There's no prior history to guide us, or answer any of our questions."

Ashley looked pale. "So, what now?"

"We wait," answered Rick. "I've blotted all the spilled coffee that I could see. Now . . . ." Rick looked helpless as he shrugged and reiterated, "We'll just have to wait."

They remained quiet for a long time.

Rick broke the silence when he said, "I figure that some of the coffee must have been absorbed into their food. So, it'll obviously become part of their diet. How that's going to effect their growth, or even their survival, is anybody's guess."

The two of them continued to stare at the remnants of the disaster. Trying to sound optimistic, Rick said, "Maybe the little fellows will like coffee. Who knows?"

"Yeah," concurred Ashley. "Maybe they'll like it so much that we can get a *Starbuck's* stand in here instead of that old coffeemaker."

*　　*　　*

"You are such a bad boy, Bruce," giggled Maria into the telephone. "Do you kiss your mother with such a dirty mouth?"

"Hey!" retorted Kreitzer. "Are you becoming the Queen of the Convent or something? It used to turn you on when I talked like that."

"It still does," said Maria, using a sultry tone. "When it comes from you."

"You know what?" asked Kreitzer rhetorically. "We're going to have a great time, you and me."

"I've missed you, Bruce. You shouldn't stay away so long. You ought to think about giving up on Chicago and moving here."

"What? Are you kidding?" joked Kreitzer. "If I moved out here to California, you and I would never leave my bedroom."

"I know," purred Maria. "That's what I'm talking about."

"Oh yeah? What about your other clients? What would you do about them, huh?"

"Baby . . . . I never met nobody that can make me feel the way you do." Maria paused before whispering, huskily, "Nobody."

"Okay, listen," said Kreitzer, mentally rearranging his schedule. "I was thinking that on Monday we'd meet for dinner and stuff, but I've got a better idea."

"Yeah, baby? What is it?"

"I want you to meet me here at the hotel at four o'clock. I'll be finished with my meeting by then, and you and I can have the rest of the afternoon to fool around before dinner."

Hearing the front door open, Maria glanced at the clock and knew that Miguel had just come home from work. Although he was aware of what Maria did for a living, he preferred not to listen to her client conversations.

It was time for Maria to conclude her call with Bruce Kreitzer. "Ooo, that sounds good, *mi querido*. Very good. But, is there any chance that I can get to taste you earlier? Like, maybe three o'clock?"

"I don't think so, baby," said Kreitzer, sounding disappointed. "You're just going to have to wait till four."

"Okay," agreed Maria. "I'll call you from the lobby at four. I'm hot for you, baby. I can hardly wait." Maria hung up the phone and listened to Miguel's footsteps as he headed toward the bathroom. She opened her date book and jotted Kreitzer's name in for Monday, four p.m.

Miguel came into the kitchen and plopped down on the remaining chair at the little table for two. "What's for dinner?" he asked without fanfare.

It was obvious to Maria that Miguel had suffered through another bad day. There seemed to have been a lot of them lately. "Pizza," she replied. "I ordered it about twenty minutes ago. It should be here soon."

"Mmm," mumbled Miguel with a nod of his head. "Did you get it with chorizo?"

Maria knew that the little sausages were Miguel's favorite. "Yes. Chorizo on half and mushrooms and onions on the other half. Sound okay?"

"Yeah. It's okay."

"So, what went on at work today?" asked Maria. "You look like the little kid that didn't get invited to the party."

"Aaww," he growled disgustedly. "It's the same bullshit. Rick and Ashley. Just the same bullshit."

"What happened this time?"

Miguel stood and walked to the refrigerator. "Rick had us all standing around a table where he's got his new GMO, and he's bragging all about it and shit like that."

In past conversations, Miguel had explained the abbreviation, GMO. "What kind of GMO?" she asked.

"Just a friggin' maggot," he said, taking out a can of cold beer. "A stupid-looking bug with a long-assed Latin name. Rick kept repeating the name over and over, just showing off and trying to make the rest of us look dumb."

"What's it for?" she asked. "What's it supposed to do?"

Miguel was becoming annoyed. Maria seemed to be more interested in the GMO's than the reasons for Miguel's anger. Also, her curiosity about the bugs was making it difficult for him to tell his story. "How the hell should I know?" he blurted. "It don't make no difference! It's just a god-damned bug!"

"Okay," she said, "So, go on. Tell me what happened."

"So, we're all standing around, and I said something funny. Then, Juanita, that stupid bitch, slaps my arm and makes me spill my coffee. The whole god-damned cup slipped right out of my hand and spills onto the freakin' maggots." Miguel shook his head at the memory. "Stupid bitch."

Maria sat up with a worried look. "Oh, Jeez!" she exclaimed. "What happened? What did Rick say?"

"Rick starts acting like he's The Man. He looks at Juanita and says," Mocking Rick Ballinger, Miguel took on a high-pitched, feminine voice, "'Don't worry, Juanita. It's cool. Don't you worry about a thing.' Then, he looks right into my face and says something about whose fault it really is." Miguel paused, gathering his thoughts. "Damn, I hate that guy! Stupid *cabrón*!"

"That was it? He didn't say anything to Juanita?"

"Not a god-damned word! He kept stroking her and telling her not to worry. That it wasn't her fault. What bullshit."

"I'll say," agreed Maria.

Miguel took a long swig of the beer and reiterated, "It was her fault. If she didn't hit my arm, I wouldn't have spilled my god-damned coffee. Dumb piece of shit."

"What happened to the GMO's?"

Miguel ignored Maria's question. "Then, that friggin' Ashley gets on my case. She's like a god-damn leech. I hate her. Her and Rick, both."

"I know, baby," said Maria soothingly. "I know." She stood and moved around to Miguel's side of the table. Brushing the hair off Miguel's forehead, she gently kissed it. "It'll be okay, Miguel. You'll see. It'll be okay."

Miguel put his arm around Maria's hips and rubbed the cheek of her butt. "When I was coming home, I ran into Gonzo. He can get us a couple of tickets to the 'Lakers' for Monday night. What do you say?"

"Monday night?" questioned Maria. "No, I can't, baby. I gotta be somewhere Monday. Can we go tonight, or maybe over the weekend?"

"They're on the road. They ain't playing till Monday."

"Then, how about we go down to *Rudy's*, and have a couple of beers?"

Miguel was disappointed. Even though he assumed correctly that Maria had made an appointment with a client for Monday, an unspoken rule prevented the subject from being discussed. The couple had long ago agreed that her work would always be kept separate from their living arrangements. "What about the pizza?" he asked.

Maria said, "Hey! If we don't feel like eating it, I'll just stick it in the freezer. The hell with it! Let's you and me get out of here. It'll be good to take your mind off Rick and Ashley."

"Yeah," said Miguel, playfully slapping Maria's rear end. "To hell with them. Besides, it's the weekend and I don't have to look at their ugly faces 'til Monday."

CHAPTER TWENTY-EIGHT

FLORIDA

The Chamber of Commerce was always crowing about two attractions that set Southeast Florida apart from the rest of the country. One was the magnificent beaches that hugged the wave-swept Atlantic Ocean, and the other was the abundance of fine dining establishments that dotted the area. Local residents, as well as some astute snowbirds, knew of several restaurants that combined the pleasures of ocean-side dining with the talents of a master chef.

In addition to *Paul's Dockside*, another of Brad's favorites was *John G's*. Located on Lake Worth Beach, *John G's* was unusual in that it was open only for breakfast and lunch. Nonetheless, menus for both meals were filled with unique and mouthwatering delicacies. Patrons stood on a long line for a breakfast that included *John G's* famous "pea meal bacon," a thick slab of Canadian bacon garnished and baked with a thin layer of cornmeal.

Brad was seated next to a window that overlooked the beach. Mondays, especially around sunrise, was a good time to enjoy the relative calm of *John G's*. Waiting for a waitress to take his coffee order, Brad laid his magazine on the table and turned to gaze out over the pounding surf. Herring gulls were crying their lonely lament as they hovered over the wet sand. A sandpiper frantically searched for its own breakfast as it darted in and out of the foamy remnants of a once turbulent wave.

"Good morning," said a pleasant voice.

Brad turned his attention away from the beach and greeted the waitress who was arranging his place setting.

"Coffee?" she asked simply.

"Yes, please," he replied.

The woman handed Brad a menu and hurried off to fill his request. As he opened it to see what items might satisfy his hunger, he spotted a young, red-haired woman coming toward him. Stopping at the table nearest Brad, she sat down.

The young woman was very attractive. With the exception of her lips, which were full and pouty, her face was small with delicate features. Her hair, pulled into a high ponytail, was held in place with a pretty, yellow hibiscus clasp.

Not seeing a wedding ring, Brad ventured, "Good morning."

The redhead looked up and smiled. "Good morning," she acknowledged.

Turning fully to face her, Brad said, "When I came here this morning, I expected to be surrounded by the sounds of the surf and the good tastes of a hearty breakfast. I didn't expect to find a beautiful woman like you sitting at the next table. My name is Brad Bishop. What's yours?"

Blushing shyly, she looked away for a brief moment. When she returned his gaze, a broad smile appeared on her face. "Thank you," she said. "That was a very sweet compliment. My name is Nicki."

"You're most welcome," said Brad gallantly. "And now for a bold question. Would you like to join me for breakfast?" Before the young lady had a chance to answer, Brad added, "I should mention that I'm harmless, I'm entertaining and I'd love to have your company."

"Thank you, again," she said, slightly beleaguered by his forwardness. "I would consider your offer . . . but . . ."

"Ah, the 'but.' There's always a 'but.'"

The redhead giggled. "My boyfriend is just parking the car. He'll be here any moment."

"Just my luck," said Brad, shaking his head woefully. "I finally meet a girl who is bright, cheerful, and beautiful, and she's taken."

"Sorry," offered the redhead.

"Oh well," said Brad resignedly, "At least, I hope the man appreciates what he has."

At that moment, the boyfriend entered the restaurant, and she waved to catch his attention. Waiting for the young man to wend his way through the tables and chairs, she turned to Brad and whispered, "I hope so, too."

Brad ate his breakfast with gusto. After the dishes were cleared away, he relaxed with a cup of coffee and tried to finish his magazine article. Unable to concentrate, he looked out the window at the gathering crowd of beachgoers. Occasionally, he glanced over at the redhead and her boyfriend. The couple chatted amiably and seemed very compatible. At one point, her delightful laughter made Brad turn in time to see the young man gently kiss her fingers.

The interactions of the redhead and her boyfriend triggered Brad to mentally review his list of past girlfriends. Following the death of his fiancée, Amy Crawford, Brad had not dated for almost a year. The circumstances surrounding Amy's death were so horrific that Brad had trouble getting it out of his mind. For a long time afterward, he blamed her death on himself.

Regaining a healthy outlook took some professional help and a great deal of personal effort.

The women who followed were an eclectic lot. There was a yoga instructor, a landscape artist, a tax attorney, and even a Russian ballerina. Shorter-lived affairs included a tennis pro, a commercial pilot, and an exotic dancer. In retrospect, Brad knew from the start that each of those unions were not meant to be. He thought about Maxine, his most recent girlfriend. The woman was a passionate beauty, voluptuous, energetic, and eager to please. The beginning of their relationship was blast furnace hot, and crackled with lightning bolts of passion. Despite all that, it didn't take long for the fascination to dissipate, and within a few short months, Brad was ready to call a halt to the affair.

Since Amy's death, Brad went into relationships knowing full well that there was a key element missing. It manifested itself as a dull pain, an ache that was caused by his own sense of loss and guilt.

Brad's mind drifted back to a recent lunch with Harry Goodenow where he had introduced Brad to Dr. Indira Jawara, and she, in turn, introduced Hannah Carpenter. Brad recalled how the animated conversation had made the time skip by very quickly. Brad could still picture Hannah, sparkling and beautiful, as she participated in the round-table discussion. He wondered what her reaction would be if he called.

"Will there be anything else?" asked the waitress.

Brad thanked her for good service and left a generous tip. Maneuvering through the parking lot, he turned north onto Route A1A. It didn't take long before he walked through the door to his office and said, "Good morning," to Rose Goldberg. "How are you this fine morning?"

"Like a spring chicken," she replied. "The temperature is down, and the stock market is up. I'm feeling wonderful."

"Yeah," agreed Brad. "I saw that. The Dow was up more than a hundred points on Friday. Were your stocks among the winners?"

"Last week was very good," she answered. "But more important than the Dow, was that the NASDAQ went up also. It gained almost ninety points for the week."

"I thought you and Seymour only invested in the Blue Chips."

"Oh, no," said Rose, sipping her coffee. "My Seymour is into everything. Ever since he sold the business, he spends his time looking for bargains. Stocks, bonds, mutual funds . . . you name it."

Brad was surprised. He had no idea that Rose and her husband were such serious investors. "Really!" exclaimed Brad. "I wasn't aware of that. Do you have any hot tips for me?"

Squinting her eyes, Rose asked, "Are you looking for something with stability or maybe a little more risk-reward?"

"I'm a bit of a risk-taker," Brad said with a smirk.

Even though most of the office staff had not yet arrived, Rose indicated that she needed privacy before divulging her recommendations. Leading the way into Brad's office and shutting the door, she said, "Two issues," she declared. "One is *Namlitz Electronics*. It's selling 'over-the-counter' for about six dollars a share. The other is listed on the Chicago Board of Trade. It's a futures issue called *NYMEX Natural Gas*, and you can also buy it for about six dollars." Rose nodded affirmatively as she added, "Both of them look very good."

"How good is 'very good'?" asked Brad.

"Seymour says that *Namlitz Electronics* is about to get a really big government contract and that several million dollars of outside money is going to be poured into the company. He thinks the stock could go to nine dollars a share. Maybe higher. And as far as *NYMEX Natural Gas* is concerned, word has it that their gas will soon be sold to the African Union. Seymour told me last night that he expects it to rise as much as two dollars per BTU."

"Only two bucks?" asked Brad, somewhat confused. That's just a thirty percent increase. It seems as though the electronic stock is a much better deal. If I buy that for six bucks and sell it for nine, I make a fifty percent profit. That sounds a lot better than your natural gas future, doesn't it?"

"You're forgetting about the power of margin," stated Rose, smugly.

When it came to investing his money, Brad had always put his trust and faith in Harry Goodenow's expertise. Consequently, Brad had put off learning about the intricacies of the various financial markets. Now, thinking about the missed seminar on commodities that Harry had suggested, Brad said, "Explain what you mean when you say 'the power of margin.'"

Rose put it in a nutshell. "Okay. Let's say you have a thousand dollars to invest. So, you buy *Namlitz* for six dollars a share and sell it for nine. You make about five hundred dollars profit, right?"

"Right," agreed Brad. "Invest a thousand and walk away with fifteen hundred."

"Okay. Now, take your original thousand dollars and leverage it with margin. The commodities market allows ninety-percent margins. That means that your one thousand dollars can buy ten thousand dollars worth of natural gas. So . . . ," Rose took an extra few seconds to run the numbers through her head before saying, "Ten thousand dollars will buy you approximately seventeen hundred units. If it goes up two dollars per BTU, you'll be able to pay off your margin debt and still get to pocket more than three thousand dollars! See the difference? Without margin, you made less than five hundred dollars. But with the power of margin, your thousand bucks turns into a gold mine!"

Brad was astonished at the simplicity of investing on margin. After asking Rose a few questions that were prefaced by "What if . . . ," Brad thanked the woman for the lesson and made a mental note to discuss the strategy with Harry Goodenow.

"Okay," said Rose. "So, now it's time to step out and take a chance. I realize that both of those investments are risky, but everybody needs to take a little gamble in this life. If you don't, you'll never be the one to find the pot of gold."

Brad nodded. "I suppose that's true."

"It's not only true of the stock market," said Rose, "it also applies to life."

With the hour hand approaching eight o'clock, Rose went to start her day. Absentmindedly squeezing the Nerf-ball, Brad realized that Rose was right. Everybody needed to take a chance. Wasn't it just this morning that Brad risked rejection when he extended a breakfast invitation to that beautiful redhead at *John G's*? And that venture was based on nothing more than a pretty face.

Brad's thoughts shifted to Hannah Carpenter. She was also a very pretty woman, but more significant than her looks, was the knowledge that she was a good reporter, intuitive and conversational. Calling her and offering to meet for lunch didn't seem to be much of a risk at all.

Flipping open his telephone file, Brad found the number for The *Sun Coast Ledger*. After connecting with a receptionist, Brad was transferred to three different extensions before being informed that Ms. Carpenter was away on assignment. When he inquired as to the date of her return, he was told that they did not have that information. Disconnecting, Brad checked his Rolodex before dialing the private number for Sidney Aarons.

"Aarons!" said a gruff voice.

"Hello, Sidney. This is Brad Bishop. Am I catching you at a bad time?"

Sidney checked his wrist watch. "It's all right," he said, leaning back in his swivel chair. "This is as good a time as any. How the hell are you, Mister Bradstone Bishop?"

"Doing well, thank you. Business is brisk and I'm managing to stay out of trouble. How about you? You seem to be in a jovial mood for a change."

"What the hell are you talking about, Bishop?" growled Aarons. "I'm always jovial."

"Oh yeah? Then, how come you have a reputation for combining the worst of Hannibal Lechter and Darth Vader?"

Sidney just grunted. "And to what do I owe the honor of this phone call?"

Brad sat upright in his chair. "You have a reporter working for you by the name of Hannah Carpenter. Do you know who I'm talking about?"

"Oh, jeez," whined Aarons. "Give me a break."

"What do you mean?" asked Brad.

"Are you familiar with the weekend supplement of my newspaper?"

Brad was a little confused by Sidney's flip-flop of subjects. Nevertheless, he answered, "Sure. I've even read it once or twice."

Sidney said, "Well, in the back of it, you'll find the personal ads. You know, 'Love-Line,' 'Find-a-Mate,' 'Boy-meets-Girl.' Do yourself a favor. Pick one up, read it, and stop bothering me."

Brad was surprised by Sidney's intuition. "What makes you think I'm asking about her for personal reasons? Maybe, I'm doing some investigative work that has led me to her. Did you ever think of that?"

"Get real, Bishop! Hannah isn't part of any investigation. You're just chasing after a good-looking skirt."

"Okay," chuckled Brad. "You win. I was calling to ask her out for lunch or something."

"Oh yeah? Well, you can't. I sent her out to L.A. to do a story."

"When will she be back?"

"Couple of days, I guess," answered Aarons. "I'll be talking to her later this morning. It depends on how the story is going."

"Okay," said Brad. "I'll call back in a couple of days."

"You do that," stated Aarons.

Brad hesitated a moment before saying, "Let me ask you a question, Sidney."

"Make it quick. I've got a meeting."

"How come you were so sure of my motives when I asked about Hannah?"

"Simple. After she had lunch with you and your weird friend, Harry Goodenow, she sat me down and wanted to know all about you."

"Really?" said Brad wide-eyed. "What did you tell her?"

"The truth, Mr. Bishop. I told her the truth."

"Oh, great!" said Brad with mock horror. "I thought we were pals. Do you think she'll ever want to talk to me again?"

"Luckily for you, she was still interested even after I told her that you were a direct descendant of Jack-the-Ripper. Now, enough of this matchmaking bullshit. I've got to go to work."

After hanging up, Sidney noted that it was 9:05, which would make it 6:05 in the morning, Los Angeles time. Hoping that Hannah would be awake, he dialed her number.

"Hello?" greeted Hannah.

"Were you still sleeping?" asked Sidney.

Hannah immediately recognized her boss's voice. "No. Not at all. As a matter of fact, I was about to jump into the shower."

"Good, but before you get all soaped up, give me a progress report."

Hannah updated the Editor-in-Chief on the events of the past few days, including highlights of her interviews.

Sidney said, "Make sure you fax me your article for the weekend edition."

First assuring Sidney that he would have the copy before noon, she then told him the story of Brother Timothy's televised brawl.

"No kidding!" remarked Sidney. "The honorable and righteous Brother Timothy Goodman was involved in fisticuffs?"

"He didn't actually throw a punch," said Hannah defensively. "But he was on the receiving end of a good shot and ended up tumbling backward over his chair. It was quite a sight."

"Call the station. Send me a videotape. I'd love to see it."

Hannah jotted a note to herself as she continued her update. "While I was interviewing him the next day, we were interrupted by a phone call from a producer at MSNBC. Get this! Brother Timothy got invited to appear on *Hardball with Chris Matthews*. How do you like that?"

"What did I tell you?" boomed the editor. "I said this guy was going to be front page news!"

"You were right, Sidney. Besides sending you my article for Sunday's supplement, I'll be faxing a separate piece on Brother Timothy. It's going to include all the details about the talk-show slugfest. It'll be on your desk before the end of the day."

"Good. How about my buddy, Thurman Lynch. You get a chance to interview him yet?"

"Oh, Sidney," said Hannah, shaking her head. "I hope he's not a good friend of yours."

"Why?"

Hannah related the man's penchant for all things sexual.

"Are you saying that Lynch made a play for you during the interview?"

"*A play*? How about multiple plays? The man's persistence at trying to sweet-talk his way into my hotel room, deserved a gold medal."

"Wow! It seems as though everybody is after you. You must be hot stuff."

"What do you mean, 'everybody?'"

"Just before I called you, I heard from a guy who wants to ask you out on a date."

"Are you pulling my leg?"

"No. You obviously have enough men waiting to do that. I, on the other hand, am being quite serious."

"So, who were you talking to?"

"Bradstone Bishop."

Hannah was silent for a moment as she processed the information. "Brad Bishop? The man that Indira Jawara and I had lunch with?"

"One and the same," confirmed Aarons.

"Oh my! Did you tell him I was here in California on assignment?"

"Listen, young lady," said Sidney sternly. "I'll tell you the same thing I told him. I'm the Editor-in-Chief of a major newspaper, not a matchmaker. Go handle your own love life. Leave me out of it."

"You know what I think, Sidney?"

"What?" he asked gruffly.

"You are such a Teddy Bear."

CHAPTER TWENTY-NINE

CALIFORNIA

The radio alarm clicked on, and the muted voice of Neil Diamond singing "September Morn" brought Rick Ballinger fully awake. Hoping not to disturb Sarah, Rick quickly reached for the snooze-button and turned off the music.

Sarah stirred, rolled over and rasped, "What time is it?"

"It's only 6:00," Rick replied softly. "Go back to sleep. I'll see you later."

As Rick reset the alarm for 8:00, Sarah mumbled something incoherent before falling back to sleep.

Saturday and Sunday had passed pleasantly. Rick and Sarah had used the weekend to visit with her parents, Marvin and Esther Levine. Despite their hospitality, Rick had been on edge. He had gone away and left his "newly hatched" genetically manufactured organisms all alone in the laboratory. Rick had been so focused on creating the GMO's that he had trouble turning his mind away and relaxing. Several times during the weekend, Rick had entertained the thought of driving back to the lab just to check on his little charges. Sarah had managed to calm his anxieties by pointing out that the round trip from her parent's home to the lab and back, would take the better part of four hours. Coupled with the time he would spend in his lab, his absence might cast an insulting pallor on the weekend visit.

Driving home Sunday night, Rick had announced that he planned on getting to the lab very early the next morning.

Sarah's reply was, "Not me. I need more sleep than that. So, do me a favor. Before you leave, give me a kiss and reset the alarm for 8:00 a.m."

Arriving at Envirogen, Rick's mind was already busy going over all the steps required to get to this point in the Kudzu Project. Walking down the hall toward Forum Lab, a dreadful thought occurred to him. It was the recollection of the previous Friday, when Miguel had spilled coffee directly into the Petri dishes that housed the newborn organisms. Were they still alive? Had any of them survived?

Rick quickened his pace. He opened the door and looked across the room at the stainless steel table where he had left the specimens. Hesitating in the doorway, Rick squinted, trying to decipher what he was seeing. The three Petri dishes were nowhere to be found. Instead, it appeared as though someone had laid out a wrinkled tarpaulin over the entire surface of the workstation. Taking a cautious step forward, Rick felt an object under his right foot. He looked down. Several large caterpillars were crawling around his feet. One of them had already made its way onto the front of Rick's shoe. Lifting his foot to brush off the pest, he was taken aback by the sight of several long pointy spines protruding vertically from the tail section of the insect. Under his lifted foot lay the crushed remains of two more caterpillars. Scanning the immediate area, Rick was astonished to see dozens of caterpillars milling around. He looked behind him and saw that a few had already crawled into the hallway. Wanting to confine the troublesome creatures to the lab itself, Rick stepped outside and gently kicked at them like soccer balls. In a few seconds, he had them all back inside the room and closed the door. Shuffling his feet in a sweeping motion, Rick moved slowly toward the tarp-covered, stainless steel table. He had only worked his way a short distance when his heart began to race. He stopped and leaned forward. The tarp-like blanket was no tarp at all. It was, in fact, moving. The entire tabletop seemed to be undulating as though it were alive. Nervously glancing around the room, he immediately noticed that the caterpillar population was denser nearer the table. Kicking a narrow path that would bring him a few steps closer, Rick suddenly felt clammy. Then, with the scope of the calamity becoming clearer, his breath caught in his throat. The table seemed blanketed with tens of thousands of caterpillars. Their numbers were overwhelming.

Breathing rapidly, Rick attempted to maneuver his way back to the door. The narrow path that he had kicked clear was now strewn with dozens of the crawling creatures. They had worked their way back around, seemingly blocking his escape. A moment of panic swept over Rick when he feared that he might be trapped. The feeling dissipated slowly as he inched his way back to the door by moving his feet in a sweeping motion.

There was no one in the hallway with whom to share the event. It was still early morning and other Envirogen employees had not yet arrived. He wished there would have been somebody to verify the strange phenomenon. Rick ran a short distance to the nearest laboratory and went inside. First assuring himself that the room did not have a similar infestation, Rick dashed to the wall phone.

"Hello?" said Sarah sleepily.

"Sarah!" snapped Rick. "You've got to get down here right away! Right away!"

The obvious alarm in her fiancé's voice brought Sarah wide awake. "Rick! What's wrong? What's going on?"

Rick spoke quickly. "Something got into the lab over the weekend. Some kind of insect. They're all over the place, and the damn things have eaten all my GMO's! These things are big, and they're everywhere! It looks like a goddamned locust infestation."

"Locusts?" repeated Sarah, confused.

"No! Not Locusts! Caterpillars! Jesus! I just said locusts because they're so damn many of them."

"All right, Rick. Try and calm down. I'll be there in twenty minutes."

"Better make it ten. And hurry!"

Sarah was about to hang up when a question came to her. "Rick?"

"What?"

"What do they look like? The caterpillars, I mean? What do they look like?"

"Oh, dear Jesus! I don't know. Uh . . . . Kind of big for caterpillars. And they have these pointy spines, like a porcupine, growing out of their tail section."

"Spines, eh? What can you tell me about their coloring?"

"Oh, God. I don't know, Sarah. Just get down here. You'll see for yourself."

"Okay," said Sarah. "I'm leaving now." Sarah was about to hang up when she heard Rick shout something. She put the phone back to her ear. "Say it again, Rick. I didn't hear you."

"I said you'd better bring bug spray, Sarah. Lots of it."

Sarah threw on jeans, a sweater and sneakers, grabbed her purse and keys, and hurried out to the car. She tried not to think about what she might look like without the benefit of her usual twenty minutes in front of the makeup mirror. Instead, her mind was racing in other directions.

Rick had made it sound as though he lost the entire Kudzu Project. The thought gave Sarah a profound sense of sadness as her heart went out to her fiancé. All those long hours and all that hard work seemed to have disappeared into a sink-hole. She was overcome with an urge to hold him. Eventually, they would have to regroup and start from scratch.

As for the immediate problem, Rick's description only mentioned spiny protrusions on the bugs rear ends. Even though Sarah knew that there was a number of species that matched that depiction, she couldn't help thinking about the saddleback.

Sarah had driven less than ten feet when she realized that she had forgotten her cell phone. Cursing herself for not thinking of it sooner, she slammed on the brakes and parked haphazardly by the curb. Running back into the house, Sarah thought about calling a colleague for help. Her department consisted of three other scientists and three technicians. Each of the scientists had his own area of expertise, including biology, chemistry and botany. None of them would be of any great help dealing with a horde of caterpillars. However, one of the techs, Becky Leconura, was a recent graduate of the University of Michigan with a degree in entomology. Sarah decided to ask her for help.

Seeing the digital clock on the dashboard clicked to 7:12, Sarah knew that Becky would not have yet left for work. Remembering that the girl would occasionally carpool with Winston Sattherwaite, Sarah dialed Winston's home number.

"Yes?" said a deep voice that barely sounded like Sattherwaite. "Who is this?"

"This is Doctor Levine. May I please speak with . . ."

"Sarah?" the voice interjected. "Sarah, it's me. Winston."

"Oh. Winston. I didn't recognize your voice."

"That's because I'm sick, Sarah. My chest hurts. My throat is scratchy and both my ears are blocked. I'm a mess, Sarah. When I stick out my tongue there are big red blotches . . ."

Sarah broke into the litany of ailments. "Winston. Listen to me. I need Becky's home phone number."

"Becky? Our Becky?"

Sarah spoke commandingly. "Yes! Get it for me! Quickly!"

Winston became flustered at Sarah's tone. "Oh, my heavens! What happened? What's wrong?"

"Winston, please!" cried Sarah. "Just get me her phone number. I'll explain later."

"Sarah, Sarah, wait! Look on my desk. Her number's in my Rolodex."

Sarah sighed impatiently. She spoke rapidly, explaining that she was enroute to Envirogen and calling from her cell phone. She took an extra moment to say that the problem involved a large number of insects that had infiltrated one of the labs. She heard Winston's little cry of alarm at the mention of an insect infestation. After clarifying that she needed Becky to assist her in the cleanup, Sarah added, "If you don't get me Becky's number, I'm going to make you personally responsible for going in there and getting rid of the creepy-crawlies."

Winston sucked in an audible breath. "Don't you dare! Don't you even dare!"

"Then, go! Go, go!" shouted Sarah. She heard the receiver drop followed by the quick patter of bare feet as Winston ran off to find Becky's number.

Within thirty seconds of Winston huffing and puffing out the telephone number, Sarah had Becky on the line and was explaining the problem.

"I'll be ready in a flash," said Becky, responding to her boss's urgency. "Give me a half-hour and I'll meet you there. Maybe sooner, depending on traffic.

*   *   *

With the comforting knowledge that Sarah was on her way, Rick Ballinger called his boss, Doug Matsushita at home. His wife answered sleepily and said that her husband had already left for work. From where Doug lived, it would take him at least a half-hour to arrive. Rick dialed the extension to Doug's office. Without giving any details, he left an urgent message for Doug to come immediately to Rick's laboratory. Satisfied that he had done all he could for the moment, he decided to go back and take another look at the weird caterpillars.

Moving cautiously down the hall, checking the floor, walls and ceiling as he went, Rick saw nothing to alarm him. Still, his heart raced as he neared the lab. The wooden door was closed. However, milling around at its base, were two of the unwelcome insects, along with a third which was crawling up the flat panel toward the door handle. Rick made a face, as he stomped the two large bugs on the floor. The compression from his shoe made a peculiar noise as though one were stepping on a brittle shell encasing a cherry tomato. He found the sound to be repulsive. Nevertheless, not wanting to touch the odd-looking beasts with his hand, he swung his foot up to kick at the caterpillar that was crawling toward the door handle. Rick missed on his first swipe and left a big smear of brownish, yellowish sludge just below the unmindful caterpillar. Rick wiped the bottom of his shoe on the tile floor and left an equally large stain. Lifting his right foot higher this time, he teetered slightly while aiming his strike at the remaining caterpillar. Rick pushed his foot hard against the door. Although the bug squished under the pressure of his right foot, Rick was precariously balanced on his left, which was sitting in the slippery ooze that had, just moments before, come off the bottom of his shoe. His action of pushing with one foot in the air caused him to clumsily slip and fall to the floor. Scampering quickly to his feet, Rick looked all around, hoping that no one had witnessed his ungainly tumble.

Rick stared at the closed door and thought about the extraordinary event that was going on behind it. Even though he told Sarah that Forum Lab had been invaded by weird caterpillars, Rick began to wonder about the validity of his statement. Of the thirty separate laboratories housed in the main building, about half were located along its perimeter and therefore had windows. Forum Lab was not one of them. It was an interior room without the benefit of a view. The previous year, Rick had been given the option of moving his equipment to a third floor corner with cross ventilation, but had declined the offer for a number of reasons. The majority of his experiments involved living specimens and would have required that the windows be kept closed and covered. Besides that, his present lab was far more spacious.

Rick thought about how such an enormous number of caterpillars had managed to enter. If windows were not the answer, then, what? A hole in the floor? A crack in the plaster? The air conditioning duct? "Right!" he exclaimed out loud. "The vents!" Running the configuration of the room through his mind, Rick recalled two separate vents plus an air exchanger, all on the wall opposite the door. Feeling a need to see if the insects were streaming in through one of those openings, Rick turned the handle and pushed open the door. The scene was like something out of Kafka's *Metamorphosis*. Caterpillars were everywhere. The big stainless steel table that had housed the original GMO's was still covered with undulating legions of bugs. What Rick found more startling was the increased number of caterpillars on the floor. When he was there less than fifteen minutes before, the area in front of the door had only light traffic. Now, the floor looked like a traffic jam in rush hour!

Standing at the threshold, Rick held onto the door jamb and kicked at the bugs. His goal was to clear a space for himself so that he could maneuver in relative safety. Despite expending more energy than he had anticipated, he eventually felt as though he had a sufficient margin of protection. Glancing up at the point where the wall met the ceiling, Rick could see one of the two a/c vents as well as the big square air exchanger. Although there were a few caterpillars on the wall, both of those openings were clear. Unfortunately, Rick could not see the remaining grate on the far right. His vision was blocked by a closed circuit TV and a fluorescent fixture that hung from the ceiling. Rick looked down at his feet and saw that the caterpillars had closed the gap. Moving further into the room and concentrating on reestablishing his circle of safety, Rick began kicking furiously at the encroaching insects. As he lifted his gaze to check the last vent, he heard the door open behind him.

"Holy shit!" cried Doug Matsushita.

CHAPTER THIRTY

CALIFORNIA

The firm knock on the door was followed by the muffled announcement, "Room Service."

Brother Timothy called out, "Be right there." He started toward the door, but hesitated as his eyes came to rest on the coffee table. "Cover up those papers," he said to Verne Smenken. "We don't need anybody seeing our business." The Preacher opened the door and greeted a young man pushing a large cart brimming with breakfast. On it were three main plates, each covered with a domed silver lid, plus an array of carafes and thermal pots with juices and coffee. On one corner of the rolling table there was a stack of cups, saucers, and silverware, while the opposite side displayed an enormous basket of breads, muffins, and breakfast pastries. The uniformed young man raised the four wooden flaps, transforming the cart into a big round table capable of seating four. Efficiently, he arranged the linen and set the table for three. Room service at the *Peninsula Beverly Hills Hotel* was more than just a meal wheeled to your room. Here, it was an extravagant production.

Brother Timothy, wearing a hunter green silk robe over a russet-colored pajama set, signed the tab before bidding the lad a good day. By the time the Preacher sat down, Verne had already filled two coffee cups. "Please pour a cup for Melanie," said Brother Timothy. "She'll be joining us in just a moment."

Verne shot a quick glance at the Preacher before doing as he asked. "This here breakfast," Smenken pointed out, "is a feast compared to the slop they fed me in jail."

Brother Timothy gave him an exasperated glance. "I would certainly hope so," he said. "And hopefully, that will be the very last time you have to spend a night in a place like that."

The aftershocks of Friday's TV talk show were still reverberating. Lawsuits had been filed, the parties involved were making inflammatory public statements and Verne Smenken had gone to jail. A powerful and expensive law firm had been retained to dig Brother Timothy out of the legal quagmire.

"Yeah," agreed Smenken. "It sure ain't a fun place."

Brother Timothy sipped his coffee before saying, "The lawyer told me that you came close to not getting out at all."

Smenken looked up from his eggs and sausage.

Brother Timothy continued. "He said that when he went to bail you out, you were in the middle of another fight."

Smenken looked down. "The guy was being an asshole. I had no choice."

The young blonde girl, Melanie, hair tousled and rubbing sleep from her eyes, came out of the adjoining room. "You say that about everybody," she said. "That's why you're always getting mixed up in fights."

"I wasn't talking to you," replied Smenken, sullenly.

Melanie folded one bare leg underneath her as she plopped down at the breakfast table. Her satin robe shifted and opened slightly in the front.

Smenken glanced at her.

Barely eighteen years old, Melanie had the grace of a dancer and the suppleness of a gymnast. Nature had also endowed her with the body of a centerfold. All those attributes aside, she had the aggressiveness of a wolverine, as proven by her willingness to jump into the fray during Friday night's short-lived, televised battle. She had known Brother Timothy for more than four years and, despite their age difference, had been sharing his bed for almost two.

Reaching for one of the muffins on the far side of the table, Melanie's robe slipped open even more, revealing a portion of a bare breast.

Smenken had difficulty turning away from the sight.

"Melanie's right," said Brother Timothy. "If you walk around with a chip on your shoulder, you'll always be getting into some sort of trouble."

Melanie spoke to Verne. "Haven't I been telling you that?" Then, turning to Brother Timothy, she added, "That's what I've been telling him."

Verne Smenken was getting upset. He felt as though the two were ganging up on him. He didn't mind if the criticism came from Brother Timothy, but found it very difficult to accept from a teenage slut like Melanie. "This ain't none of your business," he mumbled.

"Yes it is, Verne," said Melanie. "What you do affects all of us. If you keep this up, you'll take us all down with you."

Smenken had lost his appetite. He folded his napkin and tossed it onto his plate with the half-eaten eggs. "You ain't got no call talkin' to me like that. Besides, you ain't no example of goodness and virtue."

"We're not talking about me, Verne," retorted Melanie. "We're talking about you and that redneck temper of yours."

"Don't you be calling me no redneck, you slut! You whore! You weren't nothing but a street tramp until Brother . . ."

"Enough!" commanded Brother Timothy. "Both of you. This kind of bickering won't accomplish anything. It only serves to tear us apart. We need to be a family and stand united."

Smenken looked down repentantly. In contrast, Melanie squared her shoulders and threw her head back defiantly. The action caused her robe to fall open, exposing a generous portion of both breasts.

Brother Timothy put both hands on the table. "Go get dressed," he said to Melanie. "I want you dressed when we sit down to eat."

Melanie looked at the Preacher disbelievingly. She opened her mouth to say something but thought better of it. Instead, she pulled her robe closed and strode to the adjoining room.

Brother Timothy focused his attention on Verne Smenken. "There will be no more name-calling! Do you understand?"

Smenken lowered his voice to a hoarse whisper. "Why does she have to be here, Tim? You and I were doing okay. Why did you have to bring her along?"

"She was a lost soul, and she needed our help. Now, that the Lord is in her heart, she's become part of our family."

"She's driving a wedge between us," lamented Smenken. "We were doing good until . . ."

Brother Timothy held up his hand, cutting off Verne's sentence. "I hear the same complaint from you when it comes to Leila. You're not happy with either of those young ladies. I don't think it would make a difference who I brought in. You'd find fault with all of them."

Smenken tried again. "Remember when we was in Sacred Heart? And you and me swore that we'd be together forever?"

Brother Timothy leaned back and took a deep breath. He certainly did remember Sacred Heart, the Catholic orphanage where he and Verne were raised. Closing his eyes, he vividly recalled Father Shaughnessy, the visiting Priest with his hairless body and bad breath. Brother Timothy also remembered the nuns, the worst of which sanctified the Priest's perversions, and the best of which turned a blind eye to the proceedings that took place in the basement.

"I remember," said the Preacher. "And I haven't gone back on my promise, have I? We're still together after all these years."

"But it ain't just you and me. Things are different now."

Brother Timothy nodded. "Of course they're different. That's what we've been striving for. We tried with all our might to get out from under the wickedness of

231

the people at Sacred Heart. Think about what they did to you, Verne. Think about the room in the basement and the evil things the priest did to you. I've taken you away from all that. And, just as I promised, we're together. You and me."

Sullenly, Smenken added, "And Leila and Melanie, too."

"Yes. They are part of our family as well."

Smenken hung his head.

"Stop worrying about them," said Brother Timothy. "We need to concentrate on the job at hand. Our world is being turned upside down by scientists who call themselves genetic engineers. You and I both know that they are doing the handiwork of the Devil, and it has fallen to us to stop them."

Smenken looked up.

"Verne, my friend, I need you at my side during this battle. I need your strength, your bravery and your faith. God will smile on you for your efforts, and I will always be grateful."

Verne nodded approvingly. Despite Brother Timothy's weakness for young girls, Smenken loved him. Truly loved him. There were times he fought down the turbulent feelings of jealousy, especially when he heard the sounds of nighttime lovemaking coming from the Preacher's bedroom. Smenken had always harbored a secret desire to be held and comforted by this man. He longed for the day that he might sleep next to his friend, this man of God, and be blessed by the Preacher's warmth and security.

Smenken knew all about the Preacher. Back in the days of the orphanage, Brother Timothy was known as Timmy McGinty. Several years after they had escaped the abuse of the home, Timothy assumed the role of a Fundamentalist Preacher and changed his name to Brother Timothy Goodman. Smenken had been sworn to keep the secret of his friend's deception. Over the years, Verne had watched a transformation take place as Tim McGinty grew into his new persona. Brother Timothy's fervent faith in the Lord made it easy for Verne to accept Tim as a man of God, a man whose sermons exuded divine guidance.

Brother Timothy continued to speak. "You and I have a history and a friendship that transcends all others. And I cherish that. Together, we will smite the Devil."

Smenken beamed with pride and purpose.

CHAPTER THIRTY-ONE

CALIFORNIA

T raffic along Washington Boulevard had begun to build. Driving faster than she should have, Sarah thought about what she would see when she arrived at Envirogen. Rick's description of an army of caterpillars, each with a tail full of spines, was disturbing. Where did they all come from? She didn't think that the infestation came from outside of Envirogen's main building. If that were the case, there would have been some signs such as tenting or cocooning. But, nothing had been reported. Sarah's thoughts moved to a more reasonable answer.

Forum Lab had been the site of Rick's experiment in genetic engineering. He had taken the little paravulgarus and changed it. Added a new dimension. Created something different. But . . . . what?

Mulling over the facts, Sarah knew that the paravulgarus, if left alone to molt and mature, would eventually grow into a full-fledged caterpillar. Not one with spines on its tail, but a mature caterpillar nevertheless. However, the little grubs had been surgically altered on a microscopic level. From the beginning, Sarah had expressed her reservations. Manipulating these life-forms created the very real possibility of something going wrong.

Sarah understood the practical side of genetic engineering, including the benefits that could be gleaned from such an operation. Her concerns, however, stemmed from her knowledge of insects and their proclivity toward reproduction. Never giving birth to just one or two babies, insects were among the world record-holders for numbers of hatchlings. The swarms of newborns always produced a few mutations that would go off on their own and form new branches in the family tree. The resulting dilemma was that nobody could guess what kinds of problems would be generated by the new species. The same would be true if a person created a new species in the laboratory and released it into the wild. Without understanding the nature of the new creatures, could anybody predict their effect on our world?

Pulling into her parking space, Sarah walked quickly to the front entrance of Envirogen. She fumbled with her ID-pass card until she heard the soft click that allowed her to push the door open. Turning the corner of the hallway that led to Forum Lab, she spotted Doug and Rick. "Hey, you two," she called as she strode toward them. "Got everything under control?"

"Nope," said Doug, emphatically. "The situation is totally out of control."

Rick said, "Boy, am I glad to see you."

Sarah saw the look of consternation on their faces. Gesturing towards the closed door, she said, "since both of you look like you've seen a ghost, why don't you give me an overview of what's going on?"

"Wait until you take a look," said Rick. "You won't believe it."

As Sarah reached for the door handle, something caught her eye. A caterpillar had just squeezed itself out from under the door. She stepped back and caught her breath.

Rick raised his foot with the intention of crushing the bug, when Sarah shouted, "No! Don't!" Waving the two men back, she knelt to take a better look.

Doug spoke softly. "Rick and I have been talking it over, Sarah. We figure it'll be best if we keep them confined to the lab. Y'know, not let them out in the hallway or anything. At least, until we figure out what to do."

Sarah looked up from her kneeling position. "Are all the caterpillars this color?" she asked.

Rick and Doug shared a glance. "I'm not sure," answered Rick, puzzled. "I think so, but . . . ." He turned to Doug and asked, "Did you notice if they're all the same?"

"To tell you the truth," said Doug, "I was so impressed by their numbers, I didn't really pay any attention to their markings."

Sarah reached for the caterpillar.

"Be careful it doesn't bite you," warned Rick.

"Bite me? Why? Has anyone been bitten?"

"Well . . . . no," said Rick. "But you can never tell. I mean, just look at those spines."

"Caterpillars aren't known for biting people," she said. "They're strictly vegetarians. And as far as the spiny protrusions on the tail are concerned . . ."

Sarah's sentence was interrupted by someone running down the hallway. They all turned to see Becky Leconura, the technician from Sarah's department, coming toward them.

"Thanks for coming, Becky," said Sarah.

"No problem. What've we got?"

"A bunch of caterpillars crawling around inside there," said Sarah, pointing to the door.

"Not a bunch," corrected Rick. "Thousands of them."

"Tens of thousands," augmented Doug.

"Tens of thousands?" questioned Becky, as she knelt down alongside Sarah. "What kind of caterpillar is that?" she asked.

Sarah spoke softly. "My guess is that it's a new species."

"A GMO?" asked Becky in a hushed tone.

"I think so."

Joining the whispered conversation, Rick bent down to one knee and interjected. "I don't believe that it's a new species. This isn't anything like what I was working on. I think that these little devils came in from the outside. Through the air-conditioning vents or something."

"Why do you say that?" asked Becky.

"Because the ones I created were just little-bitty maggots," explained Rick. "There were only six of them. And they were all gray. Kind of a dull gray. The only similarity, between these things and the bugs I was working with, is that bright red dot on top of its head."

The lone caterpillar had been making its way toward Sarah's shoe. She took her plastic ID card and brushed the insect back. The action made it roll up into a tight little ball, fully protected and defended by the cluster of protruding quills. In that position, the spiny projections took on a needle-like quality. As the caterpillar unfolded, everyone noted the odd coloring, including the ominous red dot on its head.

"Y'know, Sarah," whispered Becky, "the coloring kind of remind me of . . ."

Sarah finished the sentence. " . . . Of a saddleback."

"Right," said Becky.

Sarah stood. Taking a deep breath before opening the door, she was again interrupted by a new arrival coming down the hall.

It was Ashley Eberhardt. "Don't try and start without me," she called, lightheartedly. "I'm the one with the marshmallows."

They all looked in her direction, but nobody smiled.

"Oh, jeez," she said, suddenly worried. "What happened? Somebody die?"

Sarah and Rick began a hurried explanation of what was going on. Ashley's eyes widened when Rick told her about the multitude of bugs crawling around on the other side of the door.

Ashley turned to Sarah. "And, you don't think they somehow came in from the outside? Maybe through a crack in the wall or something?"

Sarah started to shake her head, but was interrupted by yet another arrival. Miguel Ortiz sauntered over and announced his presence with, "Whazz-up, dudes? What's going on?"

A flurry of explanations brought Miguel up to date on the phenomenon. "Huh!" grunted Miguel. "So, let's get in there and stomp all the little mothers."

Sarah turned the handle and opened the door. Becky was beside her, as the other four peered over the women's' shoulders. Sarah was speechless, but Becky could be heard uttering a hoarse, "Holy Mother of God."

Softly, Ashley said, "Holy shit."

Doug whispered, "I already said that."

"See what I mean?" said Rick.

The telephone in the laboratory began ringing. They all just stood in the doorway and listened. After the third ring, Ashley said, "I hope nobody expects me to go in there to answer it."

Miguel's eyes darted around the room. He said, "Maybe we can call in for some napalm or some shit like that. We sure ain't gonna get it done with no fly-swatter."

Several of the caterpillars had inched their way to the threshold, and one had made its way onto the front of Becky's sneaker. She stamped her foot, dislodging the creature. "There are too many of them," she said. "They're up on the walls, and I can even see a couple on the ceiling."

Sarah half-turned to Rick. "The concentration seems to be on the big table in the center. "Every inch of it is covered."

"That's where the six little GMO's were sitting. I had them right on that table until . . . ." Rick's voice trailed off.

Sarah's mind raced for an answer. A misplaced gene? An unpredictable catalyst? Could her supplier have shipped saddleback larvae by mistake? Not likely. A more plausible explanation probably had something to do with the night she and Winston found the saddleback in the cage with the paravulgarus. She shivered at the possibility. Referring to Rick's theory, Sarah said, "I don't think that's what happened, Rick."

Everyone waited for an explanation.

"I think what we're seeing is the result of your gene-splicing experiment."

Doug addressed Sarah. "What's the basis for your conclusion?"

"At the moment, it's just a hunch. We'll have to do some testing to confirm my theory."

"I'm all for testing," said Doug, "but right now, we have a more immediate problem." He swept his hand as he said, "Right now, we've got to figure out how to control this infestation."

Rick spoke with a note of hopefulness. "You're the expert, Sarah. Any suggestions?"

"Yes," she replied, closing the door. She took a deep breath, and began issuing orders. "We'll need brooms, plastic sheeting and Vaseline. Lots of Vaseline." Sarah turned to Ashley. "I want you to head over to Ralph's Supermarket and pick up a dozen jars of Vaseline and at least a half-dozen empty cartons. They always have empty cartons for customers who want them." Next, turning to Miguel. she said, "Head over to the Home Depot on Arroyo and pick up four or five brooms and some heavy-duty plastic sheeting. Since we'll need to cut it into strips, get me a good pair of scissors, too."

"Scissors, heavy-duty plastic and four, five brooms," repeated Miguel.

"And some duct tape," added Sarah. "Got to have duct tape. Write it down."

Rick handed Miguel a pen while Becky fished in her purse for a piece of paper.

Directing her attention to Becky, Sarah said, "Gather up a couple of these critters and take them to our lab. As soon as Kim comes in, I want both of you to run a tox-screen on them."

Curiosity got the better part of Matsushita. "Who's Kim?"

"Kim Koto," replied Sarah. "She's my chemist. I suspect that the spines on the tail have some sort of poison in them." Returning her attention to Becky, Sarah added, "Tell Kim to give me the whole gamut of toxicology screens but have her pay special attention to the presence of any vesicular toxins. I need to know exactly what our little beasties are hiding in those needle-like protrusions."

CHAPTER THIRTY-TWO

CALIFORNIA

It was mid-morning before things looked as though they were coming under control. Miguel and Ashley had returned from their shopping trips and followed Sarah's instructions for reigning in the pesky caterpillars. Within the first thirty minutes, the other techs, including Darlene, Nancy, Lynn, Juanita and Britney, had arrived. With Rick and Doug pitching in, Sarah worked feverishly to direct traffic. Sarah had her troops sweep the hordes of caterpillars into the cardboard boxes that Ashley had picked up at the supermarket. Duct tape had been used to seal the boxes, preventing any insects from escaping.

Sarah's best trick was her clever use of the plastic sheeting and Vaseline. She cut the plastic into long strips, each about six inches wide by three foot long, and coated one side with a thin layer of the petroleum jelly. Laying the first strip on the floor, slick side up, Sarah explained, "Most insects, especially caterpillars, dislike oily substances. They absolutely will not cross the strip of plastic after its been coated."

Strategically placing the strips on the floor, Sarah bordered off protected pathways, allowing everyone to work in relative safety. One Vaseline coated strip lay across the door's threshold, preventing the caterpillars from exiting out into the hallway. Still, some of the spiny insects had worked their way onto the walls that bordered the door frame, thereby managing to find a way to sneak out of the lab. Doug had made it his job to stand sentry just outside the door and to pulverize each of them if they tried to escape.

Sarah directed Miguel to sweep the walls and ceiling in order to knock down any clinging caterpillars. "Pay special attention to the air-conditioning ducts," she said. Let's hope that none of the little buggers took off through there."

Miguel was standing on a three-step fold-out ladder and reaching as far as he could in an attempt to knock down a lone caterpillar crawling on one of the fluorescent fixtures. The broom's bristles dislodged the creature but, unfortunately, it fell down squarely onto Juanita's head. She emitted a short cry of horror. Not knowing how many insects had landed on her, Juanita panicked and flailed a hand wildly through her hair.

Responding to the girl's shrieks, Ashley shouted, "God-damn you, Miguel! Watch what the hell you're doing!"

"Relax, woman," he said condescendingly. "It's just a stupid little caterpillar."

Ashley, who was trying to console Juanita, fumed at Miguel's insensitivity. She barked, "You're the reason we're in this mess, in the first place. Last Friday, you spilled your coffee all over the new GMO's. And today, You're making matters worse by flinging these damn bugs at us!"

"I didn't fling no bugs at you," said Miguel defensively.

"Is that true, Miguel?" asked Doug. "You spilled coffee on the GMO's?"

"It was just an accident," said Miguel.

Sarah felt a need to nip the dissention before it grew out of control. "Ashley," she said, "we're going to need some more cartons."

There were five small cartons, each filled about halfway with the errant caterpillars. The group had estimated that each carton contained four to five thousand of the creatures. Sarah continued. "I want you and Juanita to run out and get me another six or eight cartons. We probably won't use them all, but better to be safe than sorry."

Ashley and Juanita walked the narrow path bordered with greasy plastic strips before stopping at the door. "It shouldn't take us more than twenty minutes," said Ashley. "We'll try and hurry."

"Just drive safely," said Rick. "We don't need another disaster."

Ashley led the way down the hall while Juanita hurried along, rubbing the outside of her palm.

Glancing around the room, Sarah said, "We've got the majority of these devils confined. What do you say we take ten minutes? Go wash up. Grab a cup of coffee. Whatever. See you all back here at ten-thirty."

The group's exodus was single file and in the directions of the cafeteria and bathrooms. Sarah, Rick, and Doug watched the crew leave.

Once alone, Doug turned to Sarah. "When I got here this morning, the scene looked like something out of a biblical plague. What do you think went wrong?"

Sarah replied, "I have a suspicion, but bear with me just a moment until I call Kim and Becky and find out the results of their toxin analysis." The wheeled office chair that was stationed in front of the telephone had a lone caterpillar meandering across its seat. With her ID badge, Sarah flicked the insect to an area that held thousands of its brethren, all penned in by jellied plastic strips.

Inspecting the lower half of the chair, Sarah spotted another critter crawling up one of the wheeled legs. "Give me a hand, Rick. Let's turn the chair over and see if we can find any more."

Flipping the chair, Rick was surprised to count eleven more caterpillars gripped to the chair's underside.

Doug shook his head and exclaimed, "Christ! These sons-of-a-gun are everywhere!"

Even though the chair was soon liberated from its posse of caterpillars, Sarah still hesitated before making her phone call. Peering under the table, Sarah bellowed, "Oh, crap!"

Rick and Doug bent to look. "Damn," announced Rick. "There must be hundreds of them under here."

"I'll tell you something," said Doug. "If they turn out to be poisonous, I'm going to shut down Forum Lab and send everyone home."

Holding a cup of coffee, Miguel came back into the room. He sauntered over to the little stepladder and, using it as a stool, sat down on its top rung.

Sarah said, "Better check the underside of that ladder, Miguel. We just found a bunch of these babies crawling around underneath this table and chair."

Miguel stood and, with one hand, turned the ladder over. Three of the creatures had made their way to the underside of the first rung. Stepping over to where the caterpillars were penned in, he banged it firmly on the floor, trying to dislodge them. In doing so, his coffee cup shook, causing a portion of its contents to slosh over the side and hit the floor in the midst of the insect horde.

Rick said, "Hey! Watch your coffee, Miguel. We don't want a repeat of Friday's mess."

Miguel flushed. "If Juanita hadn't . . ."

Rick interrupted. "Just be careful you don't spill any more coffee."

Miguel felt his anger welling up. He hated Rick Ballinger. Taking a deep breath to calm himself, Miguel repositioned his stepladder and sat down. Rather than say something he might be sorry for, he took a sip and gave the steaming brew a chance to alleviate his frustration.

Sarah dialed the extension to her own lab and waited for someone to answer. After only a brief moment, she said, "Becky. It's Sarah. What have you got for me?"

The three men waited and watched as Sarah nodded her head and mumbled an occasional, "Uh-huh." Their attention was momentarily diverted when the door to the lab opened and Ashley and Juanita walked in carrying a bunch of empty cartons. Starting to say something about the difficulty of completing their mission, Ashley was quickly shushed by Doug holding a finger to his lips.

"What's going on?" whispered Ashley.

Rick answered. "Sarah is trying to find out whether the caterpillars are poisonous or not."

After a short interval, Sarah said, "Okay. Call me back as soon as you get those results." Turning to face her small audience, Sarah said, "Definitely poisonous. It's a vesicular toxin that seems to be fairly potent. They're running some tests right now to determine the exact level of toxicity. Kim said she should have some definitive answers by noontime."

Juanita dropped one of the cartons she was holding. "Poisonous?" she asked, tremulously. Extending her left hand so that everyone could see it, she said, "I think I got bit by one of them. How poisonous are they?"

Sarah, Rick and Doug came closer to inspect the bite.

"My hand is starting to swell," complained Juanita. "What's going to happen?"

Sarah took Juanita's hand and examined it. Noting the swelling and the redness, she asked, "Are you experiencing any other symptoms?"

"I get a sharp pain sometimes. It shoots up into my wrist. It feels like a really, really bad bee sting."

"Anything else?" asked Sarah.

"No."

Ashley interjected. "Tell 'em about your headache, Juanita."

Juanita hesitated. "Well," she said reluctantly, "I've got this killer headache right behind my ears. But, I get them sometimes. So, I'm not sure this is from the caterpillar bite."

Sarah let go of Juanita's hand. "Is this headache the same kind you always get?"

"Not exactly," answered Juanita. "Usually I get, like, migraines. Y'know, right behind my eyes. This one is different."

Putting a gentle hand on Juanita's shoulder, Doug said, "I don't think we should take any chances. We need to get you over to the hospital."

"I'll take her," offered Ashley.

"All right," said Sarah.

Rick spoke up. "Wait a minute. I'm going to need Ashley here. Let's send someone else with Juanita."

Darlene had returned from her break and was standing in the doorway. "I'll take her," she offered. "I don't mind."

Rick nodded his approval. "Yes," he said. "That'll work."

"Okay," agreed Sarah. "Once you've spoken to a doctor, have him call me. Let him know that I'm the entomologist and that I'll fax him the toxicology report as soon as I have it."

Shortly after Juanita and Darlene had left for the hospital, the other technicians returned from their break. Sarah set them to work rounding up the rest of the caterpillars. Turning to Rick, Sarah said, "I'm going to place a call to Jake Kaminski."

"Who's Jake Kaminski?" asked Doug.

Sarah explained that she had worked with Kaminski in choosing the two species of insects for the Kudzu Project.

"If you ever meet him," said Rick, "remember to refer to him as 'Your Eminence.'"

"Really," stated Doug, raising an eyebrow.

"He's like the 'Obi-wan Kenobi' of entomology," said Rick. "And even though the whole world has to pay homage to the great Jacobus Kaminski, Sarah here, gets to call him 'Jake.'"

Sarah smirked at Rick's playful sarcasm. "Professor Kaminski is also the one who suggested that I use the saddleback caterpillar for one of my other projects. There isn't anybody on this planet who knows these bugs better than him."

"Okay," said Doug. "I'm impressed. Give him a call."

While Sarah called her own lab in order to get Kaminski's number, Ashley grabbed two of the empty cartons and carried them to a spot close to where Miguel had been sitting. Something caught her attention. She froze. "What the hell . . . !" she cried.

Everyone spun around to look. A few feet from where Ashley stood was a foot-high mound of undulating caterpillars. Thousands of the thorned creatures were rushing toward the mushrooming pile of insects. Its base, already more than three feet across, continued to expand as the miniature mountain grew in height.

Sarah and Rick rushed over to examine the phenomenon. Although Doug moved forward for a better view, he positioned himself a safe distance away. The technician, Britney, who stood at Doug's side, was unaware that she was holding a portion of his shirt sleeve. Nancy and Lynn both spotted the living, growing pile and headed for the exit.

"Damn!" exclaimed Miguel, fascinated by the sight.

Ashley spoke with a soft tremor. "Do caterpillars usually do things like this?"

Sarah answered. "I've never seen anything quite like it."

Doug asked, "Could this be their mating ritual? Is this what they've been doing to multiply so fast?"

Before the question could be answered, Rick spoke up. "Hey, Miguel!" he called. "Isn't that the spot where you just spilled your coffee?"

Miguel looked up. "What?"

"Your coffee," repeated Rick. "You spilled your coffee when you were banging that little ladder on the floor."

"No, man," protested Miguel. "I didn't spill no coffee."

"Yes you did," said Rick, pointing his finger at the mound. "I saw some of it spill onto the floor. Right there. Right there where the caterpillars are massing."

CHAPTER THIRTY-THREE

CALIFORNIA

Witnesses said that the Camaro was doing better than eighty miles per hour when the right, front tire came off its rim. Their statements told of how the car fishtailed wildly before crossing the median strip and careening headlong into the oncoming westbound lanes. When an approaching Camry swerved to avoid the inevitable head-on collision, all hell broke loose. It looked as though the damage would be confined to the first eight vehicles until the driver of a Wal-Mart tractor-trailer was forced to cut his wheel sharply. It flipped over and skidded down the highway like a scythe in tall grass. Thirteen additional cars either spun out of control, accordioned under the impact of the big truck, or burst into flames. Traffic came to a standstill.

Two miles from the accident's epicenter, Darlene and Juanita had been sitting at a dead stop for the last twenty minutes. Neither knew the reason for the holdup, nor how much longer it might be before traffic would start to move again.

"This is crazy," said Darlene. "We could be here all afternoon."

"Oh, God. I hope not," said Juanita, sounding a little desperate.

Darlene glanced at her passenger. Juanita had reclined her seat and was sitting slumped way down. With both hands tucked underneath her sweater, she looked as though she were comforting an upset stomach. Her eyebrows were corkscrewed with the pressure of keeping her eyes closed. Darlene asked, "Are you going to be all right?"

Juanita was breathing through her mouth. Struggling, she asked, "Could you turn up the A.C.? I need some air on my face."

Darlene fumbled with the controls until a blast of cool air came into the vehicle. "Is that better," She asked, repositioning the vents.

"Yeah, I guess," said Juanita, closing her eyes. Taking a ragged breath, she added, "I'm just not feeling good. I feel like I'm going to be sick."

Noting a flushed look of fever on Juanita's face, Darlene reached over to touch her companion's forehead. Not expecting Darlene's touch, Juanita jumped spastically at the contact.

Darlene drew back. "Oh my gosh, I'm sorry Juanita. I didn't mean . . . . I just wanted to . . . ." Darlene stopped in mid-sentence.

Juanita had removed her left hand from under her sweater. The palm and fingers were swollen to twice their size and looked more like a caricature of a clown's hand. Attempting to brush her hair off the glaze of perspiration, Juanita moved her hand to the left side of her face. As she swept her hair back, Darlene gasped at the sight of blood streaming from Juanita's left ear.

"Oh, my God!" said Darlene, trying to hold down a welling feeling of panic. "You're bleeding!"

Juanita didn't respond. Letting her arm fall to her side, she, once again, squeezed her eyes shut.

Concerned with the bleeding, Darlene fumbled in her purse for a tissue. As she reached to dab at the bloody ear, she froze in alarm. Juanita, arching her back in pain, emitted a deep guttural growl.

"Juanita? Juanita, what's wrong?"

Juanita's only response was a convulsive reaction that grew more contorted with each second. Frightened, Darlene drew back. "Juanita! Juanita, please . . . !"

Darlene screamed as Juanita writhed in pain and threw herself back into the seat. The throaty rasping intensified, sounding as though an obstruction was choking her. Knowing that help was needed, Darlene tried to open the car door. However, the doors were locked and, in her frantic state, she was unable to open them. She rolled down the window and hollered, "Help! Help, please! My friend needs help!" Spinning back to look at her passenger, Darlene saw a layer of foamy spittle oozing from Juanita's mouth and covering her lower lip and chin. Darlene screamed again.

*   *   *

Doug spoke softly. "Could coffee somehow be connected to all of this?"

No one answered.

Doug persisted. "I mean, you said something about coffee being splashed on the original GMO's last Friday, right? Now, coffee gets spilled again, and just look," said Doug, pointing at the mass of insects. "That damn mound of bugs is more than two feet high and growing! It sure looks to me as though the damn things are trying to get at the coffee spill."

Ashley spoke up and almost spat her words. "You're a walking disaster, Miguel! If it weren't for your incompetence . . ."

"Get off my case, woman!" retorted Miguel. "Just get off my case!"

"Cut it out!" shouted Rick. "That's enough out of both of you. We've got plenty to worry about without the two of you clawing at each other."

Sarah made a timely suggestion. "Miguel, please sweep that mound of caterpillars into one of those big cartons over there. It shouldn't take more than one to hold them all."

"And when you're done," added Rick, "clean up that coffee spill."

Sarah also suggested that the remnants of the spill be covered with a thin layer of petroleum jelly.

After putting Ashley to work at the opposite end of the laboratory, Rick turned to Sarah and said, "Now would be a good time to call Professor Kaminski."

Sarah dialed the number. It wasn't long before the connection was made.

"Sarah Levine!" boomed Jacobus Kaminski. "How nice to hear from you again."

"It's good to talk to you again, Jake, although I wish it were under better circumstances."

"Really? What seems to be the problem?"

"I'm sure you recall our last conversation," began Sarah, "when we discussed several species of insect that would . . . ."

"Yes, of course," interrupted Kaminski. "The saddleback, the paravulgarus, and the *Elaphidion skiles*."

"Exactly," said Sarah. "But right now, we're in the middle of a mysterious turn of events, and I could use your input."

"I love a mystery," said Kaminski. "Give me the details."

Sarah gave a brief description of the gene-splicing operation. She ended by saying, "The idea was to create a GMO that would eat the root of the kudzu vine without harming the surrounding environment. We thought that we had it under control."

Kaminski interjected. "Then, something happened. Something unexpected, right?"

"Right. We came in this morning to find the laboratory overrun with caterpillars. Literally, tens of thousands of them. And it all happened in less than three days!"

"Someone left a window open," offered Kaminski.

"We thought of that but dismissed it," replied Sarah. "It's an interior room without windows."

"Then, it must have been Mr. Smythe, the butler, in the library, with a steak knife."

Momentarily confused, Sarah was silent.

"A little levity," explained Kaminski. "It's just a line from a board game called, *Clue*. Anyway, give me some more details."

After Sarah spoke about the successful creation of six genetically manufactured organisms, she concluded with a description of the caterpillar.

"The coloration and spines on the tail," noted Kaminski, "seem remarkably like the saddleback. Was the saddleback part of the gene-splicing process?"

"No. However, I should tell you this. One night last week while I was inspecting the cages, I found one of the saddleback caterpillars inside the cage with the paravulgarus. I have no idea how it might have . . ."

Kaminski interrupted. "That must be it," he said. Somehow the DNA of the two species got mixed together, intertwined, and the result is this new species of caterpillar that has now invaded your laboratory. Is there any similarity to the original skiles or the paravulgarus?"

"None to the Skiles beetle, but this new caterpillar does have the paravulgarus's gray underbelly and the bright red dot on the top of its head."

"See? There you go," stated Kaminski. "Mystery solved."

Sarah hesitated before saying, "Well, the real puzzle is how they could have achieved such numbers. Procreating? Cloning? How did they manage to multiply so quickly?"

"I have no idea, Sarah. You'll need to give me more information. What do you and your colleagues think might have happened?"

"To be honest with you, Jake, we're scratching our heads on this one." Sarah hesitated a moment before adding, "Although, there has been one strange occurrence."

"Yes? What was it?"

"A short while ago, someone spilled some coffee on the floor. Within minutes, thousands of the caterpillars had formed a huge mound over the area. I've never seen anything like it."

"Coffee?" questioned Kaminski. "You said, coffee?"

"Yes," confirmed Sarah. "Coffee. And last Friday, there was a similar accident. Some coffee was splashed onto the original six GMO's."

Sarah could barely hear the Professor as he mumbled the single word, 'coffee.' She waited. Finally, she asked, "Jake? Are you still there?"

"Puerarin!" stated Kaminski with urgency.

"What?"

"Puerarin. It's the common bond that links coffee and kudzu. And, I suspect it's the catalyst that's causing your problem."

"Puerarin," repeated Sarah. "I've never even heard of it. What is it?"

Kaminski explained. "It all started around the mid-eighties when a couple of scientists from Rutgers University toyed with a variety of solutions for drunkenness and hangovers. They did experiments with various chemicals, food combinations, and oxygen therapy. Then, they heard about an old Chinese herbal remedy, a tea concocted by boiling the leaves of several different plants, including the leaves and roots of the kudzu."

Sarah stood. "Kudzu?" she asked.

"Yes," confirmed Kaminski. "After months of research, the two scientists were able to isolate a single chemical, a pure chemical, mind you, called puerarin. When they had finished eliminating all the other ingredients from this mystical Chinese tea, they discovered that it was the puerarin that worked to alleviate hangovers."

"All that is pretty interesting, Jake, but what's the connection to coffee?"

"Oh, right," said Kaminski, caught up in the telling of his tale. "Well you see, they tried to make a comparison between the effectiveness of the Chinese tea and coffee. Specifically, caffeine and puerarin. What they found was very exciting."

"You have me on the edge of my chair," said Sarah.

"When they probed into the chemical composition of coffee, they found puerarin!"

"Really?"

"Yes," said Kaminski, sounding as though he were the one responsible for the find. "Coffee contained puerarin. Just like that kudzu tea, only more of it."

A moment passed as Sarah frowned. "I fail to see how . . ."

Kaminski cut off her words. "Your new caterpillar, Sarah. It's been manufactured to have an insatiable appetite for the root of the kudzu vine. Think about it. The root system of the kudzu contains only small amounts of puerarin. Now, all of a sudden, you went and introduce something new. Coffee. All well and good, except . . . , that particular food source contains huge quantities of puerarin. Consequently, they're drawn to it like bees to honey. Get it?"

"I think I get it," said Sarah. "Hold on just a second, Jake. Let me ask Rick a question. Sarah turned to her fiancé. "What kind of nutrients were you feeding the new GMO's ?"

"Well," said Rick thinking back to the previous Friday, "Ashley and I made a blend of carbohydrates. Mostly shredded potatoes, a little ground up kudzu root, and a teaspoon of sugar."

Sarah spoke back into the phone. "Did you hear that, Jake?"

"Yes. Potatoes and a little kudzu root. Lots of starch but very little puerarin."

Sarah needed to sequence the events in her mind before they made sense. She tested her understanding by saying, "So, since the new organisms were starved for puerarin, they would have attacked anything that contained it, right?"

"Right," concurred Kaminski. "Including something as innocuous as spilled coffee."

Immersed in Kaminski's explanation, Sarah finally asked, "Are you suggesting that somehow the high dose of puerarin is acting as a catalyst for their reproduction?"

"It's definitely acting as a catalyst," answered Kaminski. "But, the sheer number of insects that you're talking about is probably due to good old-fashioned fornication."

Sarah made a face that revealed a quandary. She did not want to insult a man of Kaminski's stature, but she had to speak her mind. "With all due respect, Jake, let's not forget that these bugs are still larval caterpillars. They shouldn't be able to reproduce until they've grown to adulthood."

Kaminski chuckled. "Under normal circumstances, Sarah, you would be correct. But in this case, you're still thinking of them as larvae because that's the way they were when you started this project. However, you folks have created a brand new species. A species that only *looks* like a larval caterpillar. Based on all you've told me, I'd venture to say that it is, in fact, an adult insect, fully capable of reproducing hundreds of thousands of offspring."

There were several moments of silence before Sarah said, "Now, what?"

"Keep them contained," advised Kaminski. "If you let them out, they'll march to every supermarket in America, head straight for the coffee aisle, and ravage the shelves."

Before disconnecting, Kaminski said, "I'm serious about not letting them out, Sarah. Remember what happened to the gypsy moth and the Africanized bee."

Replacing the phone in its cradle, Sarah turned to Rick and Doug. Everyone else in the lab stopped working, anxious to hear what Sarah had to say. "It seems as though our little caterpillars enjoy the taste of coffee."

Doug was first to ask a question. "I heard you mention the chemical, puerarin. Is that the culprit?"

Sarah nodded. "Yes. It's a substance that's common in both coffee and kudzu."

Before Doug could ask a follow-up question, Sarah added, "You know how coffee is sometimes offered to help someone overcome a hangover? Well, that's because people thought that caffeine was the answer. But, researchers now think that it's the puerarin that makes the difference. It turns out, the Chinese have been using puerarin as a cure for hangovers for centuries."

Rick glanced at Miguel before turning back to Sarah. "You mean that the coffee that was splashed onto the GMO's on Friday was the catalyst for all this?" he said, sweeping his hand around the room.

"Partially. The coffee worked to stimulate the growth of the new organisms."

"How so?" asked Rick.

"You fed them a diet of starch, but very little puerarin. So, when the coffee spilled on them, it functioned like an instantaneous injection of high energy. A food source that boosted their metabolism a thousand-fold."

"Okay," said Rick. "That explains their size. But what about their numbers? What did Jake have to say about that?"

"The coffee acted like a massive dose of steroids mixed with Viagra. Not only was their circulation increased, but it also stimulated their sex drive."

Doug said, "I didn't know that caterpillars had a sex drive."

"Neither did I," said Sarah. "So, I posed that same question to Jake. Even though his answer caught me off guard, I realized that it made perfect sense. He said that these bugs are not caterpillars. They just look like caterpillars. In fact, they're a brand new species which have already reached adulthood. That's why they're able to reproduce so rapidly."

Once again, Rick flashed a stern look at Miguel. "And the proof of the pudding is the coffee that Miguel just spilled on the floor. The caterpillars were drawn to it because of the puerarin."

"It seems so," said Sarah. "Kaminski made a joke when he said, if they get out of the lab, they'll ravage the coffee aisle of every supermarket in America. But, I'm not sure that's so far from the truth."

The phone rang. Rick answered, announcing, "Forum Lab." A few seconds later, he said, "Hold on. She's right here." Handing the phone to Sarah, he said, "It's Kim."

Sarah's side of the conversation consisted mainly of 'Uh-huh,' 'I see,' and 'No kidding.' The phone call lasted several minutes until Sarah gave final instructions. "As soon as we hear from Darlene and Juanita, I'll want you to fax that toxicity report to the hospital."

After hanging up, Sarah could see the anxious looks on the faces of Rick, Doug and the rest of the crew. "Well," she began, "the news is not very good. Kim says the toxin has a matrix she's never seen before. She suspects that, after a person comes in contact with the poison, it could present itself more like a hemorrhagic toxin than like a vesicular one."

"What does that mean?" asked Rick.

Doug jumped in. "I'll tell you what it means," he said. "It means that we quarantine this room and send everyone home. I'm not taking any chances. I'm calling in an exterminator and have the lab fumigated and sterilized. That's it!"

"Doug," said Sarah. "There are some things we need to discuss."

"No problem, Sarah. We can discuss anything you'd like, but first . . . ." Preparing to address Ashley, Miguel, and the rest of the Forum Lab technicians, Doug suddenly realized that they were anxiously awaiting his decree. "I want all of you to go home," he said. "I'll see to it that each of you gets paid for the entire day. When you report for work tomorrow, go directly to the cafeteria. Rick will be there to let you know what's happening."

For a moment, no one moved.

"See you tomorrow," said Doug with a wave.

No one said good-bye. They all just left.

CHAPTER THIRTY-FOUR

CALIFORNIA

"What are you doing home so early?" said Maria as Miguel walked into the bedroom surprising her. "You feeling okay?"

"Yeah. I'm okay."

"So, why you home so early? You didn't quit, did ya?"

"Nah," stated Miguel. "They sent all of us home."

Maria held a black plastic tube in her left hand and a mascara brush in her right. Except for a brassiere that was sheer and white and barely large enough to be worthwhile, she was totally naked. "Really?" she said, turning back to the mirror and leaning in close to brush her eyelashes. "What happened?"

Miguel sat on the edge of the bed and watched as Maria resumed the process of applying her makeup. Perhaps, it was her nakedness that aroused him, although he had seen her without any clothing countless times. Perhaps, it was the odd time of day, the unusual circumstances of his being home so early, that prompted the flush of desire. More than likely, it was Maria's pose, facing away and bent at the waist, along with the provocative view of her heart-shaped buttocks that caused the erotic stirrings in Miguel. "C'mon over here, baby," said Miguel, his voice husky with lust.

"I can't be comin' over there to you, Miguel," protested Maria. "I'm gonna be late. Tell me why you're home so early."

Miguel took a deep breath and began untying his sneakers. "The lab somehow got full of bugs. So, they sent us all home."

"Bugs?" asked Maria. "What kind of bugs?"

Intending to change into shorts, Miguel had taken off his pants. On the way to the closet, he stopped and stood behind Maria. Placing both his hands on her hips, he pushed against her, allowing her to feel his excitement. "C'mon, baby," he coaxed. "C'mon over to the bed."

Maria spun around. "Stop it, Miguel," she scolded. "I'm gonna be late, and you're gonna mess me up. Go put on your shorts and tell me about the bugs."

Miguel sighed. He knew that Maria had an appointment to see a client. Her entertaining out-of-town guests was beginning to annoy him but, as per their agreement, he could not complain. "What time you coming home?" he asked.

"I don't know, baby. Y'know . . . it depends. Maybe nine. Maybe midnight." Seeing a dour look at the corner of Miguel's mouth, Maria switched to a new topic. "But I'll tell you what, *mi querido*," she said sensually, reaching her hand into his jockey shorts. "No matter what time I get in, I'll wake you up and give you the ride of your life."

Difficult as it was, Miguel sat back on the bed.

Stepping into her skirt, Maria said, "Now, tell me about these bugs. Where'd they come from? Someone leave a window open?"

Maria listened as Miguel told her the tale of the genetically manufactured insects. She had always been fascinated with her boyfriend's job, and often, asked questions that Miguel could not answer.

Although Maria was soon dressed and ready to leave for her appointment, she was reluctant to do so. When Miguel spoke of the hordes of insects that blanketed Forum Lab, Maria asked some pointed questions about how such a thing could have happened. Miguel went into considerable detail, even talking about how something as simple as a spilled cup of coffee could have been the catalyst for the strange event.

"Really?" asked Maria. "A spilled cup of coffee was the cause of all that? How could that be?"

Miguel explained. "All the big-shots were huddled together, but they were stumped. Especially Rick Ballinger, that little prick. He didn't know what to do. He was running around, squealing like a little girl. Asshole! He let his girlfriend, Sarah, make all the decisions. She's pretty smart. Anyways, she was talking on the phone to some other big-shot bug-dude, and it turns out, there's something in coffee, a chemical or something, that makes these caterpillars go ape-shit."

"Jeez!" exclaimed Maria, amazed at how weird it all sounded. "Coffee, huh?"

"Yeah," concurred Miguel. "They gotta have it. Like crack to a junkie. The last thing Sarah said to us before we left is that we should all be very careful with the little suckers. They'll eat anything to do with coffee. Coffee beans, coffee grounds . . . . even coffee ice cream, I guess."

*   *   *

Bruce Kreitzer's trip to California was a reprieve. Just getting away from the pressure cooker atmosphere in Chicago was a blessing in itself. Life under the gun of Porky Pignatano had become unbearable. Kreitzer was well aware that his problems with the Mafia loan-sharking machine weren't going to go away. As a matter of fact, the longer he ignored the debt, the deeper his troubles became. Interest on his loan was mounting at a rate that was threatening to strangle him. It wouldn't be long before Pignatano's gang of enforcers found him and . . .

Kreitzer was afraid. Having seen Porky's number one collector, the gargantuan creature, Bruno Mordello, Kreitzer had nightmares of the man breaking down his door and looming over him with his gorilla-like bulk and his meat-cleaver hands.

Besides all of that, Kreitzer's uncle and boss, Josef Ubermann, created a different kind of fear. Kreitzer knew that it was going to be impossible to keep his job and continue to avoid his uncle. The trip to California only offered a brief respite in which Kreitzer was able to catch his breath.

Despite attending the seminars sponsored by the SEC and the Chicago Board of Trade, Kreitzer found it difficult to concentrate. Instead, his mind wandered back to Chicago and to the last series of commands issued by Ubermann; specifically, his call to come up with a plan to save the company. Compounding the pressure, was Ubermann's intolerable decision to cut Kreitzer's salary.

Another segment of Kreitzer's West Coast stay had to do with the man's prurient interests. Having the names and numbers of three California based prostitutes, gave Kreitzer the opportunity to fulfill his sexual fantasies. There was Lily, an enormously buxom beauty with a sweet, southern drawl. The woman had a capacity for contorting different parts of her body, and had shown Kreitzer a few clever tricks that she could do with her breasts. The second prostitute was an amazingly statuesque model that went by the name of Bunny. With her blonde hair piled on top of a six-foot, four-inch frame, the athletic woman looked like an artistic composite of beautiful amazons. In the past, she would arrive at Kreitzer's hotel room with a small, dark black suitcase. Although Bunny was demanding and forceful, Kreitzer found her domination to be irresistible. After applying her various restraints, including spiked cuffs and leather strappings, it wasn't long before Kreitzer was lost in a delirium of convulsive pain and orgasmic pleasure.

However, for Kreitzer, it was the third prostitute who was indelibly imprinted in his mind. Maria was, by far, the youngest of the three and had what Kreitzer considered to be a perfect body. More than that, it was the woman's ability to make him feel as though he were the only man in her life. After two failed attempts to coordinate their schedules, Kreitzer arranged to skip his Monday afternoon seminar and meet in his hotel room at three o'clock.

Feeling as giddy as a schoolboy, Kreitzer bounded into the lobby of the Hilton and strode to the elevators. A voice from the front desk caught his attention. "Mr. Kreitzer!" shouted the manager. "Mr. Kreitzer, please."

Bruce Kreitzer turned. "What?"

"I have some messages for you."

Kreitzer stood his ground. With Maria scheduled to arrive shortly, his only thoughts were of her.

The desk clerk held up two slips of paper and said, "I think these messages are important."

Kreitzer sighed and walked to the desk. Reading the notes, he saw that, not only were both from Josef Ubermann, but that one had the word "urgent," written in bold and underlined. Kreitzer felt a wave of frustration as he rode up the elevator. The anticipation of Maria, with her sweet disposition and her teenage allure, had filled his thoughts to the exclusion of everything else. In his room, he sat on the bed and contemplated returning his uncle's call. Kreitzer checked his watch, calculating the time difference between Los Angeles and Chicago. Even though he figured that the time was acceptable, Kreitzer continued to have second thoughts. The word, "urgent," rang out like an alarm, making him wonder what other red flags might be waving. Maybe, the old man wanted to cut Kreitzer's salary even more. Maybe, Pignatano had been calling the office and making threats. More than likely, Ubermann just wanted to know if Kreitzer had come up with an idea to solve the company's financial woes.

A soft knock at the door broke his concentration. Crossing the room, Kreitzer opened the door to see Maria standing there. He held his breath as he took in her youthful beauty. She was wearing a white tailored jacket over a simple mint green blouse. A short, white skirt, smartly pleated, along with three-inch white heels, emphasized her shapely legs. Quarter-size, mint green earrings and a matching necklace completed her outfit.

The moment of silence was broken when Maria exhaled and, radiating the longing of a woman who had finally found her missing lover, whispered, "God, I missed you."

CHAPTER THIRTY-FIVE

CALIFORNIA

"Are you serious?" asked Bruce Kreitzer. "The place was really full of caterpillars?"

Maria nodded her head excitedly. "Yeah. Still is," she said. "I mean it. He said there were hundreds of thousands of them. Nobody couldn't walk without stepping on them because the floor was completely covered."

Kreitzer looked at Maria with skepticism. The whole thing sounded like a tall tale from some guy who was trying hard to impress her.

Maria sat naked and cross-legged on the sheet-rumpled bed. Her olive skin looked as though she spent all of her time at the beach when, in fact, it was due to her Latin heritage. Sitting in an upholstered chair in the corner, Kreitzer stared at Maria. Following the lines of her body down to her pedicured toes, he was momentarily fascinated by the contrasting whiteness of the bottoms of her feet. "Somebody leave a window open in the lab?" he asked distractedly.

"I asked the same questions," said Maria proudly. "But, there aren't any windows in that lab."

"So, how do you explain it?"

Maria slipped off the bed and walked to the large vanity mirror. Running her fingers through her hair, she said, "The place where he works is a scientific laboratory. They're always doing some kind of thing with bugs. My friend thinks that something went wrong with one of the experiments."

"Do you know the name of the place where he works?"

When Maria had originally related the story, she deliberately neglected to explain the relationship she had with Miguel Ortiz. Instead, she simply referred to him as, a friend. "Yeah," she said. "It's called Envirogen. It's over in Pasadena. He's been working there a couple of years."

Kreitzer was getting hungry. Two hours of sex prompted him to suggest that they get dressed and go out for dinner. He stood and padded his way to the bathroom. Flushing the toilet, he said, "Caterpillars up the ying-yang, eh?" He turned on the shower, adjusting the temperature of the water before adding, "It all sounds pretty weird if you ask me."

Maria raised her voice so as to be heard over the sound of the running water. "Y'know what's really weird?"

"What?"

"That the little suckers love coffee."

"Love coffee?" asked Kreitzer, lathering his hair with shampoo. "Who loves coffee?"

Maria giggled because it sounded as though Bruce was talking through a mouthful of bubbles. "The caterpillars, silly," she replied. "The caterpillars go crazy over coffee." Maria followed that statement by giving an account of how her friend and his co-workers had discovered that the caterpillars were drawn to coffee.

Kreitzer had toweled off, blow-dried his hair and was sitting naked on the edge of the bed. He was unfolding a pair of navy dress socks when Maria said, "My friend told me that one of the big-shot scientists said they should make sure that none of the caterpillars get out of the lab, or else they'll eat all the coffee they see. Doesn't that sound creepy?"

Kreitzer stopped what he was doing. He sat there, stone-still and deep in thought.

"What?" asked Maria. "What are you thinking?"

"What's your friend's name?"

Maria hesitated. "Uh . . . . Miguel."

"Well, I'd like to talk to Miguel. Do you think you can arrange that?"

Maria had a fleeting thought that Bruce might be harboring some juvenile jealousy but quickly dismissed it. "I guess," she shrugged.

"Can you do it right now?" he asked.

"You mean, you want to talk to him now? Tonight?"

"Yeah," said Kreitzer. "It's important. And, if it is what I think it is," he said cryptically, "I can really make it worth his while."

* * *

"Hardball with Chris Matthews" was a taped delay show and viewed by audiences in the Los Angeles area at 7:30 p.m. Stealing a moment from writing the final paragraph of her upcoming article, Hannah Carpenter glanced at her watch. It was already three minutes past show time. Hannah clicked the save button on her laptop and turned on the television. Chris Matthews was introducing the guests for the first half of his show. The topic was the Middle East and his two panelists were the Israeli Assistant Ambassador to the United Nations, and a spokesman for Hammas, the fundamentalist group that had splintered from the PLO. Although it promised to be an emotionally charged spitting contest, Hannah was waiting for the second segment, a discussion on the pros and cons of genetic engineering. One of Matthews' four panelists was slated to be Brother Timothy Goodman. Since Hannah had another interview scheduled with the Preacher for 4:30 the following day, she didn't want to miss the second half of this show.

The first half proved to be somewhat disappointing until it neared the end of its allotted time. The Palestinian had an accent that was so thick, it all but made him unintelligible. At one point, after a steady barrage of accusations, he became flustered and referred to himself as a terrorist rather than a freedom fighter. His own blunder made him angry and he blamed the Israeli for a series of sins that became louder and more unbelievable as his list went on. Among other things, he charged the Jews with cutting the hearts out of Palestinian babies so that they could be eaten as part of a ritual on High Holy Days.

After the calming effect of a commercial break, Matthews introduced the guests for the second half of his show. There were four panelists; Dr. Scott Allen, the vice president of genetic research at Genentech Corporation; Dr. Mark Evans, a molecular biologist and information officer for the National Institutes of Health; Lee Erickson, Republican Senator who chaired the Committee for Ethics in Science; and Brother Timothy Goodman, staunch opponent of the new science.

"Let me begin," said Matthews, "by asking Senator Erickson just how difficult is it for your committee to come up with a consensus on the ethics of genetic engineering?"

Senator Erickson squared his shoulders and said, "Chris, I'm proud to say that I am chairman of one of the few committees in Washington that cooperates on a bipartisan level. We speak with one voice. Just last week . . ."

Matthews interrupted. "Bipartisan? I seem to remember a cat fight between Senators John McCain and Hillary Rodham Clinton on the issue of stem-cell research. What do you mean, 'one voice?'"

"Well," replied the Senator, "we're bound to have some disagreements. After all, ethical standards are a matter of opinion. When it comes to . . ."

Matthews chopped off the Senator's sentence. "Isn't there a move on the floor of the Senate to have some of your committee members removed?"

"Oh, I think you're exaggerating the situation, Chris. My understanding . . ."

"Last week," interposed Matthews, "Senator Ted Kennedy told me that there was too much infighting on your committee for it to be effective. How do you answer that charge?"

Senator Erickson tried his best to answer the questions. It was a mistake. He would have been better off discussing only the goals of his committee.

For his part, Chris Matthews was just playing hardball. In his rapid fire style of questioning, he went from panelist to panelist, drawing out the most controversial aspects of genetics. Occasionally, when he sensed a rift among the guests, he would shut up and allow the combatants to bang heads. It made for great television.

The format of the program moved the show along quickly. At seven minutes into the discussion, Matthews said, "Brother Timothy, *Time Magazine* recently referred to you as 'America's conscience emanating from the pulpit,' and you, in turn, have voiced your opposition to genetic engineering. But, how can you be against research that can cure diseases like cancer, Alzheimer's and Parkinson's?"

Brother Timothy slowly nodded his head. "No one is against finding the cure to these dreaded diseases. My objection is with the road that scientists have chosen to travel as a means of finding those cures."

"What's the difference?" asked Matthews. "A cure is a cure. Interstate 95 takes you to Boston. So does the Massachusetts Turnpike. Why object to any road as long as it gets you there?"

"It has to do with the cost of traveling that road," said Brother Timothy. "We've been ignoring the warning signs, and now we're about to crash through the guardrail and go over the cliff. We can end up . . ."

Matthews interrupted. "I've listened to your sermons, Brother Timothy, and you seem to be convinced that genetic engineering is the work of the Devil. Why would the Devil be interested in stopping the suffering that comes from these diseases?"

"The Devil will use any means he can to achieve his goals. He'll even use scientists. Look what scientists did when they invented the atomic bomb. That certainly wasn't an act of God. Look what they're doing to our Earth in the name of science; polluted water, smog-laden cities, acid rain. The Devil is snickering at the havoc he's created. Worse things will . . ."

"I've got to interrupt you," said Matthews. "This talk about the Devil disappeared in the thirties along with the dust bowl, the depression and divining rods. Nobody believes in the Devil anymore. You're going to have to do better than that."

Brother Timothy said, "You may not believe in the Devil, but facts are facts. Genetic engineering creates far more problems than it solves. When scientists . . ."

"Give me an example," demanded Matthews. "Give me an example of a problem created by genetic engineering."

"AIDS," said Brother Timothy.

"What?" exclaimed Matthews, cynically. "AIDS?"

"Exactly," confirmed Brother Timothy.

A distinct murmur could be heard from the other panelists.

Brother Timothy continued. "In the late sixties, a couple of scientists from Purdue University were working under a grant from the federal government. They were doing genetic research on some volunteers who were getting a stipend of seventy-five dollars a day. That was a lot of money back in the sixties and, because of that, it attracted a number of poor immigrants into the study. Many of these guinea pigs were Haitians, and after the grant money ran out, these poor people were left with AIDS."

"That's preposterous!" shouted Dr. Mark Evans.

"Irresponsible charges!" charged Dr. Scott Allen. "You don't know your history."

Brother Timothy stayed focused on Chris Matthews. "Genetic experimentation has a record of going badly. Look at the work that was done on frogs and resulted in the deaths of millions of the poor creatures. Look at Adolph Hitler's attempt to create a master race. Look at . . ."

The other panelists were all bouncing around, calling out to be recognized by the host. "You can't make a statement like that!" said Dr. Mark Evans. "It's totally unsubstantiated!"

Dr. Scott Allen shouted over the din. "Let him give you the name of the two scientists!"

Senator Erickson called out, "I have a report that confirms this story!"

Chris Matthews raised his voice in order to be heard above the others. "You're saying that AIDS was caused by a genetic experiment gone wrong?"

"Yes," answered Brother Timothy calmly. The scientists were attempting to enhance the immune system through a series of recombinant DNA procedures. Not only did the experiments fail, but they also left our world with an epidemic of biblical proportions. Doesn't it look to you like the work of the Devil?"

The chorus of shouts from the other panelists rose in volume once again. Matthews managed to restore order long enough to recognize Senator Erickson. "You keep saying something about a report, Senator. What kind of report are you talking about?"

"I've recently received a report that confirms what Brother Timothy is saying. It explains the origins of AIDS and puts the blame squarely on the back of the National Science Foundation. I'm proposing an investigation . . ."

The Senator's words were drowned out by the loud bickering of the other guests. For a brief second, the camera zoomed in to catch a close-up of the host, Chris Matthews. He looked into the camera with an expression of wry astonishment.

In the control room, the telephones were ringing off the hook and e-mails began flooding into the studio by the thousands. Brother Timothy's remarks had shaken the viewing audience out of their complacency, and now they were clamoring to add their own yeas and nays. If the producers ever decided to televise "The Best of Hardball," this episode would have been among the top choices.

CHAPTER THIRTY-SIX

CALIFORNIA

It was just after nine p.m. in Pasadena which made it just past eleven o'clock in Chicago. Josef Ubermann answered the telephone with a gruff, "Hello!"

"Uncle Joe?" said Kreitzer, barely recognizing the voice. "This is Bruce."

"Where the hell have you been?" barked Ubermann. "I've been trying to reach you for three days!"

Ignoring his Uncle's tirade, Kreitzer went straight to the purpose of his call. "I've got it, Uncle Joe."

There was a brief pause before Ubermann growled, "What the fuck are you talking about? Are you drunk?"

"No, Uncle Joe," answered Kreitzer. "I'm calling because I've got the answer to the company's cash-flow problem."

Ubermann digested his nephew's words for a long while. Finally, with controlled anger, he said, "Listen to me, you skinny weasel. You skipped out early to L.A. without telling me. You haven't returned any of my phone calls, and I've been threatened by a couple of Mafia hit men who think that I know where you are. So, what you tell me next better be worth listening to, or else I'm going into work tomorrow morning and canceling your corporate credit cards. After that, I'm going to call Porky Pignatano and personally turn you over to the mob. Understand?"

Kreitzer swallowed. "You won't have to do any of that, Uncle Joe. What I've got . . . . it's perfect."

"Let's hear it."

Several hours earlier, Maria had made arrangements for her client, Bruce Kreitzer, to meet with her boyfriend, Miguel Ortiz. For Maria, the prospect of such a meeting had seemed incongruous, and she was becoming more anxious. At first, Miguel balked at the idea, saying that it was late and he didn't feel like driving all over town just to tell a story about some strange bugs. However, when it was suggested that they meet at the *Denny's Restaurant* on Colorado Boulevard, Miguel agreed, knowing that its location was close to home.

Although Miguel was initially wary about Kreitzer's motives, and Kreitzer was dubious about the validity of the coffee-eating caterpillars, it wasn't long before they found common ground. Miguel had been looking for a chance to get back at Rick Ballinger and Ashley Eberhardt, and this client of Maria's was offering Miguel the opportunity for a little payback.

Kreitzer asked Miguel numerous questions and came away impressed with the man's knowledge of genetic engineering. Kreitzer quickly became convinced that these caterpillars were the answer to his prayers. They were small and, therefore, hard to detect. They were lightweight and, therefore, cheap to transport. And, according to Miguel, they were unguarded and, therefore, easy to steal. Moreover, Kreitzer had the prospect of earning an unprecedented amount of cash; enough to free his neck from the oppressive weight of Porky Pignatano's boot.

The two men had struck a deal. Kreitzer offered Miguel a hefty sum of money. In return, Miguel agreed to take Kreitzer to Envirogen's lab and grab one of the cartons that was filled with the genetically manufactured caterpillars.

The three of them returned to the couple's apartment so that Miguel could get his passkey needed to open Envirogen's front door. Before they readied themselves to leave, Kreitzer had asked Maria if he could use the telephone to call Ubermann.

Kreitzer explained to his uncle, "There's a company out here, a biotech company. They've created a brand new species of insect, and guess what?"

"This better be good," said Ubermann, impatiently.

"Oh, it's good, all right. Listen to this. The damn things love coffee!"

"What?" asked Ubermann, incredulously.

"Coffee!" repeated Kreitzer. "The bugs love coffee! They eat it by the ton! Any kind of coffee. Brewed coffee, coffee grounds, coffee beans . . . they eat it all!"

Kreitzer knew by the silence that he had struck a chord with his uncle.

Ubermann's mind was working overtime, digesting the facts and mulling over the possibilities. "What about coffee plants?"

"Coffee plants?" asked Kreitzer, puzzled.

"Yes, you idiot! Coffee plants! The little bushes that the beans grow on. Will the bugs eat those?"

"Yeah," said Kreitzer, a little tentatively. "I guess so."

Exasperated, Ubermann said, "Damn you, Bruce! This is no time to be guessing! I want to be absolutely certain."

"Hold on," said Kreitzer. "I'll ask." He hollered into the kitchen. "Hey, Miguel! Come here. I got a question for you."

While Kreitzer was on the phone, Miguel and Maria had been sitting in the kitchen. She was aware of the plan for the two men to steal a carton of the caterpillars. Maria had expressed her misgivings, saying that Miguel might lose his job if he were caught. Miguel had voiced a different viewpoint. He spoke about the anger and frustration caused by Rick and Ashley. He justified the planned theft with a simple explanation. "They owe me," he said. "All the work I've given them . . ." He hesitated, searching for the right words. "They just owe me," repeated Miguel. "That's all."

Miguel heard his name being called from the bedroom. He stood and walked to the doorway. "What's up?"

Still holding the receiver to his ear, Kreitzer asked Miguel, "Will the bugs eat coffee plants?"

Miguel just stared, seemingly without comprehension.

Kreitzer tried again. "Y'know, the bushes where the beans grow . . . . Will the bugs eat those plants?"

Miguel was trying to recall the events of that day. Finally, he said, "Sarah Levine is the entomologist at Envirogen. She was talking to another big-shot entomologist. They both said there's a chemical in the coffee that the bugs gotta have. They go after it like crazy. She even told us afterward, that the bugs will eat anything that has that chemical in it. So, yeah. They'll eat the coffee plants, too."

Kreitzer resumed talking to Ubermann. "Did you hear that?"

"Yes. Now, listen to me. Here's what I want you to do." Ubermann laid out a rudimentary plan, including the things his nephew needed to do, once he got hold of the bugs.

After disconnecting, Ubermann thought about his own role. It was clear. He simply needed to take all his available cash and buy coffee futures. With his business under pressure because of overdue corporate loans, he had less than a month to pay back fourteen million dollars. Additionally, if he personally borrowed, mortgaged and hocked himself to the hilt, he could get his hands on an extra four million. Diverting all that money would allow him to invest a total of eighteen million dollars in coffee futures. At a margin rate of ninety percent, his eighteen million would buy close to two-hundred million dollars worth of that commodity. After the bugs did their work and devastated the coffee fields, the price of coffee would rise dramatically. At least fifty percent. Maybe even double. Doing some conservative calculations, Ubermann figured that, even after paying off his loans, his profit would still exceed a hundred-forty million dollars!

*　*　*

With room for more than four hundred cars, the parking lot at Envirogen was huge. However, at this time of night, there were only a half dozen vehicles, sitting silent, darkened and close to the building's entrance. Tall mercury-vapor lamps reflected off the glass walls and cast an eerie luminescence over the black-topped field of painted lines. Big block letters, each back-lit to a muted glow-green, stood atop the three-story structure and spelled out the corporate name, ENVIROGEN.

"I thought you said this place would be empty," said Kreitzer, sitting in the passenger seat of Miguel's car.

"Almost empty," answered Miguel. "Everybody goes home between five and six o'clock. These cars belong to the cleaning crew. That's all."

Kreitzer was nervous. It had been a long time since he had deliberately stolen anything. He thought about an incident that had occurred ten years earlier when he had gone into an upscale department store to buy a bathing suit. After entering the dressing room with three garments, he decided to steal the one he liked best. Leaving the swimsuit on under his pants, he walked out of the store wearing the stolen garment. But, tonight was different. The goods he planned on stealing were far more valuable than a bathing suit. Besides, he was in unfamiliar territory and partnered with a relative stranger.

The building looked as imposing as a vault. "You sure this is going to be easy?" asked Kreitzer.

"Piece of cake, man," assured Miguel, as he eased his car into a space near the front door. "We walk in, grab one of the boxes, and walk out."

Kreitzer nodded, trying to convince himself that it would be as easy as Miguel made it sound. Walking towards the double entry doors, Kreitzer glanced furtively in all directions.

"Relax, man," said Miguel. "You're jumping around like a cockroach, and you're making me nervous."

Kreitzer didn't respond. Instead, he took a series of shallow breaths and tried to calm his nerves.

Miguel slipped his I.D./passkey into the door slot. Following an audible click, Miguel entered with Kreitzer only one step behind. They walked through a small reception area before crossing in front of a bank of elevators. A long hallway loomed before them. It was empty. Miguel led the way, passing five doors, each with hand-painted lettering that established their identity. Kreitzer whispered the names as they walked the hall. "Marathon, Olympus, Centurion . . . . What do they all stand for?"

"They don't stand for nothin'," said Miguel in a matching whisper. "They're just names." Twenty paces further, he stopped in front of a door labeled "Forum." "This is it," he said. Checking the empty corridor one more time, Miguel pushed the door open and the two men stepped inside.

All the lights were on just as though it were a workday. Glancing around the room, Miguel saw the telltale signs of the morning's odd event. Cartons were stacked on the big center table, each one sealed with duct tape, while strips of Vaseline-coated plastic, used earlier to corral the caterpillars, lay on the floor. Other than that, everything still looked normal.

"Piece of cake," repeated Miguel. "C'mon with me, but watch out for those plastic strips. They're coated with some slippery shit. So, just walk on the path."

They started toward the center table when the sound of running water froze them in their tracks. Turning to look at the washroom, Miguel wondered if one of the cleaning crew was working inside. Before he could verify the thought, the bathroom door opened and Rick Ballinger stepped out.

There was a moment of awkward silence as the three men stared at each other. Looking back and forth between Miguel and the tall stranger, Rick asked, "Miguel? What are you doing here? It's almost ten o'clock."

The ability to ad lib was not one of Miguel's strong suits. "Um . . . I was just . . . uh . . . I was just showing my friend all the bugs we found today."

Rick shook his head from side to side. "That isn't such a good idea, Miguel. You and your friend had better go."

Kreitzer took over. "Miguel was telling me about what happened here," he said. "I just wanted to check it out for myself."

Rick narrowed his gaze. The tall man didn't look like someone who would have been Miguel's friend. He was dressed too well and didn't sound like one of the Mexican's neighborhood chums. "Are you a reporter or something?"

Kreitzer hesitated. "Yeah," he said. "I'm a reporter. And this sounds like a weird story. I mean, invasion of the caterpillars, and . . ."

Rick interrupted. "Well, this is no way to get your story," he admonished. "And, late at night is no time to be sneaking around my laboratory. If you want, you can call me in the morning and make an appointment to speak with Dr. Matsushita and myself. But this sort of . . ."

Miguel turned and stepped up to the stainless steel table. Snuffling a grunt of impatience, he boldly grabbed one of the cartons and spun to face Rick. "We ain't bothering you," he said.

Rick moved to block his path. "What do you think you're doing?" he asked, pointing to the carton. "You can't go anywhere with that!"

Miguel felt anger welling up inside. Rick Ballinger represented an authority which Miguel found repressive and suffocating. Impertinently, he said, "Who's gonna stop me? You, you little pussy? You and that Ashley bitch?"

The words were shocking. Pulling up short, Rick felt his heart begin to pound. "You know something, Miguel. You're coming close to losing your job."

Miguel became enraged. "You gonna fire me? You gonna give me my walking papers? Huh?"

Rick didn't respond.

"Eat me, *cabrón*!" spat Miguel and pushed forward, holding the carton in front of him.

Unwilling to allow the situation to deteriorate any further, Rick reached to take the carton. Kreitzer interceded, lunging forward and grabbing Rick's wrist. The action was unexpected. Trying to pull free, Rick inadvertently elbowed Kreitzer in the neck. The blow provoked Kreitzer, and a scuffle ensued. He stepped behind Rick and, using his height and longer reach, pinned Rick's arms behind him.

"Hey!" bellowed Rick. "What are you doing?"

Miguel sprang into action. Dropping the box of caterpillars, he leaned into Rick's face. "What are you going to do now, you little shit!" hissed Miguel.

Despite being locked in Kreitzer's grip, Rick managed to glower at his technician and say, "You're fired, Miguel! You don't work here anymore! Get out!"

Miguel's nostrils flared as he swung a roundhouse and felt his fist connect with the side of Rick's cheek. The blow opened a jagged gash and blood began flowing freely down his face. Even though Rick slumped in Kreitzer's grasp, the tall man didn't let go. Miguel leaned in just as Rick, in a burst of defensive energy, flailed out with his leg. Miguel doubled over in pain, as the kick caught him squarely in the groin. Kreitzer lost his hold, enabling Rick to wriggle free. Before Rick could turn to face the tall stranger, Kreitzer fired off a karate-chop. The blow made Rick shudder and fall to the floor. His moan became a cry of pain, which quickly turned into a wail.

Miguel struggled to his knees and called out, "Shut him up! Shut him up before someone hears!"

Kreitzer looked around. He didn't see anything that could be used as a gag. No dust rags. No old socks. Making a desperate attempt to smother Rick's cries, Kreitzer knelt down and roughly put a hand over Rick's mouth.

Rick promptly bit Kreitzer's finger.

Jumping up in pain and anger, Kreitzer grabbed the first thing within his reach. The sturdy object weighed about twenty pounds and looked like a small microwave oven with sharp corners. Before using his new weapon, Kreitzer kicked viciously, catching Rick in the ribs.

With pain washing over his body, Rick drew his knees up and hollered, "Help! Somebody, help me!"

"Shut him up!" repeated Miguel.

Raising the oven over his head, Kreitzer slammed it into its target with an explosive force. One corner of the metal casing caught Rick in his right temple. A dull thud filled the air as Rick's head smashed against the floor.

Dropping the oven, Kreitzer stared at the gaping puncture wound. Rick lay perfectly still.

The two men looked at each other with a combination of fear and incredulity. A heartbeat later they both moved quickly to the door. Just before exiting the laboratory, Kreitzer stopped short and snapped, "Wait a second, god-dammit!" He turned and strode back into the room. He picked up the compact oven and set it back on the table. Then, using his shirtsleeve, he wiped away any trace of fingerprints from the lethal weapon. He looked around, wondering if he had missed anything.

Walking back into the room, Miguel spoke frantically. "Hurry up, man! We can't stay here like this."

Not wanting to leave empty-handed, Kreitzer picked up the box that his accomplice had dropped earlier. After handing it to Miguel, Kreitzer turned and scooped up a second carton from the pile. Armed with two insect-laden cartons, the men walked quickly and silently out the door and into the night.

CHAPTER THIRTY-SEVEN

CALIFORNIA

"Rick! I'm home!" announced Sarah as she walked through the door of their apartment. Putting her purse and keys on the little entry table, Sarah called again, more loudly, "Rick?"

Rick spent much of his free time in the room that the young couple had converted into a study. It was home to his-and-hers personal computers and a single fax machine. Sarah poked her head in, hoping to find Rick engrossed in a book or a website. Not seeing him, she moved quietly to the master bedroom where she expected to find him sleeping.

"So," she mused, finding the bed empty. "Where is that man of mine?" Turning around to face the emptiness of her home, she answered, "Probably working late, as usual."

The day had been chaotic. In addition to Rick's early morning phone call, demanding that she come witness the caterpillar invasion, she found herself leading the charge in an all-out effort to control the catastrophe. After Doug sent everyone home, she offered to stay with Rick while he tried to deduce what went wrong. Since there was nothing that Sarah could do to solve the puzzle, it was decided that she should keep her scheduled appointment with an old college roommate. By the time Sarah came home, she was totally relaxed.

Satisfied that Rick wasn't hiding anywhere in the apartment, Sarah kicked off her shoes and clicked on the answering machine. There were three calls. One was a solicitation from the Police Benevolent Association. The second was from Sarah's girlfriend who gave a quick review of a sweater sale at Dillard's.

Last, was a message from Rick. "Hi, Sarah," his electronic voice began. "Got some bad news. Darlene called earlier and told me that Juanita is in intensive care. She lapsed into a coma as a result of the caterpillar bite. Darlene was a basket case and could hardly talk. Call me here at the lab when you get in, and I'll give you the details."

Sarah immediately dialed Rick's number. The telephone rang eight times before she finally hung up. She tried calling his cell phone, but only heard his recorded announcement inviting the caller to leave a message. Assuming that he had forgotten to turn on his cell phone, or had temporarily left the lab, Sarah took the time to undress and prepare for bed. In a few minutes, she plopped her tired body into the corner of the sofa and, once again, dialed Rick's number. Still no answer. Snuggling back into the folds of the overstuffed piece of furniture, she grabbed the remote and turned on the television. Sarah channel-surfed until she came to a late-night cartoon called *"South Park."* It was an adult oriented piece of animation featuring some nasty little children who spent most of the show cursing unabashedly. The mindless drivel was just the sort of thing that Sarah needed. Several times during the next half-hour, Sarah tried calling Rick. Her concerns ebbed when she rationalized that, due to the danger of working in proximity to all those caterpillars, Rick must have chosen to work in one of the adjoining labs. Knowing that, eventually he would call, she decided to wait.

Sarah turned her attention back to the television show as a commercial appeared on the screen. Her thoughts drifted back to Rick's message and its implications. Sarah didn't know Juanita very well, but she seemed quite likeable. During the morning's cleanup, she had pitched in without complaint until Miguel swept one of the caterpillars off the ceiling and onto the frightened girl's head.

Sarah recalled the conversation with her chemist, Kim Koto. The results of testing the poison were confusing. Kim related that some tests had shown the poison to be vesicular, while in others, it had presented itself as the hemorrhagic variety. Whichever, poor Juanita was feeling its full effects. Sarah decided that, first thing in the morning, she would have Kim call the hospital and talk with the doctors who were caring for Juanita. Hopefully, it would result in something positive.

As the television droned through the second half of *"South Park,"* Sarah sensed that her eyes were beginning to close. She hoped that Rick was having some luck finding answers to what went wrong.

It wasn't long before Sarah was fast asleep.

CHAPTER THIRTY-EIGHT

CHICAGO

Josef Ubermann did not trust his nephew. It wasn't that he thought that Bruce was a thief who might steal the family jewels; rather that he couldn't be counted on to design an effective plan of action. Ubermann's impression had always been that his nephew was a screw-up.

Disparaging thoughts aside, Ubermann did, in fact, appreciate the significance of his nephew's find. Discovering a brand-new species of caterpillar with an insatiable appetite for coffee was extraordinarily lucky. Now, however, the situation had reached a point upon which good fortune could no longer be relied. The next steps were crucial.

Ubermann's requirements were twofold. First, he needed to place the insects where they would do the greatest damage. That meant he had to learn which countries produced the most coffee. His second goal was to make arrangements to transport the insects to those sites.

In his last telephone conversation with his uncle, Bruce said that he and his new cohort, Miguel, a bug expert, had successfully acquired two boxes full of the coffee-loving creatures, approximately 15,000 of them. When Ubermann replied, saying that he hoped that the number of insects would be enough to damage the coffee crop, Miguel responded by explaining the bugs phenomenal reproductive rate. He said, "Once they start eating the coffee, a special chemical kicks in, and pretty soon you got more bugs than you know what to do with." When it came to bugs, Bruce's new pal seemed to be quite knowledgeable. Ubermann was glad that his nephew was utilizing the man's expertise.

It was several minutes past midnight when Ubermann began flipping through his Rolodex. The man was in the business of buying and selling commodities. That meant that he had a file full of contacts who knew everything there was to know about various crops, including coffee, that were traded on the Mercantile Exchange. He was searching for an expert who worked with coffee growers and could pinpoint the location of the world's biggest farms.

Having made a short list of people he would call first thing in the morning, Ubermann went to his computer and clicked on to the Internet. It was time to do some serious research into the subject of coffee.

As dawn broke over the Chicago skyline, Ubermann shut off his computer. Disregarding the fact that it was four-thirty in the morning in California, Ubermann dialed Bruce Kreitzer's number. His plan was coming together, and he needed his nephew's reassurance that everything was still on track.

The telephone rang a long time before Kreitzer answered. "Hello?" he said groggily.

"Wake up!" said Ubermann, sternly. "Wake up and listen to me."

Recognizing his uncle's voice, Kreitzer sat up in bed. Exhausted from an afternoon of lovemaking, and a stress-filled evening of stealing the bugs and murdering the young scientist, Kreitzer had trouble coming awake. Still, he struggled to clear his head and to speak coherently. "What's going on, Uncle Joe?"

"I'm calling to make sure you have everything under control. Do you still have the bugs?"

"Uh . . . yeah," said Kreitzer, closing his eyes. "I got 'em."

"And they're all still alive?" A long pause ensued, and Ubermann heard his nephew's breathing thicken. "Bruce!" he shouted. "Wake up, damn you!"

"I'm up," said Kreitzer, forcing his eyes open. "I'm up."

"Answer my question. Are the bugs still alive?"

"Yeah, Uncle Joe. They're okay."

"You make sure you keep them that way," ordered Ubermann. "They've all got to be in perfect shape by the time you get to Colombia."

Kreitzer still had the fuzziness of sleep in his head. "Colombia?" he asked.

"South America, you idiot!" snapped Ubermann. Then, almost to himself, he said, "Good Christ. This is who I have to work with." Louder, he barked into the phone. "I want you to call me every couple of hours. Keep me updated! I want to know every little detail of what's going on with you and those insects. I've got a lot of money riding on this. A lot of money! Don't you screw it up! If you have any questions about what you're supposed to do, call me immediately! You understand?"

Kreitzer nodded his head. "Yeah, Uncle Joe. I got it."

"This plan is starting to come together. We'll stay in touch, and I'll give you the details as they unfold."

Feeling drained, Kreitzer hung up and put his head into his hands. Besides having had to suffer through a day that included cracking open a man's skull with a microwave oven, he had to endure his uncle's Drill-Sergeant directives on only two hours sleep.

The previous night's incident at Envirogen was foremost on Kreitzer's mind. After leaving the lab, the two men had returned to Miguel and Maria's apartment. For the next several hours, they had argued about the best way to handle the situation. Kreitzer wanted Miguel to hang out with him, feeling that the technician's expertise was paramount when it came to handling the bugs. Miguel, on the other hand, said that he had to show up for work the next day, or else he would be tagged as a suspect.

Even though it was a valid point, Kreitzer didn't want to be put in the position of losing control. Nervous about how Miguel might handle himself during a police interrogation, Kreitzer tried a different strategy. He offered to double Miguel's payoff in return for not going to work.

It was a lot of cash and Miguel was tempted. However, the prospect of being fingered as Rick's killer quickly overcame the temptation. He said, "Until you know something definite about where you're gonna plant these bugs, you don't need me."

"That could take time," Kreitzer replied. "What am I supposed to do with the bugs until then? What if they die, for Christ's sake?"

"They ain't gonna die," answered Miguel. Just feed 'em some coffee grinds. They'll be fine."

The idea of handling thousands of insects all by himself gave Kreitzer the shivers. Wanting Miguel to take on that responsibility, Kreitzer doubled the offer once again.

Everybody had his price and, with that last proposal, Miguel's was met. "Okay," he said. "I'll take care of keeping 'em alive, and you take care of figuring out what we do with them."

Finally, around two a.m., Kreitzer had left the apartment to return to his hotel. He parted with a reminder to Miguel. "When you get to work, don't say anything to anybody. They probably won't even notice that the two boxes of bugs are missing."

The digital display on the nightstand blinked 4:51 a.m. as bits and pieces of his uncle's telephone call resurfaced. That place that Uncle Joe had talked about, Colombia, where the hell was that? Maybe somewhere near the Panama Canal, or something. His lack of sleep was preventing him from thinking clearly.

Kreitzer rubbed his morning erection as he shuffled to the bathroom. Afterwards, he walked back into the bedroom, opened the door to the closet, and flipped on the light. There, on the top shelf, snuggled securely between an extra pillow and blanket, sat the two boxes, unlabeled and seemingly unremarkable. There was no indication that, inside, a new life-form was swarming.

CHAPTER THIRTY-NINE

FLORIDA

Brad Bishop arrived at his office later than usual. "Good morning, Rose," he said, approaching his office manager's desk. "Anything exciting happening that I should know about?"

"Oh, look who's here," replied Rose Goldberg in mock astonishment. "I see you've decided to grace us with your presence. Are Tuesdays going to be your days to sleep-in?"

Brad sighed and looked skyward as if seeking guidance from an unknown source. "What ever happened to things like admiration for your employer, or good old-fashioned respect for authority?"

"Those concepts went out the window rap music."

Brad stared at the woman for a full second before saying, "I'm amazed that you know anything about rap music."

"I may be a Jewish grandmother, but I'm still hip."

Brad smiled. "What have you got for me?"

"A couple of messages," she said, gathering up several pink slips. "Most of it can wait, but there's one call we need to discuss." Standing, she said, "We'll talk about it in your office."

After the door was closed, Rose said, "You got a call from Doctor Caruthers."

"Doctor Caruthers?" repeated Brad. "I don't think I know a Doctor Caruthers."

"After I told him you weren't here, he introduced himself as Stephanie Ballinger's personal physician."

Brad sat back. "Really," he uttered. "What else did he have to say?"

"Not much," answered Rose. "He just kept saying that it was very important that he get in touch with you. I couldn't squeeze anything else out of the man and, believe me, I tried."

"I assume he left his number?"

277

Rose handed Brad the piece of paper. "It's Stephanie's home number." A moment of silence was followed by Rose adding, "Maybe she's got a disease or something."

"Maybe," said Brad as he looked at the message.

"Maybe, she's got dysentery, and she'll have to spend the rest of her life in the bathroom."

Brad looked up. "Why don't I call the man and find out."

"Maybe, she's got cancer of the mouth, and her tongue will have to be removed. That wouldn't be so bad."

Brad looked at Rose in disbelief. "Why don't you go back to your desk so that I don't have to listen to your vindictiveness."

As Rose walked to the door, Brad could hear her mumble, "Leprosy wouldn't be so bad, either."

The third ring of the telephone was interrupted when it was picked up and answered by a man who announced, "Carlton-Ballinger residence."

"Hello. This is Brad Bishop. Can I speak with Ms. Ballinger, please."

The person on the other end responded as though he were expecting the call. Brad was put on hold, but only for a moment. Then, a different man picked up and asked, "Mr. Bishop?"

"Yes. This is Brad Bishop."

"I'm Doctor Caruthers, Mr. Bishop. Stephanie asked me to call you."

"Is everything all right?" asked Brad.

Just as the doctor started to answer, Brad could hear a woman's voice in the background. Hoarse, strained, and barely recognizable, she said, "Is that Brad? Is that my Brad?"

The doctor continued. "I'm afraid I have some bad news."

Brad could hear the distraught woman say, "Let me talk to him."

"All right, Stephanie," said the physician, his mouth turned away from the phone. "In a moment." Speaking back into the telephone, the doctor said, "I'm going to put her on the phone. However, I want you to know that I've given her a rather powerful sedative. So, when you've finished talking to her, I'll get back on the line and answer any additional questions."

There was a muffled rustling as though the telephone rubbed against a down comforter. Suddenly, a tearful voice cried, "Brad? Brad? Is that you?"

Brad had never heard Stephanie sound so upset. "What is it, Stephanie? What's wrong?"

"It's my Richard. It's my son. He's dead. He's dead!" The shocking phrase was followed by an anguished wail and a barely discernable, "Oh my God, he's dead!"

"What happened?" asked Brad. When there was no response, he called, "Stephanie? Stephanie!"

Doctor Caruthers came back on the line. "Mr. Bishop? Doctor Caruthers, here. The sedative is finally taking effect. She'll be out of it for several hours. Were you able to understand her?"

Brad and the doctor talked for the better part of twenty minutes. Caruthers related the story from his own perspective, saying that he rushed right over as soon as she had called with the news of her son's death. He told Brad that, in her tormented state of mind, she had smashed the large mirror in the hall. Barefoot, she attempted to clean it up, but only succeeded in slicing her hands and feet. "The bleeding was quite severe," said the doctor.

Brad was about to ask a question, but the doctor had more to say.

"The young man's fiancée, a girl by the name of Sarah, called from California this morning. When she awoke, she realized that Richard never came home from work. When he didn't answer his phone, she drove to his laboratory and found him there. According to her, he was already dead."

Brad took an audible breath and swallowed. "What was the cause of death?"

"The fiancée said that Richard had been murdered. She said that someone had hit him on the head. I really don't know much more than that."

Brad asked, "When do you think I'll be able to talk to Stephanie?"

"She'll be out of it for three, maybe even four hours. But, in the meantime, she wanted me to call and ask if you would go to Pasadena. She said that you're the only one she can trust to find out what really happened."

Although the doctor wasn't able to provide any additional details, he instructed Brad to jot down two telephone numbers for Sarah Levine. "One of those numbers is her cell phone," said the physician, "but I can't recall which is which."

Brad ended the conversation by saying that he would, indeed, make arrangements to fly to California. Before disconnecting, he asked Doctor Caruthers to have Stephanie call as soon as she was able. "I'd like to stop by and hold her hand."

Hanging up, Brad sat back and thought about Stephanie. The death of a child is difficult for any parent to endure, but when that life is taken away through the brutal act of murder, the episode becomes an unspeakable tragedy. Brad knew that Stephanie would grieve forever.

Swiveling his chair, Brad stared, unseeing, out the big office window. Anguish and emptiness were burdens left for the living. Brad understood the concept. He had experienced those same feelings when he lost his fiancée in a firestorm. It had taken years for his emotional wounds to heal. Now, suddenly thrust into the midst of this tragedy, Brad realized that his past pain was mixing with the pain of the moment.

After waiting several minutes to compose himself, Brad asked Rose to come back into his office. One look told her that the problem was serious. Without saying a word, she sat and waited to hear what her employer had to say.

"Stephanie's only child has been found murdered."

Rose put a hand to her lips.

Brad continued, "She wants me to go to Pasadena and find out what happened. I suppose I'll also have to make arrangements to have the body brought back here."

Rose's eyes filled with tears. She whispered hoarsely, "My dislike for that woman has suddenly disappeared. All I feel is a cold chill, like someone stabbed me in the heart."

Brad nodded his understanding. "Call the airlines and see what flights are available. Let me know as soon as possible. In the meantime, I'm going to call Richard's fiancée, Sarah Levine."

Rose remembered the name. "She's the one I gathered the information on, right? The entomologist with all the doctorates."

"Yes. She's the one."

Rose said, "When you speak to her, remember that she's going to be a basket case."

"I know," nodded Brad. "I'm not looking forward to any of this."

CHAPTER FORTY

CALIFORNIA

Bruce Kreitzer used the remote to flip to yet another channel. CNN Headline News appeared, and the information bar on the bottom of the screen reminded viewers that it was ten-forty, Tuesday night. Miguel Ortiz still had not returned any of Kreitzer's three phone calls. Frustrated, he stopped his pacing and dialed Miguel for the fourth time.

The Mexican answered curtly. "Yeah?"

"Where the hell have you been?" questioned Kreitzer. "I've been calling you all night."

Miguel whined, "C'mon, man. I just walked in the door. What's up?"

"Didn't Maria give you my messages"

"She ain't home," explained Miguel. "What's going on?"

Kreitzer took a breath. "I think the bugs are dead."

"Dead?" repeated Miguel. "What the hell happened?"

"I don't know," answered Kreitzer, the pitch of his voice higher than he would have liked. "I put my ear next to the boxes, and there's no sound. Nothing. It's like they're all dead."

"Shit," muttered Miguel.

"You're the god-damn bug expert," said Kreitzer accusingly. "What do we do now?"

"Did you shake the box?" asked Miguel.

"What?"

Miguel repeated his question. "Did you pick up the boxes and shake them? Y'know, try and get the suckers moving?"

There was a pause before Kreitzer answered, "No."

"Go do it now," demanded Miguel. "I'll hold."

A minute passed before Kreitzer got back on the telephone. "They're moving," he said contritely. "I can hear them moving around." Then, he spoke more commandingly. "But you better get over here anyway and feed them. I don't want a bunch of dead bugs on my hands."

"It's late, man," complained Miguel. "I'll come over tomorrow."

"Bullshit, Miguel! We grabbed those bugs last night! It's already been twenty-four hours since they've had anything to eat. You gotta come over here now and feed them!"

"Listen, man . . ." began Miguel.

"I don't want to hear any bullshit from you!" growled Kreitzer. "I'm paying you a lot of money. A lot of money," he emphasized. "So, get your ass over here and make sure these god-damn creepy-crawlies stay alive."

It took almost forty-five minutes before Miguel arrived and knocked on Kreitzer's hotel room door. "What took you so long?" asked Kreitzer letting the Mexican into the room.

"I stopped at the market and bought some coffee."

Kreitzer nodded. "How did everything go at work today?"

Miguel took one of the cartons off the shelf and set it on the bed. Then, he opened the grocery bag and took out a two-pound tin of coffee and a handheld can opener. Turning the key to remove the lid, Miguel said, "It was a shitty day, man. Cops all over the place. Everybody crying and shit. I got questioned, like, three separate times."

"What did you tell them?"

The lid popped off the metal container and Miguel removed the little yellow coffee scoop. "I told 'em you were the killer. I told 'em your name and everything."

Kreitzer felt an icy wave pass through his body. "What?"

"Relax, man," said Miguel with a low chortle. "I didn't tell them shit. They don't know nothin', and they ain't got no suspects either."

Kreitzer exhaled. He watched as Miguel peeled off a corner of the duct tape that held the box closed. "What are you doing?" asked Kreitzer.

"I'm opening the box a little bit so that I can pour some of this coffee inside."

Kreitzer watched the procedure.

With the tape removed, one of the caterpillars wriggled forward and began to crawl out of the opening. Miguel took his pen and pushed the creature back inside. Taking a full scoop of coffee, he carefully tapped it, guiding the aromatic grounds into the tiny aperture.

As Kreitzer stared, mesmerized, Miguel smoothed the duct tape back into place. Then, he took down the second carton and repeated the same steps.

Kreitzer asked, "Why don't you just open the box all the way? It'll make it lot easier to pour in the coffee."

Miguel resealed the second box. "Yesterday," he explained, "when we was rounding up all these bugs, a girl named Juanita got bit by one of them. Today, I find out she's dead. They took her to the hospital, but she died anyway."

Kreitzer straightened up. "No shit! They're really poisonous?"

Miguel said, "Well, I ain't takin' no chances. That's for damn sure."

*   *   *

Walking out of the front entrance of the Downtown Marriott, Hannah Carpenter glanced at her watch. The digital display told her it was Wednesday, 11:53 a.m. She looked up at the sky. It was blue, she conceded thoughtfully, but nowhere near the color of her own Florida sky. Los Angeles mixed a little brown into their palette before painting the broad strokes of its canopy. Hannah knew that the dull blue of the Southern California sky was due to a smog layer that hung over the city. Despite all that, the air was cool and the humidity was low, both of which were refreshing changes.

Waiting for an attendant to bring her car around, Hannah noticed that traffic on South Figueroa Street was light. It would be easy to drive to the mall. Earlier, she had asked the Bell Captain for directions to the nearest department store. The man had suggested the Beverly Shopping Center on La Cienega Boulevard, a big, upscale mall that included a Macy's and a Nordstrom's. It would be a fine way to spend her time while she waited for a return phone call from her boss.

Sidney Aarons had called the previous evening to say that it was time for Hannah to come back to Florida. "You've been out there long enough," he had told her. "I can't afford to keep you indulged in the lavishness of Beverly Hills."

Hannah told Sidney that she wanted one last interview before leaving California. "Ever since Brother Timothy's appearance on 'Hardball,'" Hannah explained, "there has been a veritable uproar. The man's statements about the origins of the AIDS virus have become the lead story on the evening news."

Hearing Sidney's sigh of resignation, Hannah smiled and pressed her advantage. She knew that extending her stay was a little selfish, but meeting with Brother Timothy would add an exclamation point to what had become her six-part series. Because the article was selling a lot of newspapers, Hannah was finally gaining some journalistic recognition.

Reluctantly, Sidney agreed. "All right. You've got until tomorrow. If you get the interview . . . fine. If not, book yourself a flight back home."

The parking attendant arrived with Hannah's car. After getting directions to the mall, she confidently pulled into traffic.

Three hours earlier, Hannah had spoken with Melanie, Brother Timothy's teenage assistant. The young girl assured Hannah that her message would be forwarded to the Preacher.

Although Nordstrom's and Macy's were both having sales, it was the latter that featured a "Women's Wear Clearance." Once in the department, Hannah spotted a skirt and blouse ensemble that could be worn for work or on weekends. It had grays and whites that blended together in a smoky pattern and was set off by a razor-thin slash of bumblebee yellow that started at the left shoulder and serpentined its way to a point under the right breast. Originally tagged at $170, it had been marked down seventy-percent. At the register, the pretax total came to $51. As Hannah took out her credit card, her cell phone rang.

"Hello?" answered Hannah.

The reception inside the store was not very good, and the caller's voice was breaking up. "May I please speak with Hannah Carpenter?"

"This is she," replied Hannah.

"This is Brother Timothy. Can you hear me?"

"Oh, Brother Timothy. I didn't recognize your voice," said Hannah. "Wait just a moment until I can get a clearer signal." Hanging the outfit back on the rack, she walked to the nearest exit. Once outside, the telephone reception improved. "Sorry about that," she said. "Thanks for returning my call. I wanted to chat with you about your television appearance on . . . '"

Brother Timothy interrupted. "You asked me to let you know the next time the Devil came to town."

Hannah was silent.

"Can you hear me?" asked Brother Timothy.

"Yes," said Hannah. "I can hear you just fine. But . . . . what do you mean?'"

"Yesterday, the Devil showed up in Pasadena. If you want to see his handiwork, meet me at a place called Envirogen. It's a bioengineering facility off Washington Boulevard."

Despite the warmth of the sun, Hannah felt a chill run up her spine. "What happened?" she asked.

Brother Timothy spoke somberly. "A young man is dead. His head was crushed."

"Oh, my God," whispered Hannah.

"There is one more thing you ought to know."

"What is it?" she asked tremulously.

A short pause preceded Brother Timothy saying, "This isn't the end of it, my dear Hannah. This is merely the beginning."

*   *   *

A rising mist obscured his vision. Squinting, Brad tried to make sense of it. As he peered into the swirling fog, he became aware of a javelin-like rod perched next to his right arm. Mounting apprehension soon led to a trembling fear. Grabbing the weapon, he steadied it, poised and ready to strike at any danger that lurked ahead.

Waves of hot air swept in and spun the mist into a whirlpool of spray. Now, he could begin to make out the figure that stood in the vortex. It was a young woman wearing a garment made of layers of white chiffon. Unable to discern the features of her face, Brad found himself distracted by the diaphanous material, which ebbed and flowed in the wind.

Something heightened his fear and, instinctively, he tightened his grip on the spear. It felt slippery, almost as though the shaft were covered with a thin layer of grease. Brad tried to wrap his fingers more tightly, but he couldn't summon enough strength. The woman in white stepped forward, causing Brad to cock his arm, prepared to throw the javelin at the apparition. The haze cleared momentarily, and Brad sucked in a sharp breath of recognition. Amy Crawford, the woman to whom Brad had been engaged, was standing there!

Alarmingly, Brad felt the weapon in his hand take on a life of its own. It grew heavier and thicker, making it difficult to control. Despite the power of his grip, the lance moved forward, as its glistening point headed toward Amy. He tried to stop it, but it was too unwieldy.

Brad looked to his left and saw a stern-faced officer in a gold-buttoned uniform. What did he want? The spear was becoming a missile, moving faster and faster toward Amy. Unaware of the danger, she stood poised and beautiful and only a moment away from being struck down. Frantically, Brad turned to the officer for help. The man mouthed something, but Brad couldn't hear. Pleading for the uniformed man to repeat his words, Brad finally was able to make out the phrase: "This is your Captain." Desperately, Brad tried to understand what that meant.

The voice repeated. "This is your Captain speaking."

Opening his eyes, Brad blinked and looked around. A flight attendant walked past holding a cocktail destined for a passenger sitting two rows back.

The Captain continued speaking over the intercom. "We're approaching the Grand Canyon, which will be visible from the left side of the airplane. Visibility is excellent, and I'm sure you'll all enjoy the sight."

Brad reached up and turned the air-conditioning control to a higher setting. The dream had left him with a sheen of perspiration, and the cool air felt good on his face.

"Can I get you anything?" asked a pretty, dark-haired flight attendant.

Brad nodded. "Yes. I'll have a Diet Coke with lots of ice."

The young woman noticed Brad's glistening face and asked, "Are you all right?"

Brad smiled weakly. "I'm fine," he said. "Must be the turbulence."

The attendant stared blankly for a second, knowing that the flight had, so far, been a smooth one. Then, realizing that some passengers were never comfortable with flying, she smiled compassionately and said, "I understand."

The disturbing dream left Brad with the realization that it had been several years since the loss of his fiancée had invaded his sleep. He understood why it had reoccurred. It was this new tragedy, the killing of Stephanie's son that brought back the torment of his own loss.

The previous afternoon, when Brad had met with Stephanie, he found the woman inconsolable. There were moments between her wails of anguish that Brad found himself tuning out and thinking about his own pain.

Brad had waited until he returned to his office before calling Sarah Levine. After he had introduced himself as a personal friend of the Ballinger family, he said, "I'll be flying out to California tomorrow. Is there anything I can bring that might be helpful?"

Recognizing Brad's offer as genuine, Sarah inhaled the kind of ragged breath people take when they suddenly realize there is someone to help them in their grief. "Thank you, Mr. Bishop," said Sarah, her voice cracking with emotion. "I'm looking forward to your arrival and whatever assistance you can offer."

Brad said, "I'll be renting a car and driving to Pasadena. Where will I find you?"

"I'm not sure," said Sarah dejectedly. "I don't want to stay in our apartment, and if I go to my mother, she'll just smother me. I suppose I'll be better off going to work. It'll help keep my mind occupied." Then, she made certain that Brad had all her contact phone numbers.

Brad looked out the window, as his airplane prepared to land at Los Angeles International Airport. He thought about Sarah's parting words. "I've got to go, Mr. Bishop," Sarah had said. "One of the cops just came in and wants to talk to me. Maybe, he'll tell me that it's all been just a bad dream."

CHAPTER FORTY-ONE

CALIFORNIA

S arah's directions were clear, making it easy for Brad to find the industrial park that housed the Envirogen building. Once inside, he was greeted by a receptionist who directed him to the resident entomologist, Doctor Sarah Levine.

As Brad stepped through the door marked Department of Life Sciences, he almost collided with a man who seemed to be scurrying by on his tiptoes. Appearing a bit high-strung, the man became flustered by the near-miss. With a loud, "Oh, crap!" he dropped a small pile of documents and a metal stapler. The papers floated to the floor, landing in a wide semicircle, while the stapler fell, clunked, and bounced up into the man's ankle.

"Ow! Ow!" cried Winston Sattherwaite, lifting his foot, and at the same time, trying to caress his injured ankle. "Oh, my God!" he said dramatically, as he danced a little one-footed jig. "I think it's bleeding!" He looked pleadingly at one of the nearby technicians. "Becky?" he called in anguish. "My ankle. Is it bleeding?"

Becky Leconura barely looked up. "No, Winston," she said impatiently. "It's not bleeding. Stop being such a baby."

"A baby?" cried Winston, insulted. "You don't know what pain I'm in. This is the kind of thing that can cause infections and gangrene, for God's sake!"

"Excuse me," interrupted Brad. "Can you tell me where . . ."

Winston turned to face Brad. "You're the one at fault here, you know," he said accusingly. "You came barging in here like a runaway freight train. 'Beep, beep!'" sounded Winston, waving his arms frenetically in an attempt to imitate a locomotive crashing into the office.

Becky never looked up as she said, "Freight trains go 'toot-toot,' Winston. Not 'beep-beep.'"

A little wave of chuckling swept through the half-dozen people in the room.

Winston bent to pick up the scattered pile of papers. "Oh, my gawd," he said, stretching out the name of the deity. "My ankle's starting to swell. Before this day is over, I'm going to look like an over inflated balloon." Standing, he stared at Brad and asked indignantly, "And, what is it you want, anyway?"

"I'm here to see Doctor Levine."

Stapler in one hand, rumpled papers in the other, Winston held out his arms as though barring Brad from proceeding any further. "Absolutely not!" he said emphatically. "She can't see anyone right now." He narrowed his gaze. "Are you a reporter, or something?" he asked suspiciously.

"No," replied Brad, taking out a business card. "She's expecting me."

Scrutinizing Brad's face, Winston took the card and said, "You wait right here." He turned and started to walk away, but stopped after only a few feet. "And don't you touch anything, either," he added.

Brad watched Winston Sattherwaite's exaggerated limp, as he went off to find Sarah Levine. Glancing around the laboratory Brad locked eyes with Becky. He smiled.

"He's all right," said Becky, apologizing for Winston's behavior. "He carries on like that all the time, but he's a brilliant botanist."

Brad nodded with understanding. "Comic relief in a stress-filled environment?" he ventured.

Becky smiled softly. "Exactly," she said. "And lately, there seems to be more stress than usual."

Winston returned with a more accommodating attitude and led Brad to an office tucked into one corner of the large room. Sarah Levine stood, and they shook hands.

"Allow me to offer you my deepest sympathies," said Brad. "Strange as this may sound, I know exactly what you're going through, and my heart goes out to you. Is there anything I can do for you?"

Sarah's eyes were red and puffy. She eased herself back into her chair and said, "Thank you for that, but I don't think there's anything that you can really do."

"Richard's mother, Stephanie, asked me to come out here and do whatever I could to make things easier," said Brad. "She also asked me to find out what happened."

Sarah spoke softly. "Only his mother referred to him as 'Richard.' He was 'Rick' to me and the rest of his world." Reaching for a tissue, Sarah blew her nose. "There were a bunch of people here yesterday," she said. "They were investigating the hell out of this whole mess. Police photographers, forensic specialists, a medical examiner, teams of detectives, everybody." Sarah shook her head slowly. "So far . . . . nothing."

"I'm going to be in Pasadena for the next few days," said Brad. "I think it would be a good idea for us to get together and talk about some important issues. Events and such that you'll be sharing with Rick's mother."

Sarah held Brad's gaze, while she mulled over his words. Finally, she said, "Stephanie doesn't like me. I don't know how well you know her, but she's a very narrow-minded person. Very little tolerance for minorities and zero tolerance for Jews. I don't think I can share anything with that woman."

Brad nodded and showed a thin smile. "I understand where you're coming from," he said. "Stephanie can be tough. Even though she's been a client for many years, her intolerance has always been a bone of contention between us. Despite that . . ."

Sarah interrupted. "I'm glad to hear that you're aware of her shortcomings."

Brad tried again. "Despite those shortcomings, let me tell you about something she recently agreed to. When Stephanie found out that you were engaged to her son, she asked me to investigate your background. I did. After telling her all the details, your family, your education, your published works, and your standing in the scientific community, I convinced her that you and Rick were a perfect match. She was about to invite you to her home and accept you as her daughter-in-law."

As Brad spoke, he could see that Sarah's eyes were welling up with tears. Soon, she put both hands to her face and cried softly. "I'm sorry, Mr. Bishop," she said, reaching for a handful of tissues.

"Call me Brad. Please."

Sarah nodded. "All right, Brad," she said through a nose full of tears. "But for now, I need the time to grieve by myself."

Brad stood. "Certainly," he said. "We'll catch up with each other later. Before I go, could you tell me the name of the detective in charge?"

"Oh, damn. What was his name?" Sarah wiped the tears from her cheek with the palm of her hand. Swallowing, she said, "Uh . . . Santiago, Sagurro . . . something like that. I have his card here, somewhere." Searching her desk, Sarah suddenly stopped and said, "Y'know what? He was in the building earlier, and I think he might still be in Rick's lab."

"How do I find Rick's lab?" asked Brad.

Sarah stood and came out from behind her desk. "Come on," she offered. "I'll show you. I could use some fresh air."

They made their way through the long corridors and down two flights of stairs. As they descended, Brad said, "I appreciate your taking the time to show me the way. However, I didn't mean to disturb your . . ."

"Please," interrupted Sarah. "It's not even worth mentioning. This gives me a chance to feel useful. If I stayed at home, I'd just turn into a blubbering idiot. I'm better off here at work. At least when I'm here, I can do my share of blubbering and still manage to feel a little productive."

"Okay," said Brad.

"Besides," added Sarah, "this will give me a chance to find out what happened with the bugs."

"Bugs?" asked Brad. "What bugs?"

Sarah told Brad about Rick's experiment, the Kudzu Project. Keeping the story short, she briefly mentioned the creation of the new species of caterpillar. "A couple of us are trying to recreate Rick's experiment."

"Don't you have his notes?"

"We do," affirmed Sarah. "And they're complete. But, something went wrong with the DNA sequencing, and he ended up with an insect that he didn't expect."

DNA sequencing, entomological studies, and gene-splicing were sugjects that, for the most part, were foreign to Brad. "If you say so, Doctor Levine."

Stepping into the hallway, Sarah glanced over her shoulder and gave Brad an apologetic smile. Suddenly, she pulled up short and stared down the hall. There was a commotion in front of Forum Lab.

"What's going on?" asked Brad.

Visibly shaken, Sarah whispered, "I don't know. I just hope to God that no one else is dead."

*　　*　　*

Bruce Kreitzer paid the check after having lunch at *McCormick and Schmick's*, a restaurant within walking distance from the Hilton in which he was staying. He had devoured a seafood extravaganza that included, among other mollusks, enough stuffed shrimp to satisfy the appetite of a sumo wrestler. His gluttony forced him to loosen his silver belt buckle two full notches.

Returning to the lobby of the hotel, Kreitzer paused near the Bell Captain's desk to admire a young blonde, parading by in a tank top and high-cut denim shorts. The white cotton top was two sizes too small, and designed to show off her bare midriff. However, because it was scantily cut at the bottom, it also showed off the underside of her bare breasts. No one said a word while the girl paused to look at a brochure. Then, as she walked away, Kreitzer and the bellman followed her every move. The brevity of her shorts allowed a fleeting glimpse of the blonde's butt-cheeks that undulated with each stride. She disappeared around a corner.

Kreitzer heard the bellman sigh and say, "Life is good."

Without acknowledging the man's comment, Kreitzer made his way to the elevator and up to his room. Almost immediately, he noticed the flashing message light on his telephone. Punching in the numbers to retrieve it, he heard the recorded voice of Abby, his secretary. "Mr. Kreitzer," she said in a desperate whisper. "Call me back as soon as you get this message! This is a nine-one-one emergency! If you get in late, call me at home."

"Nine-one-one emergency?" said Kreitzer aloud. "What the hell does that mean?" He wondered if Uncle Joe had suffered a heart attack or something. Dialing the 800 number to the office in Chicago, he asked for Abby's extension.

"Abby," he said when she answered. "It's me. What's up?"

"Oh, Mr. Kreitzer. Thank God you called. Wait just a second. I'm going to put you on hold and pick this up in your office."

Kreitzer raised his eyebrows in response. He realized that, if Abby needed the privacy of his office to relay the news, it must be serious.

The extension clicked and Abby said, "Mr. Kreitzer? Are you still there?"

"Yeah, I'm here. Talk to me."

Still using a hoarse whisper, Abby said, "I got a call from Paul Pignatano. You know, Porky Pignatano? The Mafia Boss?"

"Yeah, yeah. I know who you're talking about. So . . . ?"

"He told me he needed to get in touch with you. He said it was a matter of life or death. I told him you were out of town on business. I told him . . ."

"Shit," said Kreitzer, barely under his breath. "Did you tell him where I was?"

"No. I didn't," said Abby. "But . . ."

Kreitzer interrupted. "Did he say anything else?"

"No. That was all, but . . ."

"And that's why you called? That was the big nine-one-one emergency?"

"No. There's more," said Abby.

"Well, what is it? Tell me, already."

Abby sounded frightened as she continued. "This morning," she said, "two men came in here looking for you. One of them was so big that he looked like a giant wrestler. His name was Bruno."

Kreitzer felt a cold wave of fear sweep through his gut.

Abby began weeping. "He said he was going to tear the place apart, if I didn't tell him where you were. He threatened to make trouble for my kids!"

Even though the woman was still speaking coherently, Kreitzer knew that her tears were probably flowing like Niagara Falls. "What did you tell him?" he asked.

"Nothing," sobbed Abby. "I didn't tell him anything."

"What did he do?" asked Kreitzer.

"While the big man was giving me grief, the other guy's cell phone rang, and I heard him talking about you."

"About me? Who was this other guy?"

"I don't know his name, but when he hung up, he turned to the big guy named Bruno, and said, 'We got him!'"

"We got him?" repeated Kreitzer. "What the hell does that mean?"

Abby sniffled and took a ragged breath before continuing. "When the little guy said, 'we got him,' Bruno asked, 'where is he?' And the other guy said . . . uh, he said . . .'"

"What did he say, Abby?" demanded Kreitzer. "Tell me exactly what he said.

"He said, 'The little weasel is in California. The Hilton Hotel in Pasadena.'"

Kreitzer became aware that, although his hands were sweaty, his fingertips were icy cold.

"They know where you are, Mr. Kreitzer," said Abby desperately. "They know exactly where you are."

It took him only a moment to realize that they must have traced his whereabouts through his corporate American Express card. That meant that Bruno Mordello would be coming after him, and Kreitzer would have to change his location immediately. After hastily and haphazardly packing his suitcase, he scanned the room for anything he might have forgotten. Opening the closet, he uttered a string of foul-mouthed expletives when he saw the two cartons of bugs on the top shelf. Berating himself for almost leaving them behind, he scooped them up together and plopped both of them on the bed. Then, he called to have a bellman come for the luggage, and to have his rental car brought around to the front.

CHAPTER FORTY-TWO

CALIFORNIA

B rad Bishop was only a step behind Sarah as she walked quickly down the hall. He thought about her statement, her expressed hope that nobody else had died. It seemed to carry the connotation that more than just the death of her fiancé was involved here.

Two women were standing in the hall just outside the entrance to Forum Lab. One was shouting an ultimatum. " . . . and if you don't get out of here, right now, I'm calling security!"

Sarah signaled to the shouting woman. "Hey! Ashley! What's going on?"

Ashley Eberhardt spun, red-faced and angry, to face Sarah. "God-damn bloodhounds!" she snarled. "They're in there crawling all over the place with their freakin' television cameras, and they won't listen to me!"

Sarah turned to the second young woman in the hall. "Lynn," she said firmly, "go get Doug Matsushita. He's in the third floor conference room. Tell him that I said he must get down here immediately."

Lynn nodded and began to walk away.

"Hurry!" demanded Sarah.

Lynn broke into a run.

With Ashley at her side, Sarah stepped into the lab. Brad stood in the doorway taking in the scene. Bright lights were set up around the perimeter, one of which was casting a sharp glare into Brad's eyes. With some people holding clipboards and wandering around the room, a few curiously searching under tables and chairs, and still others primping and preening a man standing center stage, the scene looked like mass confusion.

A man's voice rose above the din. "Quiet!"

Everybody stopped what they were doing. Pointing to a dark-haired woman in glasses and a business suit, the director called out, "Action!"

The bespectacled woman stepped forward just enough to block the glare of light in Brad's eyes, allowing him to clearly see the other characters in this surreal scene. At the epicenter of the action, standing tall with his perfectly coiffed, silver-streaked hair, was Brother Timothy Goodman.

The business-suited interviewer asked, "Brother Timothy, what was it that brought you to this place?"

The cameraman moved in for a close up, as Brother Timothy looked left and right before facing forward. "I'm here to do the Lord's work," he pontificated.

Brad was astonished. It was only a couple of nights previously that he watched this religious zealot on "Hardball" spout some absurdities about the AIDS virus. Now, here he was in person, and commanding center stage, once again.

Brother Timothy continued. "This place, called Envirogen, has proven itself to be nothing more than a festering sewer, a place where diseases are born. And now, two people are dead. Young, vibrant people, God-loving people whose lives were stolen away by the Devil himself."

The interviewer was playing her part well. She had an appropriate look of shock and horror as she asked, "Can you tell us what happened?"

Brother Timothy took another few seconds to survey his surroundings before saying, "Evil has invaded this laboratory. I can feel it. The Devil has slithered in and warped the good intentions of the individuals who once worked here. It made them concoct ideas that should not have been concocted, and grow things that should not have been grown."

Brad glanced at Sarah. Her eyebrows were knitted together in disbelief, and her lips were drawn tightly in anger.

The dark-haired woman posed her next question. "Some of our viewers don't understand the world of biotechnology. Could you please tell us what sort of things you're talking about?"

"I'm talking about aberrations," said the Preacher. "I'm talking about living things that should not have been created. The people in this laboratory were under the control of the Devil and, together, they gave birth to a mutated and monstrous life-form. It was that very same monster who turned on those scientists and . . ."

"All right! All right!" shouted Sarah, waving her arms and moving directly into the path of the camera. "That's it! This show is over!"

Despite everybody beginning to talk at the same time, Sarah's voice could be heard hollering, "I want all of you out of here! Now! You're here without authorization. Get out!"

The dark-haired reporter thrust her microphone into Sarah's face and asked, "Would you please tell our audience what your name is, and what you do here?"

"You're trespassing!" said Sarah angrily. "You've got less than five minutes to vacate the premises! After that, every last one of you will be arrested!"

"Arrested and prosecuted!" added Ashley Eberhardt.

While Sarah argued with the business-suited interviewer, the cameraman kept shooting his footage. With only Sarah and Ashley expending the effort to disperse the crowd, it quickly became apparent that the two women were losing their edge. In desperation, Ashley went to the wall and pulled out the plug that powered the floodlights.

Simultaneously, a loud voice could be heard from the doorway. "I want everyone out of here!" boomed Doug Matsushita. "The police are on their way! As soon as they arrive, anyone who is left will be arrested! I am authorized to charge each of you with trespassing, burglary, and willful destruction of private property!"

The sternness and timbre of Matsushita's demand seemed to have the desired effect. The majority of the intruders scurried toward the door.

"We got what we came for," said the director. "Let's get out of here." He turned to Brother Timothy and added, "We'll shoot the rest of this in the studio."

Verne Smenken was struggling with Ashley over a piece of sound equipment. Angrily, he pushed her away and yelled, "What the hell you think you're doing?"

Ashley was not one to put up with any sort of manhandling. Especially not from someone two inches shorter than herself. As Verne squatted to retrieve the fallen hardware, she gave his right shoulder a forceful shove.

He toppled over backward, cursing as he fell. "You bitch!" he spat. "You street whore! I'll kick your . . ."

Brother Timothy moved in quickly, grabbing Verne by his underarm. Lifting his assistant off the floor, the Preacher stood between the two would-be combatants. Struggling against the Preacher's grip, Smenken flailed out with his free hand. The motion unbalanced Brother Timothy, causing him to lurch sideways and step down forcefully on Ashley's foot.

Shrieking in pain and anger, Ashley lunged at Brother Timothy. His feet became tangled with Smenken's, and they both went down in a heap. Ashley screamed at the two men. "I don't give a shit who you are! Brother-fucking-Timothy or the Pope himself! Get out of here now, or I'll kick your balls halfway up your throat!"

Doug stepped between Ashley and the fallen pair. Brother Timothy, cheeks flushed with embarrassment, was first to scramble to his feet. As Smenken stood, his face crimson with anger, he coughed up a wad of phlegm, planning to spit it at Ashley. Brother Timothy put up his hand, hoping to block the vile assault, but he only succeeded in having the gob of mucus splatter on his sleeve.

"Incompetent asshole!" growled Ashley.

Brother Timothy looked into Smenken's eyes and said sternly, "Verne! It's time to go!"

Despite a seething hostility still making his nostrils flare, Smenken complied with the Preacher's command.

Doug moved through the crowd, ordering the remaining crew members to gather their belongings and to do it quickly. A couple of stragglers seemed to be hanging back, as though waiting for Brother Timothy to make the first move toward exiting the room. One of them, a tall, slender young woman, picked up her briefcase and stepped toward the doorway. Her eyes widened with recognition. "Brad?" she asked hesitantly. "Brad Bishop?"

Brad turned at the sound of his name being called. A smile creased the corners of his mouth. "Hannah Carpenter," he acknowledged with delight. "Fancy meeting you here."

"What are you doing here?" she asked with astonishment.

Brad's grin broadened. "I was just in the neighborhood and thought I'd drop by and say hello."

Hannah couldn't help but return his smile. "Seriously," she said, "what brings you . . ."

Hannah's sentence was interrupted when Doug walked up to the couple and pointed to the door. "Get going!" he ordered. "Both of you! Out of the building and off the grounds!"

Sarah intervened from across the room. "Doug!" she called. "Wait a minute." Approaching the three of them, Sarah explained, "Doug, this is Brad Bishop. He's here at the request of Rick's mother."

"Oh," said Doug. "Sorry about that. I didn't know."

Brad took the moment to shake Doug's hand and say, "And this young lady is Hannah Carpenter, a very good friend of mine."

Doug shook her hand perfunctorily and mumbled something like, 'Nice to meet you,' before returning to the business of clearing out the room.

Hannah immediately surmised that if she stuck close to Brad, she might avoid the embarrassment of getting thrown out on the street with the rest of the trespassers. The prospect of having to stay close to Brad was certainly not an unpleasant one.

As for Brad, he was happy to see a familiar face. His trip to Pasadena, along with its accompanying responsibility, was a dark burden. Hannah's presence would make things easier.

Brad refocused his attention on Sarah. "Am I right in assuming," he asked, "that the detective you were referring to isn't here?"

"Guess not," shrugged Sarah. She surveyed the disarray of the laboratory. "What a mess," she said half to herself. Momentarily closing her eyes, she sighed, "I don't think I can take much more of this."

Brad put his hand gently on her shoulder. "Why don't you give me the name of the detective, and I'll take care of things on that end. You should go home and rest. If I learn anything, anything at all, I'll let you know immediately."

Sarah called Doug over to their little group. When she asked him if he could recall the policeman in charge, Doug produced a business card with the name Detective Anthony Santero. After pocketing the card, Brad shook hands with Doctors Levine and Matsushita and left the laboratory with Hannah.

Once in the parking lot, Brad said, "I'm heading over to the police station to see how far along they are in their investigation. After I'm finished, where will I find you?"

"If you don't mind, I'd like to come with you."

Brad was silent.

Hannah explained. "The fact is, Sidney Aarons sent me out here to do a story. I've been following Brother Timothy around, almost on a daily basis. It's been one fiasco after another. Now, this," she said, cocking her thumb at the Envirogen building. "Amazing as it sounds, Brother Timothy predicted that this kind of thing would happen. I don't know where he got his information, but I do know that I need to follow it up."

Taking their own cars, they made their way to police headquarters. At the main desk, Brad asked to speak with Detective Anthony Santero. However, because the detective was on the road, the duty sergeant suggested that Brad leave his number and have Santero call.

Not satisfied, Brad said, "Then, how about Santero's lieutenant, or captain? Surely, one of them is here."

"Well, you're talking about Captain Bettencourt," said the sergeant. "He don't normally get involved with this sort of thing. You'll need to . . ."

Brad interrupted. "Bettencourt?" he asked. "Could that be Steve Bettencourt who used to be an agent for the FBI?"

"Yeah," said the sergeant hesitantly. "You know him?"

"Sure do," said Brad with a smug smile. "Tell him, Bradstone Bishop is here. I'll wait."

It wasn't long before the two old friends were pumping hands and backslapping their way into Bettencourt's office. Hannah trailed a step behind, somewhat miffed that she had not yet been introduced. The next fifteen minutes were spent catching up on events since their concurrent tours of duty with the FBI.

"What brings you out to this neck of the woods?" asked Bettencourt.

Brad explained, "We're here because of the murder of Richard Carlton-Ballinger. His mother is a good friend and client. Hannah and I are just following up."

Bettencourt became serious. "Bad business," he said. "We don't get a lot of murders out here. It's not like L.A. y'know. Maybe a couple of drifters, couple of bar fights, but that's about it. Certainly not young innocent scientists who only work with test tubes and microscopes. Got any ideas?"

Brad shook his head. "No. Not yet. What have your people found, so far?"

"Precious little," replied Bettencourt. "We've interviewed everyone at least once." The Captain shook his head. "No leads. The victim's girlfriend, Doctor Sarah Levine, told us that Ballinger was working late and never came home. Says she woke up early the next morning and went to the lab looking for him."

Brad asked, "Is she the one who called it in?"

"Yeah," said Bettencourt. "And, according to Santero's report, her only alibi is that at the time of the murder, she was visiting with an old college chum."

"How good is your Detective Santero?"

Bettencourt glanced at Hannah.

"She's okay," said Brad, alleviating the Captain's concern.

Bettencourt said, "Santero's been on the force about ten years, but he's a rookie detective. Why do you ask?"

"I don't know," said Brad, adjusting his position in the chair. "It's just that I've had a chance to talk with the Levine woman, and I'm willing to bet that she's not your killer. Have your people found the murder weapon, or any prints?"

Bettencourt gave a half smile. "You always did have good instincts, Bishop. And, you're right about Santero. Right now, he's trying to impress the hell out of me. Maybe a little too eagerly. But, as far as the crime scene is concerned, we think we have the murder weapon. It's one of those industrial microwave ovens. Somebody slammed that sucker into the side of the victim's head. Forensics has already identified hair and bone and stuff, but no complete prints."

"No prints?" repeated Brad. "Not even from the people who work there?"

"Nope," confirmed Bettencourt. "It looks as though whoever did it, wiped it clean. We've got a partial from the bottom of the oven, but the rest of it has been wiped clean."

"Could it have been a mugging?" asked Brad. "Maybe a couple of kids looking for some quick cash?"

Bettencourt shook his head. "The victim still had his money and credit cards on him. Whatever the motive for this thing, robbery wasn't it. Besides, there was no evidence of breaking and entering."

Brad thought a moment before saying, "I'm going to be out here for a few days. I'll do a little snooping. If I come up with a brainstorm, I'll let you know."

"Well," said Bettencourt, "if you're half as good as you were when we were with the Bureau, you'll probably come up with something. Just do me a favor, and don't get in the way of the investigation."

"No problem," agreed Brad. "But, I'll need you to keep me informed. I promised to do likewise with the victim's mother."

Bettencourt nodded.

Brad asked his next question. "One of the reasons I'm here is to make arrangements to have the body shipped back to Florida. How soon can I make that happen?"

"Let me check." Bettencourt tapped in an extension on his speaker phone and said, "Maggie, get me Doctor Pushkin. I need to ask her a question about the Ballinger autopsy." Waiting for the return phone call, Bettencourt studied Hannah. Without taking his eyes off the young woman, he said, "Tell me something, Bradstone. What are you doing with such a pretty girl?"

Deciding to keep Hannah's role as a reporter to himself, Brad said, "Hannah and I are both working to tie up all the loose ends of this case. Besides that, we're old friends."

"Yeah?" said Bettencourt with a twinkle. "Does she know about your drug habit?"

"Really?" said Hannah, trying to look serious. "My goodness . . . . Bradstone. I had no idea that you had a secret life. How have you managed to keep that from me?"

Bettencourt's chortle was cut short by the ringing of his telephone. It was Doctor Elena Pushkin, the Medical Examiner. After a brief conversation, the Captain hung up and said, "The M.E. is going to do the autopsy tomorrow morning. Barring anything unusual, my guess is that you should be able to ship the body sometime next week."

Bettencourt looked at his watch. It was a signal that the meeting was over. Standing, the Police Captain reassured Brad that he would be kept informed.

Brad wrote his cell phone number on the back of his business card and handed it across the desk. "Are you going to have any time for dinner?" he asked.

"Maybe," replied Bettencourt. "Give me a call tomorrow. I've got me a new wife, and I never know what to expect."

Brad and Hannah went outside to the parking lot. "What are your plans?" he asked.

"I've been thinking about that," replied Hannah. "Sidney expected me to wrap things up here sometime today or tomorrow. I was going to fly back home, but now, with this new turn of events, this killing . . ."

Brad raised an eyebrow. "You think Mister Sidney, 'play by my rules or you're out of the game,' Aarons will allow you to extend your visit?"

Hannah smiled before glancing at her watch. "We'll know in a minute," she said, taking her cell phone from her purse.

Brad listened to Hannah's half of the conversation, as she presented her Editor-in-Chief reasons for extending her stay. She dramatized the brutal murder of the young scientist working at Envirogen, and the fiasco resulting from Brother Timothy's failed on-site interview.

As Sidney responded, Brad could see the growing lines of frustration materialize on Hannah's face.

Moments later, placing a hand on her hip, she struck a defiant pose. "Sidney," stated Hannah, "This murder isn't just a page six local article. It's going to be a national headline. Brother Timothy is about to make some serious noise. He's already claiming that the Devil is in Pasadena. I'm not talking about the allegorical devil. I'm talking about the real Devil . . . . Satan, for Pete's sake! The character with the pitchfork and the horns! And, there's a huge audience out there that wants to read about it." She paused to listen.

Seeing Hannah's lips tighten, Brad knew that she was not getting her message across. He held up a hand, waving it slightly to get her attention. "Tell him who the victim is," he said.

Hannah nodded and waited for an opening. "And one more thing," she said to her boss. "The young man who was murdered? His name is Richard Carlton-Ballinger. Ring a bell?"

After only a short pause, Hannah replied, "Brad Bishop."

Another short pause and Hannah said, "He's out here at the request of the victim's mother."

Listening to Sidney postulate, Hannah began shaking her head even before he finished his thought. "No, Sidney," she said, emphatically. "Brad Bishop is not the reason I'm asking to stay longer. There's a story here. A big story that needs to be told. Now, are you going to let me do my job and tell it?"

Seeing the expression on Hannah's face go triumphant, Brad knew that Sidney acquiesced. It wasn't long before the phone call ended, and Hannah said, "Okay. I've bought myself another couple of days."

"Great," said Brad with a growing smile. "Let's have dinner."

Hannah frowned as she said, "It occurs to me that all of my interviews have taken place in Los Angeles. But now, the center of attention has moved here to Pasadena. I'll need to check out of the Marriott and relocate."

"Smart," agreed Brad. "No sense fighting the commuter traffic."

Hannah was delighted at the turn of events. Although she and Brad each had their own agenda, their goal was the same; to get to the bottom of the story. It meant that they would be spending a lot of time together.

Raising her eyebrows in graceful innocence, Hannah asked, "Which hotel are you staying at?"

CHAPTER FORTY-THREE

CHICAGO

Worldwide, there are approximately sixty countries that produce coffee. However, of those nations, Brazil and Colombia, by themselves, account for almost half of the world's production. Comparatively, Mexico, which is the fourth most successful grower, supplies a mere nine percent of the global market. Combined, Colombia and Brazil have about 400,000 farms dedicated to growing coffee.

In Brazil, the farmers, known as *fazendas de café,* are concentrated in an area of the country that the maps refer to as the state of *Sul de Minas.* The western part of that state has a growing region called the *Cerrado Vintage.* It is there that the finest Brazilian coffee is produced.

Colombia has a similar situation. *Bucaramanga* is the capital of its coffee growing region. *San Gil, Campesino, and Santander* are three of the most fertile spots within Bucaramanga. The Colombians insist that coffee was first grown in the *Santander* region. Just as in Brazil, the coffee is cultivated on thousands of small farms called *minifundios.* Although the largest of the Colombian farms is the *Narino* Vintage, there is another farm that is almost as large. It is called *Tuluni.* Located in the far south, Tuluni extends several miles into Ecuador and produces more of the very finest coffee beans than anywhere else on Earth. Experts say that the exquisite soil in the Tuluni region is due to two things. First is its proximity to one of Colombia's most beautiful natural attractions, the Caves of Tuluni. The second reason is that the land is nestled under the shadow of the great volcano Galeras. The end result of this unusual combination of geological phenomena is a rich harvest of Colombia's best blend.

Josef Ubermann sat back in his chair. He had amassed an impressive amount of information on the coffee growing regions of South America. Pulling out all the stops, he called everybody that he considered an expert in the industry. Their input, along with intensive internet research, gave the commodity broker his needed insight.

Although Ubermann was eventually able to identify those plantations that would become central to his plan, there was additional good news right around the corner. It turned out that thousands of smaller farms either bordered the fields of the main plantations, or bordered each other. When one studied a map of either the Colombian or Brazilian growing regions, it quickly became apparent that all the farms, crowded in together, looked as though they were a single, gigantic coffee plantation. Armed with that knowledge, he formulated a plan of action. It was a plan that would earn him wealth beyond avarice.

Ubermann had also completed the task of making reservations for his nephew, Bruce, and his newfound friend, Miguel. Together, the two men would take a private charter aircraft to Bogotá, Colombia. Once there, additional arrangements were made to board a smaller propeller-driven airplane, fly over their targets, and release thousands of coffee-eating caterpillars.

Experiencing a throbbing at his temples, Ubermann closed his eyes and gently massaged the discomfort. He became alarmed when he felt a vein bulging out from one side of his forehead and wondered if his nephew was going to be the cause of a debilitating stroke.

It had been almost thirty-six hours since Ubermann had heard from Bruce. Ubermann had fumed in frustration when he was informed that his nephew had checked out of the Hilton without leaving a forwarding address. Ubermann had tried calling Bruce's cell phone only to suffer through one announcement after another, asking the caller to leave a message. With each failed attempt, Ubermann grew angrier.

The phone rang, jangling Ubermann's nerves. Snatching it up, he answered, "Yes?"

"Uncle Joe? Is that you?"

Ubermann was aware of his fingertips turning cold from the pressure of squeezing the phone. "Where the fuck have you been?" he growled menacingly. "Do you realize how many times I've tried calling you?" His voice escalated dozens of decibels as he shouted, "Do you? You asshole! You're going to give me a fucking heart attack! You know that?"

Not wanting to say anything about being hunted by Porky Pignatano's henchmen, Kreitzer, in a moment of clarity, figured that it would be best not to complicate things. "I'm sorry Uncle Joe," said Kreitzer. "I had to change hotels."

"Why the hell didn't you let me know?"

"I tried," lied Kreitzer, "but I couldn't get the calls to go through. My cell phone lost its charge and needed a new battery. It's okay now."

"You could've used a pay phone, you idiot! Why didn't you just use the phone in your room?"

Kreitzer's mind raced for an answer. "Uh . . . . I . . . . I had a woman with me," he stammered.

There was a long silence as Ubermann chewed the inside of his cheek. Speaking with a subdued intensity, Ubermann said, "You're a completely incompetent jackass. I ought to cut you out of this deal entirely."

An anxious moment swept over Kreitzer. "No, please, Uncle Joe! Jeez! Have a heart!"

"Stop sniveling," said Ubermann impatiently. "You'll get your cut, providing you pull your head out of your ass and start doing the things you need to do. Understand?"

Kreitzer apologized several times and promised that he would stay on top of everything from this point forward. After answering a barrage of questions, Kreitzer felt as though he had regained a modicum of his Uncle's confidence.

Ubermann told his nephew about the flight to South America. "You and your buddy, that Ortiz fellow, will fly out of Los Angeles with a charter jet service called *Sky Transport*. I want you to call them and confirm everything."

Sitting at the little desk opposite the bed, Kreitzer began writing instructions, using key words such as South America, L.A.X. and *Sky Transport's* telephone number. Scribbling furiously, Kreitzer wrote out his itinerary, including flying into El Dorado Airport in the capital city of Bogotá. From there, he would be boarding a second plane, a puddle-jumper that would fly him and Miguel to the primary coffee plantations of Colombia where they would drop half their stash of insects. The second half of their journey involved changing planes in the southern city of Leticia. There, a crop duster would fly them to Brazil, where they would repeat the infestation process.

Kreitzer had four pages of notes by the time Ubermann was finished dictating. He made his nephew repeat everything twice before he was satisfied. "Get on this, Bruce," urged Ubermann. "Stay focused. And, don't be messing with any whores, understand?"

"No problem, Uncle Joe. I'll get right on it."

Ubermann took a breath. "How about the bugs? Are they okay?"

"Oh, yeah," said Kreitzer, enthusiastically. "Miguel said that we should feed the caterpillars some coffee in order to keep them alive. So, we got a two-pound tin of Maxwell House, and I've been shoveling that stuff into their containers. You ought to see 'em, Uncle Joe. The god-damn things go nuts every time I feed them. And, they're getting bigger, too."

After promising to call at least twice a day, Kreitzer hung up and stared at the closet that held the two cartons of insects. He thought about his own last comment, that the caterpillars *were* getting bigger. It was just this morning that he noticed a definite bulge in the side of one of the cartons. Picturing an uncontrolled growth rate, he shuddered at the thought of the cardboard boxes bursting open. "Sweet Jesus," he whispered to himself. "What the hell am I supposed to do if that happens?"

CHAPTER FORTY-FOUR

CALIFORNIA

Pasadena's Ritz-Carlton Hotel featured two separate dining rooms. "The Terrace," which was the more casual of the two, was open for breakfast, lunch and dinner, but was best known for its sumptuous Sunday brunch. The more upscale of the eateries was "The Grill," which only served dinner and overlooked a stately and elegantly appointed garden. After Hannah had accepted his dinner invitation, Brad opted for the latter.

The waiter made several suggestions from an extensive wine list, and Brad chose a German Riesling that, ultimately, proved ideal.

After the wine was served, Brad held Hannah's gaze and offered a soft-spoken toast to their new friendship. The sincerity of his words put a spreading glow in her cheeks. If asked, she would have blamed the wine, although the flush of warmth went much deeper. Relaxing in her chair, Hannah considered the moment to be a perfect end to an otherwise hectic day.

While they were still in the parking lot outside the Pasadena Police Station, Brad had called the Ritz-Carlton and asked about the availability of a room for Hannah. Once the reservation was booked, she drove to Los Angeles, packed her belongings, and checked out of the Marriott. Then, fighting the blowing horns of impatient commuters, she headed back to Pasadena and checked into the Ritz. Hannah was given a nice room on the eighth floor overlooking the courtyard and gardens.

Looking up from her menu, Hannah stole a glance at Bradstone Bishop. He had a strong jaw line that gave his face the rugged good looks of an outdoorsman. Hannah was comfortable with his height. It was an issue with which she had struggled all her life. With Brad, she could wear three-inch heels and not feel conspicuous. When he walked, she noted an athletic gait, a fluid motion that made her think about whether or not he knew how to dance.

"See anything you like?" asked Brad.

"What?" said Hannah, coming out of her reverie.

"The menu," he gestured. "What's whetting your appetite?"

"Oh," said Hannah, looking back at the selections. "Umm . . . the little blurb under the Caesar salad says that they'll prepare it at our table. It's for two. Will you share it with me?"

Brad nodded. "Yes. That sounds good. How about the main course?"

Hannah closed her menu. "The salad will do fine. I have a feeling it's going to be more than enough."

Brad smiled. "Now I understand how you maintain your figure."

"It works."

Brad said, "This afternoon, at Envirogen . . . were you there covering the story about the murder?"

"Not really," explained Hannah. "I've been doing a series of articles about biotechnology. Specifically, genetic engineering. And, because of his intractable stance on the subject, I've been focusing my efforts on Brother Timothy. This morning I received a call from him. He said . . ." and here, Hannah deepened her voice in an attempt to mimic the Preacher's timbre. "If you want to see the handiwork of the Devil, meet me at Envirogen."

"Not bad," complimented Brad. "You've almost mastered his inflection."

"Thank you," said Hannah. "I'm still working on it."

"So, you were there covering his news conference."

"Yes. The good Preacher and his little minion of groupies who always seem to be hanging around."

Brad asked, "Like the character with the short fuse who got into it with that female technician?"

"Right," said Hannah, nodding her head. "Smenken. You're talking about Verne Smenken. That man's problems go a lot deeper than a short fuse. He can be dangerous. I actually saw him in a fight where he tried to kill a man with a heavy, steel folding chair."

Brad cocked his head and asked, "What were you doing at the time? Hanging out with him in some biker bar?"

Hannah giggled at the absurdity and said, "No. It happened while I was watching Brother Timothy on a TV talk show, and an argument broke out. Suddenly, Verne charged into camera view, swinging a metal folding chair and almost killing one of the panelists."

"It doesn't sound as though you'll ever be elected president of his fan club."

Hannah made a little face of revulsion. "He's such a little slime ball. He's there every time I interview Brother Timothy. He looks right through me and gives me the creeps."

After the waiter took their order, Brad sipped his wine and asked, "What does Brother Timothy have to say about the murder?"

"Brother Timothy's point of view is limited. He sees things as a struggle between good and evil, God and the Devil. If he likes something, it must be the work of God. If something is bad, or wrong, according to Brother Timothy's gospel, it must be the work of the Devil. The man isn't really interested in solving the crime. He's just interested in furthering his own agenda."

"Which is . . . ?"

"The basis of all his sermons is that genetic engineering is evil, the work of the Devil. He uses that message to instill fear in everyone who will listen to him. He says that the young scientist who lost his life, died because of the experiments he was conducting." Hannah lowered her voice once again, pontificating in the Preacher's southern drawl. "He had the audacity to put his fingers into God's own mixing bowls of life."

"You do that very well," said Brad.

Hannah gestured noncommittally. "To tell you the truth," she said, "Brother Timothy is starting to lose his luster. When I first began interviewing him, I was fascinated by his magnetism, his ability to weave his web. He's a powerful orator."

"I know," agreed Brad. "I've heard him speak."

Hannah continued. "But lately, he's changing. Fame and fortune are going to his head. He's become demanding and seems to be out of touch. I'm beginning to question his motives."

Brad started to say something, but was interrupted by the waiter who arrived with a large rolling cart filled with all the ingredients necessary to create a Caesar salad. Hannah and Brad watched as the waiter-cum-chef rubbed the sides of the big wooden bowl with fresh garlic. He pulverized some anchovy fillets and mixed in a raw egg, olive oil and Worcestershire sauce. After squeezing in the juice of half a lemon, he added the romaine leaves. Expertly tossed, the leaves evenly coated with the anchovy and oil mixture, the waiter sprinkled the whole thing with freshly grated Parmesan cheese and flavored croutons. It looked and smelled delicious.

The meal was fine. Brad and Hannah were each savoring an *aperitif* of Drambuie when she asked, "How did you get the name, Bradstone? It's very unusual."

"It's my mother's family name," explained Brad. "She died giving birth to me, and my father wanted to preserve her memory. Her name was Merriam Bradstone."

"That's so romantic. I mean, what your father did. They must have been very much in love."

A soft smile came to the corner of Brad's lips. "My father loved her very much. He always talked about her. He wanted me to know her as he did. My dad was a straight-ahead kind of guy. Strong, commanding and loved by everyone who knew him. He always said he inherited his leadership from his father, my grandfather."

"You're speaking in past tense," noted Hannah. "Are either your father or grandfather alive?"

"No. They're both gone. And, they represented the last of my family."

"What do you mean?"

Brad related the tale of the Bishop family history. His grandfather, Webster Bishop, was a riverboat gambler and a rogue. A colorful man who had made some money in the saloons and dance halls of middle America. A win in a high stakes poker game netted Webster Bishop a deed to some property in Oklahoma, which later turned out to be rich with oil.

"Really?" said Hannah. "It sounds like a movie script."

"Kind of. Grandpa Webster got himself partnered up with Standard Oil and was able to amass a sizeable fortune. He married my grandmother and produced only one child, my father. They named him John Henry Bishop after John D. Rockefeller and his partner, Henry Flagler. In the Forties, Palm Beach, Florida was becoming a winter playground for wealthy New York families, and one particular family, the Bradstone's, built a home on the ocean. My father had moved to the area to help Henry Flagler with his railroad, and met my mother Merriam. The rest you know."

"Sidney Aarons thinks very highly of you," said Hannah.

Brad smiled. "He said some very nice things about you as well."

Hannah said, "Sidney has sort of taken me under his wing. It turns out that he knew my father. They were good friends."

Hannah went on to talk about her parents. She spoke about her mother's career as a beauty queen, and her father's fame as an award-winning photojournalist. When she mentioned his untimely death, she found herself wiping away a tear.

"I'm sorry," she said. "I don't usually get emotional about this. It's been a long time since my father died and I . . ." Her voice trailed off.

Brad leaned forward and touched her hand. "I think it's a good sign," he said. "First of all, it shows that you have a heart. It also shows that you're feeling comfortable enough to share it with me."

"Yes," replied Hannah. "Somehow, it's comforting to know we have these things in common."

Brad maneuvered to a brighter subject. "We have a lot in common, including Professor Indira Jawara. She's quite the little fireball."

"Sure is," said Hannah, dabbing her nose with a tissue before taking a sip of her scotch-based liqueur.

Brad said, "And let's not forget Harry Goodenow."

Hannah shook her head, smiling ruefully. "Harry Goodenow," she said almost to herself. "That man is persistent. You know, he's left me at least a half-dozen messages. Will he ever give up?"

"Well, you'll be pleased to know that, for the moment, Harry has found someone new to pursue. Chances are he'll leave you alone as long as she keeps his interest."

Hannah smiled. "Your friend, Harry, is chock full of charm. I hope that he . . ." Her sentence was interrupted by a muted ring.

"Is that your cell phone?" asked Brad.

"Yes," replied Hannah, fumbling in her pocketbook. By the time she managed to hunt down the elusive phone, the ringing had stopped. "Oh, well," she said resignedly, "probably not important anyway."

Looking at her face, Brad saw that she was a little distracted. "Why don't you check to see who called? I don't mind."

"Are you sure?" she asked, reaching once again for the phone.

"No problem," he answered.

Hannah checked the little display window and said, "All of that, and I don't even recognize the number."

"Did the caller leave a message?" asked Brad.

Hannah punched in the combination of numbers and listened while the caller's message was repeated. Finally disconnecting, she said flatly, "That was Brother Timothy."

"Really?" exclaimed Brad.

"Yes. He wants me to call him, right away."

CHAPTER FORTY-FIVE

CALIFORNIA

"Garden of Light," announced the greeter.

Hannah was taken aback by the unexpected title and thought for a moment that she might have misdialed. "Excuse me," she said, "I was trying to get hold of Brother Timothy. Is this . . ."

"Hannah?" asked the voice on the other end. "Is that you?"

"Yes," answered Hannah, tentatively. "This is Hannah Carpenter."

"Hannah! It's me, Melanie! How are you?"

Knowing that she had in fact dialed correctly, Hannah felt relieved to finally recognize a now familiar voice. Melanie, she remembered, was the young girl who had escorted Hannah to her last interview with the Preacher. She was the same girl who charged into battle during Brother Timothy's televised brouhaha. "I'm fine, Melanie. Is everything all right where you are?"

"You bet. Now, hold on for just a minute. Brother Timothy was expecting your call."

Waiting for Brother Timothy to pick up, Hannah mentally replayed Melanie's greeting, "Garden of Light." As each day passed, the Preacher's organization seemed more like a Hollywood production and less like an evangelical ministry. Hannah wondered about who might have been responsible for creating the new title. Her contemplation was cut short by Brother Timothy, whose voice sounded hollow as if it were piped through a speakerphone.

"Ahh, my dear Hannah," said Brother Timothy. "I'm pleased you were able to return my call so promptly."

"Well, your message had a ring of urgency," said Hannah. "Is everything all right?"

"Yes, of course," answered the Preacher. "We're all okay, but there is an issue that needs to be discussed."

Something sounded different. For the moment, Brother Timothy seemed to have replaced his commanding demeanor with one that was almost apologetic. "Yes?" Hannah queried.

"It has to do with that sorrowful event that occurred this afternoon, and the bludgeoning of that young scientist, Ricky Ballinger."

"Did you find something?" she asked. "A suspect?"

Brother Timothy's voice returned to its more familiar timbre. "I have no doubt as to the ultimate identity of the perpetrator, as well as his motives."

Hannah closed her eyes, mildly irritated by the man's pomp. She knew he was referring to the Devil, and she was tiring of his single-minded point of view. The volume on the Preacher's speakerphone was high enough for Hannah to hear the sound of shuffling papers. She also heard someone else cough once, and wondered how many people were listening to this conversation. "Okay then," she conceded, "What can I do for you?"

"Will you be doing a story about the murder?" asked Brother Timothy.

Hannah narrowed her gaze. It was an odd question. She was a reporter and the murder of that young scientist was news. "Yes, of course. Why do you ask?"

"It's a good story, Hannah. It's a story that your readers will be interested in. I'm sure you'll do an exemplary job putting it together."

"Why do I have a feeling that you're getting ready to drop the other shoe."

"Don't misunderstand me, Hannah. I think this story needs to be told. It's just that . . ." Brother Timothy paused.

"Let me guess," said Hannah. "You want me to include your point of view, that Satan is behind the murder. Is that it?"

"You're an excellent reporter, Hannah. I've told you that from the beginning. I've always given you credit for being accurate and fair. If you choose to include my beliefs in your article . . . fine. And if not, that would be acceptable, as well. However, I do have a request."

Tentatively, Hannah asked, " . . . and that would be . . . ?"

"When you write about that young man's death, I would appreciate you sticking to the facts. Discovering the corpse at a place like Envirogen, a corporation that deals in genetically altered life-forms, is a story unto itself. It certainly doesn't need any embellishment. Especially over what happened while we were there."

Hannah was having trouble understanding the meaning of the Preacher's words. "What are you talking about?"

"I'm talking about the fiasco that took place this afternoon at Envirogen's laboratory. All those people carrying on like lunatics. Being asked to vacate the premises or be arrested. I found the whole episode a little . . . embarrassing."

Hannah relaxed, realizing that this phone call was nowhere near the crisis she imagined. Smiling at the recollection of the female lab technician pushing Brother Timothy and Verne Smenken into a tangled heap, Hannah realized that the Preacher was merely trying to head off a story that might bruise his colossal ego. "Brother Timothy," she said with a lilt in her voice, "is this an attempt to manipulate the press?"

"I'm merely asking you to keep to the story. The murder victim, who through no fault of his own, was pulled in by the satanic allure of the Devil. He found himself in unfortunate circumstances and had no way to prevent his own death. The police are falling over each other searching for earthly clues, while he lies there, clubbed to death by the Devil's own demons."

"It is a good story," agreed Hannah, "and I have full intentions of writing all about it. I may not give the Devil all the credit that you would like, but I will cover the story."

"Thank you," said Brother Timothy. "I knew I could count on you."

"Wait a minute," said Hannah. "I didn't agree to turn a blind eye to the fiasco that happened in the laboratory. I consider that just as much 'news' as the murder."

Hannah heard a moan of exasperation coming from someone else on the other end of the line. Brother Timothy said, "A good reporter focuses on the story at hand. She doesn't allow herself to get bogged down with distractions that, inevitably, turn off the reader. I want you to stay focused on the story."

Hannah was becoming annoyed with his tone. "You know what the problem is?" she asked rhetorically. "You don't realize that you've become news. Big news. That means the whole story gets told. Now, you may not like the things that are being written about you, but . . . hey, that comes with the territory."

A voice in the background uttered, "I told you she wouldn't listen."

Hannah felt a chill when she recognized the voice as that of Verne Smenken.

There was an unusually long moment of silence before Brother Timothy said, "Of course, you can mention the news conference that I was attempting to hold. I just don't want you writing about . . ."

Hannah interrupted. "Listen. Tomorrow, I'm going back to Envirogen and, hopefully, getting statements from the management and staff. Their viewpoint is as much a part of this story as yours. I'm sorry you're not happy with . . ."

Verne Smenken could be heard clearly as he said, "She's gonna make us look like a bunch of hillbillies. Let me take care of it."

"Sit down, Verne," demanded Brother Timothy. Then, to Hannah, "You disappoint me, Hannah. I've been more than fair with you. I've given you access and interviews. I feel that I deserve more consideration than you're offering."

A distant memory stiffened Hannah's resolve. When Brother Timothy uttered the words, 'You disappoint me,' it brought back the cold memory of her stepfather's abuse. A sharp edge came to her words. "I'm sorry you feel that way. I'm just doing my job."

Brother Timothy sighed. "Good night, Hannah."

In the moment before the line disconnected, Smenken could be heard saying, "You gonna let it be? Just like . . ."

The line went dead before she could hear the rest of the man's sentence.

*   *   *

Bruce Kreitzer was not looking forward to speaking with his uncle. The calls always turn into bashing sessions, a time for castigation and name-calling. It was becoming intolerable. Unfortunately, Bruce had no choice. This scheme, which involved dropping bugs into South American coffee plantations, was going to make him millions. It was going to get people like Porky Pignatano and Bruno Mordello off his back and allow him to live a lavish life style. A bevy of soft, silky women and a collection of sterling silver belt buckles would suit him just fine. Knowing that he needed to put up with his uncle's wrath for only one more day, Kreitzer breathed easier.

"Did you screw anything up?" asked Ubermann.

"No, Uncle Joe. I didn't screw anything up, but we got a problem."

"Oh, Christ! What now?"

"I called that *Sky Transport* charter service. They can't fly us out of here until Friday morning."

Ubermann fumed. It wasn't just another glitch, it was a major predicament. He had made contingent flight arrangements based on the time that the two men would have arrived in Bogotá. Now, all those secondary flights would have to be changed. Scheduling changes with those kinds of people usually meant more grief, more aggravation and definitely more money. "What time did they say they could get you there?"

Kreitzer referred to his notes. "The flight leaves at 6:30 in the morning. They gotta make a refueling stop somewhere, but then we get to Bogotá a little after 4:00 p.m. local time."

Despite Ubermann cursing with vile abandon, Kreitzer was grateful that the explosive string of epithets was not directed at him. Once the fires cooled, Ubermann jotted down the new flight times and prepared to rearrange the South American portion of his nephew's trip.

"All right," said Ubermann. "Let me get on this and do what I have to do. If anything else comes up, anything at all, you call me. Understand?"

Kreitzer hung up the phone after assuring his uncle that there wouldn't be any more problems. Thinking about his mission once he arrived in Colombia, Kreitzer looked up at the closet door and silently reminded himself not to forget to take the two cartons of insects.

The thought process reminded Kreitzer that he had not fed the little critters since earlier in the day. He walked to the closet and opened the door. Bending down to pick up the tin of Maxwell House, a small movement caught Kreitzer's eye. Something wriggled between the coffee container and his pair of brown shoes. Reaching to move the round metal coffee can, Kreitzer was startled to see two caterpillars inching along the carpet. "Oh shit!" he cried backing up.

He looked up at the two cartons that sat on the shelf. One seemed to be intact, but the second box was sitting at an odd angle. As his eye swept over the sealed carton, it moved. It seemed to seesaw as though it were balanced on a marble. Kreitzer darted his gaze back and forth between the rocking carton and the two caterpillars making their way across the floor. Suddenly, another caterpillar, bigger than either of the ones on the floor, pushed out from beneath the carton.

Kreitzer panicked. He picked up his shoe, intending to pulverize the caterpillars when, alarmingly, he saw another one of the spiny beasts inside his shoe! "God-dammit!" he yelled as he dropped the one shoe and reached for the other. Checking first to make certain that no additional bugs were hiding within, Kreitzer grabbed the toe of the loafer and, wielding it as though it were a blacksmith's hammer, beat the three bugs to death. They were big! Bigger than he remembered. When he connected with the heel of his shoe, they splattered, shooting their blood and guts in all directions. The impact made a weird crunching sound and, momentarily, Kreitzer envisioned a nightmare of hundreds more hiding all over his hotel room.

He looked up, searching for the caterpillar that had last escaped from its container. He spotted it, hanging off the edge of the shelf and about to drop to the floor. Kreitzer cocked his arm, ready to swing his shoe into battle, when the big bug released its grip and fell. "Holy shit!" he exclaimed, as he suddenly realized that, if he were still bent over, the bug would have landed on the back of his neck. "You little son of a bitch!" he screamed. "You're dead!" he screamed again, as he flailed wildly at the creature. "You are fucking dead!"

Panting more from fear than exertion, Kreitzer looked up at the fragile carton. He dropped his shoe and gingerly reached for the cardboard box. Gripping it with both hands, he became aware of its fullness. The sides of the container were being pushed outward by the strain of proliferating insects.

Placing it on the desk, he turned it upside down and caught his breath. The seam down the middle of its underside had split open. It wasn't big enough for the hordes of caterpillars to come rushing out, but it was an opening that was being tested by the life-forms trapped inside. Two of the ugly beasts were desperately trying to push their bulk through the narrow slit. Kreitzer laid the box down with its bottom side up and reached for the Gideon Bible. He placed the weighty book on top and stepped back. "That ought to hold you suckers!" Then, he called Miguel.

Miguel Ortiz wasn't much help. "It's too late to go out and get bigger cartons," he said. "Just go buy some more tape and tape the damn thing shut."

"What about feeding them?" asked Kreitzer.

"They should be all right until we get there," answered Miguel, referring to their South American destination.

"What, are you kidding?" said Kreitzer incredulously. "This is Wednesday. We ain't leaving until Friday. We can't take a chance and not feed them for that long. What the hell are we supposed to do if they die on us? You better get your ass over here and do something. You're the bug expert. This is your job."

"All right," said Miguel. "I'll come over tomorrow and transfer the bugs into bigger cartons."

"And feed them," added Kreitzer.

"Yeah, yeah. I'll feed 'em, too," said Miguel, annoyed at having to take orders from someone like Kreitzer. "In the meantime, go get more tape."

Kreitzer stepped out of the elevator and crossed the lobby to the front desk. "Is there some place around here that I can get some tape?"

The adolescent-looking desk clerk replied, "I think all the music stores are closed."

"I'm not talking about CD's and shit. I'm talking about tape for wrapping packages."

"Oh. You mean, like Scotch Tape."

"Yeah. Scotch Tape. Where can I get it?"

The young man gave Kreitzer directions to a 24-hour drugstore.

"Hey," said Kreitzer, as an afterthought, "Do you know if they sell belt buckles? Silver ones?"

Having no idea, the clerk just repeated his directions, saying that the store was less than a block away.

Outside, Kreitzer stepped across the narrow, covered driveway. Standing where he was partially obscured by a cluster of broad-leafed plants and a pair of thick Doric columns, he took a moment to breathe in the cool night air. A car pulled up and stopped between him and the lobby entrance.

Wondering if it might be a late night check-in, Kreitzer turned to satisfy his curiosity. Since the driver was watching his oversized passenger squeeze himself out of the car, only the back of the driver's head was visible. A moment later, a cold chill swept through Kreitzer's belly, as he recognized the emerging hulk of Bruno Mordello.

CHAPTER FORTY-SIX

CALIFORNIA

The cocktail lounge in the Ritz-Carlton Hotel was very comfortable. Soft music emanated from a piano bar where a dapper, white-haired gentleman, replete in tuxedo, played a medley of show tunes. A small candle, casting a romantic glow, adorned each table.

Hannah sat mesmerized, listening to Brad tell the story about Harry Goodenow, single-handedly thwarting an armed robbery at his bank.

Hannah said, "He just doesn't look like the type of person to do such a thing."

Brad grinned. "I think that Harry's heroic action surprised him more than it did the robbers."

Hannah's conversation with Brother Timothy, including his impertinent demands, and Smenken's veiled threats, had made her extremely tense. However, Brad had assured her that everything would be all right. His voice had a calming effect, and Hannah soon felt better. The mood lifted completely as soon as the waitress came by to take their orders. Hannah asked for a "Bikini Martini."

When Brad said that he never heard of it, the waitress recited the recipe. "To a jigger and a half of vodka, you add some Malibu rum and coconut liqueur. Then, you mix in a splash of pineapple juice and just enough cranberry juice to give the drink a meaningful blush. Shake that puppy over some cracked ice and . . . Salute!"

"Is that your favorite drink?" asked Brad.

"I don't drink enough to have a favorite," replied Hannah. "To tell you the truth, if I had two of those, I wouldn't be able to walk out of here. You'd have to carry me up to my bed."

Brad held her gaze for just a moment before smiling and looking away.

Realizing the implications of her last sentence, Hannah changed the subject and asked, "Wasn't that a terrible thing that happened at Envirogen?"

Brad looked quizzical. "Do you mean Rick Ballinger's murder, or Brother Timothy getting knocked 'ass over teakettle?'"

"No. I meant the murder," said Hannah. "Everyone was so upset. When you introduced me to Doctor Levine, she looked as though she were about to burst into tears."

Brad nodded. "Yes, I know. You're probably unaware that Sarah Levine and Rick Ballinger were engaged."

"Are you serious?" asked Hannah.

Brad confirmed it with a solemn, "Yes."

Hannah digested this information before softly uttering, "My God. That means, on top of losing her fiancé, she had to put up with Brother Timothy's insensitivity."

Brad decided to tell Hannah the rest of the story. "Poor Sarah has been through the proverbial wringer. When she became engaged to Rick, his mother, Stephanie, contacted me. The woman was positively livid with the prospect of her son getting married."

"Why?" she asked quizzically.

Brad replied, "Because Sarah Levine is Jewish."

Hannah was taken aback. "Those beliefs should have gone out with the Inquisition and the Dark Ages."

Brad shrugged. "Obviously, the prejudice is still with us."

A prolonged silence was finally broken by Hannah asking, "Do you have a problem with Jews?"

A smile inched its way to the corners of Brad's mouth. "I live in Florida," he stated, "a state made up of two kinds of people. Half of them are Jewish and the other half want to be. So, show me a good pastrami on rye, and I'll follow you anywhere."

Hannah giggled. "Tell me, how do you manage to keep good client relations with a woman like that?"

"It isn't easy," said Brad, shaking his head. "My second-in-command, Rose Goldberg, a Jewish grandmother type, without whom I could never survive, and Stephanie Ballinger, have this personal vendetta that absolutely poisons their relationship. I spend my days refereeing a war of vitriolic barbs."

"I'm half Jewish," said Hannah. "My mother's maiden name was Blumenfeld. Rebecca Blumenfeld. Although, when she competed in beauty pageants, she used the name, Becky Bloom."

"Beauty pageants." repeated Brad. "That goes a long way toward explaining your good looks."

"Thank you," said Hannah.

"Did you ever think of pursuing a career in modeling?"

"No," said Hannah with a soft laugh. "I fell in love with writing at an early age and set my sights on becoming a reporter."

"Sidney Aarons thinks that you have the potential of becoming one of the best reporters on his staff."

"Have you two been talking about me?" asked Hannah.

"Yup," admitted Brad. "I wanted to know when you were coming back to Florida. My intention was to ask you out to dinner. Now, here we are."

Hannah felt a warmth inside. This man sitting across from her was even better than she had anticipated. He was bright, conversational, and complimentary without being trite or condescending. He also seemed to be sincere, a quality she treasured. "I'm very happy that we got to do this sooner, rather than later," she said.

Lightly touching her arm, Brad looked into her eyes and said, "Me too."

It was just two words, but Hannah became aware of a breathlessness that surprised her. Despite feeling silly and adolescent, she wrapped herself in the glow of the moment. They continued to chat, and time slipped by quickly.

Brad said, "It must be very interesting having a job that changes so dramatically with each new assignment."

"You're right," said Hannah. "I come face to face with new surprises every day. It's one of the things I love about my work."

"Give me an example."

Hannah said, "Take the story I'm presently doing. It started out as an article about a Pentecostal minister preaching fire and brimstone. Halfway through, the story took on a life of its own. Now, I'm writing a series of feature articles about biotechnology. There are so many facets to the story. It's all very exciting."

Brad said, "Driving out here from the airport, I was listening to National Public Radio. Just some talk show, but they were discussing a problem that exists with the Texas Blue Bonnet, the official flower of that state. It grows wild along the highways, and it's being pushed out by a weed, known variously as turnip weed, turnip cabbage, or bastard cabbage. Texans have been pouring huge sums of money into genetic engineering, trying to eradicate this plant. Well, it turns out that the Lady Bird Johnson Wildflower Society has discovered that planting a flower called Indian paintbrush on top of the pesky weed will prevent it from blossoming and allows the Blue Bonnet to reemerge. So, you see, there's more than one way to skin a cat."

"That's a good twist to this story. Perhaps I'll use it."

Brad asked, "Where do you stand in this controversy?"

"To tell you the truth, I've been so busy trying to write the story that I haven't planted my feet on either side of the controversy. However, I'll tell you this;

321

ninety percent of the interviews that I've conducted all dance around one central issue. Money. Even Brother Timothy, who is steeped in altruism up to here . . ." said Hannah, gesturing to the height of her forehead, " . . . is motivated by the weight of his collection box. The more fear he can instill into his parishioners, the deeper they dig."

Brad said, "So, you feel that greed is the culprit?"

Hannah nodded. "It sure is a long way ahead of whatever's in second place." Leaning forward and lowering her voice conspiratorially, Hannah said, "I interviewed a prominent research scientist who swore that one of his co-workers had engineered a new drug for diabetics. It was designed to eliminate the need for daily injections of insulin."

"Why are we whispering?" whispered Brad. "I mean, so far, your story sounds okay."

"Wait," said Hannah. "Listen to this. He told me that his company put a halt to the new drug. Then, the inventor disappeared and his notes were destroyed."

Brad looked skeptical. "Assuming that the man's story was true, why would a pharmaceutical company do that? Wouldn't they be able to make a lot of money with a drug like that?"

"According to his story," continued Hannah, "the business of insulin injections, including needles and the rest of the paraphernalia brings in ten times more than what the new drug would have generated."

"Are you really going to print that?" asked Brad.

"Unfortunately," replied Hannah, "this guy wasn't able to give me enough facts to verify his story. So, I won't be able to take credit for a blockbuster headline. But, it's interesting speculation. The best I can do is to include his tale as a titillating possibility of the dark side of genetic engineering."

Brad wondered where news ended and sensationalism began. "I'll give you this much," he said. "In my experience, money is often a motivating factor. Sayings such as 'Money talks,' 'Follow the money trail,' or 'Put your money where your mouth is' sound like clichés, but they're really the golden rule of investigative work. The reason, of course, is greed."

Hannah asked, "Do you think that money is going to be at the root of Rick Ballinger's murder?"

"Too soon to tell," he answered. "If you recall, when we were at the police station, my buddy, Bettencourt, said that Ballinger still had his cash and credit cards. So, on the surface, it doesn't look as though money was the motive. On the other hand . . . . who knows. Tomorrow, I'm planning on going to Envirogen and speaking to the people connected with the case. Maybe by then, I'll be a little smarter."

Hannah said, "I'd like to be with you when you interview those people. Would that be all right?"

Brad smiled. "I'd like that very much."

Hannah looked at her watch. "It's getting late. Care to walk me to my door?"

Arriving on the eighth floor of the Ritz-Carlton, Brad and Hannah stepped off into a plush elevator waiting area. In addition to a single window overlooking the parking lot, the eight-by-twenty foot hallway offered a choice of two elevators or the emergency staircase as exits. Turning right down the main corridor, the couple passed a dozen rooms before coming to Hannah's door. As she inserted her passkey into the slot, Brad slipped his hand into hers.

Hannah was immediately moved by the gesture. The cool strength of his touch seemed electrifying and sent a silent flutter through her. Turning fully to face him and staring deeply into his eyes, she felt his fingers intertwine with hers as he slowly moved his lips closer. Lifting her chin, she closed her eyes and accepted his kiss.

It was a soft, gentle kiss, lasting just long enough to hold a promise of passion. Taking a half step backward, Hannah whispered, "Good night, Brad. And, thank you."

Pushing the door open with one hand, she reached in and flipped the switch on the wall. The light did not come on.

"Oh," said Hannah, toggling the switch several times. "Lights are out."

Brad said, "Probably just a blown bulb."

Hannah asked, "Could you hold the door open while I turn on the one over the bed?"

Brad did as asked, which allowed a little ambient light to filter in from the main corridor. He watched Hannah fade into the blackness of the room and disappear around the corner. A low thud was immediately followed by Hannah exclaiming, "Ow!"

"Are you all right?" asked Brad.

"Ooo, that hurt," said Hannah, plopping herself onto a corner of the bed.

Brad let go of the door and reached into the bathroom for the light switch. Turning it on, the light cast enough of a glow for Brad to make his way without bumping into any sharp objects. "What happened?" he asked.

"I rapped my ankle on the bed frame," she said, standing and wincing in pain. "And thank you for turning on the bathroom light. I wish I were smart enough to have thought of it."

"Are you going to be okay?" he asked.

Susceptibly aware of how close they were standing, Hannah swallowed and said, "Yes. Fine. I'm fine. Trying to slow her heartbeat, she added, "How about you?"

"I'm fine," said Brad with quiet reassurance. "Besides, now I get to kiss you goodnight, once again."

"Oh. I guess so," said Hannah, as she became aware of Brad's hand slipping around her waist and onto the small of her back. She put her hands on his chest and slowly slid them up and around his neck. Their lips met, separated, and came together again. Hannah felt both his hands on her back, one drawing her torso tightly against his, the other slipping down low and pulling her hips forward. The sensuousness of the moment was overwhelming, and she tightened her arms hungrily around his neck.

Brad was burning with desire. The woman he held in his arms was supple and eager. He felt her excitement as she pressed against his groin, seductively undulating her hips. Her breath was sweet and hot against his face, while her breasts were heaving, yearning with the expectation of things to come. As Brad kissed her neck, he bent and scooped her into his arms and laid her on the bed.

Hannah stiffened. "Wait," she said breathlessly. "Wait. Please."

Brad pulled back. "What is it, Hannah? What's wrong?"

"I can't do this," she said. "I mean . . . I can do this, but I just can't do this now."

Brad sat on the edge of the bed. "Okay," he said, exhaling. "Anything you want to talk about?"

"Yes," answered Hannah.

Fully expecting her to say that she did not want to discuss the matter, he was surprised by her quick, positive response. Brad took a calming breath and reached for her hand. "Before you tell me what's on your mind, I just want you to know that I think you're wonderful. Now, it's your turn."

"I think you're wonderful too," she said, wiping an invisible layer of perspiration from under her eyes. "It's just that it's moving too quickly. I don't feel right about this. It's too soon."

Brad nodded, albeit with some reluctance. "You're probably right," he said, standing and adjusting his clothing. "Other than a quick lunch at Paul's Dockside, this is the first opportunity we've had to spend any time together."

"Do you really understand where I'm coming from?"

Brad reached out and helped her up to a standing position. "Tell you what," he said with a grin.

"What?"

"I'll go take a cold shower, if you'll promise me that this little episode won't put a damper on our next date."

Hannah looked into his eyes and saw the sincerity she hoped to find. She threw her arms around him and squeezed a warm and appreciative hug. "Thank you, Bradstone Bishop. Thank you for understanding."

Brad made his way down the hall toward the elevator. Just before turning the corner, he looked back and saw Hannah standing and waving a final good night. He waved back, stepped into the vestibule, and pushed the "down" button. A couple of minutes passed. Since it was only four flights down to his room, Brad thought about taking the stairs. Hoping to hear some movement from the elevators, he leaned in closely and listened to each one. Sounding as though both cars were starting their upward journey simultaneously, he decided to give his patience an additional thirty seconds. Of the two elevators, the one closest to the main corridor arrived first. Brad stepped into the empty car, pushed the button marked "four," and waited for the doors to close. Nothing happened. He could hear the sound of the second elevator moving upward. Once again, he pushed the number for his floor and followed that by jabbing at the "Close Door" button. Finally, just as the second car reached the eighth floor, Brad's doors began to slide shut.

Brad shook his head. It was either feast or famine. A person could wait all night for one elevator, only to have both show up at the same time. His thoughts were interrupted by the figure of a man emerging from the other car. Brad caught a quick glimpse of the stranger's face. While the doors to Brad's car closed, he thought that the man looked suspiciously like the character that ended up on the floor at Brother Timothy's news conference. As Brad's car lurched downward, he suddenly cried out, "Smenken! That's Verne Smenken!"

CHAPTER FORTY-SEVEN

CALIFORNIA

Bruce Kreitzer dropped to his knees. He tried desperately to curl his long, lanky body into a tight ball and hide it under one of the nearby broad-leaved plants. He kept his head down like an ostrich, hoping that, since he could not see Bruno Mordello, Bruno would not see him.

The low rumble of Bruno's voice echoed under the hotel's canopy, as he ordered the driver, "Wait here! I'll be back!" The next sound was the car door slamming shut.

Crawling backward, Kreitzer inched along until he felt that he was fully hidden by one of the decorative columns that supported the covered portico. Heart pounding, he chanced a peek at the idling automobile. Unfortunately, he had moved too deeply under the cover of the broad leaves, and it prevented him from seeing anything. Still determined to get a look at the driver, Kreitzer cautiously raised his head.

"Are you all right, Mister?" asked a voice a mere five feet from Kreitzer's hiding place.

Panic engulfed Kreitzer like a wildfire, making his body break out in a sweat. His heart pumped with such force that his shirt pulsated to the rhythm. Kreitzer jerked his head around, trying to locate the questioner.

Standing there in plain view was a teenage boy, no more than fourteen. Wearing baggy shorts, an oversized sweatshirt, and a pair of sneakers that should have been condemned by the Board of Health, he held a skateboard tucked under one arm. The sight of Bruce Kreitzer's face, looking dirty, sweaty, and fearful, made the boy take a step backward and mutter, "Holy jeez!"

Kreitzer was prepared for the worst. Since Bruno Mordello's driver was within easy earshot of the teenager, Kreitzer fully expected to be riddled by the man's semiautomatic. Kreitzer squeezed his eyes shut and waited. When nothing happened, he glanced over and quickly realized that the man in the car was totally engrossed in manicuring his fingernails. Turning back to the youngster, Kreitzer mustered all his calm, put a finger to his lips, and pantomimed a request for a conspiratorial silence.

The boy just stared.

Kreitzer took a chance and whispered a single sentence of explanation. "I'm playing a joke," he said, his words barely more audible than a breeze. He winked and smiled as though he were bringing the boy into his confidence.

The adolescent glanced at the driver of the nearby car, before looking back to Kreitzer. Wordlessly, the kid dropped his skateboard onto the blacktop and swiftly pushed his way into the night.

His clothes sopped with perspiration, Kreitzer felt chilled and shivered involuntarily. Although he fought to maintain the air of calm that he had presented to the skateboarder, a feeling of panic lay just beneath the surface. Needing to see what was happening, he decided, once again, to peek around the column.

Using the pace of a snail, Kreitzer changed positions to get a better view. He heard Bruno Mordello lumber out of the hotel lobby and call, "Hey! Carmine!"

Carmine, the driver, tore his attention away from the concentrated study of his cuticles and said, "Yeah?"

"Park the car," ordered Mordello. "He's here."

Kreitzer knew instantly to whom Mordello was referring. They had found him. Again, he folded himself into a fetal position and wriggled back into the camouflage of the dense landscaping. Kreitzer stayed stock-still for what seemed like an eternity, but in reality, was only minutes before Bruno and Carmine disappeared into the lobby of the hotel. Kreitzer pulled himself out of his makeshift rabbit hole and bolted around the corner to where his rental car was parked.

Driving several miles, Kreitzer came to an all-night diner. He parked away from the glare of lights before assessing his situation. No clothes, no toiletries, and no place to stay. He did, however, have his rental car and his wallet, which allowed him a needed sigh of relief. The fleeting feeling of euphoria dissipated in a flash when he remembered that the two boxes of caterpillars were still in his hotel room. "Oh, shit," he muttered aloud. "Shit, shit, shit, shit!" He tried to concentrate on what to do next. Bruno and Carmine would probably be staked out in the lobby, preventing Kreitzer from retrieving the bugs. Knowing that he'd be spotted in a second, Kreitzer visualized himself being stripped naked, strung up by his thumbs, and tortured with a cattle prod.

Rubbing his face, Kreitzer tried to chase away the nightmare. He considered asking the hotel's desk clerk to go get the two boxes. If Bruno and Carmine were waiting in the lobby, the desk clerk's actions would not raise any suspicions. But, Kreitzer shook his head as he thought of a problem with his plan. The desk clerk, who would probably be curious, would want to open one of the cartons and look inside. 'Then what?' thought Kreitzer. "Christ!" he exclaimed aloud, rapping the heel of his hand on the steering wheel. He pictured thousands of insects running all over the lobby. It would be like opening the gates of Hell. He needed somebody trustworthy. Someone who would not pry. Someone like Miguel or Maria.

*   *   *

As he pushed the button inside the elevator, Brad desperately tried to think of why Verne Smenken would be on the eighth floor of the Ritz-Carlton. Nothing good came to mind. Despite Brad's attempt to stop the elevator on the seventh floor, the digital floor indicator showed that he had already descended further. Quickly, he jabbed both six and five and waited. The elevator finally came to rest on the fifth floor. Even before the doors were fully opened, Brad tapped the button that would bring the car back to the eighth floor. The doors seemed to take forever to close. Impatiently, Brad jammed his finger against the buttons marked "Eight" and "Close Door," but still nothing happened.

Verne Smenken was there to make trouble. Bad trouble. Brad had witnessed Smenken's temper and knew that he was capable of inflicting harm. Unable to wait any longer, Brad bolted from the elevator and ran across the narrow vestibule to the exit stairwell. As he dashed up the three flights of stairs, he hoped against hope that Hannah would not open her door to Smenken. Brad reached the eighth floor and charged into the stairwell door. Unexpectedly. it was locked, and running into it was like running into a brick wall. He tried the handle, rattling it with the force of a noisy intruder, but it would not respond. Looking through the little window, Brad was woefully discouraged to see that the elevator he had been in had just arrived and opened its doors to reveal an empty car. Belatedly realizing the hotel's security measures, Brad cursed the policy of locking the fire doors and only allowing access into the stairwell. He knew that the only door open at this time of night would be the one to the lobby. It meant that he had to run down the eight flights of stairs and then, only then, could he ride back up on the elevator. He flew down the stairs and burst through the door to the lobby. The remaining elevator was waiting there with an open door. Thanking the gods for small favors, Brad rode up unimpeded. His mind raced with the thoughts of how much time had elapsed during which Smenken could have raised hell.

On the eighth floor, Brad charged out of the car and wheeled around the corner, hoping to see Smenken standing in front of Hannah's room. Instead, the corridor was empty. As Brad sprinted down the hallway, he heard a crash followed by a muffled scream. At the door, he saw the edge of a towel sticking out from the bottom, preventing it from closing all the way.

Pushing his way inside, Brad heard Smenken growl, "You filthy bitch! I'll slice you to ribbons!"

"Hey!" hollered Brad, darting forward.

Smenken spun at the sound of the shout. He snarled and crouched, preparing to parry the attack. "I'll kill you too, you sinner!" he spat.

The room was in shambles. The big desk was tilted backward on two of its legs and leaning against the window sill, while a wooden, straight-backed chair was upside down against the adjacent wall. The table lamp, although cracked and lying on the floor, was still shining brightly. Clad only in her white bra and panties, Hannah cowered on the club chair. Although Brad took in the entire scene, his focus was on the outstretched arm of the intruder, which held a thick-bladed knife.

Smenken lurched forward, jabbing the air with the deadly weapon and causing Brad to jump back reflexively. The attacker did it twice more in quick succession, each time taking a half step closer and forcing Brad farther back toward the bed.

"Is that the best you can do?" taunted Brad.

"I'll show you what I can do!" said Smenken with uncontrolled vehemence. He lunged again, slashing the knife from side to side.

Hannah screamed.

Brad skipped from one side to the other, avoiding the razor tip by mere inches. As Smenken's right arm was crossing his body in a wide arc, Brad leaned in and shot out a left hook, catching Smenken on the side of his cheek.

The blow stunned the knife wielder, stopping him in his tracks. Using his left hand, he touched the raw spot on his face and looked at his fingertips. Blood confirmed the open gash on his cheekbone. His eyes went wide. With flared nostrils and savage rage, Smenken spewed a new revelation. "You are the Devil!" he uttered. Pointing with his knife, he added, "You and that bitch!" In a flash, Smenken charged forward, baring his teeth like a wild animal.

Not expecting Smenken's quickness, Brad barely had time to counter the move. The knife came at him in a downward arc plunging toward his chest. Instinctively, Brad put up his arm, luckily blocking the glistening blade from finding its mark. With his left hand, Brad seized the man's wrist and held on.

Smenken reached around and grabbed a handful of Brad's hair, yanking viciously and pulling his head backward. With grim determination, Brad continued to hold tightly to Smenken's wrist, which still held the weapon. They spun together in the center of the room like two dervishes locked in a death struggle. They danced toward the opposite wall where the wooden chair lay overturned. Brad struggled to maintain his grip, but it was like holding on to a writhing eel.

Sweeping his leg, Brad tried to knock the assailant off his feet. It took two attempts before connecting. However, with their arms and legs locked in combat, the two men, together, toppled and crashed into the wooden chair. Slamming his hand into a corner of the overturned piece of furniture, Brad felt his fingers go numb. Smenken pulled his knife hand free, forcing Brad to roll away from the inevitable jab and slash. He scrambled to his feet in time to see Smenken do the same. Brad backed up to the foot of the bed where the bedspread lay in a folded heap. Smenken charged, emitting the bloodcurdling scream, "Vengeance is mine, sayeth the Lord!"

Brad heard Hannah's fearful cry, as he reached for a handful of bedspread and threw the bulky pile of fabric up between himself and the flailing maniac. A second later, Smenken ran into the bedcover, which partially draped itself over his right arm and shoulder.

Wasting no time, Brad lashed out with a kick to the groin. Smenken doubled over, crying out in agony, but still slashing wildly with his big knife. Brad pressed his advantage, kicking the attacker again, this time a downward thrust onto the side of Smenken's knee. He buckled and began to fall to the floor. Stepping forward, intending to do more damage, Brad suddenly felt the hot burn of steel. The knife had sliced the side of his right calf. Awkwardly, Brad stepped sideways, reaching out to hold onto something to keep from falling.

Screaming obscenities, Smenken writhed in pain. But through it all, he looked up and saw that his enemy was injured and holding on to the overturned chair for balance. Sensing an opportunity, Smenken, still on his knees, swung the knife in a wide arc, hoping to amputate any body part within reach.

Brad heard Hannah shriek in horror just as the knife grazed his thigh. Holding the protruding leg of the chair, Brad pivoted and grabbed it with both hands. Then, lifting and swinging it in a belt-high arc, Brad put all his strength into the whipping action. Smenken saw the chair coming and tried to duck out of the way, but it was too late. The sturdy piece of furniture pounded into Smenken's shoulder with the force of a battering ram.

The sound of the impact was sickening. Brad's first thought was that the wooden chair had split, only to realize a moment later that the noise was that of breaking bone. Emitting a guttural howl, Smenken watched his knife fly out of his hand and skitter under the television cabinet.

Despite having the use of only one arm, Smenken, snarling like a trapped animal, still managed to get to his feet and attempt a headlong rush. However, the fight had taken its toll. Smenken's dislocated knee slowed his forward motion, and Brad easily sidestepped the limping madman. Firing out a right hook, Brad's fist connected fully with Smenken's temple. Down he went. Struggling back to his feet, Smenken wavered unsteadily until his eyes rolled back in his head and he collapsed, unconscious.

Hannah unfolded her cowering body from the club chair and rushed into Brad's arms. Shaking like a leaf in an autumn wind, Hannah sobbed and tried to explain what had happened. Brad held her tightly until a semblance of calm returned.

Their embrace was interrupted by a groan from the beaten man on the floor. Brad glanced at Smenken before looking at Hannah and asking, "You don't happen to have any rope, do you?"

Hannah shook her head nervously. "No. No rope."

"All right," said Brad. "You call the police. I'll take care of this character."

As Hannah dialed 911, Brad unfolded the king-size bedspread and laid it out on the floor. Grabbing Smenken by the ankles, Brad maneuvered the man onto the spread and began to roll him up like a burrito. Halfway through, Smenken became alert and struggled to free himself. However, with his body tightly cocooned, the man was harmless. Nevertheless, he did manage to crane his neck. Seeing Hannah's half-naked body, he intoned in a deep drawl, "You are the Devil's own slut! It is women like you who set fire to the world and devour its children! It is women like you . . ."

"Shut up, Smenken, you creep!" Brad kicked the bedroll, but the thickness of the padding negated its impact.

"And you!" shouted Smenken, peering at Brad through snake-like slits. "You lust after this whore! Just like Brother Timothy." The pronouncement of the Preacher's name had a strange effect on Smenken. He began to whimper. " . . . my . . . Brother . . . Timothy." The poignant little cry quickly turned into sobs, and soon Smenken was struggling to catch his breath. However, within seconds, he swallowed hard and renewed his invectives. "Whores! Vermin! All of you conspiring to steal my Timothy away from me!"

During Smenken's ranting, Brad went to the closet and removed a wooden hanger. Returning to his rolled up prisoner, Brad rapped him on the head with enough force to rattle the man's teeth. "Enough!" commanded Brad. "I don't want to hear another word from you."

In response, Smenken spat at Brad. Instead of hitting its target, the wad of mucus landed on a corner of the spread that partially covered Smenken's mouth.

Rolling the madman over onto his stomach, Brad sat down in the middle of Smenken's back. Despite the humiliation, Smenken wasn't finished. Although his voice was muffled by the fabric and the carpet, he shouted, "The Lord's work must be done! The death of . . ."

Once again, Brad smacked the top of Smenken's head with the sturdy hanger. It made a loud "crack" and was followed by painful grumbling. Ignoring the man's complaint, Brad asked casually, "How are you doing with that phone call, Hannah?"

It took the better part of two hours, but the episode finally drew to a close. Hannah had dressed hurriedly, throwing on a pair of taupe slacks and a sweater the color of oatmeal. As she tended to the knife wound on Brad's calf, Hannah was interrupted by the arrival of four policemen, two paramedics, and a clerk from the hotel's front desk. After statements were given, the cops accompanied Smenken to jail, while Hannah accompanied Brad to the hospital.

It was just before two in the morning when the couple arrived back at the hotel. Begging her forgiveness, the hotel's management had arranged for Hannah to have a different room. Sitting on the corner of the bed in her new quarters, Hannah shivered slightly as a chill passed through her.

Brad asked, "Are you going to be all right?"

"I . . . I think so," she answered.

Brad said, "You realize that you don't have to stay here. We can check you in to any hotel. If we use my credit card, you'll have total anonymity. You'll be safe."

Hannah looked up. It was a sound suggestion. However, feeling as though she would be giving in to her fear, she shook her head and said, "Thank you, Brad. I appreciate the offer, but I'll stay here." Trying her best to put on a brave face, she looked around the large room. "It's nice here, comfortable. I'll be fine."

"Okay," said Brad, a little uncertain about her fearlessness.

"I'm more worried about you," she said pointing to Brad's dressing. "Are you having a lot of pain?"

In the Huntington Memorial emergency room, a Doctor had used nine stitches to sew up Brad's leg. "No pain at all," he said. "Not only did the doc do a good job, but they pumped me full of antibiotics and painkillers."

Hannah took an audibly ragged breath. She looked into Brad's eyes for only a moment before staring down at her tightly clenched hands. She started to speak, then hesitated, searching for her words. "He was so . . . . He looked like . . ." she paused, as her fear came rushing back.

Brad took Hannah's hands and guided her to a standing position. Feeling her tremble, he gently encircled her with his arms.

Her voice choked as she said, "I thought he was going to kill me." A single sob made her quiver. "And I thought I was going to lose you, too."

Brad held her more firmly, trying to chase away the memories of Smenken's attack and replace them with the safety and security of his own embrace. Hannah responded to his strength and wrapped her arms tightly around him. She placed her cheek next to his, savoring the calm that was beginning to wash over her.

Brad lightly kissed her forehead and both cheeks. Closing her eyes and tilting her head back, Hannah yearned for more. Sensing her desire, Brad brushed his lips over her neck and tasted the delicateness of her skin and the barest hint of her perfume. Ever so softly, Hannah moaned with pleasure and moved her lips to meet Brad's.

Suddenly aware of her vulnerability, Brad felt a wave of guilt. Quietly, he said, "I'm not sure this is such a good idea."

A puzzled expression crossed Hannah's face, as she studied Brad's eyes. Time passed. The Earth slowed its wild spin, and the tides flowed in on majestic curls, allowing her to clearly see into this man's heart, into his soul. Answering his doubts, she slid her arms around his neck and fully kissed his mouth. Then, with her lips barely brushing his earlobe, she whispered, "Stay with me."

CHAPTER FORTY-EIGHT

CALIFORNIA

Growing impatient, Bruce Kreitzer looked at his watch. It was 6:50 Thursday morning and for the past seven hours, he had been parked in front of Miguel and Maria's apartment. Just before midnight, Kreitzer had called Miguel to inform him of the situation.

Maria had answered the phone on the fourth ring. Sounding breathless, she barely had managed to say "hello." Ignoring her huffing and puffing, Kreitzer had asked to speak with Miguel. Although Maria had muffled the telephone's mouthpiece, Kreitzer heard her say, "Honey? It's Bruce. He wants to talk to you."

Miguel cursed before saying, "I told you not to answer the god-damned phone!"

"But he wants to talk to you," urged Maria.

"Well, I ain't talking to him. So, hang it up!"

Uncovering the mouthpiece, Maria said, "Miguel said that he'll talk to you in the morning."

Frustrated, Kreitzer had spent the night in his car. Face unshaven, teeth unbrushed, and still wearing yesterday's clothes, Kreitzer felt like a homeless person living inside an untended-laundry hamper.

At half past seven, Miguel finally walked out of his apartment building. Unfolding his stiff and aching body from behind the steering wheel, Kreitzer met the Mexican on the sidewalk. "We got a problem," he said without preamble.

"Yeah, we got a problem!" snapped an irritated Miguel. "We got a big problem. You! You and your god-damn phone call, right in the middle of me gettin' some poon-tang."

Kreitzer blinked. The unexpected remark made him lose his train of thought. "Uh . . . I didn't know you were getting laid," he said dumbfounded.

"Well, I was. And I don't get laid that much. So, why the hell were you calling so late?"

Kreitzer was still bewildered over Miguel's comment. After all, having the luxury of living with a beautiful prostitute like Maria meant that he should be getting as much sex as he wanted. Snuffing out the thought and refocusing, Kreitzer said, "This is serious. Real serious."

Miguel looked exasperated. "What?" he asked curtly.

"The bugs are in my hotel room and I can't get to them."

Miguel just stared, unable to comprehend what he had just been told.

Kreitzer spent the next ten minutes explaining the situation. Even though he mentioned Bruno Mordello and his greasy companion Carmine, Kreitzer changed the story slightly. Instead of admitting to owing huge gambling debts, he chose to say that the two men were there to repossess his car. Embellishing the tale so as to make it plausible, Kreitzer explained that he was driving a rental car just to keep the repossession agents off his back. And that, in actuality, his own car was parked in a garage in Burbank. "My car has been giving me all kinds of repair problems. I don't want to pay for the car until they fix it right. In the meantime, I've got two goons, waiting for me to show up, back at the hotel. All they want to do is repossess the damn thing."

Miguel understood. "Yeah, man," he said, remembering his own past run-ins with a re-po man. "I know what you mean. So, what do we do now?"

Kreitzer explained the simple plan. All Miguel had to do was go to Kreitzer's room, grab the two boxes of bugs and leave.

Miguel looked dubious. "But what about those two guys?" he asked. "What if they give me a hard time?"

"They ain't after you," said Kreitzer. "They're probably hanging out in the lobby waiting for me. You'll be able to waltz right past them. You'll be in and out of there in no time."

*   *   *

Some people move to Southern California for the weather. Along its coast, they are assured of shirtsleeve temperatures and comfortable humidity. From Hannah's viewpoint, the day was absolute perfection. The sky seemed a deeper blue, as though Mother Nature had added melted sapphires into her color palette before brushing it on to the canopy above. The air seemed cooler, softer and honey-pocked with wisps of jasmine and myrrh. With her senses heightened, Hannah basked in her neoteric surroundings, appreciating all the things that she normally took for granted.

Hannah's brightened outlook stemmed from the act of giving and receiving without reservation. Her time spent with Brad brought her to a place she had never been; a place of dizzying heights and swirling vortexes. For Hannah, the night had passed in a dream filled with passion beyond anything she had ever experienced. Their lovemaking had gone on for hours. It wasn't until almost dawn that they finally fell back into their pillows, tired and spent from their fervor. Although Brad had fallen asleep almost instantly, Hannah nestled into the crook of his arm and spent the balance of the night watching him.

During breakfast, Brad skimmed a layer of cream cheese onto his bagel, while Hannah studied his face. A warm glow spread across her cheeks as she admired his rugged good looks.

Brad took a bite of his bagel before asking, "Would you mind if I gave you a little advice?"

"Not at all," answered Hannah, coming out of her daydream.

"Last night, you suffered through the emotional stress of almost being killed. Afterward, we exhausted ourselves . . . ." Brad smiled warmly before adding, " . . . expending all that passionate energy. Then, by your own admission, you didn't get any sleep. If you don't at least eat some breakfast, you're going to fall face-first into your bowl of soup come dinnertime."

Hannah looked at her plate and realized that her mushroom omelet was untouched. Taking a forkful, she said, "Thank you. That's good advice."

Watching her eat, Brad thought about their night of lovemaking. It had been different in a way he hadn't expected. Better. More intense. Certainly more satisfying. Perhaps, it was the leftover tension of surviving Smenken's attack that heightened their passion. Perhaps, it was his audacious rescue that added to the depth of their pleasure. For whatever reason, the night had been special. He found himself looking forward to the days to come.

The waiter was refilling their coffee when Brad's cell phone announced an incoming call. It was Steve Bettencourt, Captain of the Pasadena Police Department. "Just calling to check on you after your knife fight," said Bettencourt. "How are you doing?"

"Good," said Brad, brightly. "Doc says I'll probably make it to lunchtime."

"I already got the hospital report, Hero," said Bettencourt. "Nine stitches and a tetanus shot, but no permanent damage. Can't hurt a bonehead like you."

Brad asked, "Anything new on the Ballinger murder?"

"Nothing definite, yet," said the Police Captain. "We're still trying to put it together. Santero is going back to Envirogen for another round. One of the techs is a guy by the name of Miguel Ortiz. Employees say that Ortiz and the victim were always at odds over one thing or another. Santero's going to interview Ortiz again and see if he had a real hard-on for his boss. And there's another guy we want to talk to. A supervisor, just like Ballinger. His name is Fishman. Mel Fishman. A witness said that Fishman actually threatened Ballinger's life."

"Sounds promising," said Brad.

"Yeah, well, Doctor Levine said she was there during that incident. According to her, Fishman is all bark and no bite. But, we'll check him out anyway."

Brad had been listening closely, and it didn't sound as though the cops were closing in on the killer. "Let me throw a monkey wrench into the works," he said. "I think that you should put Verne Smenken on your suspect list."

"Why? You pissed at him because he came at your girlfriend with a butcher knife?"

"That would be reason enough," grunted Brad. "But, no. I'm not a vindictive kind of guy. Fact is, Verne Smenken has motive."

"Okay," said the cop. "Let me hear it."

Bettencourt listened as Brad put forth his theory. He talked about Brother Timothy's sermons expounding on the evils of genetic engineering and Verne Smenken's blind allegiance to the Preacher. "I believe that Verne has been so brainwashed that he can't tell right from wrong. He's only interested in carrying out the Lord's vengeance, or the Preacher's vengeance, or, whatever. Either way, I think he saw Rick Ballinger as more than a geneticist. I think he saw him as one of Satan's demons, someone who needed to be destroyed. And by the way, little Verne is hopelessly in love with Brother Timothy. I think he'd be willing to do anything for that man, including murder."

"Interesting theory," said Bettencourt. "Do you have anything that might be construed as evidence?"

"Not much," replied Brad. "Couple of things he said last night, but that's about it. My friend, Hannah, has interviewed Brother Timothy several times with Smenken present. She can probably give you a better insight."

"Well," said Bettencourt, "now that he's in our custody, we'll have an opportunity to put the screws to him. Detective Santero is very good at getting perps to confess."

"Who knows?" said Brad. "Maybe, you really can get him to confess to killing Ballinger."

Bettencourt was doubtful. "Yeah, right. Maybe, the creep will admit to being the other gunman on the grassy knoll. Or . . . Hey! Better yet, maybe, Smenken is the killer that O.J. has been looking for. Ever think of that?"

CHAPTER FORTY-NINE

CALIFORNIA

Despite the confidence that Kreitzer had tried to instill in Miguel, the Mexican lost it all as soon as he entered the lobby of the hotel. He had listened to Kreitzer's pep talk and understood that going in and bringing out the bugs would be a cakewalk. Now, faced with the reality of actually carrying out the deed, Miguel felt anxious.

Before arriving at the hotel, the two men had stopped at Gelson's Supermarket and picked up two cartons and a roll of plastic tape. Since the caterpillars had outgrown their original cardboard boxes, Miguel planned to transfer the insects to the new, larger ones.

With the corrugated cartons folded flat and tucked under his arm, Miguel entered the lobby of the hotel. Hesitating, he searched the room for anyone resembling the two men who were after Kreitzer. Not seeing them, Miguel walked quickly to the elevator and rode up to the third floor.

Stepping out of the elevator, Miguel looked up and down the long corridor. Except for a housekeeping cart, which took up half the width of the narrow hallway, no one was there. Glancing behind him as he walked, Miguel made his way towards Kreitzer's room, which was past the cart, almost to the end. Apprehension was making his breathing shallow, and thin beads of sweat formed on his upper lip. From the corner of his eye, he glimpsed a lurking shadow. It made him jump, causing one of the flat boxes to slip from his grasp. A maid, standing in an open doorway, stifled her greeting when she saw the panic in Miguel's eyes. Lowering her head, she melted back into the room and returned to work.

Picking up the fallen carton, Miguel cursed himself for being so jittery. He quickened his pace and, in a moment, was standing at the door marked 324. As Miguel reached into his pocket for the key, the sound of the arriving elevator drew his attention. He was certain that the two men, looking for Kreitzer would suddenly charge out of the elevator and shout commands such as 'Freeze!' or 'Stay where you are!' Anticipating the worst, Miguel held his breath. Instead of a confrontation, a middle-aged couple emerged and made their way to the opposite end of the hall. Miguel exhaled, as a trickle of perspiration ran down the inside of his shirt. Relieved, he slid the key into the slot, turned the handle and opened the door.

"Holy shit!" uttered Miguel in alarm. "Holy fucking shit!" Two big coffee cups lay on the floor, their contents emptied and puddled into big, wet, stains. As Miguel stared fixedly at two masses of caterpillars, each swarming hungrily over the coffee spill, he shuddered in fear. The insects had grown very large. Each was now close to three inches long and much fatter around the middle.

Miguel turned his attention to the most shocking sight in the room. Between the double mountains of ravenous insects, lay the bodies of two dead men.

*   *   *

After arranging a morning appointment with Sarah Levine, Brad and Hannah made certain to get there early. It quickly became apparent that Envirogen had altered its security procedures. The young girl who normally sat at the reception desk manicuring her nails had been replaced by a uniformed man demanding to see some identification. All visitors were made to sign a log and wait while the time of their arrival was duly noted. Only then were they issued a temporary pass. A second security officer, standing guard at the elevators, scrutinized the newly acquired passes before allowing anyone access to the rest of the building. It wasn't until the couple entered Sarah's office that the air of tight security finally lifted.

Sarah, who had not yet eaten breakfast, led Brad and Hannah to the cafeteria. The couple ordered coffee, while Sarah filled her tray with a buttered blueberry muffin, a powdered sugar donut, and a large glass of orange juice. Apologizing for her indulgence, she said, "I can't help it. When I'm stressed, I compensate by eating. Losing Rick is going to turn me into a two-ton widow."

"Have you been sleeping?" asked Hannah.

"Sleep?" asked Sarah. "That word sounds familiar. I think I remember doing that in a former life."

When Hannah and Brad had first arrived, he made a point of reintroducing the two women. The previous day's event, which included Brother Timothy's attempted news conference, had been such a confusing hullabaloo that Brad doubted whether Sarah would have remembered meeting Hannah. Brad presented Hannah as a good friend and a reporter doing a feature article on Brother Timothy.

At first, Sarah seemed dubious about Hannah's agenda. However, rather than stew about it, Sarah decided to ask a pointed question. "Is your article going to include information about the death of my fiancé?"

"The focus of my story is Brother Timothy," said Hannah. "When I first met him, I was impressed with his good looks, commanding voice, and dynamite smile. But now that I've come to know him, I see a dark side. Besides having questionable morals, the man is a blatant opportunist. After he found out that your fiancé had been murdered, he jumped at the chance to use that tragedy to further his own cause. The man clearly understands words like manipulation and fear mongering, but has no concept of things such as sympathy or remorse. I do intend to mention Rick's death, but only to expose Brother Timothy for what he is."

Hannah's commentary was disarming. Moved by the woman's honesty, Sarah felt an instant camaraderie. She wiped her lips clean of any telltale powdered sugar residue and asked, "Any word on what's happening with the investigation?"

"Not much," answered Brad. "Still ongoing. As a matter of fact, Detective Tony Santero will be here later today. He wants to talk to a few more people."

Sarah sighed. "Funny, how strange thoughts keep popping into my head. It wasn't too many years ago that the term, 'closure,' began to be used. Anytime there was a televised interview with people who lost loved ones, a kidnapping, a murder, whatever, the family always talked about the need for closure. I used to pooh-pooh the idea until . . ." Sarah lowered her head for a moment before continuing. "Until I lost Rick. Now, suddenly, I understand the concept."

"If it's any consolation," said Hannah touching Sarah's hand, "the police have indicated that the autopsy should be completed sometime today or tomorrow."

Sarah nodded, but didn't say anything.

Brad said, "I'm friendly with a guy named Steve Bettencourt who happens to be the Captain of the Pasadena Police Department. He and I met when we were both working for the FBI. He said that he'll do what he can to move this along."

Sarah's eyes pooled as she returned Hannah's hand-squeeze. "You have no idea how much I appreciate what you're doing for me. I wouldn't even have known where to begin."

Brad said, "The Captain asked if I would offer my assistance in the investigation. Unofficially, of course."

"Good," said Sarah. "I feel better knowing that there's someone on the team who's looking out for my interests."

Leaning forward and lowering his voice, Brad said, "Bettencourt mentioned a name to me. Mel Fishman. He said that there were witnesses who overheard Fishman threatening Rick. What can you tell me about this guy?"

Sarah was shaking her head even before Brad finished asking the question. "Mel is just a blowhard. Very competitive. A typical overachiever. I was there when that incident occurred. It happened because Rick was chosen to head up a project that poor Mel thought he deserved. He was just lashing out."

Brad asked, "So, you don't think he might have been angry enough to plan a murder?"

Sarah shook her head again. "No." Then, she added, "Look. No one is more interested in finding Rick's killer than I am. Believe me, if I thought there was the slightest possibility that Mel Fishman was the culprit, I'd be first in line to pull the lever on his gallows. But Mel's all bluster. The first sign of any physical confrontation, and Mel would have taken off for the hills."

"How about this other guy?" asked Brad, "Miguel Ortiz?"

Before Sarah could answer, Ashley Eberhardt approached the table. "Hey, Sarah," she said, putting a hand on her shoulder. "How are you doing?"

Sarah thanked Ashley for her concern and patted her hand appreciatively.

Turning toward Hannah, Ashley said, "I recognize you from yesterday's fiasco in the lab. I realize that I kind of got into your face, but I thought you were one of Brother Timothy's groupies. I just want to apologize."

"Not a problem," answered Hannah. Then, smiling wryly, she added, "But after watching you single-handedly take down Brother Timothy and his disturbed assistant, I'm really glad that I'm not one of them."

After introducing everyone, and inviting Ashley to sit down, Sarah said, "Brad was just asking me about Rick and Miguel." Turning to face Brad, Sarah explained, "Ashley is first assistant in Rick's laboratory."

Brad asked, "How long did you work for Rick?"

Ashley said, "About two years. He was great to work for. He was more than my boss. We had become like brother and sister. The man had a heart of gold."

Sarah added, "Rick had an excellent work ethic. He loved what he did, and he did it well. Once he became focused on a project, it wasn't unusual for him to work until midnight, then go into work at five o'clock the next morning."

Ashley jumped in with her own testimonial. "This shouldn't have happened to him. The man didn't have a mean bone in his body. He was easygoing and always had a smile. If anybody had a problem with Rick, it had to have been something of their own making."

"That brings us back to Miguel," said Sarah.

"Oh, please," Ashley said, exasperated. "Miguel is an idiot. He never does anything right. Whatever he touches turns to shit. And then he points the finger of blame somewhere else."

Offering additional credence, Sarah said, "Ashley worked with Miguel every day. She could tell you more about him than I could. But, Rick did mention Miguel's temper."

"'Temper' is putting it mildly," said Ashley. "I think that the man is capable of anything."

"Did you tell that to the police?" asked Brad.

Ashley hesitated. "I told the cops that Miguel was irresponsible, missed a lot of work . . . that sort of thing. But now that I'm talking about it, I think the cops should know just how dangerous he is. If it were up to me, I'd make him the number one suspect."

"Okay," said Brad, swiveling in his chair to face Ashley. "Let's say that Miguel is our number-one suspect. Does he ever work late? Like between ten and midnight?"

Ashley had a look of incredulity. "Hell no! Five o'clock whistle, and he's the first one out the door."

"Okay," pressed Brad. "Give me a reason that he might have shown up here so late and committed murder."

"Miguel's crazy," answered Ashley. "He flies off the handle at everybody. A couple of the other techs said that he was thinking of quitting because of how much he hated Rick."

Hannah broke her silence. "Do you think he hated Rick enough to kill him?"

Ashley looked down. "I don't know," she admitted, shaking her head. "I wouldn't put anything past him, but I just don't know."

"I'd like to talk to this Miguel Ortiz fellow," said Brad. "Is he down in the lab right now?"

Ashley grunted. "Nope," she said succinctly. "He never showed up today. Irresponsible asshole."

"Take it easy," coaxed Sarah. "I don't want you getting ulcers over this."

"Sorry," said Ashley, taking a deep breath. "Anyway, it's typical of Miguel to miss work. He does that a lot."

"Maybe, I can find him at home," suggested Brad. "Any idea where he lives?"

Ashley brightened. "I know exactly where he lives. We used to carpool, sometimes. Of course, it was always with my car, but . . . yeah, I know where he lives."

CHAPTER FIFTY

CALIFORNIA

After a stop at Wal-Mart to buy a micro cassette, Brad and Hannah found their way to Colorado Boulevard, the street made famous by the annual Rose Bowl Parade. Following it west, they turned right on Marengo Avenue.

Hannah removed the directions from her purse. Reading them, she said, "Ashley's instructions are to stay on Marengo all the way. After we cross the two-ten freeway, we'll be in the Washington Park area. Then, we need to look for a street called Barcelona. It'll be on the left just past *Carballo's Market*."

The directions were clear, and it didn't take long before they were peering out their windows for Miguel's address.

Before Brad and Hannah left Envirogen, Ashley had talked about Miguel's girlfriend, Maria. Ashley had met the young woman on several occasions and always came away with the distinct impression that she was a hooker. When Hannah had questioned the presumption, Ashley replied, "Are you kidding? His whole life is made up of strippers and whores."

Brad and Hannah had discussed the best way to approach their visit. If Miguel were home, Brad intended to be straightforward. He had some pointed questions and had no intentions of putting up with any sort of deception. On the other hand, if Maria were the only one there, Hannah would fall into her role as a reporter doing a story about genetic engineering.

It was Maria who answered the door. Once she understood that Hannah had come to interview Miguel about his work at Envirogen, she invited the couple in with open arms.

"When will Miguel be home?" asked Hannah.

"Oh, he doesn't get out of work until five," answered Maria, preparing a fresh pot of coffee. "He usually walks in the door between five-thirty and six."

Hannah persisted. "How about a day like today, when he's not working?"

"Not working?" asked Maria, a look of consternation making its way across her brow.

"We just came from Envirogen," said Hannah casually. "They told us we'd find him at home."

Maria wasn't sure what to say. Fully aware of Miguel's erratic attendance, she had even admonished him for being so lackadaisical about something so important. However, the last thing she wanted to do, in the presence of this reporter, was to highlight Miguel's irresponsibility. Maria was interested in pursuing this opportunity and did not want to say anything that might cause Hannah to leave. "Oh right," said Maria, pretending to suddenly remember a missing fact. "I forgot that he had to do something today."

Hannah smiled. "Well, since I'm already here, maybe I could ask you a question or two."

It was the perfect proposition for Maria who showed an instant enthusiasm for the idea. "Sure," she said. "I know a lot about what's happening at Envirogen. Me and Miguel talk about it all the time."

As Maria poured the coffee, Hannah could hear the excitement in the young woman's voice. She had a childlike enthusiasm and an inquisitiveness that Hannah found charming. Within a half hour, they were "best friends," and Hannah knew that she had gained Maria's confidence.

When the discussion turned to engineering new life-forms, Maria's exhilaration reached new heights. "Just last week," she said, vigorously stirring her coffee, "they made a new bug in the lab. Did you know that?"

"I thought I heard something about that," said Hannah. "What was it?"

"They were supposed to make a bug that would eat the roots of some kind of plant that grows in Georgia or Alabama. I'm not sure. But then, somebody in the lab spilled a cup of coffee and . . ." Maria's eyes brightened with the anticipation of springing a surprise. " . . . and guess what?"

Brad and Hannah glanced at each other before she replied, "What?"

"It turns out that the bug likes to eat coffee more than it likes to eat that plant. A lot more!"

"What are you talking about?" asked Hannah.

Maria was so energized she almost bounced in her chair. "Miguel said that one of the really important entomologists called and said that they should lock up those bugs. The man said that if the bugs ever got out, they'd eat anything that was made with coffee. Even coffee ice cream! Can you believe it?"

"When did you say this happened?" asked Hannah.

"Just last week. Miguel said that a girl he works with, got bit by one of the damn things and ended up in the hospital."

Hannah narrowed her gaze. "And all this happened in Miguel's lab?"

"Yeah," answered Maria. "The scientist that made the bug was Rick, Miguel's boss."

"Rick?" asked Hannah. "Rick Ballinger?"

Maria's balloon of enthusiasm seemed to deflate. "Yeah," she said sullenly. "Him."

Hannah lowered her voice as though she were about to share a secret. "Did you know that he was found murdered?"

"Yeah. I heard."

"They're going nuts over there," said Hannah. "Cops are crawling all over the place. They're asking everyone for an alibi."

"I know," said Maria. "Miguel told me. A friend of mine, Bruce Kreitzer, is in town from Chicago. On business. The three of us were together on Monday night."

Brad found it interesting that Maria had felt compelled to offer an alibi. Even though she wasn't a suspect, she must have realized that Miguel was. Brad said, "These businessmen from Chicago usually stay in Los Angeles. What brought your friend to Pasadena?"

"He had to go to some kind of conference. S.E.C . . . F.E.C. I don't remember. All I know is that he's a big-shot commodity broker, and he had to be here."

*   *   *

No sign of movement. No sign of breathing. Just two bodies with absolutely no sign of life. Miguel knew instantly that they were the characters who had been pursuing Kreitzer. The hulking mass of one of the dead men matched the description of the enforcer whom Kreitzer had referred to as Bruno. Despite more than a dozen caterpillars running over each of the victims, there seemed to be a concentrated number crawling on their fear-frozen faces.

As Miguel stared at the nightmare in front of him, he saw Bruno's lips move. Suddenly terrified that this giant of a man, akin to the mythical Cyclops, would struggle to his feet and club him bloody, Miguel felt paralyzed. Watching intently for further signs of life, he saw a large caterpillar inch its way out of the dead man's mouth. Miguel gagged as he thought about how many of the loathsome insects might still be in there.

Swallowing hard, Miguel shifted his gaze to the table and spotted the source of the infestation. Kreitzer had mentioned that he had left the Bible atop one of the boxes. Now, Miguel could see that the Holy Book had been pushed aside and that caterpillars, one by one, were squeezing themselves through the small slit at the top.

Not wanting to be the third victim, Miguel surveyed the carpet around his feet before picking a clear path to the desk. Unfolding one of the flattened squares of cardboard, Miguel turned it into a new carton and, using the clear plastic tape, sealed the bottom flaps. Although his intentions were to open the insect laden containers and dump the contents into the larger ones, nervousness was affecting his concentration. The longer it took to assemble the boxes, the closer he came to the edge of panic.

Finally, Miguel was ready. He grabbed the split-seamed box and turned it upside down. Putting two fingers on each flap, he pulled them apart, allowing thousands of the thorn-tailed insects to fall into their new cardboard home. Several of the bugs missed their target and landed on the desktop. Hoping to slam and squish the creatures into oblivion, Miguel reached for the Bible. However, in so doing, the transferred bugs began climbing out of their cardboard cage. Alarmed and momentarily befuddled, Miguel dropped the prayer book and concentrated on pulling off long strips of tape and securing the carton. He swiped at the few scurrying caterpillars, knocking them onto the carpet. One of the bugs crawled to the edge of the desk and fell off onto Miguel's shoe. "God-dammit!" he cried, stomping repeatedly to dislodge the clinging beast. Once again, he grabbed the Bible and began flailing at the dispersing caterpillars. By the time Miguel had cleared a small safe-zone, he was breathing hard.

Remembering Kreitzer's instructions, Miguel went to the closet and found the remaining box of bugs. Although this one was also bulging at the top and bottom, it seemed to be relatively secure. Deciding to skip the step of transferring the insect residents to their new home, Miguel chose instead to put the old carton, in its entirety, into the new, larger one. Before sealing the outer container, he slit the top of the inner one, allowing the crammed-in caterpillars some limited freedom. Making certain that he had a clear path, Miguel picked up both cartons and walked out of the room.

The horde of insects left behind was insatiable. Devouring coffee in any form not only helped the creatures to grow in size, but it also aided the expansion of the toxin-laden sacs that lined the insect's underbelly.

Ugly beasts, mottled gray, and each with a bright red dot on its head, they scrambled over the two dead bodies until the coffee residue was gone. Strangely, when their eating frenzy ended, they all stood motionless for several minutes.

Suddenly, a lone caterpillar turned and scurried across the carpet. Then, as if blindly following the sound of a dinner bell, the others followed the leader toward the open closet. There, in the corner like an aromatic smorgasbord, was a two-pound can of Maxwell House Coffee.

CHAPTER FIFTY-ONE

CALIFORNIA

Agreeing to split a sandwich for lunch, Brad and Hannah stopped at *Trader Joe's* and ordered a ham and Swiss hero with all the trimmings. They drove to Smyzer Park, an area adjacent to the entrance to the San Gabriel Valley Boy Scout Council.

Substituting a couple of sheets of newspaper for placemats, Hannah spread out the sandwich and drinks on the redwood picnic table. Next, she arranged some plastic utensils and paper napkins before looking up for approval. She loved the idea of a picnic with Brad. The air was cool and dry, ideal for just such a midday interlude. When Brad had made the suggestion, Hannah gushed like a schoolgirl. She was experiencing feelings that made her heart sing.

Studying Hannah's face, Brad couldn't help but smile. She looked like a little girl anticipating a birthday party. Even though he was drawn to her and fully aware of her reciprocal feelings, his churning emotions made him uncomfortable. Finding it difficult to forget the pain of losing his fiancée, Amy, he told himself to slow down and be more cautious. The previous night's battle with Verne Smenken had left Brad shaken. He wasn't afraid for himself, but the thought of losing Hannah had been overwhelming. Afterwards, after the police showed up, after the emergency room, after their frantic lovemaking . . . that was when the nightmare came. Brad couldn't recall all the details, but he did remember Hannah's life being in jeopardy, and himself unable to come to her rescue. Despite having awakened with a start, the warmth of Hannah's naked body soon dissipated the remnants of the dream.

The sandwich, which was overstuffed and unwieldy, caused Hannah a giggling fit, as she tried to be ladylike with her first bite. While Brad poured the ice tea, Hannah wiped an errant piece of lettuce from his bottom lip. The moment was tender, relaxed and intimate.

A sound, distant at first, became increasingly annoying until Brad answered the insistent beeping of his cell phone.

The caller was Rose Goldberg. After getting Brad's input on an important business decision, she said, "You also have an urgent message from your friend, Harry Goodenow. He said that it's not quite a matter of life or death, but it is a choice between being able to afford the good life or a monastic one."

Brad smiled at the message. "It sounds as though he might have a hot investment tip."

"Just watch out that it's not a bordello or some X-rated Hollywood production."

"I'll be careful," said Brad.

Rose asked, "What's happening with the Ballinger boy?"

Brad sighed. "Not much. The whole thing is moving slower than I'd like. I'm dreading the call to Stephanie."

Brad could hear Rose choking up with emotion as she asked, "Oh, my. You haven't talked to her yet?"

"Not yet," replied Brad. "I plan to phone her this evening. I hope to have some news after the autopsy."

At the word, "autopsy," Rose felt overwhelmed. "*Oy*," she said, lamenting the loss of any mother's child. "*Oy, Goht zol helfen.*"

"I'm not exactly sure what that means," said Brad, "but I know the words come from your heart. Now, tell me what's going on in the office."

"Forget the office," said Rose. "Just concentrate on what you need to do out there. I'll take care of the office."

"Well, what about the Kennedy case?" asked Brad. "Who's working on that?"

"What difference does it make?" said Rose. "Everything here is under control. The office ran smooth yesterday. It's running smooth today, and it'll run smooth tomorrow."

"I'm only asking," said Brad with a plea in his voice.

"Good-bye," said Rose. "I'm hanging up."

"Wait," said Brad. "Don't hang up yet. Just tell me if you've received the affidavits from the Wurlitzer estate."

Rose was silent.

"Rose? Rose, at least put my mind at ease and tell me I won't be walking into a hornet's nest when I get back."

"Since you asked so nicely," she replied with an exaggerated air of concession, "I'll fill you in. First of all, I want you to know that the fire in your office is out. Also, some union representatives are here, and they're in the middle of organizing our staff and . . ." Rose paused for effect. "Listen, I got to go. The police are here with the warrants." Then, she hung up.

Brad stared blankly at Hannah.

"What did Rose say?" asked Hannah.

Brad poked another button on his cell phone and dialed Harry Goodenow before answering, "I think she said that I shouldn't bother her anymore."

"What are you doing in California?" inquired Harry.

"I'm here with a friend of yours," said Brad, winking at Hannah. "Remember Hannah?"

"Hannah Carpenter?" asked Harry with a note of surprise. "That luscious, leggy reporter?"

"That's her," confirmed Brad. "Presently, we are sitting in a park overlooking the San Gabriel Mountains and having a picnic."

"Is that Harry?" questioned Hannah in a whisper.

Brad nodded with a smile.

"You scoundrel!" bristled Harry. "You dastardly opportunist! I turned my back for an instant, and you stole her away from me!"

Stifling a laugh, Brad asked, "What are you so upset about? You've got your arms wrapped around that six-foot barmaid, Andrea Pepper."

"That's not the point," objected Harry, changing his indignation into a distinct whine. "You *always* get the good ones. And Hannah Carpenter is one of the good ones. Besides, Andrea left me for a bald-headed biker named Spike who works at Home Depot. Can you imagine that?"

"Life goes on, Harry. New subject. Rose told me you called. What have you got?"

Not knowing how long Brad might be on the phone, Hannah thought that now would be a good time to touch base with her boss, Sidney Aarons.

Harry cleared his throat. "There's money to be made in commodities, my boy. Pork bellies, pea pods and petroleum. Gold for the taking."

Brad said, "Okay. You've piqued my interest. Now, be specific."

"Corn futures," stated Harry.

"Corn futures?"

"More specifically, Nebraska corn. I've received a little . . . uh, advance information, if you will. It turns out that there is a growing blight on Nebraska corn. If they don't get the problem under control quickly, it will devastate this year's crop. That, my dear Bradstone, will drive the price sky high."

"What kind of blight? And how reliable is your source?"

"My source, who shall remain anonymous, happens to be an impeccable rogue. He tells me that the problem is a pesky little critter called a corn-borer that gets under the husk and ruins those delicate, golden niblets."

"All right," said Brad. "When do you want a decision?"

Harry became serious. "This is the kind of thing that requires immediate action. You'll need to make a decision today. Tomorrow may be too late."

Over the years, Brad had learned to trust Harry's judgment. His track record had proven very profitable for Brad's bottom line. Without further hesitation, he authorized the banker to buy a hefty chunk of the speculative commodity. "If you're right on this one, Harry, I'll buy the next round of stone crabs." Disconnecting, Brad looked around to see Hannah, still on the phone and pacing a path in the grass.

"All right, Sidney," said Hannah with a mixture of exasperation and submissiveness. "You're the boss." Hanging up, She returned to the picnic table.

"What was that all about?" asked Brad.

"What did Harry want?" asked Hannah.

"I asked you first."

Hannah sighed. "Sidney wants me on a plane tomorrow. I have to be in the office at nine a.m. on Saturday."

"What's the urgency?"

"The President, along with the Secretary of the Treasury, is going to be in Palm Beach. They're giving a speech at the Breakers Hotel, and Sidney wants me there for coverage."

"Can't he send someone else?"

The look on Brad's face made her smile. "You're sweet," she said, "but there's going to be an impromptu news conference afterward, and he wants me there."

"Is that what you were aggravated about?"

"Not really," answered Hannah. "It was more his attitude."

"Why? What did he say?"

An embarrassed smile appeared on Hannah's lips.

"What?" persisted Brad.

"Sidney said that he doesn't want our little tryst ending up on an expense report that he has to pay for."

Brad shook his head with mock disappointment. "That man has no sense of charity."

CHAPTER FIFTY-TWO

CALIFORNIA

S arah Levine was in her office composing a letter. It began, "*Regretfully, I must withdraw my name from the list of speakers at the upcoming International Conference on Entomology. Due to a tragic incident in my personal life . . .*" She looked up to see Winston Sattherwaite standing in her doorway.

"Sarah?" said Winston timidly. "Your 'two o'clock' is here. I told them they were early, but you know how pushy some people can be."

"It's all right," said Sarah. "Show them in.".

Given that it had been only a few hours since Brad and Hannah had met with Sarah, salutations were brief. Afterward, Brad detailed his and Hannah's visit with Miguel's girlfriend. "Maria is an interesting sort. Once she found out that Hannah was a reporter doing a piece on genetic engineering, she opened up like a faucet. All in all, it was pretty informative."

Sarah asked, "Did Miguel show up?"

"No," answered Brad. "But, when the discussion got around to Rick's murder, Maria somehow felt compelled to come up with an alibi for Miguel. She said that on the night in question, Miguel was with her and a friend from Chicago."

Sarah's shoulders seemed to slump. "I guess that means the police will have to look elsewhere."

"There is something else," added Brad.

"What's that?"

"Maria talked about a new species of insect that Rick had supposedly been working on. She referred to it as a bug that loved coffee. Also, she mentioned a girl named Juanita and said something about her being bitten by the insect and having to be hospitalized. What can you tell me about that?"

Sarah nodded her head. "Juanita Fuentes," she said confirming the information. "She wasn't bitten. She was stung."

"How serious was it?"

Looking at both Hannah and Brad, Sarah realized that neither had been told the full story. "She died," said Sarah. "The caterpillar produces a potent toxin, and she died within hours."

Brad was dismayed. "A potent toxin, indeed."

Sarah related the events that led to the development of the new life-form, and the discovery of the insect's insatiable yen for coffee. "Once the toxin was isolated and we confirmed that it was something new and extremely virulent, a decision was made to destroy all the remaining genetically manufactured insects."

"Were these bugs originally in the lab?"

"Yes," answered Sarah. "There were tens of thousands of them. Over the course of one weekend, they infested every square inch of Rick's lab."

CHAPTER FIFTY-THREE

CALIFORNIA

"What the hell's a matter with you?" hollered Miguel. "Are you stupid or something?"

"Don't you call me stupid!" cried Maria, slamming the door on the kitchen cabinet. "You ain't got no right to call me stupid!"

"Bullshit!" said Miguel, kicking one of the wooden chairs across the floor. "You must've had your head up your ass!"

Ten minutes prior to the blowup, Miguel and Kreitzer, each carrying an insect-laden carton, had returned to the apartment. Greeting them excitedly, Maria had begun telling the tale of the two reporters who interviewed her that morning. Kreitzer interrupted when he said, "Wait a minute. Why would two reporters come all the way out here to talk to you?"

Maria explained that they were really interested in talking to Miguel but, since he wasn't home, they spoke with her instead.

Kreitzer didn't buy it. "That doesn't make any sense. Envirogen has all kinds of lab technicians. Why the hell would reporters drive all the way out here just to talk to Miguel?"

The question had made all three fall silent.

Kreitzer continued. "Did they ask you anything about the murder?"

When Maria nodded affirmatively, Miguel lost his temper. Shouting profanities in Spanish and English, he demanded to know what the reporters had asked, what Maria had told them, and why she had acted so stupidly. Miguel's anger escalated as he yelled, "They were cops! Didn't you figure out that they were god-damn cops?"

Maria wasn't having any part of it. "You're crazy!" she shouted. "They weren't cops! They were just doing a story on genetic engineering, for Christ's sake!"

"If they were just doing a story on genetic engineering," screamed Miguel, "why the fuck were they asking about Rick's murder?"

"I don't know!" answered Maria, shrilly. "But, I did what you told me. I told 'em we were all together Monday night."

Turning to face Kreitzer, Miguel asked, "What the fuck are we supposed to do now?"

Before an answer could be offered, Maria looked from one man to the other. "Did you guys have something to do with that?"

Miguel half-turned and barked over his shoulder, "Shut up, woman!" Readdressing Kreitzer, Miguel asked, "What do we do if they come back?"

"Answer me!" shrieked Maria.

Miguel spun to face her. "I said shut up, *hija de una puta!* Just shut up!"

Maria stepped forward until they were only inches apart. Choking with anger, she screamed, "You can't tell me what to do! Get out! Get out of my . . ."

Miguel cut off Maria's demand with a vicious slap to her face. Never expecting the blow, it threw her sideways into the row of base cabinets.

Kreitzer called out, "Hey! Knock it off!"

Maria caught the edge of the sink and held on, as a thin trail of blood trickled from her nose. Wiping it with the back of her hand, she stared at the red smear before glaring at Miguel and hissing, "*Chinga tu madre, Cabrón!*" Knocking over a wooden chair, Maria stormed out the front door.

The men stared at one another. Kreitzer asked, "Should we go after her?"

Miguel picked up the toppled chair and muttered, "Shit." Then added, "Dumb bitch. Let her go. She'll calm down. She always does."

Kreitzer looked around. "I don't think we should stay here."

Trying to compose himself, Miguel ran both hands through his hair. "Yeah," he agreed. "You're probably right."

Kreitzer thought about his uncle's plan, including the airline reservations with Sky Transport and tomorrow's trip to South America. "Let's just find someplace to stay the night," he suggested. "We'll be out of this town first thing in the morning."

Miguel nodded. "Okay, but where do we go? We can't go back to your hotel. There are two dead bodies and the place is crawling with these bugs."

Kreitzer chewed his lip before saying, "Let's head over to L.A. We've got to be on the plane at six in the morning. So, we might as well get a night's sleep somewhere near the airport."

"What about the bugs?" asked Miguel.

"What about them?"

"I don't know. Shouldn't we feed them or something?"

Kreitzer looked at his watch. "Yeah," he concurred. "That's a good idea. We won't be landing in Colombia until late tomorrow afternoon, So, let's feed them one more time."

Miguel opened a cabinet and removed a large tin of ground coffee. Lifting the plastic lid, he said, "This is almost full. We can dump half of it into each box."

They removed the plastic tape before carefully opening the top and peering inside.

"Holy shit!" said Kreitzer. "Those suckers are big."

"Yeah," said Miguel softly. "I saw how big they've gotten when they were crawling all over your dead buddies."

Grabbing the coffee tin, Miguel poured half its contents into the middle of each container. The reaction was instantaneous. The bugs quickly began scrambling over each other in a furious attempt to get at the food. Unexpectedly fast, their swarming movements startled both men.

"Holy Jesus!" cried Kreitzer, jumping back.

"Motherfucker!" cried Miguel, as he snapped the lids shut. "Did you see that?"

Wide-eyed, Kreitzer said, "I didn't know caterpillars could move that fast."

With the feeding of the new life forms complete, Miguel grabbed the roll of Scotch tape. "This tape you bought is for shit. It ain't sticking very good. Maybe, we should go buy something stronger."

Kreitzer used his thumb to press a loose piece of tape to a corner of the cardboard cube. "Nah," he said finally. "Don't worry about it. It'll hold till we get to where we're going."

CHAPTER FIFTY-FOUR

CALIFORNIA

B rad made two phone calls. One was to Steve Bettencourt, the Captain of the Pasadena Police Department, and the other was to Stephanie Ballinger, the mother of a murdered child.

The first call went well. Filling Bettencourt in on the meeting with Maria, Brad spoke about the woman's need to offer an alibi for her boyfriend's whereabouts on the night of the murder. Brad presented Maria's claim that she and Miguel had been with a friend of hers who had flown in from Chicago.

Bettencourt said, "That one's going to be tough to disprove. Her testimony alone validates his alibi."

"Why not check it out anyway?" suggested Brad. "See if she's lying about her friend from Chicago. She told us his name was Kreitzer. Bruce Kreitzer. I'm not sure of the spelling but, supposedly, the man's a commodities broker and in town for a convention of some sort. That should be enough information to get started. You never know. If he doesn't corroborate her story, you've got an opening."

Jotting down Kreitzer's name, Bettencourt said he would have Detective Santero check it out.

Brad said, "There's something else that you might want to ask Detective Santero."

"What's that?"

"When I first arrived at Envirogen, I noticed that the entry door was fitted to be opened with a key-card, and that all the employees had them pinned to their lapels."

"Yeah . . . So?"

Brad continued. "So, that means that every time someone enters after hours, their arrival should be registered on a computer printout somewhere in the building."

"You're right. I'll double-check with Santero. What else you got?"

Brad brought up his conversation with Envirogen's entomologist, Sarah Levine, and her news flash about the new species of insect that Rick Ballinger had engineered. Emphasizing the potency of the poison, Brad said, "I know that the Medical Examiner is supposed to look at everything when they do an autopsy, but could you make sure that the doc has tested for toxins? I'd hate to think that we're all looking in the wrong direction, when in actuality, Rick died from a bug bite."

"First of all," replied Bettencourt, "don't sweat the autopsy. Doctor Pushkin is as good as they get. She taught pathology at Montefiore Medical Center in New York before she moved out here to get away from all that traffic and violence. I trust her to do a thorough job. Besides, I've already got her preliminary report where she confirms the forensics." Bettencourt shuffled through a pile of papers. "Here it is. It says, 'Victim died of a cerebral hemorrhage brought on by severe trauma to the head.' And further down the page, Pushkin goes into the victim's blood analysis. Let's see . . . It says . . . 'Toxicology, negative.' There you go, Brad. No poison."

Changing the subject, Brad asked, "How are things going with Verne Smenken?"

Bettencourt snorted an unhappy sound. "I don't think it's going to make a difference what we charge him with."

"Why not?" asked Brad. "What's the problem?"

"He's crazy," said Bettencourt. "Nuttier than a fruitcake. He's been interrogated a bunch of times, and everybody comes away with the same conclusion: He might as well be howling at the moon. Even if we get a confession, it'll never stand up in court."

"So, what are you going to do with him?"

"We're letting the D.A. handle it. He'll figure something out."

Brad's next call did not go as smoothly. He had been in Pasadena for barely one day and had spent an inordinate amount of that time worrying about the inevitability of this call.

As soon as Stephanie answered, Brad closed his eyes. He was listening to a frail voice, frightened and filled with anguish. Brad started to speak but hesitated when he heard her whimpers of despair. It was like listening to an ancient woman, suddenly fearful at the thought of being left alone. It didn't take long before she broke down completely and dropped the phone.

"Stephanie?" called Brad. "Stephanie! Are you all right?"

A man's voice came on the line. "Mr. Bishop?" he said. "My name is Cory. I'm one of the staff here. Ms. Carlton-Ballinger is okay. Kind of. The doctor told me to give her a sedative if she got this way again. Could you hold on?"

Brad waited. Afterward, Cory said, "It would probably be best if you told me of any pertinent information. When she wakes up, I'll relay the message."

Because Cory had sounded reasonably competent, and because Brad was still three thousand miles away, he decided to give Cory the information on the disposition of Rick's body. Afterward, Brad was thankful that he had been spared the emotional roller coaster of having to explain it all to Stephanie.

Looking around his hotel room, Brad thought about what he should do next. He took a deep breath and tried to shake himself out of the doldrums. His abbreviated conversation with Stephanie had been a morose affair, and now he wanted to sweep it away and step into the sunshine.

Brad turned his attention to Hannah. Their upcoming dinner was less than an hour away, and he was looking forward to it. Earlier, when the couple had returned to the Ritz-Carlton, Brad asked the concierge to make dinner reservations at *JJ's Steak House*. Bettencourt had recommended the restaurant, which was located nearby on Colorado and De Lacey. Feeling better about the rest of his day, Brad stripped and brushed his teeth before reaching into the shower stall and setting the water temperature on "cool."

Alone in her room and unhappy at the thought of having to return home, Hannah called the airline and reserved a seat for a flight back to Florida. Her plane would be leaving at noon the next day, which meant that she would have to be at the airport by ten a.m. In turn, she would have to leave the hotel no later than nine. All that would barely leave enough time to share breakfast with Brad. He had become a very special person in her life, and she found herself wanting to spend more time with him than was practical.

Sitting on the edge of her bed, she drenched herself in melancholy. "Well," she mused aloud, "at least we'll be together tonight." The thought liberated Hannah from her mood, and she brightened at the prospect of meeting Brad within the hour. Undressing quickly, she brushed her teeth before stepping into the shower and setting the water temperature on "hot."

CHAPTER FIFTY-FIVE

CALIFORNIA

The lounge at the Ritz-Carlton was well-appointed and, like so many others, this one also had a large-screen television behind the bar. It dominated one corner and hung down from the ceiling at an angle that made for easy viewing from anywhere in the room. At the moment, it was set to the channel that featured CNN Headline News.

Due to all the tables being occupied, Brad and Hannah opted to sit at the bar. They were soon noticed by a young man in a crisp white shirt and a black silk bow tie who said, "Good evening, folks. Welcome to the Ritz. What's your pleasure?"

Hannah asked for a White Russian, while Brad requested a spicy Bloody Mary. The bartender placed two coasters in front of them, along with a crystal dish filled with dry-roasted nuts. Quickly, efficiently, and artfully, he combined, blended, poured, and finally served two perfect cocktails.

"I'd like to make a toast," said Brad raising his glass, "but so many good things are happening, I'm not sure which one to toast first."

Hannah smiled broadly. "Then, allow me."

"Okay," said Brad, pleased to be relieved of the responsibility. "Fire away."

"I offer this toast to you," she said, "for being my knight in shining armor. For coming to my rescue and slaying the proverbial dragon."

Brad said, "Aw, shucks, ma'am. T'wern't nothin'."

Hannah became serious. "It most certainly was," she said. "I become frightened every time I think about what might have happened if you hadn't come charging in."

Brad stared into her eyes for several moments before saying, "And I'm thankful that I was able to be there for you."

Hannah touched his hand.

Brad said, "Speaking of the proverbial dragon, Steve Bettencourt doesn't think that Smenken will end up in jail."

With her drink halfway to her lips, Hannah froze. "What are you saying? Are they going to let him go?"

Brad replied, "Bettencourt believes that Smenken is mentally unbalanced. Looney tunes. Whenever he's questioned, the man just rants and raves. Bettencourt told me that he had turned the whole thing over to the district attorney."

"So, what does that mean?"

"It means that Old Verne will stay locked up until the system verifies his lunacy. Then, they'll transfer him to a mental facility."

Hannah looked down.

Brad touched her arm. "Either way, he'll be locked up and you'll be safe."

Deep in thought, Hannah nodded and took a sip of her drink. "I've never been that afraid in my entire life," she said. "The look in his eyes . . . It was so scary. It was like . . ." Hannah paused, groping for words that might explain the depth of her fear. "I never really thought much about the Devil, but if someone were to ask me to sketch his likeness, I would draw a picture of Verne Smenken standing in my room."

Brad swiveled his chair so as to face Hannah straight on. Softly, he said, "He can't hurt you now."

As though she hadn't heard Brad's words, Hannah continued. "When he barged into my room, slinging his vile curses like handfuls of mud, all I could think of was how weird he looked. It was like looking at somebody through shattered glass. His face seemed to be all distorted, and . . . and even his words were strangely distorted."

"What do you mean?"

"It was like . . ." Hannah paused, struggling to find an analogy. " . . . as though I were listening to an audiotape of Brother Timothy speaking sideways. Brother Timothy talks about genetic engineering and tries to strike fear into his audience. Verne, on the other hand, has the message all screwed up. He just lives inside his own nightmare."

It was the first time that Hannah had discussed Smenken's assault, and Brad could see tears beginning to well. Coming off his stool, Brad put his arm around her shoulder and whispered, "It's all right, Hannah. He's gone. Everything will be all right."

Hannah took a ragged breath and tilted her head until it rested on Brad's chest. After a full minute, she looked up and said, "Thank you, Brad. I'll be fine."

"What do you say we finish our drinks and head out for dinner?"

Hannah smiled weakly and said, "That sounds good." Lifting her glass to take a last sip, Hannah glanced at the television behind the bar. "Brad!" she said with a note of urgency. "Look!"

Brad followed her pointing finger and saw that CNN had a split screen format. On one half, an anchorwoman was reporting the news, while the other half displayed a photo of Brother Timothy Goodman.

Brad called to the bartender. "Excuse me. Could you please make the television a little louder?"

The young man with the bow tie reached for the remote control and, within seconds, adjusted the volume.

The anchorwoman, whose commentary was picked up in mid-sentence, said, " . . . part of his ongoing program. Despite that, Brother Timothy was called in by the Committee to testify on the dangers of genetic engineering." The picture switched to a full screen shot of Brother Timothy sitting at a table with a small microphone in front of him. The setting seemed austere, as though it were taking place in a courtroom or a Capitol Hill Senate Chamber. The upper right-hand corner of the screen flashed the words "Videotaped Earlier." Brother Timothy was speaking. "We need our scientists to act responsibly. We need laws, like the Ten Commandments, that must not be broken. Otherwise, we risk opening the Gates of Hell. Corporations like Envirogen will continue to create monstrous things that will eat our food, drink our water and, ultimately annihilate our children."

The CNN camera cut back to the anchorwoman who declared that it was time for a commercial break. Brad said, "Well, Brother Timothy is right about one thing."

"What's that?" asked Hannah.

"Envirogen has already created a new life-form that's showing a real interest in devouring one of our food groups."

Hannah smiled as she said, "You mean the curse of *Starbucks*?"

"Yeah," said Brad, getting into it. "A plague on *Dunkin' Donuts* coffee."

Hannah giggled. "A blight on *Barney's Coffee*."

Suddenly, Brad's smile vanished. His face slowly contorted as an idea unfolded itself into substance. Speaking softly, he repeated, "A blight on *Barney's Coffee*."

"Right," said Hannah, not yet following his train of thought. Then, puzzled with his expression, she spread her hands in a gesture of noncomprehension. "Talk to me," she urged.

Brad blurted, "It's coffee!" He spoke the two-word statement as though it explained it all.

"What are you talking about?"

"Coffee!" said Brad excitedly. "You said it yourself, Hannah. All your interviews about genetic engineering have had one common thread. Greed. All this time, I've been looking for the money trail. And guess what? It's coffee. Coffee and that damn coffee bug. That's what this whole thing is all about."

"I'm not following you," said Hannah. "Give it to me again. Slower this time."

Brad snapped open his cell phone. "Okay. In a minute. Just let me make this one call." A few seconds after dialing, Brad said, "Harry. Do me a favor. I want you to find out if there have been any major trades of coffee futures in the last month."

Brad briefly listened to Harry's reply before interrupting. "No time for that, Harry. This is very important. It truly is a matter of life and death."

After receiving a promise of a return call, Brad hung up and turned to Hannah. "Think about it. Rick Ballinger was trying to create an insect that would eradicate the kudzu vine. Instead, he inadvertently engineered a creature that will devour any kind of coffee. From mocha latte to Maxwell House. Now, if somebody had that bug in his possession, and wanted to make a lot of money, what would he do?"

Hannah's eyes were wide with anticipation. "Tell me."

Brad said, "He would buy coffee futures. But, unlike my giddily investment in Nebraska corn, the possessor of the bug would invest big bucks into coffee futures. And then one night, when nobody was looking, he would sneak into a couple of the major coffee warehouses and release the bugs. If Sarah and Maria are right about what they told us, the bugs could devastate a good portion of the nation's coffee supply in no time. And just as Harry said, that would drive the price sky high."

"Oh my God!" uttered Hannah.

Brad continued. "It all makes sense. Everyone testified that Miguel hated Rick. But more importantly, Maria told us about her friend from Chicago . . ."

Hannah interjected with a sudden sense of clarity, "Of course! The commodities broker! The three of them were together and probably hatching their scheme."

"It may not have been premeditated," offered Brad. "It's quite possible that they only intended to steal a box of bugs. But, unfortunately, Rick was working late that night, and one thing may have led to another."

Hannah's mind was churning. "Rick died between ten and midnight. And Miguel and his Chicago pal would have been able to get into the building at that hour because Miguel has a pass."

"Right," said Brad. "That would explain why Maria felt compelled to offer an alibi, even though . . ." Brad's sentence was interrupted by his cell phone.

It was Harry. "Bradstone, my good friend. Have you ever considered becoming a clairvoyant?"

"What have you got, Harry?"

"Amazing," stated Harry. "You were so right. There has been a major purchase of coffee futures, originating from a Chicago firm called Ubermann Trading

Group. The buy is bigger than anything I've seen. More than 170 million dollars worth of coffee. Now that's what you call a hill of beans!"

A call to Steve Bettencourt was the next obvious step. Speaking at length with the Police Captain, Brad detailed his theory.

After hearing about the extraordinary purchase of coffee futures, Bettencourt said, "I'll send Santero out to Miguel's place with a couple of uniforms. We'll bring them all in for questioning. Is this Kreitzer character staying with Miguel and his girlfriend?"

"I'm not sure," answered Brad. "But there's something else I want to talk about."

"Yeah? Like what?"

"It might be a good idea to get the FBI involved," suggested Brad. "I know you don't like the idea of anyone muscling in on your jurisdiction, but I was thinking in terms of a plot that could wipe out a big portion of the country's coffee supply. We might be talking about economic disaster."

"Yeah," said Bettencourt. "Probably a good idea. As it happens, I still keep in touch with one or two of the mucky-mucks. I'll make sure to bring them in on this."

Brad said, "One more thing; nobody knows more about these bugs than Doctor Sarah Levine. She's the resident entomologist at Envirogen. You're going to need her help."

Bettencourt agreed but asked Brad to make the initial call. "Since she knows you, it'll be better if you're the one to ask for her help."

Brad and Hannah discussed the best way to handle the conversation with Sarah. Brad opted to keep it short. His theory about what might have happened to Rick Ballinger was, in fact, just a theory. The last thing he wanted was to give Sarah any false hopes. Brad said, "I think it'll be best if I only talk about the coffee bugs. I'll let the police handle the rest."

Hannah offered a different point of view. "You're not giving Sarah enough credit. She's a smart woman. Once you tell her that you think some insects were stolen from Rick's lab, she'll put two and two together. She'll know instantly that the theft of the bugs might have been the motive. I think you should be honest with her."

Hannah's suggestion turned out to be valid. When Brad asked Sarah if she knew the exact number of bug-filled cartons that were in Rick's lab, the woman stayed two steps ahead in the conversation. She quickly surmised that it might have been Miguel who was responsible for Rick's death. Also, once Brad explained the buying and selling of commodities, Sarah quickly understood the enormous value of the coffee bugs.

Sarah asked, "So, you think that this Bruce fellow might have had something to do with it?"

"That's my guess," said Brad. "Trading in commodities is what he does every day. I think the idea of using the bugs to further his own fortune would have dawned on him right away."

"Okay," she said. "I guess I'll just sit tight and wait for a call from the FBI."

"Right," said Brad.

A short silence was followed by Sarah saying, "Thank you, Brad. I appreciate your keeping me informed."

"You're welcome, Sarah. It's the least that I can do. I hope you have a good night."

"Good night," said Sarah. Then, with a short, tired grunt, added, "Sleep tight, and don't let the big bugs bite."

CHAPTER FIFTY-SIX

CALIFORNIA

Dawn arrived as a fleeting shaft of light seeped its way through a crack in the wide bank of gray clouds. The telltale sound of distant thunder spoke ominously of a low-pressure system building to the east. The air felt thin, ethereal, almost temporary as though waiting for some catastrophic event that would make it all disappear.

It was still dark when Bruce and Miguel drove the rental car along the one-oh-five before exiting onto Sepulveda Boulevard. Since the crush of metro traffic had not yet reached the point of hysteria, the drive to Los Angeles airport was relatively uneventful. Dropping the car off, the two men boarded an airport shuttle and made their way to the Sky Transport Terminal. Miguel was wearing the same thing he normally wore to work; dark green twill pants and a white pullover shirt. Kreitzer, who had shopped the night before, had on tight western-style jeans with loops wide enough to accommodate his new leather belt and big silver buckle. His shirt was a matching blue denim. Each man had one carry-on suitcase and a nondescript cardboard carton. They were the only two passengers at the gate.

The thick-waisted woman behind the ticket counter had a blonde hairdo that did nothing to enhance her square face. Going about her business in a professional manner, she spoke only when necessary. Several taps on her keyboard activated a printer, which produced boarding passes for Bruce and Miguel.

Putting the boarding pass in his breast pocket, Kreitzer asked the agent, "How we doing time-wise?"

She glanced at her watch and said, "Right on time. You can board now."

"What about the pilot and co-pilot?" asked Kreitzer.

"What about them?"

Kreitzer leaned an elbow on the counter. "I mean, when do they show up?"

"They're already on board. You should be landing in Houston a little before eleven-thirty."

"Houston?" exclaimed Miguel. He turned to Kreitzer. "We're supposed to be going to Bogotá, Colombia."

The blonde, seemingly bored, answered anyway. "Houston, Texas is just a refueling stop. From there, it's direct to Bogotá."

"You sure?" asked Miguel.

The agent tossed the Mexican a mild look of disgust. Then, pointing, said, "Right through that door and down the stairs. Can't miss it. It's the blue and white Gulfstream."

There was a 737 jumbo jet parked a mere forty yards from the Gulfstream IV. The disparity in size made the plane they were about to board look puny. In spite of that, the little jet was a most substantial aircraft. The Gulfstream IV had a range of more than 4800 miles, a cruising speed of better than 500 miles per hour, and could attain an altitude of 45,000 feet. It most definitely was a globe-hopper.

The two men climbed the rollaway staircase and walked to the first two available seats. After storing their small carry-ons in the overhead, each man, still holding tightly to his own cardboard carton, slid into a seat. A pretty young woman appeared from the rear of the aircraft and greeted the two passengers. Late twenties, maybe thirty, she wore a short navy skirt and matching blazer over a simple white blouse.

"Are you the stewardess?" asked Kreitzer from his seat on the aisle.

She smiled pleasantly. "Yes," she said. "Only these days we're referred to as flight attendants. My name is Lisa. If you need anything, just let me know."

Kreitzer looked over his shoulder. There were only nine additional seats. "There's not a lot of room here. How many more people are we expecting?"

"Just one more," said Lisa. "But, he'll be with us only as far as Houston. After that, you fellas have the plane to yourselves."

Kreitzer asked, "Will you be serving drinks like a regular airline?"

Lisa's smile faded as she nodded and said, "Sure. Breakfast and lunch, too." Then, changing the subject, she pointed to the boxes and asked, "Why don't we take those cartons and put them in the overhead? You'll be much more comfortable."

Miguel turned, unsure of Kreitzer's reply.

Kreitzer shook his head. "Nah, that's okay. They're real light," he said hefting his box to show Lisa.

"Well," she shrugged, "it's a long flight. I just thought you'd be more . . ." Lisa's attention was diverted by the arrival of the final passenger. "Good morning, Mr. Pate," greeted Lisa. "Nice to have you back on board."

Several inches over six feet, Pate had a nice head of gray hair, a jutting jaw, and a deep Texas drawl. "If it weren't for you, you pretty little thing, I wouldn't even be flyin' this bucket of bolts."

Lisa laughed and headed to the rear.

Pate made his way to the seat across from Kreitzer. "Howdy boys," he said as he maneuvered himself into a comfortable position. "I'm Kevin. What're your names?"

Despite being put off by the man's gregariousness, Kreitzer cautiously answered, "I'm Bruce. This is Miguel."

"What do you have in the boxes?" asked the Texan.

The cartons were attracting far more attention than Kreitzer wanted. Exasperated, he said, "Samples."

"No kidding?" said the big man, genuinely curious. "What kind of samples?"

Kreitzer was feeling closed in. "Uh . . . Styrofoam pellets," he stammered.

"Styrofoam pellets? Like the kind used for fragile stuff?"

Kreitzer had had enough of this conversation. "Yeah," he said curtly. Then, deliberately ignoring the Texan, Kreitzer turned and whispered something to Miguel. Getting the hint, Pate sat back and unfolded his copy of the *Wall Street Journal*.

At six-fourteen a.m., the Gulfstream IV received permission to take off. A rush and a roar accompanied the plane as it sped down the runway and ascended into the overcast sky. Not more than ten minutes into the flight, Miguel said, "This is bullshit, man! I ain't holding this god-damn box for the next ten hours!"

"Yeah. You're right," said Kreitzer. "We can slide them under our seats."

"What, are you kidding?" complained Miguel. The whole friggin' plane is empty. Let's just set 'em on an empty seat." Miguel watched as his partner unbuckled, stood, and stacked both cartons on the seat behind them. Stretching out, Miguel said, "Wake me when the food comes."

Lisa poked her head into the cockpit. "Can I get you boys anything?" she asked.

The pilot, Wally Bannerman, was first to answer. "No thanks, Lisa," he said, pointing to a large nearby thermos. "Carol whipped up my special blend." He was referring to his wife's recipe of strongly brewed coffee mixed with a couple of tablespoons of Kahlua liqueur.

The co-pilot, Jesse Burnett, said, "Hey Lisa. If you slip off your panties, I'll take one of them ee-rotic lap-dances."

Lisa rolled her eyes. "Let me tell you something, asshole. The expression, 'Coffee, tea or me,' is just a joke." She turned on her heel and made her way to the back of the aircraft.

Climbing rapidly on an easterly heading, the plane approached thirty thousand feet. Wally, preparing to reach for his coffee, asked Jesse to take over the controls. The old-fashioned thermos was a big, clumsy affair capable of holding almost six cups of hot liquid. "I'm just gonna pour myself a cup of Carol's brew. Want some?"

"Nope," said Jesse. "I'm waiting for Lisa to come on back. I'm going to have her bring me something to eat."

Wally chuckled as he unscrewed the big plastic lid that doubled as a cup. "Get you something to eat? Ha! You'll be lucky if she ever talks to you!"

Jesse glanced over at the pilot who was fumbling with the three separate parts of the thermos; the lid, the cap, and the wide-mouthed insulated container. "I just haven't plucked the right strings," said Jesse. "But she wants me. I'm sure of that."

Wally looped the forefinger of his left hand through the thin plastic handle on the ancient lid. Then, balancing the thermos on his knee, he unscrewed the cap. Using his already occupied left hand to grip the container, Wally looked away for a place to set down the cap. The inevitable happened. The thermos slipped out of his hand and tumbled upside down, striking the center console. Then, like a circus acrobat, it bounced and flipped, sending sprays of steaming hot coffee over everything.

A cupful of the scalding liquid landed on Jesse's hand and leg and formed blisters on contact. He cried out in pain, as he tried to get out of harm's way. Twisting his body in the cramped cockpit, he inadvertently banged into the "stick," the steering assembly that controls the ailerons and rudder. The plane lurched violently, pitching far to the left before tilting forty degrees to the horizon.

Trying to right the aircraft, Wally grabbed the controls. In his first attempt, he overcompensated and the wings tilted far to the opposite side. The thermos, rolling from side to side, emptied its contents onto the carpet.

In the passenger compartment, Kreitzer, Miguel and Mr. Pate screamed in fear and shouted profanities as they grabbed on to anything that might save their lives. One row behind them, the stacked cardboard boxes toppled into the aisle. The impact was too much for the poorly sticking tape, and their top flaps swung open. The contents burst forth like an erupting lava flow, scattering thousands of the huge caterpillars.

Finally managing to regain control of the aircraft, the pilot took a deep breath and turned to Jesse. Before Wally could ask how his co-pilot was doing, a piercing shriek came from the passenger compartment.

Standing at the rear of the aircraft, Lisa pointed and screamed a high-pitched wail. The object of her fear was a massive horde of ugly gray bugs, each more than six inches long, and each with a tail full of sharp, poisonous thorns. Like an army of vicious marauders, they scrambled forward, single-mindedly streaming towards the cockpit.

CHAPTER FIFTY-SEVEN

CALIFORNIA

At 8:33 Friday morning, the Channel Five Anchorman was handed a news bulletin. Taking two seconds to look it over, he stared back into the camera and said, "We have some breaking news." Then, glancing only occasionally at the copy, he read, '*A private chartered jet from Los Angeles Airport reportedly went down earlier today in a rural area about sixty miles east of Pasadena. It is believed that all those on board died in the crash. The pilot, Walter Bannerman, was employed by Sky Transport for more than five years. Other people on board included the co-pilot, Jesse Burnett, and three businessmen. Their names are Bruce Kreitzer, from Chicago, Kevin Pate, from Houston, and Michael Ortiz, a resident of Pasadena.*' The newsman returned his full attention to the camera before adding, "Sally Pinto is on her way out to the crash site. We will, of course, update you as more details become available."

Fifteen minutes later, Brad's cell phone signaled an incoming call. It was Steve Bettencourt. "Did you hear the news?" he asked.

"No," replied Brad. "What happened?"

"Plane went down," said Bettencourt. "Bruce Kreitzer and Miguel Ortiz were both on it. Want to guess where it was headed?"

Brad hesitated a moment before saying, "Why do I have the feeling that your answer is about to frighten me?"

"Bogotá, Colombia," said Bettencourt dramatically. "The heart of the world's coffee supply."

Brad whistled softly. "I guess I didn't give those boys enough credit. I was thinking in terms of infesting a single coffee warehouse, and all this time they were plotting to eradicate the world's supply."

Bettencourt filled Brad in on the progress of the investigation. "Maria admitted to lying about Miguel's alibi. Of course, her confession may have had something to do with a bright red hand print on the left side of her face. I suspect it was put there by Miguel."

Bettencourt went on to say that Ashley Eberhardt had been fairly certain that two boxes of the caterpillars were missing from the laboratory. "It looks more and more like your theory is going to hold up. Santero and I, plus two guys from the FBI, are heading out to the crash site. Want to tag along?"

"You bet," said Brad.

"Okay. Do me a favor and call Doctor Levine. Have her join us out there. I think we might be needing her expertise."

Disconnecting, Brad turned to Hannah and said, "You're going to hate this."

"What?" she asked, anticipating bad news.

"Bruce Kreitzer and Miguel Ortiz were passengers on a plane that just went down about sixty miles east of here. Bettencourt thinks that they had the coffee bugs with them." Brad paused for effect. "The plane was headed for Colombia, South America, the epicenter of the world's coffee supply."

Hannah looked bewildered. "I'm sorry to hear that the plane crashed and sorrier still that some people may have lost their lives, but why am I going to hate that?"

"Because I'm heading out there to join them, and you're heading back to Florida."

"Oh, damn!" said Hannah, reacting to the shortsightedness of Sidney Aarons. "Damn it!" she said again. Staring at Brad, she declared, "I can't miss this opportunity. This incident is part of my story." Hesitating, she said, "No. That's wrong. This is the *culmination* of my story!"

"What are you saying, Hannah?"

"I'm saying that I'm going with you. I'll call Sidney and tell him that I'm going to stay here and finish this story."

"And, what if he says, 'No?'"

Hannah's brow wrinkled at that possibility. Then, her worry lines faded and were soon replaced with a coy smile. "Got any room on your staff for an ace reporter?"

*　　*　　*

The Gulfstream had crashed in a rural section bordering the outskirts of a town called Moreno Valley. It was located about ten miles south of Riverside. After calling Sarah, and passing on Bettencourt's directions, Brad and Hannah left for Moreno Valley. Hannah spent the better part of the sixty-mile drive trying to convince Sidney that her doing the follow-up on the plane crash was in the newspaper's best interest. Finally, after a five-minute harangue, the editor gave his reluctant approval.

The couple followed the 210 Freeway out of Pasadena and exited onto the Corona Parkway. From there, it was just a short hop to Route 60 and on into Riverside. Finding Route 91, they followed it south for ten miles. Moreno Valley was one of those little towns that was quickly growing into a major suburban area. Between the explosion of the middle-income population and the accompanying shopping malls, Moreno Valley was becoming recognized. However, once past the neon signs and billboards, the farming communities loomed large.

Hannah read the directions aloud. "We have to look for a sign that says, 'Arroyo Verde Park.' It should be up here on the . . . Hey! There it is. Right up ahead."

Brad turned onto a rough macadam road, barely wide enough for two cars to pass, and drove for almost a half mile. Rounding a bend, they came to a clearing that extended for at least a half mile. Brad slowed the car.

The scene that presented itself was incongruous. A gigantic old warehouse, more than 200 feet in length and at least half again as wide, stretched out in front of them. The structure had a badly rusted tin roof that probably didn't do much to keep the rain out. Broken boards and missing windows made up the outer walls of the unstable-looking building. A weathered sign in green and gold said, "Cibolo Equipment." Jutting out from the center of one wall of the ancient warehouse was the sleek tail section of a blue and white Gulfstream jet aircraft.

Hannah put a hand to her mouth. "Oh dear God," she said softly.

Slowly coasting toward the building, Brad scanned the area. "Look there," he said pointing away. "You can see where the plane taxied along the ground." His finger followed the track directly to the point of collision. "For some reason, the pilot wasn't able to apply the brakes."

Hannah said, "They must have been going too fast. I mean, look . . . They went right into the building."

"I don't think that was the case," said Brad. "That warehouse is so old and rickety, it wouldn't have taken any effort at all to crash through the wall. If the plane had been going fast, it would have gone right through and come out the other side. I think it was moving slowly."

"Then, why didn't it stop?" asked Hannah.

"I don't know," replied Brad. "Maybe the pilot was hurt. Or . . . maybe worse."

There were four cars parked near the building. One was a white Ford Explorer with a sign designating that the vehicle belonged to a local Riverside television station. A young man with a bushy mustache was setting up his audio and video equipment. Watching him was an attractive, shorthaired blonde in a dark green business suit.

One of the other automobiles was a patrol car. A fresh-faced cop, not yet old enough to have developed chin whiskers, was standing alongside the two-person television crew. The officer's thumbs were hooked, macho-style, into his gun belt, and he was talking to the blonde. She, however, didn't seem to be paying any attention to what the patrolman had to say. The remaining two vehicles were an old Ford pickup truck and an even older Chevy that was minus a hubcap and had one fender painted in red primer. The occupants were nowhere to be seen.

Brad and Hannah got out of their car and approached the trio. "Hi," said Hannah, holding up her press credentials. "I'm Hannah Carpenter. This is Brad Bishop." As she came closer, she turned her attention to the rookie cop. "What's the story?" she asked. "Any survivors?"

The cop shrugged. "I don't know."

Brad asked, "Who's inside the building?"

The cop shook his head. "Nobody. We were told not to go in there."

Brad and Hannah both turned to stare at the accident scene. Although the airplane was half-buried into the side of the old structure, there was no sign of fire, or smoke, or anything else that might have prevented someone from searching for survivors.

"What do you mean?" asked Brad, a tightness coming to his words. "Why can't you go in there?"

The cop shrugged again and turned to look at the shapely backside of the television reporter. The young man's cavalier attitude was beginning to annoy both Brad and Hannah. Finally, the cop said, "They told us that the building might collapse. They said to wait right here until they send out one of them . . . uh, y'know . . . engineers. Building engineers."

Brad took several steps toward the warehouse. Huge sliding double doors, big enough to accommodate a dump truck, were open and inviting. They looked as though they hadn't been moved in a century. From a few yards away, Brad peered inside. "Listen," he called over his shoulder to the policeman. "This building may be old, but I don't think it's going to collapse."

"You better get away from there," said the rookie.

Brad took another few steps closer to the opening and pointed inside. "Look here! There are steel girders holding this place up. It'll be all right."

The cop was becoming irritated. Enunciating each word, he said, "We ain't supposed to go in there. Now, get back here."

Two more steps and Brad was standing on the threshold. The darkness inside was lessened by shafts of light seeping in through small holes in the walls and roof. Brad knew that the nose and cockpit section of the airplane must have been jutting in to the interior of the building, but a big piece of farm equipment covered in an even bigger tarpaulin, blocked his view.

Unhooking his thumbs from his gun belt, the cop took two steps toward Brad. "Hey, look, Mister! I'm the law around here! And you ain't supposed to . . ."

The cop's attempt to exert his authority was broken by a scream emanating from inside the warehouse. A woman's scream, fearful, bone chilling, and shrill.

CHAPTER FIFTY-EIGHT

MORENO VALLEY, CALIFORNIA

With Hannah on his heels, Brad bolted through the double doors. Thirty feet inside, they stopped and listened, trying to determine where the scream might have originated.

Two stories high and almost as big as a football field, the building was absolutely cavernous. Besides its unending floor space, it had a network of catwalks that crisscrossed the high ceiling. The unidentified wail, echoing through its vastness, could have come from anywhere.

Tucked away in the far left corner, barely visible in the dim light, was a large block of administrative offices. A closed door designated the entrance to the lower rooms while, off to the right, an open staircase led to the second floor.

Brad put a hand on Hannah's shoulder and faced her toward the corner offices. "You go that way," he said. "Keep calling out to her. I'll check the airplane. Be careful."

Scanning the area, Brad could see that the majority of the floor space was used as storage for big, used farm equipment. Tractors, backhoes, combines, and bulldozers were all scattered haphazardly throughout the interior. Considering the size of the search area, the bad light, and the farm equipment, his task was, at best, daunting.

Trotting toward the Gulfstream, Brad called, "Hello? Hello!" He heard Hannah doing the same as she made her way in the opposite direction. Stepping around a makeshift partition, Brad saw the front of the aircraft, bent and broken from its lost battle with the warehouse wall. The open side-door to the aircraft allowed Brad to peer inside. However, due to the aircraft's standing high off the ground, the lip of the doorway came level to Brad's shoulders, thereby limiting his view. Placing his hands flat on the floorboards, he hoisted himself up and inside.

To his right was the passenger compartment, consisting of only eleven seats. They were all empty. Beyond that was a separate lounge area, dominated by a small, armless sofa. In front of it was something that looked like an odd pile of discarded clothing. Unaware that he was holding his breath, Brad moved toward it.

He exhaled noisily when he realized that the rag pile was actually two bodies, face down, one partially lying on top of the other. Kneeling, Brad felt for a pulse on each victim. Their skin was cold, indicating that rigor mortis had already set in.

Brad started toward the cockpit, when a short rustling sound made him turn and glance to the back of the plane. Thinking that he heard it again, Brad called out, "Hello? Anybody there?" A door at the rear was marked "Restroom." The impact of the crash had caused its framework to buckle, resulting in a substantial gap around the upper half of the restroom door.

Brad tried to open it, but it seemed to be stuck. Slipping his fingers into the gap, he gripped the door tightly, preparing to yank it open, when he heard a voice coming from inside. Tremulous and pleading, the speaker said, "No! Please, no!"

Brad pulled the door open and found himself staring at a young woman whose face was blanched with fear. Dressed in a disheveled white blouse and a navy skirt that had ridden up high enough to reveal her bare legs and white panties, she had somehow managed to wedge herself into a tight little area next to the toilet.

Brad knelt and said softly, "It's all right. Take it easy."

The young woman was not looking at Brad. Her eyes were riveted on a point somewhere above his right shoulder. "Come on," he said, holding out his hand.

Rather than allowing Brad to help her up, the flight attendant shook her head and hoarsely whispered, "No." Then, without taking her eyes off the spot, she put a finger to her lips and mouthed, "Shhh. Don't move."

Brad turned to see what was capturing the young woman's attention. His mouth fell open and he sucked in a breath. Two giant caterpillars, each the size of a small rolling pin, were on a little shelf just above his head. One of the creatures had accordioned its way over the edge and hung there precariously, ready to drop onto Brad's neck. Eyeing the lethal-looking thorns on its tail, Brad jumped up quickly. His action came just in the nick of time. The woman shrieked as the gray beast released its grip and fell to the floor. Brad kicked at the red-dotted aberration, catching it fully on its side and booting it out of the tiny bathroom. Looking up, Brad saw that the remaining caterpillar had not moved from the spot on its perch. Turning back to the young woman, Brad commanded, "Come on! "We've got to go!"

Overwrought and shaking badly, the woman had to be lifted and practically dragged to her feet. To get to the plane's exit door, Brad half-carried her past the two dead bodies. Forcing the attendant to sit down with her legs dangling out of the aircraft, Brad jumped to the ground, grabbed her by the waist and pulled her out. Whimpering like a child just awakened from a nightmare, the young woman clutched at Brad as she fell into his arms. As he hustled the limping flight attendant toward the building's double door exit, he heard a deep groaning sound like metal against metal. That was followed by a loud boom. He glanced over his shoulder at the heavy scaffolding hanging twenty feet in the air and wondered if the young cop had been right about the building's imminent collapse.

$$* \quad * \quad *$$

While Brad had been in the plane, Hannah made her way across the wide concrete floor to the darkest part of the building, which presumably housed the office. Its door was flanked by a pair of stacked wooden crates, each piled to a height of twelve feet. Expecting it to be locked, Hannah half-heartedly tried the handle. Surprisingly, it turned without resistance, enabling her to pull it open. The only light in the room came from the door that she had just opened and from a dinner-plate-size hole that sat above a fire door in the far corner. It looked as though there once might have been an exhaust fan that fitted that round opening. A row of light switches sat on the wall to her left. She tried them all. Nothing happened.

Hannah called out. "Hello? Anybody?" As her eyes adjusted to the meager light, she could see that it was not an office. Rather, it was a large open area that probably served as a combination conference room and cafeteria. On one side was a pair of six-foot tables, laid out end to end and surrounded by metal folding chairs. The remaining half of the room was dotted with round lunch tables, each designed to seat four or five comfortably. Besides the fire door at the rear, the far wall had four additional doors. Although Hannah couldn't be certain, she thought that they might be bathrooms and storage. The wall to her right had a length of stainless steel countertop, upon which sat a couple of restaurant-sized electric coffee percolators.

Hannah was turning to leave when she heard a distinct moan coming from somewhere in the room. She spun, stood still and listened intently. Nothing. She called out again. "Hello! Where are you?"

The only response was a metallic creaking. It came from somewhere above and sounded as though a very heavy weight had just been placed on the roof. Reverberating throughout the warehouse, the noise was followed almost immediately by a sharp "ka-boom!" Startled, she instinctively ducked her head.

When nothing more happened, Hannah listened again for the moaning. She wondered whether it actually came from a person, or if it were just a sound that preceded the boom. Intending to check behind each of the four doors, she walked to the rear of the room.

*   *   *

The television cameraman was filming the blonde newscaster who was droning on about the frequency of plane crashes. Her monologue was interrupted when Brad came through the doors and rushed the frightened and bedraggled flight attendant into the arms of the rookie cop.

Witnessing the rescue, the newscaster, reenergized and excited, barked at the cameraman to swing around and film the exchange. Keyed up to the point of yelling into her microphone, she said, "We are actually witnessing the heroic efforts of a man rescuing a young woman who might be the only survivor!" Waving her hand, the reporter stepped closer to the double doors and called out to Brad. "Sir?" she bellowed. "Sir! I have some questions for you. Sir . . . ?"

Confident that the cop had a grip on the flight attendant, Brad turned and ran back into the building, ignoring the pleas of the newscaster. He could hear the fading voice of the cop yelling, "You get back here! We ain't supposed to go in there!"

Now that the flight attendant, along with two dead bodies, had been accounted for, Brad was tasked with discovering the whereabouts of the remaining three people who were reported to be onboard. Consequently, he returned to the plane and climbed back in.

The cockpit door, only a couple of steps to his left, was partially blocked by an empty cardboard carton. Tossing it aside, Brad opened the door. Instantly, he took a half step backward. The sight in front of him was like nothing he could have ever imagined. The little cabin was crammed with thousands of cucumber-size caterpillars, all crawling over everything and almost obliterating the view of the two bodies. Smelling the pungent odor of stale coffee, Brad recalled Maria's prophetic words of warning; "They'll eat anything to do with coffee."

It was impossible to get near enough to the victims to check for signs of life. Despite that, Brad had no doubt as to their state of health. Transfixed as he watched the sharply spined beasts eat their way through the cockpit, Brad wondered why Sarah Levine hadn't said anything about the size of these monsters.

Suddenly alert to a new movement, Brad leaned to one side and caught a glimpse of a steady stream of insects making their way out of a hole in the cockpit floor. His concentration was broken by a scream that pierced the air.

"Hannah!" cried Brad, aloud. Spinning on his heel, he stepped to the plane's exit door and jumped out. Even before he hit the ground, he was alarmed by a loud creaking noise immediately followed by an earsplitting "cra-ack!" Looking in the direction of the rooms where Hannah was investigating, Brad saw a steel bracing girder jerk before breaking loose from the ceiling. The massive length of metal I-beam detached from one end, swung down in a graceful arc and collided with one of the twelve-foot columns of wooden boxes that stood on either side of the cafeteria's door. The stack of crates toppled over with a thunderous clatter.

*   *   *

While Brad had been trying to assess the disaster in the cockpit, Hannah had made her way to the far wall and opened the first of the four doors. Inside, was a large restroom with three separate toilets and a glass enclosed shower. Seeing no one locked or hiding in any of the stalls, she stepped back into the main room. Behind the next door was a second, but much smaller bathroom. It, too, was empty. As Hannah came out of the little lavatory, she, once again, became aware of the moaning sound. She was certain that it came from the woman whom she and Brad had originally heard. Not knowing which of the remaining two doors might be concealing the woman, Hannah ran to the closest one and threw it open. She screamed!

Holding her hands out as though warding off a demonic evil, Hannah sucked in a breath and stumbled backward, finally falling over one of the metal chairs. The open door revealed a pantry filled with foodstuffs and coffee. Now, it was also filled with bugs. Huge, spray can-sized bugs. Hannah scrambled to her feet just as a resounding crack came from somewhere above. She started to run to the exit door, but froze in her stride as the big stack of wooden crates toppled. One of the boxes crashed against her half-open escape route, slamming it shut with a force that Hannah felt in her bones. At the heavy door, she grabbed the handle, twisted and pushed. It didn't budge. Not even a millimeter. She slapped furiously at the vault-like closure and yelled, "Help! Brad! Help me!"

Brad charged across the width of the warehouse. As he ran through the dim light, he looked everywhere for the spike-tailed bugs. Halfway to the cafeteria, he spotted the column of caterpillars, moving purposely in that direction. Except for the red dot on each of their heads, their natural coloring worked as a camouflage against the dirty gray of the concrete floor.

Running, his mind flashed back to the dead bodies on the plane. He desperately did not want Hannah to become part of that gruesome statistic. As he approached the corner room, Brad saw the problem. Several of the stacked crates had landed in front of the door, effectively blocking anyone from going in or coming out. Shouting through his cupped hands, Brad called, "Hannah! Can you hear me?"

Scared as she was, Hannah fought back tears of joy. Brad was there. "Yes!" she hollered from her side. "I can hear you, but I can't open the door!"

Brad gripped the side of one of the clumsy crates and tried to push it out of the way. It seemed to weigh a ton because it barely moved. Frustrated, Brad called, "Hannah. Is there another way out?"

Hannah turned to look at the fire exit against the back wall. "Yes," she answered, her voice cracking with renewed fear. "A fire door. But, I'm afraid of the bugs."

Brad experienced a flood of anxiety. The caterpillars were in there with her. Attempting again to move one of the boxes, Brad pushed at it with everything he had. Although he only managed to tilt it a few inches, it immediately fell back and wedged itself among the other containers. "Hannah. Listen to me! The bugs are after any coffee that might be in there. Can you pick yourself a clear path to the fire door?"

Hannah turned to look again. Going out the fire exit meant that she would have to come awfully close to that vile swarm of bugs. Things were bad. With the main door blocked shut, the light in the room was cut in half. She could barely see the far wall, let alone any errant bugs that might be blocking her path and waiting for her. "Oh, God," said Hannah in quiet desperation. Then, steeling her nerves, she said more loudly, "Okay. I'm going to try it."

Taking as wide a berth as possible, Hannah bolted for the rear exit. The horizontal bar on the fire door needed to be pushed in order to release the latch. With both hands outstretched, she hit the bar at full stride. The door was either locked tight or rusted shut. "Brad!" she yelled, crossing back to the main door. "The door is jammed! It won't open!"

Brad had used those precious moments to assess the situation. He had looked for a crowbar or something similar with which to move the tumbled stack of boxes. His eyes swept the warehouse and, suddenly, focused on the farm equipment parked throughout the building. "Hold on, Hannah. Let me see if I can get something that will help!"

Hannah closed her eyes. Realizing that she wasn't going to be rescued in the next instant, her shoulders slumped, and she cried out in despair, "Hurry! Please!" Her strength felt sapped. She leaned against the door, hoping that her knees wouldn't buckle. "Please hurry," she whimpered softly.

A backhoe was sitting no more than thirty yards away. The front of it had a small dozer attachment. If it would start, Brad thought, it might do the trick. He sprinted to the machine and looked into the cab compartment. An ignition key dangled from a hook on the dashboard. Climbing up into the driver's seat, Brad inserted and turned the key. Nothing. "Dead battery!" he seethed aloud.

*   *   *

Hannah was shaken out of her terror by another moaning sound. Louder this time. She looked up and thought that the woman must be trapped behind the fourth door, the only one that Hannah hadn't opened. Trembling at the prospect of what she had to do next, she made her way across the room. Opening that last door meant that she would be within two feet of those horrible creatures. Yet, she couldn't just let the woman stay trapped in there. Hannah had to help.

*   *   *

Brad tried several buttons before locating one on the opposite side of the steering sticks. Trying it, he felt exalted as the earth-mover roared to life. He put it in gear and accelerated, only to have the bulldozer lurch backward. When he tried to stop it, the vehicle, which was an older model with a split-brake pedal system, responded by turning in a tight circle.

*   *   *

Hannah inched her way toward the last door. The moaning had become deeper. She could hear the piece of farm equipment as it fired up, but she had no idea what Brad was doing. Keeping an eye on the mass of scrambling insects, Hannah approached close enough to see what they were after. Two of the shelves held big, three-pound coffee tins. One of them was already lying on the floor with its contents spilled. The bugs seemed to be in a shark-like eating frenzy, fighting to get at the food source. Hannah was terrified that, at any moment, the bugs would turn toward her and attack.

*   *   *

Brad finally managed to get the vehicle moving in the right direction. It lumbered across the warehouse and plowed into the pile of wooden boxes. The action of the little bulldozer pushing the heavy crates along the concrete floor made a loud, screeching sound. It caused Hannah to turn and take a step toward the blocked entry door. She was overcome with a rising feeling of hope, realizing that Brad was out there clearing a path for her escape. Turning back around to check the last of the four doors, Hannah stopped, frozen in horror. Standing directly in front of her was a man, swollen and bloodied, with his lips drawn back like an animal threatening to attack.

Hannah screamed. The monstrous entity before her emitted a bizarre sound, something between a bark and a bray, while sputum, mixed with blood, sprayed out of his mouth. Naked from the waist up, the aberration wore only a pair of torn, blood-spattered jeans held in place by a wide belt and an oversized silver buckle.

He crouched and forced out a guttural growl that morphed into a regurgitating, chest-heaving cough. Then, drooling spittle, he charged forward.

His stride, although loopy and unsteady, still caught Hannah off guard. She shrieked in panic. Having only a split second to avoid his rush, Hannah still managed to do so by stepping sideways. As his momentum carried him past her, she spun to face him. The man circled, preparing to lunge again. One eye was swollen shut, while the other seemed to be bulging out of its socket. His neck and torso had puffy sacs that were engorged and raw. One, near the man's collarbone, burst and a greenish pus began oozing from the wound.

Reaching for a nearby metal folding chair, Hannah held it up in front of her. Even though she had no idea what she would do if the man grabbed it, for the moment at least, she felt a modicum of protection. He came at her again, emitting a hoarse groan of pain and torment. Hannah jabbed at him with the chair, catching him high in the chest. The impact wasn't severe but, for some reason, it tore the man's skin as if it were tissue paper. Blood, the color of old oil, trickled down his chest. Bellowing an explosive sound, he grappled at the chair, pulled it out of Hannah's grip and threw it at her. She ducked, and it landed behind her with a raucous clatter. Then, with his arms spread claw-like, the deviant headed straight toward his cowering prey.

*   *   *

Brad pushed the last crate out of the way before leaping off the backhoe and opening the door. Hannah was screaming, as she was being edged backward toward the mass of giant bugs.

"Hey!" snapped Brad, directing his shout at the man's back. "Stop!" Brad yelled louder, running forward.

As the cretin spun to face the new intruder, Brad pulled up short. The shock of seeing this vulgar distortion of a man made Brad hesitate. From the corner of his eye, he saw Hannah move off to the side, away from the frenzied caterpillars. It was Brad's turn to grab a chair. Holding it in two hands, Brad moved forward with determination, jabbing viciously at the man's pus-pocked face.

The walking infection tried to swat the chair away, but Brad was too strong and too quick. Jabbing again and again, Brad forced the antagonist toward the open pantry and closer to the swarming bugs. As the ogre lurched backward, he banged his heel on the chair that had been thrown at Hannah. It slid along the floor and bumped into the pantry's threshold. Brad continued his relentless forward motion.

Bleeding from numerous places, the man made a last ditch effort to fight back. Brad swung the chair in an upward motion, catching his opponent under the chin and knocking him off balance. With his feet tangled in the metal folding chair, the half-naked man took two spastic steps backward before falling into the pantry and onto the pile of unsuspecting caterpillars. Landing on them was like landing on a bed of poisonous thorns. But, the worst was yet to come. Mesmerized by the unfolding scene, Brad and Hannah watched as the remaining can of coffee teetered precariously before tumbling off the shelf. Three pounds of ground coffee emptied and scattered and covered everything. The man's skin was wet with perspiration, pus, and blood, causing the coffee to cling like feathers to wet tar. The reaction was immediate. The needle-tailed creatures swarmed over him like a living blanket. His gut-wrenching roar was stifled by the smothering action of thousands of voracious coffee bugs.

Brad hustled Hannah out of the cafeteria. Racing across the wide expanse of the warehouse and toward the open double doors, Brad caught sight of the Gulfstream. He realized that the young cop had been right when he said that the impact of the airplane had weakened an already unstable building.

As the couple dashed to the light, a big stretch of the suspended catwalk let go of its moorings. With the metal walkway falling from a height of two stories, a tangle of pipes crashed deafeningly onto the concrete. Brad and Hannah ducked their heads and veered sharply to the right but never slowed their pace. Then, two steel beams directly above the airplane broke loose. Hinged together like a two-piece battle-axe, it swung through the air, smashing into the top of the Gulfstream with obliterating force. The section of roof, held up by those steel girders, sagged, creaked and finally collapsed in an explosion of dust and debris that engulfed them. Running hard and focusing on escape, they ignored a reverberating "clang" that detonated just yards behind them. Bent low to avoid the maelstrom, Brad and Hannah charged out of the double doors and fell to their knees, coughing and wheezing from the trailing dust cloud.

CHAPTER FIFTY-NINE

MORENO VALLEY, CALIFORNIA

Distant sirens foretold of the imminent arrival of fire trucks and ambulances. A small crowd had gathered outside the building, mostly onlookers, curious to see an actual disaster in person rather than on the six o'clock news. With each shift, or tilt, or collapse of another section of the long warehouse, the crowd "oohed and aahed" and moved further back.

Captain Steve Bettencourt and Detective Tony Santero were first to reach Brad and Hannah. After getting reassurance from the exhausted couple that they had no broken bones, Bettencourt asked, "Any survivors?"

Brad stood and shook his head. "Only the flight attendant."

Sarah Levine ran up to them. "Oh, my God! Are you two all right?"

Brad extended a hand to Hannah and helped her to her feet. She took a deep breath before answering. "As good as can be expected," she replied shakily.

With her cameraman in tow, the blonde reporter rushed over and breathlessly began her interview. "This is Sally Pinto, reporting live from the Cibolo Equipment warehouse just south of Moreno Valley." As would be the pattern over the next several days, Brad and Hannah assured the questioner of their reasonably good health.

When Sally Pinto got to the part about Brad rescuing the flight attendant, Captain Bettencourt pulled rank. He shooed the media people back out of earshot and asked Santero to work with the young local cop to keep everyone at bay.

After a short discussion about the couple's harrowing experience, Sarah asked, "Any sign of the bugs?"

Hannah nodded toward the crumbling building and said, "They're in there. Thousands of them."

Brad interjected. "More like tens of thousands."

Turning to Bettencourt, Sarah said, "We've got to try and contain them." She pointed to the hills surrounding Moreno Valley. "Once they get out into the grass and the trees, we won't be able to see them. They're too small."

"I disagree," said Hannah, nervously chewing her bottom lip.

Sarah looked at Hannah and asked, "What part do you disagree with?"

Brad squeezed Hannah's hand. "They've grown," he said.

Bettencourt said, "Grown? What the hell does that mean?"

Sarah glanced over her shoulder to make certain that no one else was within listening distance. Quietly she asked, "How big?"

Brad held his hands apart, indicating a distance of some eight to ten inches. "They're monstrous," he said. "Each one is almost as big as a football."

Sarah closed her eyes and let out a breath of defeat. "Oh my God." She turned to stare at the collapsing warehouse which, for the moment, seemed to have stabilized.

Bettencourt was puzzled. He asked, "Didn't you say that they were just . . . caterpillars?"

Before either Brad or Hannah could reply, Sarah suddenly blurted, "We've got to set fire to that building! It's the only way to be halfway certain that we keep those things in check. If they get out . . ."

"Whoa!" said Bettencourt. "Hold on! We just can't be setting fire to something like that," he said, pointing to the half fallen structure. "Besides, I'm out of my jurisdiction. This is something you need to talk about with the local authorities."

Hannah offered another suggestion. "How about F.E.M.A.? They could probably do it."

Thinking of the bureaucracy involved with bringing in the Federal Emergency Management Agency, Brad shook his head. "By the time you fought through all the red tape, it would be too late."

Sarah sighed. "It's probably too late already. Insects have an unusually strong survival instinct, and the collapse of that warehouse is threatening their existence. I can guarantee that those critters are scrambling to get out of there."

They all turned to look at the disaster scene. Their silence was broken by Sarah's soft pronouncement. "Those bugs are already making their way into the wild."

CHAPTER SIXTY

PALM BEACH, FLORIDA

F ive months had passed since Brad and Hannah's ordeal in Moreno Valley, California. The couple had discovered the contentment of holding hands whenever and wherever they walked. A common thread of values, reciprocal consideration and mutual support gave their relationship an unparalleled chance for success. Even Harry Goodenow was happy for his friend.

In the third week of July, Brad received a phone call from Professor Sarah Levine, saying that she would be coming to Palm Beach to, among other things, have lunch with Stephanie Ballinger. Although Brad felt surprised, he kept it to himself. He vividly recalled that five months earlier, when both Sarah and Stephanie attended Rick's funeral, nary a word had been spoken between the two women.

Time, however, has a way of healing old wounds. And when Sarah called Brad to say that she had accepted Stephanie's invitation, Brad felt good. When Sarah asked about the proximity of any local hotels, it was quickly decided that Hannah's apartment would provide the weekend's accommodations.

Professor Levine's fame had been growing. She had left her job with Envirogen, and taken a position with a Washington, D.C. based think-tank. Their mission was to provide information about biotechnology and help lobby for sensible legislation.

Sarah had recently received her second doctorate along with news that her latest book had reached number eighteen on the bestseller list for non-fiction. Ominously titled "The Gates of Hell," it was a treatise on the dangers of genetic engineering.

As Editor-in-Chief of the *Sun Coast Ledger*, Sidney Aarons loved to rub elbows with the rich and famous, and had arranged a dinner party in Sarah's honor. Besides having the presence of Hannah and Brad, Sidney had invited a number of guests that were bound to make the evening lively, interesting, and fun.

"Sarah! Over here," called Hannah, waving her arms.

Sarah spotted Hannah and Brad in the crowded airport, and came rushing over to a flurry of welcoming hugs. Brad took charge of Sarah's carry-on, while the two women climbed into his vehicle. The dialogue was nonstop chatter, as each of the three passengers tried to catch up on the last five months.

"Wait," said Sarah, putting her hands in the air. "Let me ask you guys a question."

Brad and Hannah relinquished the floor. Sarah asked, "Did either of you suffer any ill effects from your heroics in that collapsing warehouse?"

Although Brad assured Sarah that they were fine, Hannah added an addendum. "To be honest with you," she said, turning to look at the entomologist, "I've been having these recurring nightmares. Some of them have to do with that Verne Smenken character, but mostly, it has been those damn bugs."

Sarah reached up to the front seat and touched Hannah's arm. "I'm sorry to hear that. Hopefully, in time, the nightmares will dissipate."

Brad spoke up. "Any of those creatures survive?"

"I don't know," answered Sarah. "When I left Envirogen, I also left Pasadena. These days, I'm living in Bethesda, Maryland, a thirty-minute commute from the Washington Monument."

"Just this morning," said Brad, "I spoke with my buddy, Steve Bettencourt. I asked him about the bugs, but he didn't have any information either."

The dinner party at Sidney's home was a great success. Professor Indira Jawara was pleased to finally meet Sarah. Both women were now working for a common cause and had a deep-rooted respect for one another.

"It's comforting to know," said Jawara, "that I won't be the only woman standing on the firing line."

"Believe me," said Sidney, "those mega-corporations have enough ammunition to shoot a hundred Indira Jawaras and Sarah Levines. The two of you standing side by side only serves to give them a bigger target."

Sergei Popov was another guest. As a Russian scientist, he had worked for years developing biological warfare agents for the Soviet Union. He did it by using gene-splicing techniques to combine various strains of bacteria and viruses. After defecting to the United States, he did a one hundred eighty-degree reversal, and now worked on projects designed to increase the human immune system. "In Russia," said Popov, "they would first paint a bulls-eye on your forehead."

The party continued with good-natured banter floating around the dinner table. The food was delicious, the wines perfect and the dessert brought on a spontaneous round of applause. Sidney had arranged for a special treat. A friend of his, a master pastry chef from Brussels, Belgium, was in Palm Beach, and owed a favor to the Aarons' family. Sidney accepted repayment by having the man whip up one of his award winning confections. It was a three-inch square made of alternating layers of soft, dark Belgium chocolate and white almond mousse. Before serving, each piece of that exquisite enchantment was drizzled with warmed, French chocolate truffle sauce.

One taste of the mouthwatering *patisserie*, and Harry Goodenow said, "If there are any diabetics in the room . . . pass your plates over here."

It was well past eleven when the dinner guests finally went home. All that were left besides Sidney and his wife Lenore were Hannah, Brad, and Sarah. Retiring to the study, Sidney offered a round of aperitifs. Three snifters of Napoleon Brandy were served, with only Hannah and Lenore declining.

"Everybody have a good time?" asked Sidney, taking his seat next to Lenore.

"Great party, Sidney," said Brad. "And an outstanding selection of dinner guests, too."

Sidney chuckled. "I was thinking of inviting Brother Timothy and his band of merry men just to add some spice."

"Oh, please," said Hannah. "Him and his 'Holier than thou' attitude. That would have made me lose my appetite."

Brad sat forward. "I suppose this is as good a time as any."

"Uh-oh," said Sidney. "An announcement from Bradstone Bishop."

"Well, nothing earthshaking," said Brad. "It's just that I was telling Hannah and Sarah about my conversation with Steve Bettencourt." Brad took a moment to tell Sidney and Lenore about Bettencourt. "He's the Captain of the Pasadena Police Department, and he told me the latest news about Verne Smenken."

Sidney said, "I know all about him. Hannah filled me in."

Brad looked at Hannah as he continued. "It seems that your old friend Brother Timothy got Verne a good lawyer who, in turn, managed to get the creep released from jail."

Hannah's eyes went wide. "What?" she said with a mixture of panic and incredulity. "Why didn't you tell . . ."

Brad's hand went up, signaling that he had more to say. "But, this past Monday, Verne was rearrested and charged with the murder of a teenager named Melanie Owen. She was one of the young concubines that Brother Timothy kept nearby."

Hannah put a hand to her lips. "Oh, no," she whispered. "I knew her."

Brad nodded solemnly, but went on. "Bettencourt assured me that Smenken wouldn't beat the rap this time. It turns out that Brother Timothy showed up at the tail end of the killing and witnessed the gruesome affair. Now, the Preacher himself is a witness for the prosecution. This is one of those things that will get Smenken life in prison without parole."

Hannah nodded her head. "Good," she said with a tightness to her words. "Very good."

Brad took a sip of his brandy. "He also told me that the FBI finally traced that Bruce Kreitzer fellow back to Chicago. He was a vice president of a company called Ubermann Commodities Trading Group. It turns out, that the CEO of the company, a gentleman by the name of Josef Ubermann, has left the country. Bettencourt also found out that Kreitzer was Ubermann's nephew and that the old man skipped out on debts of more that sixteen million dollars."

"Thicker than thieves," mumbled Sarah.

"What's that?" asked Sidney.

Sarah sat up. "I was just thinking about the dishonesty of people like Bruce Kreitzer and his Uncle Ubermeister."

"Ubermann," corrected Brad.

"Yeah, right," said Sarah. "People like that are only motivated by greed. It's the reason for most of the ills of this world."

Sidney added, "Unfortunately, money is the grease that makes the world go 'round."

"I know that now," said Sarah. "I'll admit, I was a little naïve when I was working for Envirogen, but when I found out that my fiancée had been murdered over some bugs that liked to eat coffee, I woke up real fast."

Hannah touched Brad's hand. "When I wrote that series of articles about genetic engineering, I was shocked to learn how everything, I mean everything reverted back to money."

Sarah raised her brandy snifter. "I agree," she said. "And Envirogen was just like the rest of them."

No one spoke for the moment.

"Yep," continued Sarah. "Just like so many of the world's corporations, they're only interested in the bottom line."

Sidney offered the view of a businessman. "From what I understand," he said, "Envirogen stood to make hundreds of millions from the development of that little bug, and profits are an essential ingredient in the growth of any business."

"True," said Sarah with renewed animation, "but you see where it got them."

Brad said, "A new breed of insect that could have destroyed a vital segment of the world's economy."

"But that's not the worst of it," said Sarah. "The worst part . . ."

Sidney interrupted. "The worst part was the death of your fiancée."

Hesitating, Sarah looked from one face to the other before saying, "That was the worst for me personally, but that's not what I was going to say."

Everyone was now fully attentive to her next words.

"I was going to say that the worst part is not knowing what's going to happen next. You see, once a new species of insect gets out into the wild, there's no more controlling it. It just goes its own merry way and does its own thing. It mutates. It evolves. But then . . . then, it reproduces. And, since it's a new life-form, it might try and mate with anything that will hold still. Once that happens, you have real trouble. Insects give birth to enormous numbers of offspring time and time again. Subsequently, we're left with something out there that's bizarre. Something that might do irreparable harm to our environment in ways we never even imagined."

The little group's quiet introspection was broken when Sidney said, "You're talking about the coffee bugs, aren't you?"

With a grave nod, Sarah said, "Yes."

Hannah spoke, as if from a distance. "Maybe they all got crushed to death when that warehouse collapsed."

Sarah swirled the last of her brandy. "Let's hope so."

EPILOGUE

T wo months later, on the 19th of September, the following article appeared in the *Los Angeles Times*:

Associated Press. Mexico City, Mexico. Zoologists from the National Autonomous University, along with a group of scientists from the National Museum of Anthropology in Mexico City, have been studying a new species of animal discovered recently by a farmer in the little mountain village of Pueblo del Cielo. The animal, dubbed, *"Una Creatura con Muchas Piernas,"* (A creature with many legs) was shot and killed by a cattle farmer when he found it scavenging the carcass of one of his cows. In an interview given by Professor Luis Escobar, Department Head at the University, the animal was described as " . . . a strange creature that may have lived sixty million years ago, during the Pleistocene Era." Escobar went on to offer the following assessment: "Occasionally, zoologists will uncover phenomena such as this, where a creature, thought to be extinct, suddenly reappears alive and well."

In a separate interview with Emilio Llanos, a Ph.D. in paleontology, he said that no such animal ever existed during the Pleistocene Era. "As a matter of fact," Professor Llanos continued, "you can go back to the Cambrian Era, and you still won't find any evidence of such an animal ever existing before."

The farmer who shot the animal told Associated Press that over the past couple of months, his village has been constantly plagued by those animals. Farmers from all around the area have been complaining that huge swarms of the beasts, sometimes numbering in the hundreds, have been attacking and mutilating the local livestock. "When we go after them," said one farmer, "they burrow into the ground."

The as yet unnamed species looks something like a cross between a giant caterpillar and a rat. The dead specimen weighed in at slightly more than sixteen pounds, and had a cluster of quills on its tail that Escobar thinks would have been extended at a time that the animal felt in danger. Although the creature's coloring was predominantly battleship gray, a prominent red dot was clearly visible on the top of its head.

ACKNOWLEDGEMENTS

David Most, Ph.D, for his unique perspective of the commodities markets. His commentary allowed me to gain an insight into the helter-skelter world of trading Coffee Futures. His plot suggestions gave me a smile along with some good ideas.

Ilisa Stillman, for representing the quality of "Bulldog Tenacity" better than anyone I have ever met. Her willingness to stand toe-to-toe and argue for what she believes is right, resulted in long ardent discussions that kept both of us up past our bedtimes. Strangely, all her viewpoints ended up in this novel.

Howard Silver. As C.E.O. of one of the world's largest coffee conglomerates, Howard offered invaluable information that helped round out this novel. Introducing me to the people who control the global coffee markets, allowed me to learn, first-hand, all about the power of the international coffee cartels.

George Reisch, master Brewmaster at *Anheuser-Busch*, for his eclectic talent on the fine art of making beer. George's attention to detail and his vast scientific knowledge of the craft makes him a standout in the world's second oldest profession.

Vicki Fiorille's youthful exuberance was always a highlight in my day. As a fifth generation Californian, she had no trouble showing me all the nooks and crannies of Pasadena. No one could have asked for a better tour guide.

Elena Puszkin, Ph.D. If a novel is going to have a murder, then it stands to reason that the author will need the services of a pathologist. No one could have asked for a more delightful, intellectually stimulating or adorable example of such a profession.

Natalie Vandenberg, for her willingness to share ongoing research regarding the use of insects to control such things as the Kudzu plant.

Bob Hobbs, for his phenomenal ability to manipulate a paint brush. Creating the front cover, including the illustration of The Coffee Bug from just a few lines of my descriptive prose, is a testament to a mind that is home to a wide-eyed child, an impish sorcerer, and an authentic genius.

Rebecca Scheidet, for her unabashed delight in being part of this project. As a bug-loving entomologist, Rebecca worked tirelessly, burning the midnight oil and coming up with dozens of odd species, some of which made their way into this book.

Larry Goodson. As a man of unyielding principles Larry stands tall amidst a growing number of capitulators. True friend that he is, Larry saved my sanity by concocting an occasional batch of dry martinis.

Dr. Rosalyn Secor, friend and editor, *merveilleuse une amie*, for her taskmaster's desire to make this novel as grammatically perfect as I would allow.

Dan Davidow for his expertise in the world of finance. But more than that, he possesses a mind capable of convoluted perambulations that he couples with a rather wicked sense of humor, the results of which pepper this novel.

Pearl Davidow, for her encyclopedic brain, and for allowing me to rummage through it and pick out some of the most obscure facts imaginable.

Dr. Charles Stillman, for his time, energy, sense of humor, and gusto. His amazing storehouse of knowledge was put to good use when it came to correcting all my technical errors. Additionally, his aptitude for making certain that I kept a continuity throughout this novel, was extraordinary.

Barry Astroff, Ph.D., for his vast knowledge about the world of poisons. Left to my own devices, I would have settled on merely describing a skull and crossbones. Barry, however, opened my eyes to an enormously wide variety of toxins. The result was a far more intriguing novel.

Douglas Seemann for his expertise regarding practical entomology. He gave me a wealth of information about the habits, mindset and lifestyle of dozens of species of creepie-crawlies.

Angela Varricchio for divulging her secret recipe for "The Bikini Martini. Her willingness to toast anything and everything, was a sight to behold.

Judy Rapp for many things, including her love, devotion, strength, enthusiasm, and sense of humor. Additionally, her input was not only appreciated, but worked wonders to improve this novel. Last, but certainly not least, was her unending patience and her willingness to put up with the innumerable hours that I spent saddled to my keyboard.

Michelle Stillman, for her perceptive intellect that ultimately led to an astute viewpoint. Her ability to see things that are not there, is an amazing talent; a talent that directed me to create certain keystones within this novel.

Dr. Alana Grajewski, for her enthusiasm, her vibrancy, and her sense of humor that becomes so apparent when she laughs. As a world-class opthamologist, she worked tirelessly to save whatever little eyesight I had left. Combining knowledge, expertise, and compassion, has allowed her to achieve the phenomenal results for which she is deservedly revered.

Ruth Bloom for her ability as the world's best spell checker. Burning the midnight oil, Ruth worked with the dedication of a Twelfth-Century monk, enhanced, of course, by the style, flair and beauty of an erudite movie starlet.

Bobbie Barton for her unabashed innocence, her child-like view of the world, and the intricate soap operas that flowed from her resourceful imagination.

Maggie Gulley for her good nature and good humor, despite her darkened world. The magnanimous gesture of offering her son Tory's expertise, allowed this blind writer to complete this novel.

Carole Feldman for her unyielding passion when it comes to matters of faith. Her view from the pulpit added a much needed dimension to one of the key characters.

Misha Sperka for his willingness to give me, a total stranger, so much of his time. He schooled me in the art and science of coffee growing. Hawaii is lucky to have him.

Jesseca Salky for her ability to wander, unscathed, through an abstract world. Offering precious moments of her time, she waved her magic wand, allowing me to see my manuscript from a viewpoint I never knew existed.